THE ARCHERS

AMBRIDGE AT WAR

Catherine Miller

**SIMON &
SCHUSTER**

London · New York · Sydney · Toronto · New Delhi

First published in Great Britain by Simon & Schuster UK Ltd, 2020
This paperback edition published by Simon & Schuster UK Ltd, 2021

1 3 5 7 9 10 8 6 4 2

Simon & Schuster UK Ltd
1st Floor
222 Gray's Inn Road
London WC1X 8HB

www.simonandschuster.co.uk
www.simonandschuster.com.au
www.simonandschuster.co.in

Simon & Schuster Australia, Sydney
Simon & Schuster India, New Delhi

A CIP catalogue record for this book
is available from the British Library

Paperback ISBN: 978-1-4711-9550-1
eBook ISBN: 978-1-4711-9549-5
Audio ISBN: 978-1-4711-9551-8

Typeset in Palatino by M Rules
Printed and bound by CPI Group (UK) Ltd, Croydon CR0 4YY

To June Spencer and everyone who listens

The PARGETTER FAMILY of Lower Loxley

Alec	*Local landowner*
Pamela	*His exacting wife*
Gerald	*Their wayward teenage son*

The HORROBIN FAMILY of Broom Corner

Stan	*Poacher, drinker, fighter*
Connie	*His beleaguered wife*
Cliff	*Gentle-natured oldest son*
Vic	*Chip off the old block*
Bert	*Baby of the family*

The DIBBEN-RAWLES FAMILY of Noon Cottage

| Kitty | *Impoverished young widow* |
| Caroline | *Her tiny daughter* |

The BROWN FAMILY of the Ambridge store

| Frank | *Doughty shopkeeper* |
| Nance | *His unmarried daughter* |

The SEED FAMILY of Homestead House

| Morgan | *Trusted village GP* |
| Magsy Furneaux | *His spinster sister-in-law* |

| **Peggy Perkins** | *Gutsy Londoner* |
| **Billy & John** | *Her evacuee brothers* |

The ARCHER FAMILY of Brookfield

Dan	*Tenant farmer*
Doris	*His wife and village stalwart*
Jack	*Their son, newly conscripted*
Philip	*Their schoolboy son*
Christine	*Their precocious young daughter*

The GABRIEL FAMILY

Walter	*Genial friend to all*
Annie	*His busy-bee wife*
Nelson	*Their little son*

The GILPIN FAMILY of Woodbine Cottage

| Blanche | *Bedridden older sister* |
| Jane | *Mild-mannered younger sister* |

The BISSETT FAMILY of the vicarage

| Henry | *Vicar* |
| Frances | *His energetic wife* |

| **Denholm Kaye** | *Very much a bachelor* |

| **Emmeline Endicott** | *Genteel widow* |

| **Dottie Cook** | *Evacuee and mother-to-be* |

Winter

1940

All our songs went up and out the chimney

THOMAS HARDY
At the Entering of the New Year

JANUARY

In a small stone house in the crook of one of England's elbows, the old year petered out, and a new one was welcomed by a man unsteady on his feet, waving a cup of something strong.

Walter Gabriel rarely saw midnight. But it turned out he liked it just fine, with the fire burning and the parlour full, and a fiddle being tuned. 'And a happy new year to you all!' he shouted.

St Stephen's bell was quiet, stilled by the new war. Instead, his guests counted down the chimes of the old, unreliable grandfather clock in the hall.

'Twelve! Eleven! Ten!'

In other houses, scattered in the dark, some of Walter's neighbours were drunk. Most of them were asleep. One snored like a brass band.

'Five! Four!'

Some sat by hearths. Two argued eloquently. There was love being made in old wooden beds, and up against a cow byre. Whisky was drunk. A dog's ear was scritch-scratched.

Walter Gabriel sat down. Or toppled, rather. The wooden settle almost gave way, but it held, as the clock struck twelve and Ambridge was new again, a baby, just seconds old.

The moment shimmers.

Walter thinks of his father, dead just two days, another felled oak in the forest.

Across the fields, Kitty Dibden-Rawles hears a creak from the floorboards. She opens her arms to her daughter, three years old and frightened of the dark. Little Caroline's warm bulk is delicious in the bed. *My first turning of the year as a widow*, thinks Kitty.

In the yard of The Bull, the landlord's son leans his hot cheek against the pitted wall and remembers his grandmother telling him how the blind can see in their dreams.

Mrs Endicott, beneath a quilt and a blanket and another quilt, feels the cold and bitterly regrets accepting that barley wine. With her delicate constitution she can't be too careful and she can already feel it settling on her chest. *Will I see another year out?*

His doctor's bag to hand, just in case, Morgan Seed is accustomed to the emptiness of his bed. Mrs Seed died two decades or so ago but he fancies he can still hear her commentary on his habits. Tonight she is silent. *Does she disown me for what I did on Friday?*

As Dan snores beside her – honestly, it's too much, the cat has left the room in disgust – Doris Archer tries to sleep. Nineteen forty, with all its spitting anger from abroad, the great vague *over there*, is a vast wave gathering out at sea. She's prepared to swim hard.

As she drops off, Doris remembers she can't swim.

Nineteen forty was six days old.

Ambridge was in the grip of a freezing January. It had seen many winters, and weathered them all. An unassuming triangle on the map, its ribbon of lanes centred around a green, it was scribbled on by the meandering signature of the river Am. A church, of course, and its vicarage, sat tidily to the south. A pub and a store served the people who lived in the red-brick houses and the squat cottages. Some dwellings were unsteady on their feet, others had the snug, smug look of spoilt children.

As Alec Pargetter made his way through Ambridge he held his head high.

He was the latest of a long line of men who had done so. Tall, angular, with a moustache as genteel as his manner, Alec was bred to feel, not superior, he would never want to be that, but certain of his position.

Like Lower Loxley, the house on higher ground he had inherited along with fallen arches and self-confidence, his position was exalted. The house was stuffy with the log fires and candles demanded by Christmas, and he was taking a brisk turn around the village. *His* village, his wife called it, but Alec didn't put it like that.

A drover passed him. Looked twice. Quite rudely, really.

Alec passed a protective hand over the blackened skin around his eye, cursing the fellow.

So many new faces about since the war began. Alec commanded respect in Ambridge. He was only keeping Lower Loxley warm for the parade of Pargetters who would come after him. They were a still point in the whirring world; Alec believed that everyone liked it that way.

Swerving by on his ancient bike, the postman dinged his bell at Alec. There was an impertinence to its cheerful noise; Whitey White seemed to approve of Alec's black eye. The vicar's wife was so startled by the bruises she forgot to offer one of her mousy hellos.

Kitty, passing him outside the village hall, was somehow comical in her dead husband's old coat. Her slender neck, sticking out of the outsized collar, looked as if it might snap.

'Morning,' said Alec, noticing how she decided not to stare.

Her little girl, wearing two coats, one on top of the other, pointed. 'Ouch!' she said.

At the entrance to The Bull, Alec paused. January was proving to be a scathing month, cold and relentless, and the pub radiated warmth and sweaty humanity. He pushed at the door.

The pub was full. All in funereal black, many of them Gabriels, most of them drunk.

'To Jonjo!' bellowed Walter. 'A better father no man ever had!' He was maudlin, and his feet folded beneath him, making him lurch, like a dresser about to topple.

'And,' added a small old woman with not one tooth to call her own, 'the best blacksmith Ambridge ever knew.'

There were sombre nods at this.

The last *blacksmith Ambridge will ever know,* thought Alec. The war, that grinding engine, would mechanize the forge and render the Jonjo Gabriels of this world obsolete. In truth, the man had been an indifferent blacksmith, his main virtue being that he was local and therefore handy. Irritable, surly, he was now sanctified by the act of dying.

Even though, thought Alec, *we all do that.* There was no real skill to it.

Six-year-old Nelson, the great man's grandson, was under Alec's feet as he pushed to the bar. 'Yes, Bob, just matches,' he said, as the landlord asked if that was all.

'As you wish, Mr P.'

Alec held the landlord's gaze. Saw the question in his wince. 'Ah. Yes. My glorious eye. My own fault. Walked straight into the damn stable door.'

'That must hurt.'

'Like the very blazes.' Alec left, matches in his pocket and a novel feeling in his chest.

For the first time since his father died – and took his riding crop with him – Alec felt humiliated.

Jane Gilpin gave little Caroline a toffee as Kitty passed her front door. Woodbine Cottage was a small and lovely house, with a thatch that leaned over the porch like great bushy brows.

'What do you say?' said Kitty.

The child's thank-you was mangled by the toffee and the women smiled at each other.

'You look very smart,' said Kitty.

'Do I?' Jane went pink, and not from the cold. She so rarely received a compliment. This lovely young woman must *swim* in them, she thought, with that complexion, and a dancing Irish accent to boot. Kitty had noticed the effort Jane had gone to. The touch of illicit rouge. The careful curl of dark hair that nowadays was striped with pewter. 'Very smart? Goodness,' said Jane, unsure how to respond to being seen.

'Off somewhere nice?' Kitty stamped her feet. Her shoes were thin, not fit for purpose. She knew exactly how many pennies were in her bank account, and each one was accounted for. Shoes for herself came very low down on a long and crushingly banal list.

'Only, just to, a visit, a ... friend.' He was more than a friend. He might soon be much more. Jane was proficient in bed baths and crochet, but bad at men, yet even she had noticed a change in the weather around Mr Denholm Kaye. She felt a spring all of her own approaching. She was unfurling. Reaching out timid shoots.

Most of Jane's metaphors were horticultural; she was known for her hollyhocks.

'And your sister, is she keeping well?'

'The same.' Jane gave a shrug. 'The same, you know.'

They both looked up at the small window that peeped out of the thatch, like a beady eye under the brow. The face was there, as ever. A pale smudge behind the lace curtain. A hand waved.

Kitty waved back. 'How,' she asked Jane, 'does she manage to keep so cheerful?'

'Blanche is an example to us all.' Jane could have been more honest, turn the question around, ask why on Earth wouldn't Blanche be cheerful when she had a willing and able handmaiden on call day and night? 'Did you happen to bump into Mr Pargetter?'

'You mean . . .' Kitty gestured to her face. 'Yes. Poor man.'

'Probably some silly accident,' said Jane. She let the statement fall slightly, turn into a hopeful question.

'Not my business,' said Kitty, and Jane felt chastened.

As these women talked – or rather, didn't talk – of him, Alec stood at the lychgate of St Stephen's. He only took notice of the church on Sundays, when he had to, but today his name leapt out at him from a fluttering piece of paper pinned to the gate.

He read. He stared. He went very still. A statue of himself. Then he was all action, snatching the paper and balling it in his hand.

The church was lit, the organ wheezing into life. People more devout than Alec had filed into St Stephen's to celebrate Epiphany. How many of them had noticed and read the careful capitals? Perhaps the note had been ignored, mistaken for one of the vicar's interminable notices, women's guff about flowers or tea urns.

It was only when one got closer that the message revealed itself.

> DEAR FRIENDS
>   IT'S ONLY RIGHT THAT THE
> PEOPLE WHO LIVE IN THE BIG HOUSE
> SHOULD LOOK DOWN UPON US ALL.
> SO WHO DARED TO BLACK ALEC
> PARGETTER'S EYE?
>   POSSIBLY IT'S SOMEONE WHO KNOWS
> ALL ABOUT THE GAMES THIS HIGH
> AND MIGHTY GENT IS PLAYING WITH A
> CERTAIN LOCAL LADY.
>   GET WELL SOON, ALEC!
>   SIGNED
>   YOUR NEIGHBOUR

Alec hurried away, head down, out of the village.

The snowdrops had no idea that there was a war on.

They massed in happy white clumps alongside the tracks as Doris Archer awaited the 11.42 at Hollerton Junction. Important though it was to Ambridge, it was a flyspeck of a place, just a single platform. A flyspeck made cheerful by the snowdrops.

The flowers could be envied their innocence, yet Doris found the war hard to find in her daily life. Change had come, small and manifold and significant, but there was no carnage. Bombs had not rained on the village hall, or even on Leicester Square. Alongside the hushed nation she was waiting, as the tinsel memories of Christmas receded and January hit its stride, for the other shoe to drop.

Petty troubles ignored the war; they lacked the manners to take some time off. Doris had agreed with her aunt over Christmas that, yes, 'something must be done' about Doris's mother. The two women, the only relics of the generation above Doris, had shared a house for years, but the arrangement, beneficial to all, had soured.

'I can't cope with her, Doris,' her aunt had said in an urgent whisper. 'You'll have to take her in.'

As if Mum's a stray cat.

With rude speed, the old lady had been handed over. This morning, Doris had left her in the kitchen, with the children. It would probably be fine. She looked at her watch. She tapped her foot. She hoped the train would be on time.

She had left her eldest, Jack, waiting by the farm truck. Doris tried to catch his eye. No luck; he was too busy accepting the slaps on the back his new uniform inspired. The damp-eyed women and the dour older men weren't to know that so far all the boy had done was march and eat Spam.

'Tank gunner. Training at Ripon,' he said in answer to a stranger's question as he lounged against the truck. He had an apple-shaped face that shone with health, and penny-round hazel eyes. Jack's was a life without incident; it had made him unimaginative. Perhaps it was that lack of imagination that inspired him to sign up the day war was declared; Jack couldn't tell you why he did it. He had to, really. That was as far as his thinking went. 'Well, they're bloody big,' he laughed when a fat little woman asked him about tanks. Not that he'd been near one yet.

He joined in with the gossip about the strange letter pinned up on the church board. He had opinions – on this, on everything – and he said he reckoned snooty old Alec Pargetter was too long in the tooth for that type of thing. 'He must be getting on, like at least forty,' he said.

Brookfield's sheepdog sat sagely, tolerating pats on the head but not deigning to fawn. He glanced up at Jack.

'I know, Glen, we've got better things to do than ferry evacuees around. We could be at home, lounging about, but you know my folks. *Worthy.*'

The 11.42 was on time as it approached the final curve in the track.

In the Ladies' Carriage, a passenger lit a match.

'Don't mind if I smoke, do ya?' Dottie Cook's voice was distilled London; she was, she had already told her companions, from deepest Fulham. 'Only it's doctor's orders. For the baby.' She patted her tummy; somewhere in her mysterious insides was a two-month-old foetus she had decided was a boy.

'Don't mind me,' said the girl opposite.

'You could have knocked me down with a feather when I heard I could be evacuated for being in the family way. A nice free holiday! I don't have to organize a thing. We're being met by a, whatsit, a billeting manager. Do they do ciggies in the country? I've never been to proper countryside before.' Dottie pulled her thin coat tighter around her shoulders. 'And how big are cows? I mean, are they like dogs or more like horses?'

'Dunno,' said the girl, who looked as if she did know, but didn't care to discuss it. She looked out of the window at the barren ash tones of winter. 'This is nowhere,' she said.

The black eye was fading. The self-consciousness was not. Alec patted down his hair, a nervous habit his wife liked to chide him for. His hair longed to wave and bounce, but Brylcreem kept it in check. Like his eyebrows, which hung bushy over reticent eyes, his hair was less polite than the well-mannered rest of him.

Since finding the letter, he had avoided the village. There was always someone hanging around the manor he could send down for errands. Lower Loxley ran on a small platoon of people, usually the offspring or grandchildren of earlier platoons.

Now the time had come to run the gauntlet of the village store.

There was no way of knowing how many of his neighbours had read the slur. Jonjo Gabriel's funeral had ensured a packed house at St Stephen's; mourners would have filed past it, in and out. He was reduced to relying on their lack of curiosity.

In a village fuelled by chatter, that was risky.

Who the hell wrote the blasted thing? The impudent capital letters gave no clue. Never keen on grey areas, Alec could only hope that if anyone *had* seen it before he tore it down, they would know it to be preposterous. The accusation would sound outrageous to anyone who knew him. A man like him, a Pargetter, would never risk his social standing for a tawdry little affair.

As if looking in on his own life, he wondered who he was supposed to be having an affair with. There were precious few contenders; this was Ambridge, not Kensington.

Passing Agnes Boundy he tipped his hat. She ignored him, just as a mistress would, in order to throw the gossip hounds off the scent, but it would take mental gymnastics for anyone to believe that Alec and lady's maid Agnes were lovers. She was a dachshund, he a Great Dane.

Far more obvious a suspect was Nance Brown, who stood in front of her father's shop, beating the doormat as if it had insulted her. She was unshowy, unadorned, a thoroughly English creature with strawberry cheeks and hair that was no proper colour, and a diffidence that touched Alec's heart. She smiled at him. It was contained, reserved, as if she had a private smile of higher quality she shared only with intimates.

No, wait, here came perfect casting. Kitty Dibden-Rawles stopped to pass the time of day with Alec. She looked up at the sky and said yes, he was right, they might be in for some rain later. Her looks and her otherness – *aren't the Irish supposed to be racy?* – made Kitty the obvious choice for the role.

Until, thought Alec, *one recalls that Kitty is the widow of one*

of my oldest friends, and I am up to my neck in British cement, with
a wife and a son and an estate to manage.

Surely, the poison-pen letter would be met with the derision it deserved. Read. Forgotten. He could, Alec felt sure,
front out the whole damn business.

In the clamour of train doors opening and slamming, Doris
saw her evacuees. They were easy to spot. The two Perkins
boys were standard issue with snotty noses and skinned
knees. The older one had gappy teeth, and hair that stood
out like a dandelion clock. This was Billy, she learned, and
he was ten years old and eighteen days.

On closer inspection the little one, John, was a miniature
movie star. Blonde, sparkly-eyed, trembling with feeling, he
was more Shirley Temple than Clark Gable; for a second, less
than that, Doris thought, *I'll take these two home with me*. Their
vulnerability almost overrode the fact that her farmhouse
was already full of people who needed her.

'And you are?' said Doris to the girl, no, woman, no, girl,
who stood by the boys.

'Their sister.' The teenager was evidently sick of her
charges. She was dark and pert and fizzing. 'And this is
Wizbang. You've gotta find a home for him and all.' She
explained that the stick-thin mongrel was an evacuee. 'He's
next door's dog. Everyone in London's killing their pets, the
government said to, no rations to feed them, see?' Her own
father, the girl offered, had ended the family cat with a tin
of red salmon. 'Ironic, really, that was her favourite dinner.'

15

'I'll do my best.' Doris knew that an extra mouth to feed would be unwelcome. 'And you, dear? I don't have you on my list.'

'I'm not an evacuee!' the girl blazed. 'Mum made me come along, to see them settled in, she's up the wall about this so-called war. I'm *fifteen*,' she said, with great emphasis. 'I'm looking for a job.'

Dottie plonked down her cardboard case and held out her hand. 'All right, missus? Your fella away, is he? Mine's in France. Or somewhere.'

'Farmers can't be called upon to fight.' Every time Doris said that she tried to look grave, but she wanted to throw her hat in the air. She looked over the heads of the straggling little crew who were filing off the platform, looking for Jack. 'Besides, my husband's over the age limit.' The generals only wanted men between eighteen and forty-one; Dan Archer was officially past it. 'He's doing his bit, though.' There was a 'bit' for everyone to do, it seemed. Not doing your bit was tantamount to a war crime. 'He's very busy, setting up the local War Ag.'

'The what?' Dottie, who hadn't much in the way of a chin and whose eyes were somewhat hard-boiled, screwed up her face.

Doris explained, losing her audience early on, that the War Ag was a government-appointed local committee. They would see that the many, various, damn silly at times war-time farming regulations were implemented. 'It stands for War Agricultural Executive Committee.'

''Ere,' said Dottie, amused, her default setting. 'With your old man running this War Ag and you being Billeting Manager, you're like the king and queen of Ambridge!'

Doris stood on tiptoe and spotted the funny little triangular khaki hat and let out a loud 'Jack! Over here!'

Jack's shoulders sank. He flicked away his cigarette. He saw the girl. He straightened up. 'Let me,' he said, taking her rucksack and leaving Dottie with her enormous suitcase. He ignored his mother. He ignored the boys.

'What'd you bring Glen for?' Doris pushed at the dog's snout. He adored Doris; she was the fount of all food, giver of scraps.

'He ain't listening, missus,' said Dottie, rounding up the boys Peggy had left behind.

Jack said, skipping to keep up with Peggy, 'I'm Jack. Jack Archer.'

'I'm very pleased for you,' said the girl. She sighed and acquiesced. 'I'm Peggy,' she said. 'Peggy Perkins.'

'Lovely name,' said Jack.

Peggy rolled her eyes, and Jack thought what lovely eyes she had.

Only one potential host family turned up to Ambridge's village hall to meet the evacuees. The one family Doris didn't want to see. 'Stan,' she nodded. 'Connie.'

No nod back. The Horrobins were short on social niceties. Outliers by inclination, they flickered like shadows, mutating and changing, always taking the crooked road. 'Crims,' was Dan's prosaic take. Doris couldn't argue, but she knew Connie was also a victim. Married at seventeen to the hulking Stan, Connie had spent the last twenty years churning out children on nought pence a year.

'You comin' home with us and all?' Stan sent his eyes on a leisurely tour of Peggy.

Peggy said, 'You'll know me if you see me again, won't you?' and looked Stan up and down in return, with the clear message that her tour wasn't so scenic.

Doris fixed Stan with one of her stares. John had inched behind her. She felt the boy lean into her and she reached back to take his hand. 'You sure about this, Connie?' Doris held on tight to John's hand. It was so small and hot in its mitten. She thought of the dejected Horrobin smallholding, the featherless hens, the cat who gave birth in Doris's handbag the last time she was there. 'You've your own to be getting on with.'

'What you trying to say? You think I can't look after 'em?' Connie was pugnacious, her temper in direct contrast to her skin-and-bone build. Her youngest, Bert, four years old in a handknit, edged towards Billy and John.

'We can't play with *you*,' said Billy. 'You're too little.'

At the back of the hall, Jack snorted. He'd been told he could get home but no, he'd said, he'd wait and take Doris home. 'Thanks, love,' she'd said, amused at his sudden help-fulness, and aware it wasn't her who inspired it.

'How much do we get for 'em?' Stan Horrobin, scowling around a roll-up, cut to the chase. 'Ten and six for the first one, then eight and six for the next two, I heard.'

'You heard right, but ...' Doris looked at the door. Where were the patriotic locals?

'How much do them little ones eat?' Stan sized up the two pipsqueaks. He poked Billy as if the boy was a sheep at the county fair.

'Oi!' said Billy and Peggy in unison.

John began to cry. Quietly. Into the back of Doris's coat.

'What about me?' Dottie was plaintive. She had been befuddled by the drive from Hollerton Junction, asking why weren't there pavements, and was this really *it*, was Ambridge just a straggle of houses with no cinema and no dance hall and no nothing? 'I'm two months gone. I shouldn't be kept hanging around.'

'You're mine, dear!' Mrs Endicott, round as a scone and quite as dense, hurried in from the cold. Her face, once the muffler had been unwound and the shapeless felt hat removed, was unmemorable except for its animation. 'I'll look after you until baby comes, if God spares me that long. With my delicate constitution I am always one bad herring away from death.'

The hug that Dottie gave Mrs Endicott was tight and prolonged.

'There, there.' Mrs E was bewildered by the sudden sobbing. She patted the young woman's narrow back. 'Now, now.'

'Don't,' gulped Dottie as she recovered, 'let the sheep get me, will you?'

'I give you my word,' smiled her hostess.

'Just some paperwork and you can all get along home.'

Doris was keen to get along home, too. She would have to get to grips with Brookfield, shake it and straighten it out; the stitching of the farm came loose whenever she left it. If there were two of her, two Dorises in doughty coats and tightly knotted headscarves, that would be good. To the Horrobins she said, 'Are you willing to take Wizbang?' She waved her clipboard at the dog, who was cowering. Or perhaps that was just Wizbang's usual stance; he was a natural underdog. 'He eats an awful lot,' she added, watching the door and hoping for another local to turn up and offer for the Perkins boys.

The door creaked open, and Doris's heart rose. Jane Gilpin stood framed in the opening. Doris's heart fell.

'Do you need any help, Doris dear?'

The Gilpin sisters could no more take in two boisterous boys than Doris could backflip across the Marmoleum. 'Everything's under control, thank you.' Then, when Jane lingered, and the moment seemed to demand it, 'Off somewhere nice?'

'To see Denholm.' Jane spoke in a rush. The awful flower on her awful hat quivered.

'Just the two of you?' Doris and Dan had watched the bachelor Denholm circle Jane with some kind amusement. Since his mother died, the village's most dedicated bachelor needed someone to keep house for him.

Jane was shocked by this question, as if Doris had hinted at bestiality. 'He's a gentleman, Doris!'

If you say so. To Ambridge at large, Denholm was

self-absorbed and poor company. And a little stained, as if he needed a good going over with a stiff brush.

As the Horrobins grumbled and the boys chased Glen up and down the stairs to the rickety stage where, many moons ago, Doris had played Juliet to Dan's ad-libbing Romeo, Jane milked her moment. 'Denholm may be about to ask an important question. Very important. The most important question of all.'

'You mean ...' Doris cottoned on. 'But Jane, you can't—' She was glad of Peggy's sudden shout of 'Oi! Boys!' Poor Jane knew she couldn't marry, and didn't need Doris to point out why not.

Jane went off to meet her destiny. Dottie went off on Mrs Endicott's arm. Billy, John and Wizbang were officially signed over to the Horrobins.

The war demanded much. It meant following orders, obeying baffling new rules. Doris found herself signing the form slowly, as if those extra few seconds would make time for the cavalry to arrive.

Peggy was brisk. She squatted in front of her brothers. 'Now you behave yourselves.' She wiped noses and tucked in shirts. She belted John's macintosh even tighter.

'Me wellingtons hurt,' he said. His voice was unfeasibly small, as if he was doing a music hall trick.

'Wear two pairs of socks tomorrow.' To Billy she said, 'You look after your little brother, you hear?'

The ten-year-old pulled a face. He disliked soppiness. 'We'll be all right, sis,' he said.

'Of course you will.' Peggy looked at John for a long time, as if memorizing his face.

It was Stan who put paid to the farewells. 'Billy, Jim, get a move on,' he said.

'He's John.' Peggy straightened up. She laid her hand on John's golden head. 'He's John, mister, you call him John.' She lifted her hand. 'And you look after him, right? Or you'll have me to answer to.'

Neither boy looked back as their new guardians took them out to the horse and cart Stan still used. Wizbang was almost abandoned. Doris whooshed him out of the door. Nobody was left behind on her watch.

Peggy turned to Jack, who stood to attention in a way he never managed in Ripon. 'So, you taking me back to the station or what?'

Her kitchen. Her fiefdom. Cabbage boiling and little Christine drying dolls' clothes in front of the fire. Doris went from scullery to range to dresser, tying her overall tighter and pushing back her hair, and pulling together a robust meal.

She pushed the Perkins boys from her mind. She would keep an eye. It would work out. There was much to do, besides wonder how long Jack would take dropping Peggy to Hollerton Junction. It was the men's last supper, before they scattered. *Her* men. This time tomorrow, they'd be in uniform.

'Your mum was good as gold.' Dan Archer dried his hands on the wrong towel, his labours finished for the day. He wasn't much taller than Doris. He was undistinguished.

He was a template for Normal Man. Lovely eyes, though, if you looked harder. They were usually squinting through the curling smoke from his pipe. He put a hand, a paw, on her shoulder. 'We'll manage, love.'

'Shush.' Doris glanced over at eight-year-old Christine. This topic was not for childish ears.

Dan tapped the side of his nose with his finger. Truth be told, he was in no mood to discuss his mother-in-law either; Lisa scared him, and that was not a nice thing to admit. He leaned back, folded his arms, unaware he was in his wife's way, and said happily, 'You should have heard the talk in The Bull last night, love. Stan Horrobin reckons the letter writer's some *other* fancy woman of Alec's, jealous of the newer model!'

'Dan!' Doris jerked her head in Christine's direction a second time. 'For heaven's sake.'

'Sorry.' Dan sagged. Then perked up. Marvellous powers of recovery. 'Have I time to stick up some fresh cardboard over that window before dinner? Now that I'm War Ag we can't be contravening the blackout.' He pushed Mother Cat off the draining board.

Doris dithered behind him. She needed to get to the sink. She caught Mother Cat's eye. *Men*, they both seemed to say.

Hollerton Junction was not romantic. Neither was Peggy. Yet, as they waited on the empty slab of platform, Jack wanted to kiss her. He wanted to bend her backwards like in the movies.

Peggy was silent. She stared down the track. This gave Jack

time to study her shining hair, and the headlamp gleam of her large eyes. He went for blondes usually, a taste nurtured by the aforementioned movies. He also went for easy, and this girl was anything but. Words that Jack rarely used occurred to him as he surreptitiously took in Peggy's shape beneath her coat. Haughty. Imperial. Imperious? One of them. She was a queen, a gypsy queen, she was . . .

'Eyes front, soldier boy,' said Peggy.

'I was thinking, like, if I'm ever up in London . . .' A distant hoot. The train was drawing near. 'Can I look you up?'

'Why would a country mouse like you go to London?'

The neat chug of the train grew louder. The engine formed in the dark.

'The army might send me, or I might drive up there.' They both knew there was nothing to drive; family cars sat idle on bricks. 'Here, let me.' Like a Frenchman, he opened the heavy carriage door, hoping she'd push down the window and lean out to him. Those movies again; they misled him.

Peggy laughed as she jumped up the step. All was movement, steam, whistles. Her eyes glistened like an animal's. 'This is the last time you'll see me, Jack Archer.' She extended an ankle. 'These shoes'll never touch Borsetshire soil again.'

She slammed the door. And Jack felt himself grow smaller and smaller as the train took her away from him.

Lower Loxley was a house of many windows, and many views.

It was the sort of house, dignified, historic, that obligated its owners to offer a tour to guests. The view from Pamela's desk, in the room they called the office, was always a highlight.

Acres of green. And much of it owned by her husband's family. Pamela had little time to relish its beauty, and besides, the morning's drizzle turned the green to greige.

Invitations to respond to. Cheques to write. An admonishment to Borchester council via the letters page of the *Borchester Echo*. Pamela's pen was quick and sure, the double P's of Pamela and Pargetter sword-swipes.

Alec passed the window. He looked worried. His forehead had creased just after Christmas, and remained that way. Three weeks had seen off the bruising around his eyes – *How clumsy of him to walk into the stable door!* – but he still seemed damaged.

Nobody would know he was two years younger than her. He sometimes teased her about that. Pamela felt her neck. A stroke, a checking motion. Still firm. And long.

Pamela was a long woman. She had the unlikely limbs of a fashion illustration, and clothes hung just right on her. She had given up London for Alec – that's how she put it – but she dressed as if on her way to drinks in Mayfair. Clinging green wool today, with a gathered neck and a fabulous brooch from a long-dead Pargetter.

Whether or not he's over the age limit, that man needs to be at war, thought Pamela as her husband knelt to kiss Hero. His black Labrador was a shadow, a spirit guide, and was kissed a lot. Pamela felt her own mouth with a forefinger.

She wasn't given to self-doubt. She wasn't given to wondering whether she should be softer or warmer or sweeter. *Does he want an actress?* She rubbed harder against her lips; they were fashionably thin, like the rest of her. *Does he want me to pretend to be what I'm not?* Pamela slid a nail into her mouth and bit down hard.

'There now,' she snapped as she surveyed her ruined manicure. 'Look what you made me do.'

FEBRUARY

The Archers rarely disagreed.

They prided themselves on it, the way Mrs Endicott prided herself on her cherry tree and Stan Horrobin prided himself on never being sober during the hours of darkness. But today they disagreed.

'It's character-building.' Dan sat at the table, frowning at War Ag paperwork. The cold morning was done, lunch finished, and Doris's mum was napping, safe and quiet upstairs.

'It's cruel, is what it is,' said Doris, from the sink. 'Yes, Dan, I know, I know, you grew up helping out at Brookfield, but there's a difference between helping out and proper work.' She'd put Phil to bed exhausted the night before; *an eleven-year-old shouldn't be spreading dung*. Doris checked her tiny gold watch, an engagement present that never lost a second. It was ludicrously dainty on her wrist, yet had endured and survived decades of farm work and house work. It just kept going.

She had half an hour before she had to go and pick up the new labourers at Hollerton Junction. 'Mind you, Phil did well. Him and Dusty out there together.' The horse had known what to do when the boy didn't. 'The ground's perfect right now. This frost's good for something, at least.'

'Dusty'll be retiring soon, if the powers that be have their way.' Dan was offhand, totting something up with the stub of a pencil.

'How'd you mean?' Doris paused, her hands in water. Her hands were always in water.

'Mechanization, old girl! The war's bringing change. You remember the winter we had two years ago.'

She did. Neither of them went any further; the word 'bankruptcy' was taboo. Dan had worked so hard to found the dairy herd, and they had come so close to losing it. Along with the house and their dignity. *The war saved us.*

Now *there's* a gristly bone to gnaw on.

The government – the great They – needed to feed a blockaded nation. With the ports seizing up, They looked to the farmers, and paid them well. 'For once!' Dan liked to say. 'And about time.' But the equation bothered Doris; the government overpaid them for food, then swallowed the cost to offer it cheaply to the nation. It was an inducement; they deserved it, they worked hard, but it felt a little like profiteering.

Whatever the ins and outs of it, the Archers – and Brookfield – were back in business; they had Adolf to thank for Doris's new handbag.

'I heard, on the War Ag grapevine, that Red House Farm's

already put in for one of the new tractors.' Dan tried hard not to be prideful about his War Ag connections, but didn't always manage it.

'Are we going to get a tractor? What about the horses?' Doris imagined mechanical horses shitting rusty washers out in the stable. Before that moment she hadn't known she loved their horses. Not like she loved the kids or Dan or her mum. But she loved them all the same, their chestnut solidity. The cold air they sneezed out over their bran.

Dan didn't answer.

Doris pulled on her scarf, knotting it as if it would keep her head on. She passed the old piggery and saw its roof needed mending. She followed the fence and saw where it sagged. Everywhere she looked she saw jobs, jobs, jobs. She'd never had to mend a fence before the war. That was men's work. And materials were so hard to come by. It used to be Dan's territory.

The hated truck stood where she'd parked it, skew-whiff. Doris loved driving their car, but that was strictly War Ag use only these days. She showed her well-worn knickers each time she clambered up into the truck's cab; she really should practise the manouevre. Or maybe ... trousers?

Good Lord, no. There were limits.

Nance saw that Doris was in a hurry, and turned neatly from serving Alec Pargetter to ask what she needed. Solid and bonny, the shopkeeper's daughter had kept house for her father since they moved to the village. Nance conveyed intelligence the way an animal might, by her calm regard, her unflurried composure. She never drew attention to herself, and seemed to need no flattery. Linen apron, nicely pressed collar, that was Nance.

'Soap flakes! Can you believe I forgot them when I come in earlier.' Doris was astonished by her own idiocy; *if I worked for me I'd sack myself.* 'Sorry to barge in, Alec,' she said.

'Not at all, Doris, do go ahead.'

Such calming manners. Such reserve. Doris felt calm around Alec. A gent, he was silky, like Mother Cat. In some villages, an Archer might not be on first-name terms with a Pargetter. She was proud of Ambridge's egalitarianism, even as she side-eyed Stan Horrobin browsing a tray of apples and wondered if he was about to nick one. Obviously, the Archers were never invited to Lower Loxley, not like the vicar or Dr Seed; Ambridge's egalitarianism only went so far. Doris was relieved; she'd be sure to let herself down socializing with the likes of Alec and Pamela Pargetter.

Nance reached down beneath the counter; she could put her hand on anything in the shop. Her father relied on her to keep track of the sewing needles, the Oxo cubes, the starch. 'How's your mum doing, Doris? I heard she's not so well and she's come to stay.'

Doris looked into her purse, poking around the big round pennies. *You can't blow your nose in this village without it becoming the talk of the town.* Looking up into Nance's docile smile she reproached herself. It was a kind question. 'Yes, it's her legs. She's decided to stay on, indefinite like. In case she has a fall.' Doris gambled on Nance not knowing her mother had lived with family, rather than alone.

'You *are* good. It'll be lovely to see her again. Such a nice lady, your mother.'

'Yes, well, she gets tired, her legs, so, maybe no visitors for a while.' More espionage.

'There you go.' Nance handed over the box of Lux. No money changed hands. The slate was settled monthly.

Nice hands, thought Doris, whose own hands were scarlet mitts. *And nice soft hair, all pulled back like that.* There was something pleasingly bovine about Nance, now that Doris noticed her. She was emitting light in a way she never used to. If the woman wasn't already in her thirties, Doris would suspect she was in love.

There was nobody to love in this village. All the younger men at war, all the older ones spoken for. Or, if she was honest, long past such energetic emotion. 'There you go, Alec,' smiled Doris. 'She's all yours.'

The bell over the door sang as Doris left Alec and Nance alone together.

'Where were we?' Alec's eye was no longer a bloodshot dot in a blossom of bruises. It was sad, though. Sad and witty; quite the combination.

'I was looking out your account.' Nance pulled out a ledger, and ran a finger down a long line of figures. At Alec's insistence, Pamela patronized the Browns' shop for all their more basic, homely shopping needs. Supporting Ambridge was as ingrained in Alec as letting ladies go first, or believing himself to be right.

They were interrupted again. Caroline Dibden-Rawles waddled in. Brown hair like a conker and the bouncy gait common to three-year-olds.

Kitty chased in after her. Then chased her out again, as Caroline pirouetted. She laughed a 'sorry!' at Dottie as they bowled past her in the doorway.

Nance's voice was low. 'Terrible, really, to be made a widow so young.'

'Tragic,' agreed Alec. He had his wallet ready.

'He was a handful, that Noel,' said Nance. 'But to die like that, on holiday. Bournemouth, it was.' She seemed to stop herself. 'Oh, Mr Pargetter, I shouldn't go on, he was your friend.'

'An old friend, since school. But don't worry, Nance, Noel *was* a handful.'

Noel Dibden-Rawles had died as he lived – foolishly. The story had the simplicity of fable. During a week's 'recuperation' by the sea, a drunken Noel announcing he would go out with the night fishermen, and a fatalistic Kitty knowing better than to try and stop him; there was no stopping Noel.

And then the sad deputation of men in sou'westers at the door of the lodgings. Noel had stood up in the boat. They'd tried to stop him, but he said he wanted to kiss the moon's reflection.

He fell in. He drowned. That's how it went if you cheeked the sea.

'I heard,' said Dottie, bustling over, 'that the poor girl was left destitute. He drank every penny.'

Both Nance and Alec tried to semaphore with their expressions that this manner of gossip was beyond the pale.

Dottie didn't notice; she had the thick skin of a rhino. A rhino from Fulham, to be precise. 'His horrible stuck-up family disowned her, according to Mrs E. She gets by on a pittance of a life insurance. Some people! And her so nice. Ooh, mind out, here she comes.'

It was as if two children dashed in. Kitty was as breathless and excited as her daughter. The pointed woollen hat and the oversized coat added to the effect. But Kitty was never less than beautiful. It was as much to do with her vivacity as her freckled skin and the burnt-copper hair that escaped from the hat. She was after powdered egg, she said, would Nance have such a thing?

'Ooh, dun't she talk pretty? I love that accent. Is it Dublin, love?' Dottie's laugh sent her shoulders upwards. 'Only place I know in Ireland!'

'Actually, yes.'

'You ain't had one of these nasty letters, have you?'

'Me?' Kitty put her hand to her throat. 'Why? I haven't done—'

Dottie laughed, looked repentant. 'I didn't mean nothing. You're as pure as the driven snow, even I can see that. But,' she said, her tone changing, becoming thrillingly dark, 'I reckon where there's one, there's another.'

Nance's head was down; she took a long time finding the powdered egg.

Alec's nostrils dilated, like a horse shy of a gate. He looked at the ceiling, and Dottie looked at him. Unlike her Ambridge hosts, she had no deference. She had only a sense of fun that seemed downright dangerous to the others in the shop. 'What you bin up to, eh? Eh? Which lovely lady are you canoodling with on the sly?' She guffawed loud enough to make Frank pop his head in from the back room. 'Your face! God love you, Mr P, I'm only teasing.'

'Ha ha,' managed Alec, placing a pound note on the counter.

Kitty was beleaguered, holding onto Caroline, delving into the sack of a bag she carried, the collar of Noel's coat riding up over her chin.

And then Caroline began to wail. Like a siren. She'd dropped her marble. Her favourite marble. Her only marble.

It rolled. Caroline strained to run after it. Kitty held on to her, said desperately, 'Oh, whisht, darling!' Alec stopped the fluorescent ball with his shoe, and handed it to Kitty.

And there it was. Today's jolt of electricity.

Just his bare fingers on her glove.

That was all it took to remind him of yesterday and her bed.

'Me old pal, me old beauty.' Walter bent to pet Glen on the junction platform. The dog leaned into him; they were old friends. 'Who you waiting for, Doris?'

'My new men.' Doris stamped her feet, as if that might help with the biting cold. February had snuck in hard, Mother Nature showing everyone who was boss. 'I lost my whole team, Walter, to the war. And now they're sending me replacements.'

'You had a good gang on the go,' said Walter. 'You miss 'em?'

'I do.' Doris inhaled Walter's eau de cologne: stale beer and roll-ups. The Gabriel smallholding was neglected in favour of The Bull. 'How's your mother getting on without Jonjo, may he rest in peace?'

'She's all right, she's all right, not so bad, you know.' Walter said it like the gentle mantras he used on cattle. He was better with animals. Glen was in a trance as Walter felt his ears.

It must be nice to be Glen. Absurd thoughts like this had begun to intrude on Doris. *Getting petted and fed, and responsible for one thing and one thing only.* No dog could beat Glen at his job; the Brookfield flock did as they were told. She wondered, suddenly, if the sheep's future was hanging in the balance as they chewed stolidly on hay back in the great barn. Two of the largest fields had already been ploughed up for spring wheat. Perhaps England's insatiable mouth would require all of the grazing pasture to go.

Only two of the people alighting were men. They were evidently *her* men. One of them was a teenager, his face a dot-to-dot of pimples. He limped, she noticed.

'Hey, you! You for Brookfield?' called Doris to the other, a dark, wiry fellow.

He was.

In the truck he sat up front. 'So, Doris, can I call you Dolly?' His low, sandpaper voice was stubbly like his face.

She couldn't place the accent. 'No,' said Doris.

They were plainly not country people. The teenaged Eugene was on a sabbatical from Oxford. Doris had had to help him up into the cab; his foot seemed deformed. 'I had a complete nervous collapse after mods,' he said defiantly, and then, 'I shouldn't be here, I should be studying. This is a waste. This is madness.'

'None of us should be here,' said the other man. Jez was unsympathetic. He took up a lot of space, legs spread, arm out of the open window even though Doris would have preferred to keep out the cold.

'We'll make the best of it,' said Doris. She was rallying herself as much as them. She thought of the three hale and hearty local chaps she'd waved off a month ago. Brawny, canny, can-do.

'The journey,' said Eugene, 'has quite worn me out.'

Doris felt Jez study her. She fidgeted at the wheel. Jez was the natural leader of the pair, she understood that and sensed Eugene felt the same. 'Do you have much experience?' she asked him.

'What a very personal question, Dolly.'

'I meant . . .' Doris turned the unwieldy steering wheel to take the fork for Ambridge. He knew what she meant. Doris braked hard and her passengers jerked forward.

'Whoa, Nelly!' laughed Jez.

Jane Gilpin, one inch from death in front of the truck, mouthed 'sorry!' at Doris and carried on down the lane until she reached the last house on the row.

*

The silver in the cabinet was tarnished. The cabinet itself wore a fur stole of dust. The whole of Turnpike, a handsome house set a little apart on the edge of the village, spoke of neglect.

Jane first sat at the long oak table but reconsidered and positioned herself carefully on an upholstered chair, so as to look both elegant and serene when Denholm returned with the tea things.

She regretted the navy suit she'd chosen. Too severe. Jane pushed at her hat, a chiffon something that seemed soigné in her looking glass but felt foolish in this forbidding room. It was a room still dominated by the dead lady of the house.

Denholm's mother had been rather like her furniture. Austere. Outmoded. Caring little for comfort and much for intimidation. He was, all agreed, 'lost without her', a catch-all term that could mean the silly man couldn't boil an egg without supervision, or that he was the nearest thing Ambridge had to a Heathcliff.

Jane, alone of all his neighbours, favoured the latter.

It fitted with her image of herself. An unplucked flower. A neglected artefact, covered in cobwebs, that really should be taken out and polished and admired. Not idolized; Jane was modest. Just some notice would do.

Today was the day. It had to be; she would surely collapse if Denholm didn't ask her today. So many false starts over the preceding weeks. So many ellipses in their discourse that turned to prattle about the weather.

He had never mentioned love. She had waited. She had

decided such flowery talk wasn't necessary. She had made many small concessions along the way. Jane was accustomed to making concessions.

'This isn't my forte.' Denholm backed into the room with a tray. His clothes were putty-coloured, droopy; it was as if a sofa had come to life. 'Do you take milk? I've no milk.'

'Black will be perfect.' Jane had never drunk black tea. *Such a bachelor*, she thought fondly.

'It'll have to be.'

Jane tittered.

Denholm looked surprised. He didn't make jokes. And yet this Jane Gilpin kept laughing. The tray went down with a bang on a low table. Waggling his jowls, he pawed at cups and spoons until he'd managed to pour a cup of tea. 'Here. Take it. Take it.'

'Delicious,' she said, after a sip. 'Mmm,' she added. She did hate silences and Denholm tended to favour them. 'How have you been?'

He was again surprised. 'You know how I've been,' he said. 'We spoke only yesterday.'

'How true. You see through my feminine gambits.' Jane bore the silence as long as she could before resorting to the one topic that surfaced over every teacup and every tankard. 'We're still no wiser about who wrote that dreadful letter at Christmas.'

'It's been weeks.' Denholm was gruff. 'Why does it matter?'

'I see you are made of sterner stuff than I. To me it matters enormously. Someone we trust, a friend in our midst, reached out and slandered dear Alec. Who's next?'

'Why should anyone be next? I assumed Pamela wrote the note.'

Jane was startled. Denholm so rarely said anything she didn't expect. 'But Pamela's a lady, she would never stoop to such behaviour.'

'She might if she wanted to punish her husband.' Denholm didn't push his theory with any passion.

'No, no, no,' said Jane. 'I can't countenance that.'

'Do as you like,' said her lacklustre swain.

'I fear, sometimes, that the letter writer's pen might target me.' Jane shook with her own daring.

'Why, what have you done?' Denholm looked properly at her for the first time that afternoon. Or possibly ever.

'Nothing, why, nothing,' said Jane. She wasn't being truthful. The letter writer would never unmask her, however. Of that she was confident. 'I meant, well, you and I, our tête-à têtes.'

The silence again. Jane persevered with the bitter tea, and then, suddenly, it all came good. Denholm stood up and said the words she'd fantasized about in her narrow bed at Woodbine Cottage. And some other words, too, perhaps not quite so à point but Jane disregarded those.

'Since dear Mother died,' was how Denholm began, 'I've been alone in this house. It's not good for a man, Jane, being alone. I need a lady, a woman, not a young lady with silly ideas, no, but a lady of, well, not young. A lady who understands that life isn't all roses and, um, jaunts, and what have you. That kind of lady. A lady like you, Jane. Who wouldn't expect much.' He looked down at her, and seemed to soften. 'You remind me of Mother. Don't blush, it's true. One doesn't have to be beautiful, Jane. I'm not that kind of man.'

'Thank you,' said Jane, uncertainly.

'What?' Denholm scowled. 'Don't interrupt, please. This is far from easy. Do you know what I'm trying to say?'

Jane did. But she shook her head. She wanted to hear him say it clearly and precisely. So she could flatten the memory like a dried rose and keep it for ever.

'I would appreciate it if you could see your way clear to being my, well, my, in a way, no, not in a way, my, yes, that's it, my wife.' Denholm fished in his pocket and took out a ring box. He opened it. He took out the ring and waggled it at her. He fixed Jane with a stare that was close to belligerent. 'Well?'

The ring was, she knew, his mother's engagement ring. Emeralds and diamonds. 'Yes, Denholm.' Jane closed her eyes. She was ecstatic and so didn't see Denholm slump with relief into a chair. She milked the next few seconds for every last drop of goodness before opening her eyes and saying, 'But alas it cannot be.'

Wringing her hands, Jane launched into a much more polished speech than his. 'I can't leave my sister, Denholm. Imagine Blanche, confined to her tiny bedroom with those poor wasted legs. I am a woman of honour, Denholm.' Here, as rehearsed, she struck her sparrow breast. 'Do not beg. I have my duty and I must fulfil it, even if it means relinquishing . . .' Jane whispered the word. '*Love.*' She let that hang in the air alongside the dust motes. She could easily hold two distinct thoughts in her head at once. She could know that Denholm had asked her to marry him so she could be his bulwark against a lonely old age, at the same time as she could believe he was desperately in love with her. That they cancelled each other out was neither here nor there.

She had more to say, and she said it, to his baffled face. She had a card to play, and if she worded it just right, perhaps Jane could snatch her life back, own it, *live it*. 'I hardly dare ask, but I must. There is one way out of my, *our*, predicament. If you could take on the burden of Blanche . . .' Jane peered up at Denholm from beneath the chiffon veil. It was a strangely forensic look for such an emotional moment. A tiny malnour-ished hope flared, that he might say it would be his pleasure to take both Gilpin sisters under his wing.

Denholm was mute.

Jane immediately set about the kind of work in which she had become expert; she doused the hope and insisted to herself that it was too much to ask. Even a man in love would refuse. It wasn't that Denholm wasn't keen to give, it was that she asked too much.

'Can you ever forgive me?' Jane was still only in the foothills of the scene she'd prepared. 'I have misled you, Denholm, this I know.' Their bittersweet story deserved a long, satisfying final act.

'No, no, don't you worry about that.' Denholm was on his feet, moving very swiftly for a sofa. He stood by the open drawing-room door, expectant.

Jane felt she must be mistaken; he wouldn't usher out his

almost-fiancée like a cat who'd climbed on the furniture. 'Absolve me, please! I can't live with myself if I feel I have broken your heart.'

'Don't you worry about my ticker.' Denholm was in the hallway now. He was taking her jacket from a hook.

'Oh. Well.' Jane picked up her bag and her umbrella. 'Promise me one thing,' she said as she passed him, unable to whisper in his ear because his belly was in the way.

Denholm shrugged. He was querulous. 'What?'

'Do not take your life, Denholm.'

'Righty-ho.'

When the door slammed behind her, Jane peeked through the window. She knew a man such as Denholm would never blub in front of a woman.

He sat in an armchair and lit his pipe. He shook out that day's *Times*.

'So brave,' whispered Jane.

Doris braced herself as she approached the shack.

It was a good five minutes' walk from the house. The door had fissures in it she could see through. Figures moved within. The men – her men – were in there. Eugene, with his soft flannel trousers and his soft Surrey voice, had been appalled by the accommodation, but Jez said he'd stayed in worse.

'Morning!' she called, and let herself in.

She would know better next time. Jez stood in his

drawers. He didn't hurry to get dressed. Doris stopped herself admitting he had nice legs before the thought had time to form itself.

'I've brought you a kettle.' Farms run on tea. Doris put the black iron kettle on the grate. 'Settling in?'

It was a strange scene, like childhood memories of out-of-kilter dolls'-house rooms. Pamela Pargetter had mobilized the collecting of fixings for the area's incoming labourers. A dainty chair from Lower Loxley sat beside a truckle bed rescued from Mrs Endicott's spare room. Rumour had it that the Valley Farm pig man slept between satin sheets.

'Better now you're here,' said Jez.

Eugene sniggered at that. Paying his due to the boss-man.

Doris wondered how Jez always had stubble. Four days he'd been at Brookfield and he never showed a bare face, and never a whisker. Always that dusting of soot. 'You can get stuck into clearing out the ditches today. We need to keep the land drained for spring. Oh, and one of you can run over to Brampton Green with three of our weaned piglets. Dan's selling them to the new pig club.' She had to explain that too, but pig clubs were a war thing; Doris hadn't known about them until yesterday.

All very sensible, very War Ag, a pig club entailed neighbours clubbing together to buy and feed a number of pigs. Then, when the animals were slaughtered, they shared the meat, or maybe the profit. Nicely common-sensical, it appealed to Doris.

'Jez? Could you take care of delivering the pigs?'

'If I have to.'

Sullen as ever, Jez was still her best worker. Eugene seemed to resent every request, and his hands were those of a girl. The limp, which didn't matter when he was reading the days away at Oxford, put him at a disadvantage on a farm.

'By the way, Sunday services are eight o'clock and midday. Reverend Bissett, Henry, he's ever so nice. Gives a belting homily.'

Eugene let out a loud 'Ha!' and got back to his book.

Jez said, 'I won't be bothering God.'

Plump and sweet-smelling, like an uneaten apple left to rot, Blanche Gilpin lay among her bedclothes in frou-frou night attire. Her powdered face rose out of ostrich feathers.

'Agnes!' Quite a hearty voice rose from the invalid. 'Get up here, girl.'

'I'm no girl.' Agnes bobbed at the door, the curtsey a relic of ancient times when she had behaved like any other maid. 'They can hear you next door in The Bull.' As Blanche opened her mouth, she said, 'Before you ask, no, I will *not* massage those great lumps of meat of yours.'

'I pay your wages, you ingrate.' Blanche referred to Agnes behind her back – and to her face – as her crow. The black dress of severe material never changed. A brief stand-off ended as it always did. 'Half a crown.'

'Done.' Agnes applied her strong thin fingers to Blanche's doughy feet.

'What's up with my sister?' Blanche swooned on pillows

that cost twice what Agnes earned in a week. 'I mean, I know I'm a burden and I know she's a saint, etcetera, etcetera, but Jane's face is particularly long this week.' She opened one eye to study Agnes, but the maid's expression was neutral. 'You know everything, Crow. What's the jig?'

'Dr Seed'll be here in a minute.'

'Ow,' said Blanche languidly, as Agnes bent back a toe.

Blanche had been in bed for thirty years. Not through choice, as anyone who visited knew. And everyone visited.

At fifteen, young Blanche, presumably less sarcastic and more biddable than the current version, had been chosen by an aunt to accompany her on a trip to the United States.

Jane had been stiff with jealousy as she waved them off on this adventure, then consumed with guilt when Blanche arrived home alone, in a wheelchair, looking as if she'd been through a mad scientist's shrinking ray.

Poliomyelitis, storming through America, had caught Blanche a glancing blow. Her legs never recovered. The aunt had keeled over, clutching her heart, and only her ashes had chaperoned Blanche on the voyage home. It was the great saga of the Gilpin family, dividing their history into Before Polio and After Polio.

Now, Blanche could only drag herself around like a land-bound fish. The bed was by the window, and beyond that window was Ambridge, a.k.a. the world. Blanche's face was always at the glass, and the world did not neglect her.

'Hello, hello, hello!' Dr Morgan Seed took off his soft hat as he stood at the end of the bed and filled the room. He was wide rather than tall. A man in his late prime who ate a little too much and whose moustache was not quite under his control, he was full of vigour, and therefore out of place in this muggy, pastel boudoir. Like all British people in February, he appeared to be all coat. 'Apologies for my lateness, Blanche. I had to pop in to Mrs Endicott. She has a tingling sensation in her knee.'

Hungrily, Blanche asked, 'And what was this tingling sensation, Morgan?'

'It turned out to be . . . a tingling sensation.' Morgan twinkled. For a man of his age he had a good twinkle. Kindly rather than romantic.

'Mrs Endicott will bury us all,' said Blanche, acquiescing as Agnes persuaded her into a quilted bed jacket. There were many of these in her wardrobe, some lacy, others fluffy, all of them exquisite. 'She's already outlived two husbands.'

'Look who's come to help us today!' Morgan sounded theatrical as feet were heard on the stair. 'It's Nance, Nance Brown from the store, so kind of her!'

A different woman out of her overall and with her hair wound round her head in a Tyrolean plait, Nance was still diffident. She had met Blanche when delivering goods, whistled up at all hours to bring chocolate or Turkish Delight or both.

Agnes and Blanche exchanged a glance. Morgan didn't notice this glance, but Nance did, and she bit her lip.

'How pretty you are in your natural plumage, Nance,' said Blanche. 'Don't you agree, Morgan?'

'Pretty as a picture,' said Morgan. He nodded, and said it again, taking in Nance, who kept her eyes cast down.

Very particular about how they manoeuvred her down-stairs, Blanche gave step-by-step instructions. 'My arm, dear doctor, my arm! Nance, you're pinching me. Good God, Agnes, you're not transporting a sack of potatoes!'

On the comfortable leather back seat of Morgan's car, Nance fussed over Blanche's blanket to such a degree that the patient relaxed. 'Thank you, my dear,' she said. 'Morgan's right, you're a great help.'

The regular drives were Morgan's way of airing his shut-in. A kindness and an atonement; he could do nothing to help her core condition and it frustrated his desire to help. He considered his extra petrol ration well spent in rescuing Blanche from her sickroom once a fortnight.

After a bit of 'Shall I sit with Blanche? Or up front?' and an 'Oh, as you wish' from Morgan, Nance sat beside the driver. She dropped a glove and when he handed it back it was with an old-fashioned gallantry that made both the dropper of the glove and the hander-back of the glove glow.

Behind them, Blanche filed it all. Each look. Each polite word.

'Off we jolly well go!' said Morgan. And off they jolly well went.

The Austin 12 passed St Stephen's just as the noon ser-vice ended.

Dottie was first out, on Mrs Endicott's arm, wondering aloud if she was 'showing yet'. Sometimes, she said, she worried the baby was just wind. 'What if I'm not expecting at all and it's just a giant belch?' She had sung loudly despite not knowing the hymns. Her hamster cheeks were rosy, her goggle eyes were clear. The countryside, with all its hazards, was doing her good. 'I never go to church in London,' she told the Reverend Henry Bissett as he pressed her hand in the porch. 'But there's sod all to do here. Apart from wait for the next anonymous note. 'Cos where there's one, there's two, you'll see.'

This was an unpopular opinion. The poison pen was a one-off, people assured each other in whispers. If they kept a lid on the matter it would blow over. It would soon be forgotten, a secret buried in the soil, alongside all the seeds and bodies and carrion.

It was certainly *not* to be joked about at church.

The vicar, diplomatic to the point of being a contortionist, floundered. 'Oh dear, well, the letter writer will find Ambridge barren ground indeed! There's little sin here to inspire him.'

'Codswallop,' said Dottie. 'Oh, Rev, we've all got secrets. I know I have.' She nudged him, and Mrs Endicott tugged lightly on her arm. 'I bet you and the missus have some little bits of business you'd rather keep to yourselves.'

The missus went pale as she avoided her husband's eye and helped an old man of unguessable age down the step.

'It could be any one of us,' said Dottie. 'I reckon he's just biding his time, waiting for the best moment and then—' She snapped her fingers and the crack made the vicar jump. 'Bingo! Another letter, and another secret shared with the world.'

Oblivious to Dottie's provocative commentary, Doris found herself picking through the gravestones with Pamela. She was among the faction that disbelieved the scurrilous letter, and found herself all the more afraid of another anonymous declaration. A lie can rear its head and strike at anyone.

Now, passing a weeping cherub whose nose had been gnawed off by Ambridge winters, she made conversation, for some reason desperate that the chic lady of the manor should like her. She took extra care with her remarks, dusting off ten-bob words she rarely used back at Brookfield. 'The vicar has a lovely reading voice, doesn't he? *Lift up thine voice like a trumpet.* I'm very partial to the book of Isaiah. Very, erm, rousing.'

Pamela, whose mink stole suggested she wasn't an avid Bible student, said, 'Pity Frances is so unassuming. She doesn't *lead* the parish as a vicar's wife should.'

'Well, there's you, and you lead, so ...' Doris hoped that didn't sound rude. She was wearing her second-best scarf, and keenly felt it.

'You do too much for the vicar,' said Pamela. They stopped to let Bob Little from The Bull go by. He led his son, poor blind Jimmy, over to the newer graves, by the wall. There, the lad would fumble to his knees and leave his customary posy at his grandmother's dead feet.

'I do too much?' This was an alien concept to Doris.

'You have quite enough on your plate without running yourself ragged for St Stephen's.' Pamela lit a cigarette she

49

extracted from a slim gilt box which she extracted from a slim crocodile-skin bag.

Doris, dazzled slightly by the accessories, said, 'Oh, but the vicar's such a lovely man and—'

'A lovely man.' Pamela seemed to find that amusing. 'But just a man. He's not God, Doris.'

Doris was shocked. Some pedestals were concrete; you did not push or shove at them. 'With a war on, I feel the need to—'

Pamela interrupted again, exhaling smoke out of the side of the red slit of her mouth. 'Is there a war on? Or is it just men posturing in uniform? Apart from the irksome shortages and the petty privations this doesn't feel like war.' She raised her hand suddenly and shouted, 'Hey! You, boy! Philip Archer! Stop that!'

Doris wheeled to see her son's head locked in young Gerald Pargetter's arm.

'No rough-housing, Philip,' snapped Pamela.

The injustice was too much. Pamela's son, Gerald, was sixteen years old to Philip's eleven, and a much bigger and bolder boy in every way. 'You all right, Phil?' called Doris, adding tartly, 'He didn't hurt you, did he?' hoping Pamela caught her drift.

Mortified by his mother's concern, Philip sloped off. He was hoping to slope off as far as the gate, and then slope a little further, right down the lane, and home. Avoiding Sunday School was a weekly game; one he never, ever won. His mother had the all-seeing eye more commonly attributed to The Almighty.

The mothers walked on in silence.

'Give my best to Alec,' said Doris, as they parted at the lychgate. 'Where is he?'

'Attending to estate business,' said Pamela.

'Even on a Sunday.' Doris was impressed. The poison pen hadn't tarnished Alec one jot; she knew it was nonsense. 'What a wonderful husband you've got there.'

Kitty was all feeling and no body. She felt like one of the feathers in the mattress beneath her. She sensed Alec was staring and opened her eyes.

He said, 'You *like* doing it, don't you, old girl?'

He was so different naked. She loved his clothes, the quality of the wool and the tweed and the flannel, their colours like fading leaves. But she adored him in his skin, as they said back in Dublin. Lean and strong and with all those male details that made her pulse jump. The width of his shoulders. The sudden narrowness of his hips. The legs that took up the whole bed.

'I do. I *love* doing it. I could do it every day and twice on Sundays. But could you please not call me "old girl", Alec? It makes me feel like one of Doris Archer's old nags out in the meadow.'

'Ha!' Alec's peremptory laugh was an accolade.

'I heard one of them was put down.' The older horse used to amble over for an apple from Kitty's hand.

'Another casualty of war.' Alec lay back with a dramatic

whump. Kitty's bed was a cloud of pillows and comforters and blankets. It would be easy to become entangled and doze for ever. She was a siren, luring him onto the rocks of Noon Cottage with her song. Even on a Sunday; he had never taken such a risk before. 'I should be at church. It'll be noticed.'

'I'm off the hook. There's no Catholic church for miles,' said Kitty. Petrol rationing had made a heathen of her. 'I prefer our way of praying, anyway.' She knew that would earn her a scandalized gasp and she enjoyed it. Kitty was already en route to hell for this affair, and for the inescapable, horrible fact that she was glad Noel was dead.

He'd been gone for seven months.

Kitty and Alec – this new and outrageous iteration – began in shared grief that one day mutated into something else; Kitty couldn't say who made the first move. It had been inevitable. Kitty, who strove to be honest, conceded that it *felt* inevitable. Therefore, it was right, and clean.

Kitty badly needed to be clean.

She loved to stare at Alec. He allowed it these days; at first it had made him uncomfortable. She liked to describe him to himself. *You're a Navajo, with that great hawk nose. Your lips are so thin that you seem to disdain us mere mortals, but then you pout in a smile and you are all goodness.*

'C'mon, Bella.' Kitty called to the tortoiseshell madam strolling by. 'Hup!' Bella ignored her. The cat resented Alec's presence, not knowing she had him to thank for her sinecure. She had been his gift to Kitty, a furry stand-in to keep her company when Alec couldn't be there. Bella was over-loved and had character defects as a result. 'Alec, do you think this war will fizzle out? I've started to disbelieve in it.'

Alec made a rule of not discussing the war with women. It never went well. He asked, instead, 'Where's the little one?' Alec lit a cigarette and looked around for an ashtray in this feminine temple. None was to be found. He tapped the ash into a saucer.

'With Mrs E. She took her so I could have a nice rest.'

They both laughed at that. He kissed her. Put down his cigarette and pulled her against the length of him.

With Kitty, Alec felt like an engine that was constantly renewable. They made love over and over; he was more energetic after each bout.

The woman was slippery and fulsome. Suddenly erupting with flesh and then spare again. Like an alpine walk after his route march across the desert of Pamela.

Kitty pounced. Astride him she laughed. From that angle her throat was a soft column and had to be kissed.

At first Alec had shied from comparisons between Pamela and Kitty. Too caddish. Now he revelled in them. In some small way they justified his presence in a bed that didn't contain his wife.

Pamela was a folding deckchair; she took him, rather than the other way around. With none of Kitty's pagan abandon, and always according to her schedule.

The schedule! Not on this night but always on that night. And never, ever during the day, since that one exception during a honeymoon afternoon by Loch Tay. Not like this, except on his birthday when it was permitted.

And one must never, ever mention *that*.

All the while his Kitty, his Kitkat, opened out to him like an endless hall of mirrors. A blur of skin and hair and tiny white teeth like pearls.

They never discussed the letter with one another. In fact, nobody had brought it up with Alec at all. He was at the centre of the cause célèbre, yet was never consulted. The village had fallen into line and formed a protective circle.

At least, he assumed it was protective. He lived in fear that some busybody would scuttle up to Lower Loxley and whisper in Pamela's ear. He and Kitty had made, he believed, a tacit decision to ride out the genteel furore. Most people didn't believe the claim, and those who did consider him capable of infidelity didn't know Kitty's identity.

They were more careful. It was only sensible. Front door quickly opened and closed. Curtains firmly drawn. The blandest of masks in public. Another man might feel it added spice, but Alec hated it.

He hated that somebody knew. That somebody had seen through him, past the sheen of his exterior, into his real self.

Because this Alec, the sweating animal, was the real one.

He remembered where he was, what he was doing, and grinned up at Kitty.

She was staring down at him, hands on his chest, the crazy hair undone and falling over them both. But she was serious, and almost unrecognizable.

'What's up, old g—' Alec stopped himself and smacked her bottom. Only lightly. Just to see the wobble that so delighted him.

'What's the endgame here, Alec?'

'We're not playing chess.'

Aren't we? thought Kitty. She gave his penis a playful flick.

It was like pressing a reliable button on a piece of equipment. He tossed her onto her back. Kitty was, to tell the truth, exhausted, but his mouth tasted clean but dirty with cigarettes and her own self mixed up in there somewhere.

He tasted like life.

It was quiet in The Bull.

Thick walls kept out the morning rain and the trundle of carts and the very occasional burp of an engine. The smell of last night's log fire floated above the bass note of ale. Bob Little was content. All was as it should be.

Inside and out, the pub was whitewashed. In the bar, thick beams sliced through the clotted cream of the walls, and outside black timbers criss-crossed the gable. It was a distinctive place, proud and necessary.

The Littles were well thought of in Ambridge. He knew a lot about his customers – now, *he* could write a *string* of poison pens! – but there was no mud to be slung at his family.

Tragedy, yes, they had that in abundance, but no shame. He polished the last of the glasses and tucked a bottle of stout into the ranks on the middle shelf. He whistled.

When he heard dragging footsteps on the stairs he stopped.

Jimmy wasn't easy to be around these days. He loved his boy, Jimmy was a good boy, but he wasn't really coping. To lose his nan, and then his sight, it was too much for Jimmy, who had never been what Bob would call tough.

'There he is,' said Bob mildly as Jimmy crept into the bar. He winced as his son knocked his knee on a table.

'Damn,' said Jimmy. He dropped heavily onto a stool.

'Bit of bread? Bit of dripping?' Bob wasn't the housewife his wife had been, but he remembered to check now and then that Jimmy ate. 'There's a sausage. Somewhere.' Bob panicked: *was* there a sausage?

'She's given me this.'

Bob went over to take the large stiff studio photograph Jimmy held out. Who was this 'she', smiling stiffly in a formal portrait? Bob's frown went unregistered by Jimmy. Bob had grown accustomed to his mother's blindness. It had been an unquestioned factor of family life since he was a nipper. Jimmy's sudden loss of sight was more like a curse, and sometimes Bob forgot his son couldn't see.

Inseparable: that was the only word that did for Jimmy and his nan. Jimmy had been her eyes, that was how the village put it. The boy had grown up leading her around, the two of them nattering. He'd never had to be scolded into helping her. Bob had been so proud.

I still am, he reminded himself.

Two days after the old lady's funeral, Jimmy's own personal darkness had fallen over him. He'd screamed the house down. He couldn't see. Dr Seed had been emphatic. It was temporary, 'hysterical'. It was a reaction to losing old Mrs Little.

The doc had been proved right. The blindness lifted as suddenly as it struck. Jimmy could see his bed when he woke up one morning. He probably saw Bob's tears. And then the nightmarish reversal last September.

Jimmy's blindness wasn't temporary this time. Acute-angle glaucoma ran in families, Morgan Seed explained. It was incurable. For now. There was research, but . . .

The 'she' in the photograph was Hilda, Jimmy's newly minted fiancée. In black and white she was rather more glamorous than in the prosaic flesh; Bob recognized her only when prompted. The Land Army uniform suited her. *To Jimmy*, she'd scribbled just below her chin. 'So, she joined up,' said Bob.

'She dumped me,' said Jimmy. He stared at nothing. Well, at a tea towel hanging on the wall, but he wasn't to know that. 'She goes "nobody can expect me to throw away my life on a blind man".'

'Silly bitch,' said Bob, and saw how Jimmy started. The boy's instinct was to defend Hilda. Who had terrible buck teeth, but perhaps now wasn't the time to mention that.

'And then she gives me a *photograph* to remember her by.' Jimmy's lips worked as if trying to keep in the bile. 'A photograph, Dad, and me blind.'

He stumbled back upstairs.

Bob was lost for a moment, then shouted after him, 'You

pull yourself together, Jimmy! Don't let this set you back. You hear?' He threw down the cloth he'd been using. 'Bloody silly bloody girl,' he said.

The tray was wide and Agnes was small and the stairs were narrow.

She tutted as Whitey White came out of Blanche's room and hurtled past her, making the china rattle.

'Oi!' she said.

'Oi yourself,' said Whitey White. He was big, corn-fed and cocky with it. Agnes remembered him bombing about on a bike when they were both at school; he still went everywhere by bike, delivering the mail.

'Is it quite decent,' she said, struggling into the room, 'to be alone in your room with a married man?'

Blanche laughed. 'Roll up, roll up, hear all about the torrid carry-on between the postman and the lady with the withered legs! He brings me my magazines and my letters and my postcards. Whitey keeps me *alive*.' Blanche slapped both palms on the sateen eiderdown. 'He's full of news and he's always pleased to see me because of your lovely tea and the lovely cake you magic up despite all this deadly rationing.'

Agnes sniffed. The crow was anyone's for a cake-based compliment.

'If it's not a scandal for the vicar to sit with me, or Morgan, why is it improper for Whitey to lie across my bed?' They felt sorry for her, Blanche knew. And she didn't mind. It helped.

She hoarded the pity and gloated over it. It tasted sweet in a time of shortages; if they ever stopped pitying her they might stop visiting and then she would be reduced to Jane and Agnes and nobody would wish *that* on her.

Closing the door, Agnes dropped her voice to a whisper. The room grew even smaller as the delicious fog of gossip closed over their heads. 'I found out what's up with Jane.'

'Sit. Tell.'

'She's received a proposal of marriage from Mr Kaye.'

'Marriage?' Blanche's arch expression vanished. She tore details out of her maid as if gutting a rabbit. 'She said no, surely? She can't marry *him*. She can't marry anyone. Is it over? Quite over? You're sure of that?'

'Dead as a dodo.' Agnes pursed her lips. 'What *is* a dodo?'

'Shut up and fetch her for me.' Blanche raised her voice. 'Jane! *Jane!*'

Jane sprinted from the parlour below, and Agnes folded herself up even smaller, so she could stay and watch.

'Blanche, dear, is anything the matter?' Jane was startled when Blanche took her hand. 'Oh!' The grip was tight. It reminded her of Blanche's return from Massachusetts, when Blanche lay on Mother's chaise longue and grasped Jane's fingers and wept and wept. 'What is it, dearest, tell me, Blanche. You're frightening me.'

'I'd do anything for you, Jane.'

Jane hated scenes. Blanche was always so self-assured; this Blanche was combustible. 'I know that, but I need nothing from you, Blanche.'

'Are you happy?'

'Are *you* happy?'

'So long as I have you, Jane. Promise me you'll never leave me.'

'Never, Blanche.' Jane found herself crying too. There was so little visible emotion in Woodbine Cottage and now she was overwhelmed with it. She felt real; she felt alive; she felt trapped.

'Never, ever?'

Head bowed in the corner, Agnes fumed. *Say you're buggering off with Errol Flynn!*

Jane meant every word when she said, 'I'm here for ever, dear.'

She loved her sister, but that wasn't why she stayed. She stayed because there was no exit sign from her responsibilities. Because the only suitor she had ever had didn't care enough to take on those responsibilities. Jane was no fool; of course Denholm didn't love her, not in the way she dreamed about, but she had stitched the fantasy together and it had sustained her. She would have to do without it from now on. She was needed in this stuffy house.

'For ever and ever and ever.'

MARCH

It was too hot in the kitchen and too cold in the scullery.

Doris trundled between both, blotting her face with a cloth, or rubbing her hands together.

Christine, delighted with having her grandmother on tap, sat by Lisa as she rapped on the shell of a boiled egg with a teaspoon. 'I brought you that egg,' said Christine. 'My favourite hen laid it. I think. I can tell by the shape. Each hen's bottom makes a different egg and that one came from the hen with the bald patch. She's lovely.'

A plait was coming undone. Doris yanked it gently as she passed.

'Doris, love, you shouldn't let me sleep so late,' said Lisa as she pulled a delighted face at the first spoonful of the bald hen's offering. 'It's not right.'

'You deserve it, Mum.' Lying in was a cardinal sin for farming families. 'But I'll get you up tomorrow and you can give me a hand with the first breakfast.'

Lisa wasn't listening. She had laid her palm across

Christine's face and was staring at the child as if she'd never seen her before. 'My Chrissie,' she finally said, and her Chrissie smiled the very specific smile of an indulged granddaughter.

'That's me!' she said. Chrissie could be pert; Lisa never told her off for this or any other felony.

'How do, missus,' nodded Jez, as he came in without knocking. Eugene followed, folded paperback tucked into his jacket pocket. Their noses were red.

Jez sat without being asked; Jez seemed to own everything, everywhere, despite his shabby trousers.

Doris smiled Eugene into his chair at the table. Time for second breakfast. The men were already worn out. It takes a while for the farm to harden you up, make you its own. They would get used to it; Doris barely even noticed her exhaustion some days until her legs sent a firm message to her brain: *Sit! Now! Before you topple!* They were all farm-tired, a relentless ache that never quite lets go. Like every other homestead in Borsetshire, the Brookfield men worked round the clock. Hedging and ditching and mucking out. Dan had gone out to tackle a frozen drinking trough that morning straight from his bed, not knowing whether he was coming or going. 'I've set aside a nice bit of ham for you, Eugene,' she said.

'Okay.'

Eugene's attempts to mimic Jez's coarseness amused Doris. She knew he was too gently brought up to follow through, and allowed herself a smile when he was impelled to add, 'Thank you'. He loved his ham, that one; Doris always knew what 'her' people liked to eat. She had no say in the war that bubbled in the distance like a chicken carcass boiling for stock, but she could make sure everyone at Brookfield was fed.

'How's me favourite girl?' Jez addressed not Chrissie, but Lisa. 'Looking lovely, as ever.' He lifted his voice. As if talking to a child, or a cat.

'Oh, you.' Lisa simpered.

Christine, who was not cut out to simper, said, 'Why do you talk to Grandma like she's a baby?'

'We all end up as babies, if we live long enough.' Jez looked at Doris as he spoke. 'Don't we, Doris?'

She didn't answer. Jez constantly sidled over Doris's boundaries, but never in a way she could point to or complain about. She took down plates. She sliced bread. She watched the pan.

Christine was fascinated by her mother's new men. 'What's wrong with your foot?' She had been saving this question ever since she clapped eyes on Eugene.

'That's rude, Chrissie!' Doris hid her mortification in the steam from the pan.

'She's been dying to ask that,' said Jez. 'S'only natural.'

'It's called a club foot,' said Eugene. He was condescending to the child but he was condescending to them all. With the exception of Jez. 'Or *talipes equinovarus*. My foot rotates inwards at the ankle.'

'Did you wear calipers?' asked Jez, swiping a doorstep of bread as Doris put the plates down.

'It's called a foot brace,' said Eugene. For one given to oration, that was all he said.

His economy was noted over by the frying pan. Doris had seen the same reticence in her father and uncles when asked about the Great War. The one that had been meant to end all wars. It was so recent; men who fought back then were being called up again. Eugene, for all his milksop ways and his lily hands and his horror when called upon to shovel manure, had fought a war of his own.

Doris supposed that they all did, before filing that away as not useful.

He's so posh, thought Doris, wondering at Eugene sharing the shack with Jez. *Lots of long words in that young head.* Only the other day she'd heard him describe his hangover as a 'general malaise'.

Christine wasn't satisfied. 'Will your foot get better? Or drop off?'

Jez laughed.

Eugene put his head down.

'Chrissie!' Doris was sharp.

'I didn't mean anything!' Chrissie fled, ashamed.

'Sorry,' mumbled Eugene.

'Don't apologize. She's precocious, that one.'

Doris had heard rumours of a land girl. *We could pal up*, she thought longingly, as she dished out plain food on plain plates.

Jez stood. Noisily; it always involved the scrape of a chair. Wiping his mouth with his forearm he said, 'Let's eat this on the hoof.'

Even though Eugene clearly wanted to sit for longer by the range, he trooped out after him. Bundling up hot ham and cold tongue and a wedge of cheese in a cloth, Doris felt the insult of it.

Her mother went for 'a little lie-down'. Christine sulked in a distant corner of the house. Only Mother Cat kept Doris company as she cut up an old pair of trousers into neat rectangles. She made them all the same size; she had no idea why. They would come in useful.

Doris had named the cat. Or rather, the beast had named itself, swaggering in with a teeming tummy and giving birth to her kittens under the table one wet night. 'Is oo my best girl? You is.'

Doris placed the grey flannel rectangles in a pile, tweaking them until they were neat. Orderly. She trimmed edges to make them all the same. Turned the rectangles and snipped, trying to get them perfect.

If they were all the right size, then ... *what?* Doris had a superstitious feeling that she was protecting Brookfield from some calamity. Brookfield was no more nor less vulnerable than any other house. They must trust in God, Doris's old friend. The old friend who had blighted her mother's mind, and shaken the world like a snow globe.

All those prayers – where did they go? Were they boxed up? Because they weren't being answered.

'Only us!' The knock was loud but perfunctory.

Doris jumped to her feet, as if the police were at the door, come to arrest her for blasphemy. It was only Dottie, who let herself in, teeth chattering, taking off her scarf and loosening her coat down over her arms. Mrs Endicott was at her heels, smiling, coughing. Sheepish behind them, Jane seemed keen to point out they had met in the lane, she hadn't wanted to disturb, they could go, this was impertinent.

'No, no, sit, ladies, you sit.'

'I brought this.' Dottie made herself comfortable. The baby had altered her outline, adding a curve beneath her cardigan. Her chin, never adamant, was quite gone. 'For your old mum.' She flourished a lap blanket of knitted squares as if it was a toreador's cape. 'Me and Mrs E made it from odd bits.'

'When my arthritis allowed.' Mrs E, formal in hat, bag, nice shoes, looked down at her hands. 'If I'm spared another summer I'll make you one for Christmas, Doris.'

'It's beautiful.' Doris felt the weight of the blanket. It wasn't beautiful. It was, however, soft and useful, and represented hours of feminine work. 'Mum'll love it.'

'Wheel her out then.' Dottie was frank; she'd come to gawp. 'A new face here is like a night at the flicks. I've heard your ma's a real lady, with loads of the old chat.'

'Well, her legs,' began Doris. She mimed something – even she didn't know what – with her hands. 'Best give her some peace.' Her visitors didn't move. 'I'll tell her you called,' she said.

She would sit them out. She would see them off.

'Tea, ladies?' she asked.

* * *

Less than twenty-four hours later, Dottie was pumping out her latest bulletin as she held out her special green ration book to Nance. She was entitled to cod liver oil, when what she wanted, she liked to say, was cake and a nice G & T.

The subject of today's newsflash was Lisa. 'Legs still bad, apparently,' she told the queue in the shop. 'Poor old duck.'

'If I might just . . .' Morgan, hat against his chest, was trying to buy a box of candles from Nance. 'Bit of a hurry.'

'By the way, Doc, it's definitely a boy!' Dottie patted her stomach through layers of poplin and wool. 'Mrs E tied her wedding ring to a piece of thread and held it over me and it went back and forth, like a pendulum-thingy, so that means it's a boy. Round and round'd be a girl. I'm glad. I want a boy.'

'Not particularly scientific.' Morgan winked at Nance, who quashed the smile it invoked.

'Oh, you and your silly old science,' said Dottie. 'Explain this to me, if you can, with your *science*, Doc. Jane Gilpin's house is haunted.' She opened her boiled-egg eyes even wider, delighted. 'Yes! How d'you like that? Ghostly children laughing in the walls, apparently.'

'Jane said this?' Morgan frowned.

'She's taking double her sleeping draught to get away from them.' Dottie shuddered happily.

The doctor was thoughtful, almost forgetting to pick up his change.

The bell above the shop door announced Agnes. 'Is the rumour true?' she whispered, nose twitching. 'Rhubarb?'

Emerging from the back room, Frank Brown held a box of

the stuff in his arms. 'Yes, it's all true. The only thing Walter Gabriel's good for: his rhubarb! Fetch the other boxes in, Nance, there's a love.'

'Let me help,' said Morgan.

'Erm, all right.' Nance hurried out, and Morgan followed her to the cold yard.

'What a gent,' said Dottie, elbowing Agnes out of the way to get at the Christmas-red stalks.

'At least they can't ration Walter's rhubarb,' said Agnes aggressively. She barked out comments like gunfire. 'How'd they expect us to live with all these new rules? And nothing's happening, is it? *Is it?*' She repeated herself when she was ignored. 'This war's a flop. So why d'we have to live so mean, eh?'

'I'm sure,' said Frank, 'the government knows best.' There was a Union Jack hung above the onions. A portrait of the king leaned against the shredded suet. Frank Brown was a reserved man, opaque to his customers. His patriotism was the most noticeable detail of his personality.

'The government?' Dottie's patriotism was more robust, more given to complaint. 'They don't give a stuff for the likes of us.' She rifled through and sorted the rhubarb. 'Bet Chamberlain doesn't queue for sugar. All them bulletins on the BBC, they make me nervous, even though they're only reporting that nothing's bleedin' well happened.' She held up a gigantic stalk. 'What does Walter *do* to his rhubarb to get it like this?'

'Best you don't ask,' said Frank.

Dottie saw a crumpled something among the rhubarb. 'A letter!' She ferreted it out, triumphant. The other shoe had finally dropped, and she, Dottie, was at the white-hot heart of the news.

She read it out, with all the gusto of a poor man's Bette Davis.

The weak Easter sunshine touched the pewter and the silver and the porcelain on the long, polished table.

Lent, most Protestant of months, was finally over. No more fasting and reflection; time to feast. As much as one could in wartime.

There was a linen napkin beside every plate. *All that ironing*, thought Doris, as she eyed the chorus line of cutlery and hoped Dan wouldn't dive in and use a grapefruit knife for his fish, or something.

Doris had no idea what a grapefruit knife might look like.

The invitation to Easter lunch at Lower Loxley had sat, throbbing like a poisoned apple, on Brookfield's mantelpiece for a week. Thrilled to be invited, the Archers couldn't help thinking the universe had made a mistake. A lever had slipped, a button had been pressed at the wrong time. The likes of Dan and Doris didn't hobnob with the likes of Alec and Pamela.

'It's the war,' Dan had decided. 'It's making us all pull together, and quite right too.'

'All very well for you to say,' Doris had sighed. He didn't have to do his hair or tut over his wardrobe.

'To friends,' said Pamela, raising a glass.

'To friends,' said her guests. Frances, the vicar's wife, said it a little late. Her husband gave her a look.

No, not exactly a look, Doris corrected herself. Next door to a look. She noticed how heavy her glass was, how pleasant it was to hold. The rich – and the Pargetters *were* rich – led such different lives, where everything they touched was smooth and perfect and just so.

On one side of her sat Morgan, on the other, the vicar. She was grateful not to be beside Alec. She admired him, yes, but could never think of a thing to say to him. For the moment, as a girl Doris knew from the village lumbered in with a tureen of spring vegetable soup, the woman opposite her did all the talking.

Magsy Furneaux was comfortably built, un-showily made. Only her brooches and earrings and the watch that sat like a diamond-studded tourniquet on her plump wrist gave the game away. Magsy was a Borsetshire Furneaux, from a prominent family that had provided the area with landowners and members of parliament down the centuries. It had also provided Morgan Seed with his wife.

This wife, a good woman and Magsy's sister, died when the two Seed boys were small. And there and then Magsy found her vocation. 'I love them like they're my own,' she used to say, before they flew the nest. Now, as ever, she fussed over her brother-in-law as if he was a hothouse orchid. 'A touch of soup, Morgan, on your chin. Just *there.*'

He ignored her. Not unkindly. Despite Magsy's insistence

that 'poor' Morgan was struggling since the boys grew up
and she moved out, he seemed to be doing well enough, with
his comfortably upholstered frontage and his pink cheeks.

'I've always loved this room, Pamela,' Magsy went on. 'It
has such charm. The panelling is so handsome.'

'Bit dark, if you ask me,' said Dan, whose manners had
been left at home. 'Soup's top notch, though, Pamela.'

Pamela, who had done nothing to the soup beyond order-
ing it to be made, inclined her head at the compliment. She
had never chopped an onion in her life.

'What did we all give up for Lent?' Morgan asked this
with the assurance of a man who never gave up anything. 'I
gave up telling my patients what to do. They all ignore me
anyway, which is sometimes just as well. I can be rather a nag.
No smoking, no rich food, a daily walk! A doctor's advice is
seldom welcome.' He leaned towards Alec. 'I'm assuming
we'll enjoy one of our customary cigars after lunch, sir?'

Alec patted his breast pocket, where two Cohiba Robustos
sat like hot dogs.

Dan wasn't invited to this private gentleman's club of two,
much to his relief. He was a pipe man.

'I didn't consider giving up anything this year,' said
Pamela. 'The war, surely, gave everything up for us.'

Doris agreed. 'Phil and Chrissie usually give up sweets,
but ...' The suggestion that they make do with carrots, as
advised in *Woman* magazine, had not gone down well.

'Was that young Gerald I saw loitering on the drive?' The
vicar asked this gravely; Henry was great for funerals but

not so hot at weddings. 'Surely he's old enough to join us at lunch these days?'

A slight current ran the length of the table. Alec looked at Pamela who did not look back. She said, smooth as silk and quite as slippery, 'Dear boy's not been at all well.'

Well enough, thought Doris, *to yet again shove my Phil into a ditch this morning.* The only heir to the Pargetter estate erred towards Pamela's family in his looks, which were finely sketched and wary. His physique, however, was that of a cuckoo in the nest. Gerald was overblown, ham-armed, with a ripe menace in his not-at-all gentlemanly demeanour.

Cloth-eared to nuance, the vicar wasn't done with the topic. 'Gerald's at your old school, Alec, isn't he? You're a Marlborough man.'

'No, Rugby, and yes, Gerald followed my lead.' No need to fill them in on Gerald's progress or lack thereof at Rugby, where he inspired letter after letter from his tutors.

Alec poured water for Magsy, who was over-grateful. She brought to mind a dog that craves a caress but fears a kick. She made Alec uneasy; *such a soggy woman*, he thought. 'Dig in, do,' he said, knowing how Pamela loathed colloquialism at the table. At Lower Loxley, hospitality was generous – *but we must all behave.* 'What do you think,' he asked Dan, 'of these artificial fertilizers Whitehall's pushing?'

'Artificial what?' Magsy's question was ignored; the miracle feed was discussed above her greying head.

'Powerful stuff,' was Dan's take.

'Science is the future of farming.' Alec waved a butter knife to underline his point.

It was easy, thought Doris, to forget that Alec was a farmer; there was rarely mud on his bespoke clothes, and no other farmer smoked like a film star.

'Those are broad powers you have with the War Ag, Dan.' Alec was wry. It suited him. He was made of wry materials. 'You can requisition people's farms, I understand, if you suspect some abuse, if they're not using the land to maximum capacity.'

As Dan nodded, Doris cut in. 'Not that my Dan'd ever take anybody's farm from them!' The very idea.

'I would,' said Dan. 'If I had to, love. If there was no option.'

'No option?' Doris was shocked. These were livelihoods they were discussing.

Pamela said, 'Dan might not have a bayonet but he does have War Ag forms in triplicate.' She changed the subject; shop talk was also unwelcome at her table. She turned to the vicar, and said, 'Henry, as the days begin to lighten at last, I suppose it's time to start planning Ambridge's midsummer pageant.'

The vicar, mid-chew, put down his bread roll, coughed and agreed. 'Although, given the present crisis, is it *appropriate* to plan something as frivolous as a pageant?' He often couched his opinion in a question. It was one of the reasons other men avoided him like the plague when he dropped into The Bull.

'The pageant's vital!' Doris surprised herself by disagreeing publicly with Ambridge's man of God. She generally backed him up, even when he was silly, which did happen. 'I mean, Henry, forgive me, but the village needs something to look forward to.' She registered how he blinked at her breach of etiquette. *You're not a god.* Pamela had been right when she said that; the vicar was, after all, just a man. 'They're saying this war might last as much as a year; we need to keep cheerful.'

'The war,' said Alec, 'will last considerably more than a year.' When he tried to join up he'd been told instead to put his affairs in order, and wait until he was needed. The conscription age would inevitably go up. More and more men would be sucked into the whirlwind tearing up Europe. 'I do detest hearing newspapers describe it as a phony war. It's perfectly real.'

'Now, now, no doomsday talk.' Morgan glanced at his sister-in-law, at her stricken face. 'Not in front of the ladies.'

As the soup plates were cleared – noisily, the village girl was no waitress – and the lamb brought in, Doris felt Pamela bristle. Not all ladies had to be protected. That's what Doris would tell Morgan if she wasn't so, well, ladylike. The moment of affinity with her hostess surprised her; Pamela was exotic to Doris, who lacked her poise, her control, her ability to wear such tight clothes. She said, 'What I say is, let's poke that old Hitler in the eye. I'll be your first volunteer for the pageant committee, Pamela.'

'As if it's a matter of volunteering,' murmured Alec into his moustache.

'My husband's quite right.' Pamela was unapologetic.

'I'll requisition the usual personnel. But we need some new blood. How about that sweet Irish gel? Kitty Dibden-Rawles. She seems a little isolated since Noel passed away.'

Afterwards, Alec would congratulate himself on not jumping out of the chair at his wife's casual mention of Kitty. He could have kissed Doris Archer when she speculated that Kitty might not be keen, her being so young and gay and what have you.

'Nonsense. It'll get her out of the house.' Pamela was firm, as ever. All her opinions came chiselled on tablets. 'She deserved better than that wastrel, Noel. Although my husband had an unaccountable fondness for him, didn't you, Alec?'

'Everybody was fond of old Noel. Loveable rogue, you know.' Towards the end, when Alec saw Kitty's life pared thinner and thinner by Noel's behaviour, Alec had stopped using that sort of euphemism; the lovable rogue was a selfish bastard. A drinker, a sadist and, Alec suspected, *handy*, to use another euphemism. Kitty had worn long sleeves in summer and there was a newish scar on her freckled nose. 'Lamb's a touch tough,' he said, by way of deflection.

A chorus began in defence of the lamb, as he knew it must. Magsy was especially fulsome. The woman was so grateful, and yet so demanding; she confounded Alec.

Unmarried women of Magsy's age, even when they were solvent, drifted through village society like waifs. Always included in Sunday lunch invitations or birthday suppers, but never anticipated with any real pleasure. She was a duty, in her mauve-ish, dated frock. *And the poor old girl knows it.* Perhaps that was the real reason Magsy Furneaux unsettled Alec. He paid her great attention for exactly three minutes, and saw her purr.

A call-and-response from that morning's service came back to him. Landed smack in the middle of his thoughts, with all the vicar's dour sing-song enunciation.

Wash me thoroughly from my wickedness and cleanse me from my sin.

'Lord have mercy,' he'd mouthed. Doris had been more enthusiastic. More confident of a sympathetic ear up there.

'That rocking chair is ever so inviting.' Doris pointed with her fork, then felt vaguely embarrassed for doing so. There were rules to eating here; she didn't know them all, and felt they lurked beneath the Persian rugs waiting to trip her up.

'It was Alec's great-grandmother's.' Pamela, who had taken three mouthfuls of her meal, laid her cutlery on her plate. Straight, pointing to twelve o'clock. Abiding by the rules. 'Some of the house's older furniture is a trifle heavy for my taste.'

'Heavy,' said Frances, and laughed. The vicar's wife often did this; laughed at something that was not, by anybody's standards, funny.

'You know the superstition, don't you?' said Doris. 'If a rocking chair rocks on its own that means a ghost has come to sit in it.'

'Whoo!' Alec provided a spectral sound effect.

'It's not out of the question,' said Pamela. 'There must be any number of ghostly Pargetters in this house.'

Beneath the table, Hero, the black Labrador, licked Alec's hand. As if to reassure his master that Alec wasn't one of those ghosts.

'My favourite!' The vicar clapped his hands when rhubarb crumble appeared. 'You spoil us, Pamela.'

'My pleasure,' murmured Pamela. All one word: *mayplesha*.

The war, thought Doris, as she decimated her sugary dessert, had yet to reach this table. Perhaps the inherited panelling kept it out.

Dan finished his before Pamela had picked up her spoon. 'That's what I *call* a pud,' he said.

'There's plenty more,' said Pamela.

Doris didn't know whether to be proud of Dan's appetite or to prod him under the table with her uncomfortable 'good' shoe. At home, she loved to see him eat, but here it was unseemly. His elbows were on the table; wasn't that wrong too?

'More! More!' Dan was giddy on crumble.

Doris kicked him.

Magsy spoke, and her piety suggested she knew she was about to dampen the mood. 'Dear Anthony,' she said, 'adored my crumble so.'

'God rest his soul.' The vicar put down his spoon, and there are those who would say he did so reluctantly. He blessed himself. 'A fine boy, Magsy, and a credit to you, Morgan.'

It was still fresh, the wound. Anthony Seed had been one

of the war's first casualties. Morgan's younger son had been twenty-three and handsome (and growing more handsome after death; memory is indulgent) when he signed up.

On his first day on the Saar front, near the French border with Germany, in a place Doris couldn't pronounce, Anthony had walked into a British booby trap intended for the Germans. His own countrymen had shot him to death.

'It doesn't seem fair,' said Magsy, still mild, but struggling. 'The whole patrol followed him, but Anthony was the only one to die that day.'

'It's *not* fair,' said Alec. He felt for her hand. It was damp.

'Still, we must—' Morgan's eyes flitted everywhere. He wasn't allowed to finish; Magsy had more to say.

'D'you know, my George hasn't shed a tear.' Magsy blurted it out as if confessing some unspeakable crime. 'Not one. Over his own brother.'

Morgan's bedside manner was stretched thin. 'George is a grown man, Magsy, with a very busy life to lead. Important government work. Of course he grieves, we all do. He lost his brother. I lost …' He couldn't say it. Then he could. 'I lost my son.'

'I'm like a mother to those boys.' This was how Magsy described herself to herself; it was first and last in her autobiography. 'I feel their hurts as my own.'

The emotional scaffolding around Magsy needed constant upkeep; Doris remembered the scene at the funeral when George Seed had shaken off his aunt and screeched, 'You're not my damn mother!' No doubt everyone else at the table remembered, too. 'You gave your all to them,' she said.

'Worrying about children is mandatory,' said Alec drily. As if on cue, Gerald thundered down the stairs and bayed at the housekeeper for his boots.

A change of topic to something blameless was needed. Doris was serene, knowing Pamela would supply it, with her usual finesse.

But no. Frances got there first. With her usual hobnailed boots. 'These letters!' she said, with relish. 'Two now! Can you believe it? I wonder when the next one will turn up? Are they what you call poison pens?'

Alec stiffened. Another letter. He felt like screaming. What had it said about him? Had it outed Kitty?

Not for the first time he fantasized about throwing the vicar's wife in the duck pond; the Bissetts were above a certain water line in Ambridge, and were therefore mandatory lunch guests. But good heavens, they were dull.

Nobody expected men of God to be *thinkers*, but surely they could be relied upon not to lob grenades among the cut glass. The letters had never been discussed at Lower Loxley. Pamela operated on a level above village gossip, and Alec clung to the hope that she was ignorant of the accusation against him. He hadn't realized there was a second note doing the rounds. He prised at his collar. Had his neck got fatter? He was hot suddenly, and constricted.

'Written all in capitals,' said Doris, who was definitely not above village gossip. 'Cunning, that.'

A second one means they're a series. Alec took a great interest in his crumble. There would be more. *Will they all be about me?*

'I have it here.' Morgan held a piece of paper distastefully between two fingers. 'I managed to extricate it from Dottie Cook.'

Pamela queried this with the merest wrinkle of her nose; she couldn't be expected to know a Dottie Cook.

'The London evacuee,' explained Morgan. 'The one who's expecting. I felt I should hand the note to you, Alec.'

'Me? Why?' *Good God, I've turned soprano.* He had actually jumped.

'Or perhaps you, Dan, now that you're War Ag.'

Dan put on his glasses and studied it. 'My word,' he said. And then he looked at Alec, and said again, 'My word.'

'Read it, man, for God's sake.' Alec's tone let him down. Pamela glanced sharply at him.

Dan read the note aloud, in a stuttering monotone.

DEAR FRIENDS,
   IT WOULD TAKE A HEART OF STEEL
NOT TO FEEL COMPASSION FOR A LADY
WHO HAS LOST THE USE OF HER LEGS.
   WHITEY WHITE'S HEART IS SO
TOUCHED BY BLANCHE GILPIN'S
PREDICAMENT THAT HE VISITS HER
DAILY IN HER BEDCHAMBER.
   SURELY NOTHING GOES ON? SURELY
IT'S ALL INNOCENT? SURELY THEY

ONLY SHUT THE DOOR SO THEY CAN
TALK IN PRIVATE?
  SIGNED
  YOUR NEIGHBOUR

'Nice quality paper,' said Magsy, as Alec went dizzy at his reprieve.

'A woman's hand or a male hand, do we think?' The vicar steepled his fingers. 'Hmm?'

'A woman's,' said his wife, emphatically.

'A man's,' said Magsy, emphatically.

'Certainly this venom could not emanate from an innocent child,' said the vicar.

Well, obviously, Alec would have liked to say, were there not a holy force field around his guest. Relief made him heavy-handed as he poured himself a restorative glass of burgundy. So, Blanche Gilpin, of all people, was in the firing line this time.

'Could it . . .' Magsy crept along her line of thought. 'I mean, I can hardly believe I'm saying this, but could it be true?'

Doris made a noise in her throat. 'Blanche? And the *postman*? That'd be ridiculous.'

'Ridiculous things do happen.' The vicar's wife did her best to sound regretful and not zealous. Frances leaned forward, avid, *starving*. 'That letter's the reason Blanche's sister, dear Jane, sent her apologies and couldn't make it today. I met her on The Green and she was very nervous. She asked me did I feel like the windows in Ambridge had all become *eyes*.' Frances tittered.

'Enlighten me, someone,' said Pamela. 'Am I the only person in Ambridge who's unaware of these letters?'

Alec's bowels did something complicated.

'Show me,' she said, and held out the kind of long-fingered hand familiar from Tudor portraits. She frowned, her pencil-thin eyebrows meeting. 'What a sewer of a mind.' She dropped the letter onto the tablecloth. 'You say it's the second one? What bilge was in the first?'

Polite amnesia befell her guests. Alec's bowels were dancing by now. He bent down to rub Hero's snout, and heard his wife say, amused, 'Aha! I deduce that my family was the subject. Come now, it's cruel not to tell me what our bad-minded friend had to say about the Pargetters.'

'Darling, it's not worth hearing.' Alec had considerable sangfroid and he called upon every morsel of it to sound so casual.

With great gentility, Pamela insisted, and the weak link, bloody Frances, the bloody vicar's bloody wife, filled her in. To Alec's relief, she only mentioned the portion about Alec's black eye. The adultery was censored.

Pamela was dry. 'Darling, I told you people would suspect we'd taken up fisticuffs.' She allowed the tittering an exact four seconds. 'The truth was too dull; who wants to believe you walked into the stable door? And yet, that's exactly what he did.'

'I dread the next letter.' Frances's thin nose quivered. 'Who will they target? What do they *know*?'

'They know nothing.' Pamela was languid. 'They were

wrong about Alec, and so it stands to reason they're wrong about Blanche and her paramour. I, for one, plan to ignore the next epistle. Pay no mind to the nasty little brute and he'll go away.'

Raising a glass, Alec said, 'To my wife, who really should be running the country.' As the compliment was echoed, Alec thought, *I don't compliment her enough.* He staved off a fresh wave of guilt with another gulp of wine. *I should be nicer to her*; when had Alec stopped telling Pamela she was clever or funny or good at things?

At the other end of the table, Pamela shushed them all.

Trouble was, complimenting Pamela was like touching the lizard Gerald had once insisted on keeping; neither party really enjoyed it.

Talk veered towards Doris's mother, and those infamous legs of hers. Alec didn't understand old ladies' legs and didn't care to; the wine carried him softly back in time, to three hours ago.

He'd taken the back way to Noon Cottage; the letter writer might keep watch on front doors.

Kitty's bed was cold; they warmed it up. She smelled of soap, and then of him. So charming and so needy, often in the same breath. She'd rebutted that: 'I'm not needy, Alec, you just find it hard to give.' And then that hot whisper in his ear as he lay trying not to surrender to a sleep that couldn't last.

'I am your safe place,' she'd breathed.

'You big silly, I don't need one,' he'd murmured.

'Don't you agree, Alec?'

Doris's nice plain voice and her nice plain face brought him back. He was glad he'd persuaded Pamela to invite her. They needed to be seen to engage with the normal folk, the ordinary folk. 'Yes,' he said, wondering what he agreed with.

It seemed he agreed that the prime minister had 'a lovely speaking voice'. Doris's assertion was promptly taken up by Magsy and Frances; it felt obvious to Alec that 'a lovely speaking voice' was lady-code for 'I fancy Neville Chamberlain somewhat'.

Proud of subverting any detailed discussion of her mother, Doris checked her watch. It was seductive, this house, with its air of unstoppable correctness and its layering of comfort upon ease. She would have liked to watch the evening stroll in across the rolled and righteous lawn. But no, back to Brookfield for Doris, back to the tang of new milk and the buzz saw of the children's complaints about how queer Grandma had been while they were left alone with her. 'Dan,' she mouthed. She jerked her head towards the door.

'Eh?' Dan could be slow on the uptake.

The doctor let out a barked laugh. 'Your wife's right, Dan.' Morgan turned to Pamela. 'Thank you for another delightful lunch, but it really is time we left you in peace.'

Napkins were discarded. Coats were found. Gerald was whistled up to say a surly farewell. Hero barked. Morgan stayed behind for the promised cigar, and Dan commented approvingly on the freshly dug vegetable patch by the terrace as he and Doris set off on foot. 'Digging for victory, that's the ticket!'

The rows of cabbage and turnips had previously been a rose garden of thirty years standing. Alec's mother, long dead, used to breed roses. She named one 'The Boy Alec'. It was fat, the colour of sticking plasters, and smelled pleasingly of butter. There were acres available to Pamela in which to dig for victory, but she had churned up the Cherry Parfaits and the Blush Noisettes and the only extant example of The Boy Alec.

'Lovely-looking brassicas,' said Doris.

'Is it rude to say thank God they've gone?' asked Pamela. She took out a hairpin and then pushed it back into the shiny roll that hung over her forehead.

'It is rather, old thing.' Alec would have dragged all their guests back again if he could. The house was so quiet, the ticking of various clocks mocking them both. This hour in the drawing room with a book and his wife was the most Sunday-ish part of Sunday. A heavy mass of an hour, it sagged in his hands. Alec feared Pamela could read his mind. See right through his brilliantined skull to his base thoughts.

A Pekinese wobbled into the room. Mavis liked to spread herself flat on the carpet like a neglected bathmat. She panted. Her flat nose was runny and her eyes stood froggily proud of her face. Mavis loved Pamela, but the dog's relationship with Alec was less warm. She rolled over and he saw the horrid scaly patches on her back legs.

Pamela said, 'Magsy does nag old Morgan so.'

'Old?' Alec was touchy; Morgan sat comfortably in the next decade along, and Alec preferred to think of old men as being twenty years ahead of him.

'She sees Morgan as her vocation, I fear. He's very patient with her.'

'Yes, he is.'

'That boy of his, George . . .'

'Hardly a boy, Pamela.'

'He's a wild card, I've heard. Drinks.'

'I've heard the same.'

Silence. Silence. Another silence. Alec coughed just to make some noise. Pamela should know better than to try and involve him in discussing their guests. He was incurious about the interior workings of other people, and had been trained from birth not to comment.

Every crossing of his legs, every turn of a page, sounded loud as gunfire in the drawing room.

The fire petered out.

'Should I?' Alec cocked his Agatha Christie at the embers. 'Or is it a waste?'

'There's plenty of coal,' said Pamela. 'But maybe . . .' Everything was a matter of conscience these days. 'Leave it.'

'Don't want you catching cold.'

Silence.

Hero farted on the Persian rug. Alec didn't smile. There was no space for Hero's farts in Pamela's dominion; they unhappened the moment they happened.

As he reread some dialogue, and tried to care who had

killed whom, and why, Pamela said, with a lilt to her voice which signified amusement, 'So, the whole village knows who really blacked your eye.'

He kept staring at the book until it became farcical to do so. He looked up, as if only then realizing she required a response. 'What? Oh, darling, he didn't, I told you how my eye happened. It wasn't Gerald.'

'You told me two different versions, darling, both of which took place the very same day Gerald needed his knuckles bathed and dressed.'

Best to look straight at her. Even though it was dangerous, like looking at the sun.

It had been a hell of a way to end the old year. The last day of 1939 had been cruelly cold. He'd pulled Kitty tight against his side as he saw her to the bus stop in Felpersham, just a street away from the modest hotel where they had laughed at the grubby furniture and kissed each other and sat about in the altogether. She read to him, her beloved Hardy, and slapped away his desperate hands until she reached the end of the chapter. They were, like the characters, Far from the Madding Crowd.

Just before the bus took her away she whispered into his ear a line Hardy had given to Gabriel Oak. 'Love is a possible strength,' she said, inviting him to end the quote.

He was a good student. 'In a possible weakness.'

Turning into the sleet, it had taken a second or two for Alec to recognize his son in the shop doorway. Gerald was from his other life, the one in sepia. The boy pounced. Never a fighter, he was easily smothered by Alec, but not before he'd landed a lucky punch on his father's eye in the middle of the crowded pavement.

Bundling him down an alley, Alec let Gerald rage, let him spit and splutter about how he'd followed him out of the house for days on end, followed him to 'that tart'.

'Don't tell your mother,' said Alec.

'As if I would! If Mummy—' Gerald paused at his slip of the tongue. 'If Mother ever finds out I'll kill you!'

Here and now, in the room that smelled of polish and, suddenly, his own sweat, Alec said, 'Don't judge him too harshly, Pam.' *She hates being called Pam! Why did I call her Pam?* 'I leaned too hard on him. All this business with the school. Probably overdid the stern papa speech and he lashed out. Don't think ill of the boy.'

'I don't think ill of him. If I could pull the odd punch and get away with it, I would.'

'Goodness, I'd better watch out!' Alec stood up. 'I'll fetch more coal. Just this once.'

'Ring for it, darling.' Pamela gestured to the ribbon pull by the mirror.

'May as well stretch my legs.' *And vomit up my lamb.*

When he was at the door, his hand on the brass knob, Pamela, her back to him, spoke without looking up from her magazine. 'I know, Alec.'

'What's that?' His voice sounded girlishly surprised.

She flicked a page. 'I've known for some time.'

He closed the door and leaned against it. 'I see.'

'Do you love this girl?'

'What?' Alec flattened himself against the painted pine. Stared at the back of his wife's head. 'Pamela, I, that's absurd.' He was hot. He was cold. He was not himself; he was that lowest of things, a man caught in a lie.

Mavis stared at him, bug-eyed.

'I can wait, darling, but not for ever.' Pamela turned down the corner of a page. 'Do not humiliate me.' She twisted in the high-backed chair to look at him. She smiled. 'Coal, Alec. More coal.'

Hero was walked good and proper that evening. Round The Green, past the church, past the dark Sunday windows of The Bull. And then another circuit, the dog still sprightly and his owner less so. Their odyssey didn't take in Noon Cottage.

Love!

Alec was appalled by Pamela's question. The brazenness of it. The foolishness of the idea. She'd read too many novels. There was no room for love in his life. It would be like planting an oak tree in a geranium pot.

Affection, yes, and admiration, and wild desire. All of that. Kitty deserved to be treated with gentleness and to be worshipped, even; that had been a revelation, the way she made Alec admire her and even envy her in a peculiar way that, come to think of it, was too odd to dissect. He had never told her he loved her; he had never had the thought.

They were not lovers in that sense. They were friends who loved, yes, could that be a way of pinning it down? Alec shied from anything sleazy; he was not taking from Kitty, they were giving to each other. And while it was secret, it was innocent. The vacuum kept it free from taint; if nobody was hurt, then there could be no blame.

But Pamela knew.

Alec had assumed she took no notice of him; her cool eye never seemed to settle on him. And yet she knew. *She knows.* Nothing could be the same, now. It was as all-encompassing as the declaration of war.

It was an odd juncture to appreciate one's wife's emotional wisdom, to realize she knew more about him than she let on.

Alec made his way round to the back of Lower Loxley. He appreciated, too, Pamela's self-control; if she had sobbed he couldn't have borne it; he'd have given up Kitty there and then.

SPRING

1940

And which will my Bride be?
The right or the wrong? 'The wrong.'

THOMAS HARDY
The Echo Elf Answers

War was good for the legs.

Doris walked much more these days; wasting petrol was punishable with imprisonment and she was too busy to go to jail. She used up all her available puff toiling to Broom Corner, where the Horrobins' smallholding squatted, and had to lean on where the gate should have been to catch her breath.

A piece of paper tacked to the gatepost made her lose that breath again. *Not another of those horrible things,* she thought, before reading 'KEEP OUT!' It was merely the Horrobin version of a welcome mat.

'Hello there, boys.' It took her two goes to get the words out.

'Go 'way!' The taller Perkins boy threw a stone at her. Wizbang barked his encouragement.

'Now, now, Billy,' said Doris. 'That's not nice.'

'*I'm* not nice,' he told her. He threw a stone at a chicken, who dodged it neurotically.

'I'm nice, Mrs Archer,' said John.

'I can tell,' said Doris, straightening her hat. It was a hat, not a scarf, today; she was on billeting business. Boxes must be ticked and dark corners enquired into. She didn't relish poking Horrobin dark corners, but duty called. As did the memory of little John's tears in the village hall. 'Connie in?'

The boys pointed to the house that leaned to one side and whose chimney stack was jagged. They were filthy, but well fed; Doris couldn't ask for more than that in such an imperfect world.

'Connie?' She waited on the step for an invitation. Archers weren't necessarily welcome here. There had been run-ins. Dan had warned Stan he'd have to plant up at least two of their fields with sugar beet, and Stan had told Dan to piss off.

'Who's that?'

Doris followed the voice into the dark interior. No signs of spring in there, despite bluebells rioting only feet away. It was sooty, an Alice in Wonderland chaos with a bed on its side in the hall and plaster shrinking away to expose the wooden guts of the house. It smelled, too. Of slopped ale and spoilt milk. In the cell of a kitchen sat Connie.

'In, in,' said Connie by way of hello. 'Sit, if you're staying.'

Knitting needles were busy in her hands. She wasn't knitting socks for our brave boys, Doris knew; Connie was making a flam, a net for Stan to fling over a rabbit hole. The terrified rabbit, flushed out by Stan's evil ferrets, would rush out into it, and meet the tiny club which fitted so well into Stan's hand.

Two and six a rabbit, and thruppence for a skin.

'Tea?' Connie did have some teeth, but Doris couldn't make them out in the gloom.

It would be preferable to murder somebody than refuse

tea in their kitchen. Doris nodded. She took out a Manila folder from her bag, which was large enough to house such an item and much more besides. There was string in there, and a comb, and a very old wrapped humbug. She tried not to look at the cups Connie took down from a shelf and wiped on her greasy skirt.

'Carry on,' said Connie.

Doris opened her mouth, but before she could ask Connie the first question on her list – *Are the young people in your care free from lice?* – a voice came from the corner.

Connie had not meant that Doris should carry on: a male voice, fluid and naïve, but with sympathy for the prose he carefully read out, carried on instead. Doris recognized Dickens. Her favourite of his, *David Copperfield*. 'Is that you, Cliff?'

It was. It was the changeling Horrobin, the shy one, whose mild eyes and introverted manner set him apart from his feral folks. Doris squinted and made him out. 'God bless your eyesight, Cliff. Don't know how you can read in that light.'

'There you go.' Connie's tea looked surprisingly good. Strong enough to trot a mouse on. Connie looked far older than her thirty-seven years. Being a baby factory and a punchbag will do that to a woman. 'Them boys you give me is no trouble. I just feeds 'em and turf 'em out of a morning. Not a sneeze nor a cough out of either of 'em.' She looked over at the corner. 'My Cliffy loves them, don't you?'

The shadow nodded. 'That Billy's a card,' he said.

'The money's handy and all. Times is hard.'

'For all of us,' said Doris. She felt Connie bridle; bottom of the Ambridge pile, Connie didn't want competition. 'And Stan?' So many questions in the two words.

'Drinking less,' lied Connie.

'Does he let you keep the evacuee money?'

'Tell you what, why don't I come to your house and ask you questions about you and your old man, eh?'

Point taken, Doris raised her hands in surrender. 'I only want to help.'

'You Archers love helpin'.' Connie stood with her arms crossed and her legs apart, like a scrawny pirate. 'I don't need no help.'

Doris lacked the bravery or the stupidity to ask if the boys had lice. She saw Connie scratch her head – a really determined scratch, like the ones Glen the sheepdog enjoyed. She decided to choose her battles, to write 'satisfactory' on her paperwork, or even 'good' as poor Connie needed a boost, and then stood up. She gulped down the tea and made noises about leaving.

'Say a proper goodbye, Cliff.' Connie encouraged the 'good' Horrobin out of the darkness. 'You'll be setting off tomorrow, and it might be a while before Doris claps eyes on you again.'

Dipping his head, the boy emerged, reluctant. He held out his hand stiffly, not making eye contact.

Doris didn't take his hand immediately. The khaki took her by surprise. Cuffed trousers. Heavy boots. Pockets and flaps and a stiff collar. 'Congratulations,' she said. It came out feebly, hampered by the bad taste in her mouth. Battledress was the most patriotic outfit Cliff could wear, but to Doris it seemed more like a shroud. 'Where are you off to? My Jack's in Chatham now, bored stiff and hating it.'

'I'm off to France. With the BEF. Labour division.'

British Expeditionary Force: Doris knew that meant no training. Cliff would be put on a boat and decanted in France in no time. At his feet, his dog Stacey, a distant mongrel relative of Brookfield's Glen, beat a tattoo with her feathery tail. She stared, rapt, at her master. Dogs were, Doris knew, reliable judges of character. 'Your mother'll miss you.'

The empathy undid something in Connie. 'Who'll read me *David Copperfield* when he's gone?' It was desperate, nothing like the light remark it might have been.

'And all the juicy murders out of the Sunday paper, Mum. Don't forget them.'

'Not one week into his apprenticeship and called up.' Connie approved Doris's tut. 'How'd you like that? They think the world of him at Warnes and Killick. That printing place over Felpersham. What was it you were going to be, Cliffy?'

'Die stamper, Mum. And I still will be. Don't you worry.'

Stacey put her head on her paws.

The mahogany desk at the window – nineteenth-century, leather-topped – was Pamela's.

Or, she used it; somebody had passed the desk down to Alec; somebody else had passed it down to that passer-on.

In many ways Alec considered himself the curator of their furniture, as if it was all on loan until he passed it down to Gerald.

Pamela preferred to feel she owned it. She had brought many antiques to the house, but none of them were legacies. They were bought and paid for with her father's money; *his* inheritance from his parents had been nothing but a ferocious desire to live lives nothing like theirs.

Pamela smoked as if paid by the cigarette. She paused now, between a thank-you and another letter to the *Borchester Echo*, this one about a bus route that was failing her estate workers, and she sparked a match on a mother-of-pearl matchbox cover.

The scene beyond the window had, with pleasing predictability, updated its detail. Beyond the terrace and the lawn, the sheep were back out, fluffy polka dots on a green background.

She thought, as she seemed to do all the bloody time these days, about her husband. Wondered if he was with his mistress. Her imagination had become pornographic. Such images were unwelcome, but when Pamela replaced them with more innocent ones – Alec and Kitty talking, Alec and Kitty handing each other a glass of something – they were infinitely more offensive.

The cigarette glowed angry red as she pulled on it, her cheeks turning cadaverous. For the sake of understanding the wave which had overturned her marriage, she attempted to look at Alec through the girl's eyes, as a prospective lover.

Pamela saw only a husband, and a shop-soiled one at that. *What does Kitty see in him?* Yes, he was handsome, but so was Pamela's horse.

Bit of a stick insect out of his clothes. Those stiff shoulders, as if he'd left the coat hanger in his jacket. And the hair that wouldn't lie flat, and an awful way of sneezing that could be heard all over the house. He was just another man; the world was stuffed full of men, many of them trying to kill each other for no good reason Pamela could see.

Possibly Alec's only distinguishing trait was the fact that he was hers. She would never whitewash their history; she was neither sentimental nor a liar. But they had built something important together.

'Gerald!' The boy was passing the door. He either skulked or sped, and this was a skulk. 'Come here, do, darling, come *on*.' Beneath the chair Mavis stirred. Very little inspired the Pekinese to activity but her profound rivalry with Gerald forced a yip out of her. 'Quiet, Mavis. Bad girl. Gerald, darling, it's so sunny out, why not—'

'I don't care about the sun, Mother.'

'All right, well, why not invite a chum over?'

'Got no friends round here.' Gerald was hunched and beefy, a hormonal stew of resentment. Next to his leaf-slender mother he looked like a performing bear.

'Somebody from school, then. I could call up their parents. It'd be fun, you could sleep up in the attic, or make a camp.'

'School?' Gerald recoiled as if from a cobra. 'School chucked me out.'

'They did *not*, darling. It's just a suspension. Daddy's sorting it out. You really must learn not to solve problems with *these*.' She held up her fists, laughing.

Gerald didn't laugh. 'Are you stupid, Mother?'

Even an expert like Pamela sometimes struggled with her composure. 'Now, darling, that is *not*—'

'You *are* stupid. You're blind. As blind as Jimmy Little.'

'Let's not speak so glibly of poor Bob's son. I see *you* well enough, Gerald Pargetter.' She risked touching him; it didn't go well, he shook her hand off his arm. 'I see a fine young man not fulfilling his potential.'

Gerald toed Mavis, who snapped at his shoe. He slunk out.

Pamela shook her head and her hair didn't move.

In the porcelain ashtray her cigarette had burned down to a fragile ash worm. She lit another.

Brookfield's back door – to all intents and purposes the front door – always made the same noise and it always reminded Dan that he really must get an oil can to its hinges. 'Love?' he called, scraping his feet on the mat.

'She's out.' Lisa wore the pinny of power. She was in charge of the kitchen with all that this implied. In recent years she had shrunk somewhat, and she wore her iron-coloured hair in a severe bob that was at once geriatric and child-like. A clip held it back from her face. Lisa wasn't given to vanity.

'Where's she gone?' Dan was wary. He had approached a sick ewe with this expression just an hour earlier. But his mother-in-law seemed sharp. Seemed herself.

'Off to the hospital in Borchester. That poor Eugene had a fall. Oh, it was awful, Dan. Fell awkward, on his bad foot, and hurt his wrist. I said to them, off you go, I'll sort Dan's lunch, don't you worry. She doesn't half look after you, my Doris. You know what they say about you in the family. Doris and Dan, never a cross word. Two peas in a pod, they say.'

'They're right.' Dan was proud of his marriage. In a quiet way. He didn't go around bragging, but ye gods, he was grateful for it when he saw how other couples tore chunks out of each other. 'You raised a good 'un there, Lisa.'

'My Bill, God rest his soul, used to say to me, you're good for two things, Lisa, cooking and babies. He wasn't wrong.' Earlier, Lisa had roamed the house looking for Bill, weeping when she couldn't find him. 'Now, here we go.' She took up a knife. 'I know what my son-in-law likes. A nice ham sandwich, thick bread, lashings of piccalilli. Am I right?'

'Spot on!' Dan was reassured. His were broad shoulders, and he took responsibility for the farm and his family and, these days, his community. But being in charge of Lisa felt shamefully heavy. She was unpredictable; Dan liked to keep things in order. Farming had taught him that; you let things slide at your peril. A loose horseshoe this week would be a lame animal the next time you looked. With Lisa there was no plan, no forecast, just a future of being eternally on your toes. Your tired toes.

He would bring it up again with Doris. How they needed to let people know about Lisa's problems. To ask for help.

He washed his hands in the cold, cold water, dried them on

a chequered towel and sat at the table. He shoved Mother Cat until she had no option but to jump down. 'I've been over to Robin Farm.' He watched Lisa slice the loaf Doris had taken out of the oven that morning. Watched her spread two slices with pale butter. 'Making sure the new tenants are on top of things.'

'There you go.' Lisa slapped down his lunch.

No plate. Two slices of buttered bread, one with a bite taken out of it.

'Where's my ham?'

She laughed, and he laughed with relief and because, God knows, it was funny. But he didn't like the way she waved the big sharp knife around as she took out the ham from the coolest corner of the pantry.

Kitty pulled on her cardigan and went to the gate.

Shoulders up, head down, a brisk scuttle in her thin-soled shoes.

She stared down the road as if sheer need might make Alec appear. The hedgerow on either side, fattening up now that it was spring, showed her only a narrow empty funnel.

It was dicey to step out so often, to allow her face to show so clearly how she suffered, when someone among them was taking notes.

Again, she recited Alec's last words to her, whispered against her cheek just before he delivered himself unto the jaws of Easter Sunday lunch with the vicar. She'd asked when she would see him again, and his reply had become a prayer after a week of no contact. Drilled into her like the Hail Mary.

I'll be there for our Saturday, if not before.

He'd never called it that before. 'Our Saturday,' she murmured, like her grandmother mumbling at Mass. If she'd had rosary beads she'd have turned them over in her fingers. 'If not before.'

There had been no 'before'. Usually, Kitty and Alec contrived to bump into each other most days, but all week Alec had been absent from The Green, the shop, the pub. 'Our Saturday,' she said again, loving the possessive, shared nature of the phrase. Saturday visits from Alec had become constant; a handhold in her craggy week. An hour or two of togetherness, of passion, of seeing herself in his eyes, and then sweetness. Oh, that sweetness, all of it bottled up inside Alec until she popped his cork and out it gushed, pure and nutritious.

She relied on it to keep her going. 'Our Saturday.'

'Mammy!'

Kitty trotted back to the cottage, arms tightly wound around herself. A straitjacket she recalled her mother wearing often. 'Here I am, musha!' She pushed at Caroline's cowlick and bamboozled her back to bed with tickles. 'Nighty night, hen.' She was everything to Caroline, and the responsibility pleased her. Widowhood hadn't changed anything; Noel was wont to ignore his daughter for days, only to cry over her with brandy breath, prattling that he loved her and she was his angel until the poor little thing burst into hot tears and had to be prised away from the man-baby.

That's how Kitty thought of Noel. A baby, escaped somehow from his pram, and wearing a suit. Fooling the others, but never fooling his carer, his *victim*. She had learned to expect less and less from Noel, until she expected nothing.

And that's what he gave me. In spades. One day she would get around to feeling sorry for Noel, for the waste he represented, the ruin of his own hopes, but before Kitty could indulge in such generosity she had to scale the slagheap of want he had left in his wake.

Creditors had tipped their hat at Kitty the moment the last mourner left on the day of Noel's funeral. He'd spent money he didn't have on schemes that made no sense. A plot of land in Wales. Half-share in a racehorse that may or may not exist. Noel had had the fun of daydreaming about these get-rich-quick pipe dreams, but it was Kitty who was handed the bill.

There was no help to be had from the Dibden-Rawleses. They had made that clear, in their glacially polite manner. So she begged for terms from the debt collectors and lived on a strictly managed schema which sometimes allowed some air in, but mostly didn't.

Poverty was nothing new; Kitty had grown up with little. It was facing it alone that demoralized her. Keeping up appearances was exhausting, and surely pointless, but pride ran through her like the stripe in a stick of rock.

Her country life, so charmingly soft-edged and prettified by leaves and ferns and blossom, was more of a cage when closely examined. Certainty? It was nowhere to be found. Not even on Saturdays.

Unable to settle, Kitty paced Noon Cottage. This discomfort could only be cured by the arrival of Alec, smelling of the cool outside air, Hero at his side, maybe in that awful cap she hated. A book didn't help. A glass of gin made it worse. She went to the step again, and begged the night to hand him over.

'Our Saturday,' she whispered.

The empty week had brought more gossip about the letters. Kitty had presented a serene mask while Dottie read out the second one; the woman had actually written down the wording and stashed it in her purse.

The first letter – 'the Pargetter letter', Dottie called it; she was Ambridge's scholar on the topic, keeper of the archive – seemed designed to force Alec's hand. A perfect tool to nudge him into confessing to Pamela. Would that be good for Kitty? Kitty couldn't tell; perhaps he'd already told Pamela and that was why he was missing. Or, what did they call it in the army? AWOL. Absent without leave.

Because something was very wrong. This was their Saturday, and she was alone and Noon Cottage was shrinking by the second.

Out to the gate again, to the corner and back.

Kitty let out little sighs that helped for a fraction of a second. The dismal vegetable patch, a needy plot beneath the square-paned window, was flat and wretched in the darkness. No great broad leaves or rude-coloured berries.

She had no green thumb, and besides she resented the patch. It was a fig leaf placed over her Irishness and her neutrality, a way of semaphoring to the village that she was in step, and doing her bit.

It was hard to take war regulations seriously when Kitty's personal battle for survival was so intense. She was on a secret mission. She was in search of a harbour.

And my boat is full of leaks. There was no way of knowing what Alec was in search of when he came to Kitty. He had no need of a harbour. Yet she wanted to save him; it was an urge as strong as her urge to rush to Caroline when she fell over.

He might be drifting. Just passing through. *Should I have refused to have sex with him?* The great no-no of her religion, and the great turbine of life. She could have withheld, the feminine gambit.

She hadn't wanted to withhold; she was tired of scrimping and saving and eking out. She had spent herself lavishly on Alec. No questioning, no strategy. Everything was cleansed by love, she had decided, in the face of all she'd been taught.

That she loved Alec was a fact of Kitty's life. He didn't even have to do much to earn it. Whether he knew about her love wasn't clear; he was, even when naked, or perhaps especially when naked, hard to read on that subject. She had chosen an opaque man to spend her love on.

She wondered, as she scanned the road again, if she was a courtesan. Fluffy word, but it meant prostitute. She was certainly what her grandmother would call a 'bad girl'. *Bad ged-el*, in Dublinese.

A story came back to her. Of her grandmother telling her, apropos of nothing, that 'bad girls' were taken to the mattress factory and squeezed to death between two of the best quality mattresses.

Kitty had looked for a moral there, and come up empty-handed. For all she knew – Dublin was a kooky town – it might be true.

She drifted back in. Upstairs, where the attic rooms folded inwards like origami. To the kitchen where she put away a pan and leaned her forehead against the cupboard door. There was a pattern of holes, punched into the wood to let air circulate among the dried goods. Kitty poked her fingers in, and then took them out again.

A knock at the door sent her hurtling through the house. No need to pinch her cheeks; the blood rushed to her face. She paused for a second to shuck off her knickers. She must be gay, she must be bright. The courtesan must earn her keep; if Alec wanted to walk away the whole of society was on his side. Nothing tied him to her except his desire.

It was Jane Gilpin at the door.

A breeze floated up Kitty's dress as she listened to Jane ask if she had seen a kitten, silly really to get so attached, but you see Jane had christened it and fed it and now the dear little chap was nowhere to be found, so she was knocking on doors and asking if a fluffy little something wandered into the garden would they be so kind as to bundle it up and bring it to Woodbine Cottage?

'Yes, yes, of course, Miss Gilpin,' said Kitty.

'It's very furry. Almost looks as if it's wearing pantaloons! Answers to the name of, well, *Denholm*.'

Kitty closed the door, and put her knickers back on with great solemnity.

April

'I do so love our tootles in the car,' chirped Blanche from the back seat.

She watched Morgan's eyes with their great thatched brows in the rear-view mirror. Saw how diligently he watched the road. How often his eyes slid to the passenger up front beside him.

'Nance, you're too good,' said Blanche, 'giving up your Sundays for a sour old dame like me.'

'No, no, don't be silly.' Nance was inoffensive. In her manner, which was gentle, and her speech, which was demure. Even the neat bun at the nape of her long neck was neither 'done' nor casual. She smelled good, better than Blanche would expect of a woman who spent seventy per cent of her day in close proximity to ham and cheese and sawdust shavings.

'They'll be planting potatoes there, too,' said Morgan, waving his arm at a field that stretched up and away from the edge of the road. To Blanche it looked like every other field;

she heard Nance murmur something. What? *What does one reply to such a comment?*

'Potatoes everywhere, thanks to Dan Archer and the War Ag,' Morgan went on. 'Carbohydrates will win the war for us, ladies!'

'That, and blood,' said Blanche. News of Denmark's invasion had broken. The phony war was over; it was all too real now. The trance that held them in thrall since September had released them into garish Technicolor. Blanche had always thought of Denmark – if she thought of it at all – as a clean and sensible little country. It was a shame. A great shame. And there was no going back.

The privations and the inchoate fear would continue. There would be an ending that would be written about in black and white in future history books. Blanche wasn't among those who wondered what the books would say. She was engrossed in the moment. In herself.

The car hopped over a pothole.

'All right in the back?' Morgan was solicitous.

'It's like a fairground ride. Tell me, Doctor, what were you talking about so mysteriously to my sister while Agnes was dressing me?'

'Were we mysterious? Jane's very tired, she's suffering with disturbed sleep. Says the house is haunted, that she can hear dead children padding about at night. You and I know, Blanche, that it's Jane's nerves that are the real problem.'

'It's me who's the problem, you mean.' Blanche ploughed through the pooh-poohing. 'I know what it takes out of Jane, looking after me.'

'Miss Gilpin loves you,' said Nance. 'She's happy to do it, I'm sure.'

'Such tact,' said Blanche, enjoying the condescension. 'Do you know what you'd make, my dear? You'd make an excellent doctor's wife.'

'Oh, I—' Nance laughed. As if Blanche was being preposterous. 'Goodness.' Even her voice was blushing.

Morgan ignored the comment, and said, 'I don't believe in ghosts but I do believe in the restorative power of a good night's sleep. I prescribed Jane a stronger sleeping draught.' As Ambridge's doctor he had proved unwilling to mete out medicine on demand; this was often met with consternation. Instead, he tended to be, as some of his patients put it, 'dreadfully talky'. 'It's powerful stuff. You be my eyes and ears, Blanche, and make sure she doesn't overdo it.'

'My sister never overdoes anything. I am considered a debauchee if I suggest a second small sweet sherry.'

'And look, on our left—'

'Morgan, please don't tell me what's planted in that humdrum little field that looks just like all the other little fields. Let the poor thing maintain some mystique.'

Morgan laughed. A big 'Ha ha!' He glanced at Nance when she laughed too. 'I have to ask, Blanche, if you're entirely over that whole unsavoury business with the anonymous letter.'

Nance's laugh was cut off as if somebody had pulled out her plug. 'Those horrible things!' It was the most animated either passenger had ever seen her. 'They should be made to pay, whoever they are, playing tricks like that on their neighbours.'

111

Blanche was far less energetic. 'Over it, Morgan? I was over it before I read the end of the first line. I won't pay some silly troublemaker the compliment of losing sleep over their fibs.'

'You're very brave,' said Nance, twisting her neck to look at the brave, prone woman behind her. 'They're so *mean*. I dread the next one being about me.'

'Why? What have you done? Oh, don't colour up, Nance. Isn't she pretty when she blushes, Morgan? I don't suspect you of having a past.' Blanche hesitated, enjoying the power this conversation had handed her. 'Or do you have hidden, racy depths, miss? Some secret love? Oh, Nance, what have I uncovered?'

'No, nothing, I, I just go pink easily,' said Nance. She was tormented, as if Blanche was a cat and she a little field mouse.

'We all have secrets,' said Blanche. 'Even our beloved doctor here.'

'Me?' Morgan let his mouth hang open in mock amazement. 'But I'm an open book.' He put his foot down imperceptibly and the car picked up speed. 'Yes sirree,' he said, more to himself than to the ladies. 'An open book.'

'I wondered at first if the letter writer could be some enemy of mine,' said Blanche.

Nance smothered that. 'How could you have enemies? No, no, no.'

'Even a cripple can rub people up the wrong way.' Blanche enjoyed the slight cringe Nance gave at her use of 'cripple'. *That's what I am*, she thought, confident it wasn't *who* she was. 'For that theory to hold water, I'd have to share an enemy with Alec Pargetter, and that feels unlikely.'

'Neither letter is true,' said Morgan. 'Which makes us all potential victims. This character just makes up stories and broadcasts them. Not a damn thing we can do about it.'

'Worst part is,' said Blanche, looking out at, yes, another field, 'Whitey doesn't come up and lie on my bed anymore. I miss him.'

Nance gave a discreet *Ahem*.

A soft night.

Clouds like eiderdowns.

The sky a warm lilac turning to the blue of RAF uniforms above the hills.

The moment shimmers.

Jack is nowhere near the blue hills. In Chatham barracks, he lies on the camp bed nearest the window. It hit him today that there really is a war on, and he really is a soldier. A man at the far end snores, and Jack can smell the incense of a dozen mingled farts as he thinks of Peggy Perkins, and the snapshot he has in his head of her. She is turning away from him on the platform at Hollerton. Her hair swings and her eyes half-close and she could be smiling but no, she's almost certainly laughing at him. She does this again and again, the soft susurration of her hair singing him to sleep.

Morgan sits on the end of his bed. No trousers. One shoe already off. He feels oldest at this time of day. The bed is big. He doesn't always allow himself to acknowledge that he still misses his wife. He misses her scoldings. They were a kind of absolution. He would confess if he could, but this isn't one for the vicar.

Dottie kicks off the covers. Mrs E is a great believer in layers of blankets and sheets and quilts, but Mrs E doesn't sleep with a passenger. Dottie pulls up her nightie. From below her breasts her body is a hillock in the moonlight. Bigger and bigger it grows, making her feel out of sorts and then sleepy and then suddenly full of pep. Arms growing in there, fancy that. And a winkie too, if it's a boy. *Stay in there as long as you can, mate,* she implores the baby. The later the birth the easier it will be to pass it off as her other half's.

Avoiding the creaky board outside Christine's door, Doris hears her daughter's voice. It's one of the great joys of Doris's day, listening to Christine's doll, Miss Grizelda, on the receiving end of another life lesson. *Better than the wireless, it is!* Doris stops. Smiles. Strains to listen. 'And then you kneel down, that's right, Miss Grizelda, and you start off by saying "Our Father who art in heaven".' Doris jerks away from Christine's door as if the old wood burns her cheek. She doesn't want to hear her child's prayer. Can't stand the trusting confidence in Christine's voice as she speaks the words Doris taught her. She hurries down the hall. She climbs into bed beside Dan, who says, 'Doris, it's been a while, love, how about a spot of—' and she snaps 'No!' and punches the pillow and closes her eyes.

* * *

It was clear the first anonymous letter, the one accusing Alec, had only made things worse for Kitty.

Almost three weeks had passed since Easter. Since then, Kitty had encountered Alec in the shop, on the street, by the pond. Each time his face was closed, a public disguise. He had greeted her blandly. They had nothing in common, no secret code, and he offered no scrap for her to pore over. She was reduced to this piracy, stumbling across The Green, dragging Caroline by the hand, hoping he might pass with Hero.

'That child should be in bed,' said a woman as she passed.

Kitty knew that. 'We're visiting the ducklings,' she said. She had applied her lipstick carefully. She had curled her hair with the poker, having burned her finger on the gas hob. She had added a beauty spot by the edge of her mouth with the licked end of a pencil. All for the ducklings.

In her pocket was a letter to Alec: a proscribed and terrible act. On the envelope she had sharpened up her curly letters, rendering them as masculine as possible. She had rewritten the note many times, until she was satisfied that it would not give them away should it fall into enemy hands.

Dear Mr Pargetter,

I hope this finds you well.

Please do not forget the business matter we discussed. I am ready to proceed at your convenience, and can be found at the usual address.

Yours, G. Oak Esq.

The name had jumped out from *Far from the Madding Crowd*. The book had tripped her up on the rug, where she had thrown it after an evening spent trying to escape into its pages. She had run out of gin. She had run out of all but the most basic of food. Noon Cottage was a place of famine.

On the back of the anodyne note, Kitty had written something in tiny letters. A dare. A lure. Small enough to go unnoticed unless he looked for it. Surely, *surely*, he would look for it.

Kitty was jumpy. Disconnected. As if her shoes were on the wrong feet. She disappointed her little girl, who was accustomed to a merry playmate, not this anxious mother who went through the motions of hide and seek, and who cried when she sang the end of day lullaby.

If Kitty truly was a boat then she was drifting through wreckage in a night sea. The lighthouse she relied upon was dark, no longer casting a cheerful stripe on the waves.

There he was. The far side of the pond. With Hero. And there was Dan, too. And, oh sweet Jesus, there was Mrs Endicott and Dottie coming from the other direction. *Why?* she thought, her face hot. Why did they all choose this moment to step out of their doors?

Kitty hurried around the pond's uneven bank. She ignored the ducklings. If she sped up she could intercept him. 'Come on, hen.'

Caroline stumped along, her feet slipping in the mud. 'Ducklings,' said the girl. 'Babies!'

'I know, later. Oh! Alec!' Kitty was toothy, over-loud. 'Hello there!'

Dan beamed at her. Dan always did. She cheered him up, she could tell. 'Look who it is!'

Whereas Alec looked hunted. His eyes, always so soft when they looked at her, were pinwheels of confusion. His fear of exposure was the only thing that made him stop and listen to her; she could tell he wanted to run away, knees up, zigzagging, like the partridges who used to scatter in front of Noel's car. 'Hello, Kitty.' He lifted his cap woodenly.

He was such a bad actor; good thing Dan was too guileless to suspect.

'Alec, could you do me a *huge* favour and pass this note to your wife? I need to borrow a bicycle and Mrs Endicott told me Pamela has one she rarely uses and never minds lending it out.'

Mrs Endicott had stopped, her arm through Dottie's. 'That's quite right, I did tell you that. But Kitty dear, do reconsider. A bicycle is a deathtrap. A cousin of mine fell off one in Wootton Bassett and can only take soft foods from that day to this.' She turned to Dottie, stricken. 'Even a boiled egg is an effort.'

'Could you?' Kitty folded Alec's hand over the cream envelope. 'I'd be so grateful.'

'Of course.' Alec pulled his hand away.

No electricity.

* * *

Mr Frank Brown

Requests the honour of your company
at the wedding of his daughter

Nancy

To

Dr Morgan Seed

at St Stephen's Church, Ambridge
on Saturday the second of June
at 4 o'clock

and afterwards at The Bull

Whitey White delivered the wedding invitations early on the morning of the twenty-fourth of April. By midday, it was standing room only at Blanche's bedside.

Jane shared a low chair with Mrs Endicott. She was

disentangling a gold chain; she'd been jubilant to find it in the bottom of her jewellery box. It might take up half an afternoon if she was lucky.

Dottie leaned on the back of the chair, while Magsy filled the window. Doris had looked in, then backed out.

They all talked at once, until Blanche let out a roar. 'Ladies! One at a time!' She had powdered her face and the crow had curled her hair. Agnes curled the front with care and the back badly, which was very Agnes. 'Am I being indelicate to point out that there's quite an age difference between bride and groom?'

'Twenty years or so?' speculated Dottie. 'If he's fifty summat and ole Nance is thirty-ish. Not too bad. Better than the other way around, Blanche! It'd be like you marrying Jimmy Little.'

A copy of the invitation lay on the bed. It was flimsy, a corner already torn. The ink was faint. Jane took it up and smoothed it out on her lap. Poor quality, of course, like so much else since the war began. 'I for one think it's awfully romantic.'

'Hear, hear!' Dottie slapped her on the shoulder. 'Every old sock needs an old shoe. Besides, the doc must make a few bob. Nance is set for life.'

'One interesting kink of this new development,' said Blanche, 'is that Nance will be stepmother to Morgan's two boys.' She pressed her lips together. 'Excuse me. I misspoke. To George. Not poor Anthony, God rest his soul.'

All present blessed themselves except Magsy, who was

too agitated to do so. 'She will *not* be his stepmother. George had a wonderful mother in my sister, and another in myself. How can she perform that most tender of roles for a young man who is, I'm sorry to say, nearer her age than Morgan? I have nothing against Nance, she's a good and kind person, but she's just a girl.'

Dottie, who considered Nance a little long in the tooth to be a girl, said, 'She *is* lovely though, in't she? Lovely hair, lovely way of talking. You'd never know she grew up over a shop. I reckon old Morgan did well for hisself, the randy sod.'

'I wish them both happiness,' said Magsy, strangling a handkerchief in her fingers. 'I really do. But I confess it's a shock. I mean, everyone, *everyone*, thought he'd marry me.'

She silenced the room with that remark.

First to take pity, Jane buckled. 'Of course, of course,' she said, her eyes slithering so Blanche couldn't find them. She would be teased later for propping up Magsy's silly notions. But sometimes, Jane knew, silly notions were all that kept a woman going.

The door opened and Agnes sighed on the threshold with an enormous tray. The lace cap the sisters insisted she wore when company visited had slid down over her fringe. 'I swear,' she said, 'if I have to keep coming up the stairs with this blessed teapot I'll never make a start on the pie.'

'Pie?' squeaked Mrs Endicott. Rationing ensured they were all obsessed with food. Mrs Endicott dreamed nightly of eating up a sugar-paste likeness of Cary Grant and woke licking her lips. 'Did she say pie, Blanche?' She sounded shocked, as if accusing her old friend of keeping slaves, or showing her knees.

'Doris left a rabbit for me. People are so kind,' said Blanche.

'To you they are.' Agnes elbowed her way through the pleats and wool and stout hosiery.

Still fingering the invitation, Jane said, 'It's all so out of the blue.'

'Not to me.' Blanche let that ripple travel round the room.

'Don't fib, Blanche dear.' Jane found she had ripped the invitation. It was so hard not to wonder how the invitations to her own wedding might have looked. This non-event was real and solid in Jane's mind; she planned it, rethought it, sat and considered the merits of trimming her good blue suit with white fur or splurging all her vouchers on a new frock. *Denholm would have insisted on thick, heavy card for the invitation*, this she knew. *Nothing but the best, he would have said.* In the loneliness of her narrow room beneath the eaves, Denholm had been reinstated to dashing hero status. It had been simple, an old habit resurrected. She had long since designed their monogram, a J and a D entwined, crowned by rosebuds. Or foxgloves. No, rosebuds.

'I'm not fibbing,' said Blanche. 'I may rarely leave this room but I know more about the ways of the world than most people.'

Agnes made a noise that could have been a sneeze, but was more probably derision.

'Whatcha mean, Blanche?' said Dottie. She was milking and sugaring and doling out china cups.

'Those Sunday drives. Nance doesn't give up her day of rest for *me*. I brought Morgan and Nance together.'

'A regular cupid,' said Agnes as she left the room.

'That's right, Agnes!' Mrs Endicott was not at home to nuance; she thought everyone as straightforward as herself. 'What a lovely way to put it.'

'She's a treasure,' said Jane, as the door closed behind Agnes. 'What we'd do without her I don't know, the dear plain little thing.'

Agnes, whose ears had evolved to hear through doors, stuck out her tongue. She assumed Jane had deftly forgotten how she'd shrieked at her treasure that morning because the milk had turned. None of the ladies around the bed would recognize *that* Jane Gilpin.

'I can't help fretting,' said Mrs Endicott, 'that our poison-pen writer will find some way to spoil the wedding.'

'Ooh, what a thought.' Dottie moved to sit on the side of the bed, with a wince that came naturally to her in her second trimester. 'D'you mind me perching, Blanche, only you know how it is.' She pointed to the dune asserting itself through her dress.

'I don't know how it is, actually. That boon was stolen by my disease, but do go ahead and make yourself comfortable, Dottie.'

'Ta. It's like this letter writer has cameras in all our houses, innit? Watching. Listening to our private thoughts. Especially the bad ones.'

'Those are the only sort I have,' said Blanche. 'Don't let him get to you. Or her. Or *it*. Dear old Whitey and I certainly don't. We say *fie* to the poison pen!'

Jane sank over her teacup. She had hoped to keep this secret. She disagreed vehemently with the restoration of the postman, and earlier that day had tried to make her point to Blanche, but her sister was a cliff face of indifference. Jane had stomped downstairs full of bottled anger, only to find the milk had gone off. She would buy Agnes something nice to make up for the regrettable scene that followed. A little something from Frank Brown's limited doodah selection.

'I'm safe from the letter writer, now,' said Blanche. 'I've been *done*, as it were.'

More feet on the stairs. A weak knock, and Jimmy Little came in, to a cloud of coos and some clucking. The women allowed him to grope his way to the bed, knowing better than to try and help.

Dottie mimed smacking his bottom as he passed.

Mrs Endicott let out a loud *Tsk!* and there was synchronized shaking of heads. Jimmy's tragedy, an echo of his grandmother's, was a fundamental chapter of Ambridge folklore.

'My dad sent me to say,' said Jimmy, his cap in his hand, 'about the wedding, you're not to worry, Miss Blanche, he'll come next door and personally carry you downstairs and get you to the church and the do afterwards.'

'Bob's a diamond,' said Dottie.

'Oh, and Dr Seed sent this for you.' Jimmy took an orange out of his pocket.

It shone, that orange. It emitted light. Possibly it had its own soundtrack; certainly nobody present would have been surprised to hear a harp.

'An orange,' said Jane, in a strange voice. She hadn't seen one since last year.

'It's full of, um, vitamin C, or vitamin something,' said Jimmy. 'The doctor told me to tell you it's good for people who've got what you've got.'

'Polio,' said Blanche. 'Poliomyelitis.' Her long nails tore into the skin. Juice spritzed the eiderdown.

Her guests leaned in. Lust lay heavy in the air. They watched as she slowly separated each segment and dropped it between tiny teeth that curved inwards, like a shark's.

Jane knew they were waiting for Blanche to offer them some; she knew better than to wait. She daydreamed instead; if she did it intensely enough it was almost as if her day-dream was real.

She imagined herself in a new costume; hang the imaginary expense. A two-piece. Soft bouclé. Her bust was a little larger in this daydream. Denholm wore a well-cut suit in pearly grey. He was a little less portly in this daydream. He kissed her. She took off her blouse. Denholm was struck dumb by her beauty. They came together, their bodies, well, *wriggling.*

It always grew vague at this point.

'Yum,' said Blanche, and tossed the peel. Her lips were sticky.

* * *

If her plan worked, Kitty told herself, he'd come that night. But if night tipped over into tomorrow, then that was that. She had overplayed her hand by writing to Alec and she would never see him again. A superstitious creature, this all made perfect sense to her.

Just as she had once chosen to believe in the baby Jesus, she chose to believe that her letter would work its magic. She believed it as she tucked in Caroline, and put the kitchen to rights, and chivvied the dejected cushions on the couch. She believed, and that would get her through the evening; if it didn't work, well, she put off the mourning until tomorrow.

Tomorrow could take care of itself.

She missed roofs. When she looked out of her window back home – and Dublin was home, however long she ended up staying in England – Kitty saw the city unfold in grey slates. So many people. So much brute personality. 'Here, it's just you and me and a whole load of *nature*,' she whispered to Bella, who was curving her tail around the gatepost like a question mark.

Kitty didn't give up. Not then. Not yet. She had scheduled when to give up and she would stick to her timetable. At midnight she would cry and fantasize about drowning herself. For now, she'd sew.

All of Caroline's knickers needed to be patched, with big rectangles of contrasting stuff across the back. She'd saved scraps – scraps of scraps; life was all scraps – and she was hunting out a needle and thread, about to go upstairs in search of them, when she heard something. A disturbance in the quiet outside. Slight, not a shout. Something only neurotic ears would hear.

It had worked.

Alec materialized in her hallway. Hero sat, as instructed, on the step. Alec held out her note. 'You do like to test a fellow,' he said.

She stepped towards him. Took it from him. His hand was so big. She knew how his fingertips felt on her skin. 'I had confidence you'd be up to the task.' She turned over the piece of paper and read aloud what she'd written on the back. 'Love is a possible strength . . .'

Kitty backed away, up one step of the stairs. Hands behind her back. Her head tilted in a way she knew worked on him. 'Can you finish the quote?'

From the door he said, 'In an actual weakness.'

'You're a good student.' She took another step, backwards, her feet sure as a goat's. 'Hardy knows we're all equal when it comes to love,' she said. Another step back. Another. 'All equally afraid.' She was above him now, forcing him to throw back his head, as if worshipping.

Alec didn't move. He preserved the space between them. To Kitty, it seemed to glitter.

'Are we in love, Alec?'

'I can't afford love.' His face was in shadow. 'I have responsibilities instead.'

It was time to be bold; this is easier when you have nothing to lose. 'Yes, you do have responsibilities, and I'm one of them now.'

Alec's face was still a blank in the shadow. He had bucked against this, tried to withstand the pull of her, but he had had to come, despite Pamela's declaration that she knew all about Kitty. *Or because of it?* He wondered if he was that much of a swine.

Kitty turned. She walked slowly up the remaining stairs. She was still alone as she pushed at the bedroom door.

Then he ran. Two steps at a time.

'D'you remember?' Kitty, sinking onto the bed, shrugging her shoulders out of her cardigan, pointed at the wardrobe. A big ugly old thing, some Dibden-Rawles aunt had given it to them; she'd been a big ugly old thing, too. 'That game of Sardines?'

He remembered, of course.

A raucous party – the only sort Noel knew how to throw – in this very house. Some idiot suggested Sardines. Some idiot always did.

Never one of life's game players, Alec feigned enthusiasm and hid in the wardrobe, wondering if Pamela would be amenable to going home before things got out of hand around the punch bowl. The parties they threw at Lower Loxley were discreetly luxe affairs, with ice-cold cocktails and impeccable frocks; Alec was alarmed by the high jinks at Noel's.

Guests stormed up and down the stairs, and across the landing. There were shrieks and bumps until the wardrobe door burst open and Kitty jumped in beside him.

A fur coat was between them. There was no greeting. He had an urge to grab her pale hand and pull her to him against the coat's slithery pelt. Had Alec ever noticed before that he noticed her? As the whites of her eyes flared in the darkness, he confessed all to himself. Neither knew who kissed the other; they both knew it was the first time they had kissed somebody other than their spouse.

Her little tongue crept into his mouth.

The door had opened again.

Morgan had no idea what he'd interrupted, what he'd averted. Luckily he was both drunk and unsuspecting. 'Room for a little 'un!' he cried, and pushed aside the fur.

The coat was sold long ago, for less than it was worth. It had translated into shoes for Caroline and new pipes in the toilet and whitewash for the cottage's mouldy back wall.

Their embrace had not been repeated until after Noel's death.

Now, as he wavered on the threshold of the bedroom, and the threshold of something else altogether, Alec said, 'Stop.' Then, more gently, 'Stop, darling, please.'

Kitty dropped her fingers from the second pearl button on her blouse. 'Something's happened. You're different. You disappeared. What? What happened?'

'Nothing.'

'But you stayed gone and now you're peculiar with me.'

'I can't always get away.' Alec was brusque. 'It's not easy. This isn't *easy*.'

'I know, darling. I hate being your problem. I wish I could live in your pocket, all snug. And you'd reach in and feel me there and know I'm for you. It *is* easy, if you break it down.

I just want you to be my man and I want to be your woman. Because what are we doing here if we don't both want that?'

Now that she could see Alec's face she didn't much like it. It was unhappy. Tortured. Maybe the wind had changed and the Old Wives were right; he was stuck like that. 'Let me hold you, darling.'

Alec let her dash to him and press herself against him. He didn't speak. Or he couldn't. That would mean admitting he didn't know what to do.

The Alecs of this world always know what to do.

Her head on his chest, the shiny chestnut mess of it, touched him. He couldn't tell her any of the various truths that boiled in his head. He could no more tell her that Pamela knew about them than he could tell her that Gerald had seen them together. He was hammered into the sloping floor-boards with indecision and lust and another fizzing element that the fool of a man didn't recognize. 'Kitty,' he said, 'must we name this?'

'Yes.' Kitty could feel his heart jitterbug. She pulled away and glared up at him. 'Otherwise I'm just a hobby. You're passing time with me like I'm a Bridge game, or some poor game bird you're taking a potshot at.'

'Do you know what I really want to do right now?'

Sullen, Kitty said, 'I can bloody guess.' Her hand went back to the button.

Alec stopped her fingers. 'I want to watch you cook bacon and eggs and then I want to eat them with you.'

She laughed. She made the decision to laugh. She elected

to let him pull her out of her funk. Even though all he had really done was distract her. 'We can do that. Except I don't have any bacon. And I don't have any eggs.'

Meanwhile, if you trudged away from Noon Cottage, crossed a bosomy dip and went through Brookfield's gate, you would find Christine standing stoic on the kitchen table as her mother, pins in her mouth, worked her way round the hem of her dress.

It was Doris's wedding dress, dyed a muted blue, and about to be taken in and taken up to ballerina length so it could live a second life as a bridesmaid's dress. After that was done, Doris would take in and take up the wedding dress worn by Nance's mother.

All in all, Doris would have pins in her mouth for some time to come.

They didn't stop her talking. 'According to Dottie,' she told Dan, 'Blanche never offered one of them so much as half a segment of the orange, and she licked the juice off her fingers right in front of them. She can be a right Queen Bee, can Blanche.'

In the corner of the kitchen her mother dozed on the rocking chair. Phil was upstairs, doing boy things; they kept him very busy and involved apple cores, string, a rusting penknife. Glen was by the range. Mother Cat was by Glen. The livestock were in their niches. Doris surveyed the dress's hem.

'Well, blast it to hell,' she said gently, and prepared to creep round again, rectifying the asymmetry.

From the skirting boards, the mice mocked her. They ran and scratched, they thrived; Doris hadn't time to wet corks and sprinkle them with pepper and ram them into the holes they nibbled in the farmhouse's mealy wooden structure. It was her mother's tip, and it had always worked.

'Is your mum invited to the wedding?' Dan was at the table in his vest. Below the neck, he looked uncivilized; above it the trimmed moustache and the smarmed-down hair was worthy of a bank manager.

'Mmm.' Doris nodded, with a warning nod at Christine. If they'd spoken French she would have said *Pas devant les enfants* but Doris would no more speak French than she would pluck her eyebrows. 'Should be fine if we don't stay long, so Mum doesn't get worn out.'

'Isn't it time we told people about—'

A sharp shake of Doris's head cut Dan off at the pass. He did try, but his wife bested him each time. It was never the right moment to say, again, that mightn't it be better to tell their friends about Lisa's forgetfulness. Mood swings. Oddness. There was no catch-all term for the fog of old age which rubbed smooth Lisa's edges. No easy way for them to discuss it.

This gully between them displeased Dan. Only when their amity failed did he realize how much he relied on it to feel, well, *himself*.

'We'll pop into the reception,' said Doris. 'Just have a little something to eat, then slip away.' She was decisive, brooking no argument. This tone was a trump card she played rarely;

Dan was well aware that their family was a matriarchy, that Doris was the power behind the mucky throne of Brookfield, but she generally let him pretend he was in charge.

'But we have to stay for the dancing!' Christine was stricken. She rarely tuned into her parents but when she did there was often talk of something not happening, something being 'too much', something classified as 'not for the likes of us'. 'And I'll be in my new dress, Mum!'

'You won't go at all, my girl, if you don't behave. Now, stand still, Chrissie, or we'll never get this finished.' Doris felt Dan's mild surprise and heard Christine's hot har-rumph at the injustice. She folded the newly blue satin between her fingers. The waist of the dress would not fit over her thigh these days. All that farm butter. She was and was not the same person who had married Dan two decades ago.

A perceptive teacher had once made Doris write out lines for some schoolyard misdeed. Thirty times, in tall capitals, she'd copied out *Pride goeth before a fall*. She'd been puzzled at the time, but sometimes she glimpsed the truth the teacher had been trying to show her.

She didn't bend, Doris. She stood tall. Sometimes she stooped, but that was to help others, something she did unthinkingly and generously. That wasn't the problem. The problem was with accepting help. She studied it, couldn't believe it came with no strings attached. Looked for the hidden cost, which was, generally speaking, *pity*.

The change of atmosphere in the warm kitchen was all her

doing. Doris set about mending it, the way she mended their shirts and underthings.

'Here, Dan, you and Alec have any inspiration about the letter writer?' People looked to both men to *do something*.

'Not a clue, love. We just have to sit and wait for number three. We're keeping our eyes peeled, mind you, and looking out for irregularities.'

Doris was too loyal to laugh at such talk. 'Very good,' she said.

'I came across Alec on my way home. Almost stopped and had a chat about it all but I was too hungry.' He held up the sandwich she had made him. It was, possibly, the best sand-wich he had ever eaten. But then, Dan felt that way about every sandwich his wife made. 'He was out with Hero. He *loves* that dog, always walking it.'

The back door shook. The knob rattled.

'Are we locked in?' laughed Dan.

'It'll be Jez. Just see what he wants.' Doris stabbed her thumb with a silver pin. '*Don't bring him in!*' she hissed, know-ing her amiable husband would welcome Jack the Ripper if he came knocking.

'Evening, son,' said Dan. As he dealt with Jez, Doris and Christine carried out a conversation with their eyes. Neither wanted Jez in the house, and neither could have articulated quite why to Dan. It was girl stuff. Knowledge carried in the bones. Or the ovaries, perhaps.

'Right you are, Jez!' Dan waved him off, none the wiser about his womenfolk's relief.

The dress was pinned. A pot of tea was brewed. Mother Cat browbeat a mouse in the scullery.

Christine, in an old pyjama top of her father's, sat on the arm of his chair as he held forth about the new people over on Garlands Farm.

'Two whole fields lying fallow.' Dan was close to outrage. 'No wheat, no barley, no nothing. Blatant disregard, Doris, *blatant* disregard for the new regulations. Talking about breeding horses when they should be growing food to put in our mouths.'

'*My* mouth,' suggested Christine, who had a bone to pick with Hitler about rationing.

'Exactly, love,' said Dan. 'Lord knows it's a last resort, but I may have to seize the farm. After all, they don't own it, they only lease.'

'*Only?* Like us, you mean, and your parents before us?' Doris washed some striped crockery, laid it face down on a tea towel to dry, washed a pot, wiped a jug that had somehow acquired a crack behind her back. 'Who told you all this? That Charlie Logan? You know he's had his eye on Garlands for years?'

'Oh.' Dan's mouth made a perfect circle.

Christine, leaning against her dad, said, 'Mum, who's Janet?'

Doris stopped wiping. The jug froze in her hand.

'Is she pretty? I look like her, Grandma said.'

'She did *not*.' Doris slammed down the jug so hard another crack snaked across its base. 'Don't you tell fibs, Christine Archer!'

Off ran the child, suddenly sobbing, and almost tripping over Glen's outstretched paws.

'Doris.' Dan sat up. 'You know our Chrissie never tells lies.'

'She has to learn,' said Doris. That didn't make sense; it was just something to say while Doris got a grip on herself.

She slammed the broken jug into the basin of water. She didn't feel like explaining herself.

Dan lowered his voice. 'And let's be honest, your mum does mix folk up. Who is this Janet, anyway?'

'She's nobody, Dan. Drop it, will you?' The handle of the jug came off in Doris's hand and she squeezed her eyes shut. When she opened them there was no slumbering farmyard through the window, just the empty rectangle of the black-out curtain. 'I've so much to do, and this blessed wedding isn't helping.'

In her corner, Lisa twitched; Doris stiffened. Lisa was quiet, safe, but so often she was neither. Always, always in Doris's peripheral vision, like a spirit in an M. R. James story. 'Sometimes, Dan, it, well, it gets a bit much.' She leaned on her hands. The water was slightly too hot; that helped.

'You keep going, old girl, just like you always do.' Dan was blithe, pipe jammed back between his teeth and news-paper shield raised once more. 'Everything'll be fine. Hasn't it always been?'

Doris's knuckles were red through the suds. She hadn't heard that name out loud in decades. Had never heard Christine say 'Janet' before.

No, my sweet lovely man, she thought. *It hasn't always been fine.*

They got the name wrong, even though they'd lived in the village – or on its margins – for months now.

Billy called it Anbridge and John called it Hambridge.

It was all right. The fields around the house were great, and the cow Connie kept was great, and Wizbang was great; the boys had plans to smuggle the mongrel back to Mile End with them when the war was over, next week or in ten years' time or whenever the grown-ups got fed up of it.

They liked Walter Gabriel and they *loved* Connie, but they stayed well out of Stan's way. Vic, the oldest kid now that Cliff was gone, told them ghost stories. They were brilliant. Until the light went out, and then the boys wished he hadn't been quite so eloquent about the dead people who clawed their way up out of the graves around St Stephen's, bits of flesh hanging off and skellington faces.

All in all, being an evacuee wasn't bad, Billy told anybody who asked. John stayed quiet; he preferred to stand just behind his brother and let Billy do the talking. John didn't like answering questions – he could never find words, they rolled away like marbles – and he was sick of compliments about his golden hair and his cherubic face. *As if*, he thought, *I'm a girl or something.* John missed his mummy. His *mum*. Do. Not. Say. Mummy.

One saving grace of country life was the freedom, and it turned out that Borsetshire had just as many dangerous places to mess about in as London. They had fallen in the Am, and aimed their catapult at broken bottles out on Jiggins Field, and prodded a bull with a stick.

Then, most spectacular of all, they had found a hut.

Deep in Heydon Wood, in a clearing defined by a thick hedge that reminded John of Sleeping Beauty's castle, the hut's roof just about held, and the floor was brick. It was, if you squinted, a proper little house. They chased away the spiders and filched a spoon, then a cup, then a pot lid from Connie's kitchen.

It took a whole morning to cover the roof that sloped almost to the ground with branches and moss and organic debris. The thorns kept them safe from wild animals, from Vic's ghoulies and any German pilots that might be wandering about looking for a British kid to take hostage.

It was HQ.

John didn't know that stood for headquarters until Billy told him.

Doris hoped this wouldn't take too long.

While the women chatted and shook off jackets and put down handbags, she tried to get comfortable on the upright settee with spindly legs that stood in the middle of the parquet.

Getting comfarty, Dan called it when she squirmed like that at home. No getting comfarty on this antique. Its elegance rebuffed her efforts.

'Innit lovely 'ere,' said Dottie. She ran her hands over a blue and white vase on the mantelpiece. 'All so posh.'

'Is it?' Pamela was among them suddenly. Straight-backed and motoring, tart, precise. 'Oh dear, I do hope not.' She clapped for no good reason and Mrs Endicott jumped. 'Are we all here?' She greeted each woman by name. Like a visiting president of somewhere important. 'Magsy dear, good morning. And Jane, too good of you. Doris, as ever. Frances, you're an angel. And a special mention for you!' Pamela took Kitty's hand and closed her other over it. Her engagement ring shrieked in the sunlight refracting off the chandelier. 'We're so glad to see you out and about and taking part, Kitty. You are *very* welcome.'

Kitty smiled, thanked her, or began to, then heard how stupid she sounded and shut up. If only Pamela was an ogre she could hate. *Thank Jaysus you don't know about me and your husband*, she thought, as Pamela swept Caroline onto her lap.

Caroline behaved. She was meek. She knew Pamela was boss.

As did everyone else. The women listened as Pamela outlined the outline of the meeting. 'Let's make some basic decisions, such as date, theme, and so forth. Then we can delegate the various tasks, according to our strengths. Doris will oversee the costumes, of course, our resident workhorse, and Magsy can . . . well, we'll think of something, dear. This year, I beg of you, we must take proper minutes of these meetings. Any volunteers? No? In that case, Frances, you can do it.'

The vicar's wife looked startled. Doris, the workhorse, wondered if this was a wise move. Frances was, bless her, dry and rather literal. The minutes were likely to be long, and useless.

AMBRIDGE MIDSUMMER PAGEANT COMMITTEE MEETING MINUTES

Date: 26 April 1940
At: Lower Loxley
Chairwoman: Pamela Pargetter
Present: Frances Bissett, Emmaline Endicott, Margaret Furneaux, Doris Archer, Dorothy Cook, Kathleen Dibden-Rawles, Jane Gilpin
Note to self: Do I include little Caroline?

1. Pamela asked for suggestions of suitable dates for the pageant. Pamela decided it would be 2 June. Jane said midsummer falls at the end of June though and this is a midsummer pageant. Pamela said that was a mere detail.

2 Pamela noted that Morgan's wedding day is the same day as the pageant but refused to take a vote on changing the date. She said that as the wedding ceremony doesn't take place until teatime there is ample time for both events. Magsy asked if it

would be nicer to space out two such happy gatherings and Pamela said 'Bless you' and also 'No'.

3. Dottie asked how many months gone did she look. She said she is five months pregnant. She showed the committee a photograph of the baby's father. She said he was 'a smasher'. Doris said 'he is certainly a looker'. Magsy said he had a look of Mr Kirk Douglas. Kitty said he was more like a Viking, blond and tall with flashing blue eyes. Pamela told everyone to calm down.

4. We all agreed to pool some of our rations for Dottie as she is expecting. Dottie had a little cry. Magsy had a little cry. Jane said, 'Oh no, don't, you will start me off'.

5. Caroline knocked over a figurine of a lady shepherd with a lamb. Kitty scolded her. Pamela said it didn't matter, the figurine should not have been on a low shelf and gave the dear tot her watch to play with.

6. Gerald ran in and ran out again. His language perturbed at least one of the ladies present.

7. Pamela said could we please get back

to business and suggested we ask Walter Gabriel to supply this year's maypole from the trees in the south-west patch of his smallholding.

8. Mrs Endicott said could they discuss what on Earth to give dear Morgan and Nance as a wedding present as she is fearful of appearing too showy at a time of national crisis. Dottie asked will they have a real wedding cake and she said she thinks Nance will look a knockout if she actually does her hair properly for once. Kitty said it was the most romantic thing she could think of, getting married in wartime. Pamela said weddings do not fall within the remit of pageant business.

9. Dottie asked what we all thought of Dr Seed. She mistook Magsy for Dr Seed's housekeeper. We all had a lovely giggle at that. Dottie said she doesn't want Morgan delivering her baby as she doesn't trust a doctor who couldn't cure Jimmy Little's blindness or Blanche's polio. Kitty said he delivered Caroline. Jane said Blanche is incurable. Doris said that poor Jimmy has Acute Angle Glaucoma (note to self: check sp) just like his granny and is beyond the help of medicine. Magsy said Dr Seed cared

for Jonjo, Walter's father, when he was ill before Christmas. Dottie said 'Yes and now Jonjo is brown bread'.

10. Pamela said that was quite enough about Morgan and tapped Jane on the knee with a rolled-up copy of the *Lady*. Jane said 'I was not asleep, I was resting my eyes'. She said she is tired because Agnes is terribly cheeky and gives her the runaround. Dottie said that Blanche cannot be easy to live with. Jane said no, no, no, her sister is a saint. Jane had another little cry and said she can't stop thinking about the cruel letter and what must people think of Blanche. Doris said that the first letter wasn't true so neither was this one. Something went down Kitty's throat the wrong way and Pamela asked her if she was quite all right and fetched some water. Jane began to cry again and said she was v worried about the war and that she listens to all the news broadcasts on the wireless but she felt as if all the soldiers were somehow her boys and what she would really like is to have the prime minister in the airing cupboard so she could ask him questions once an hour about what was happening

and if the Nazis really do plan to take
over Ambridge.

11. Pamela said this really wouldn't do
and they must all focus. She asked for
suggestions for the theme. She said the
theme for the pageant is Elizabeth I.

12. Jane said she was sorry to be a
nuisance but she didn't seem to be able to
stop crying and she asked don't we ever
just want to cry at the awfulness of the
war and when nobody answered she just
kept crying until Pamela said we may as
well wrap the meeting up and reconvene
when Jane is quite well.

Outside Hero zigzagged about the lawn behind his master,
a man who was coming to terms with lying to both his wife
and his mistress.

If he told Kitty that Pamela knew about them, she would
end the affair. That was certain. The poor girl was inside the
house now, all unknowing, sitting up straight in Pamela's
presence. Alec had noted how carefully Kitty had fixed her
hair, how sedate her choice of dress.

Life was complicated. It never used to be. Was it the war or
was it Kitty? Alec didn't remember being dissatisfied, until
Kitty came along and excited him. He had sleep-walked all
the way to her bed.

The front would be easier than this. He had loathed

soldiering, but he had understood it. The Alec he faced in the mirror during the Great War had been whey-coloured, terrified, but he didn't recoil from him. That Alec hadn't been a liar. He hadn't even been a coward; one of the horrible facts he'd learned in 1917 was that everyone is scared.

He wondered, for a second, no longer, how Rupert had felt before the battle that killed him. The loss of Alec's older brother had been one of countless commonplace tragedies. He had few memories of the restless, cavalier Rupert. A decade older, Rupert was a visitor to Alec's nursery, then a figure on the edge of his school holidays. He had loved Lower Loxley, grown up expecting to inherit. And then he 'fell', as the euphemism had it, gargling his own blood in foreign mud.

They had never really been men together. Alec minded about that.

The call-up will come. Of that Alec had no doubt. The country was hunkering down for a long war. When it came, what would be left of him? Would he simply walk towards the bullets?

He reached the terrace. The stones were clean, bright. The pinkish things in the urns were perfect. He wasn't very good with flower names. Everything at Lower Loxley obeyed his wife; they read her mind and pretended to themselves it was what they wanted to do. That's why the white climbing things along the back of the house came into bloom just as her garden parties began, why the soufflés rose, why he visited her quarters at the allotted times.

A thought landed. It gave no warning, and he wondered where in his mind it had been born.

Could Pamela have written the first letter in order to shame him into giving up Kitty?

Alec realized he had no idea what Pamela was capable of. He couldn't even say if she was a good person or a bad person. If that was even a useful way of classifying people.

Am I a bad person?

Around the corner of the house came a figure. Furtive, hunched, it was Connie Horrobin, who was always furtive and hunched. She carried a bolt of fabric that sparked silver in the sun. 'Your missus about?'

'She's busy just now.' Alec kept his distance. He sensed Connie was fearful of men. She was all spikes. An angry little hedgehog who might curl into a ball at any moment.

'I'll wait.'

The material under her arm, comically glamorous against Connie's limp clothes, could only be black market. Alec looked about him; the furtiveness was catching. 'Does my wife . . . do business with you, Mrs Horrobin?'

'No business, no. I'm just doing her a little favour.'

'The penalties for black marketeering are serious.'

'Black what?'

'First, a fine of five hundred pounds.' Alec saw her jump at mention of such a sum. 'The authorities can go further, you know, and fine you again, up to three times the value of the goods you sell. Some people end up in jail.' Alec thought of Dan, his War Ag zeal. He half-expected him to leap out from behind an urn, take his pipe out of his mouth, and shout *Gotcha!*

'I'm not going to jail.' Connie was unperturbed.

'Have you heard from young, err, Cliff, is it?'

'Not a word.' Connie turned, and her currant eyes blazed like the fabric. 'D'you know where he might be, Mr Pargetter? He's with the BEF, he's labour, not regular army, he's doing the donkey work.' At first Connie had been reassured by Cliff's lowly status, but latterly she'd begun to fret that he was near the front with no idea how to use a firearm or fight off a filthy rotten Hun.

'Don't fret, Connie. The army's pledged to protect their labour divisions.' Alec hesitated. He wasn't sure how to speak to Connie. The words he used seemed to confuse her. Sometimes he couldn't quite catch what she said in her low, muttering local accent. 'I'm sure you're very proud of your son.'

'Proud? I was proud of my Cliff long before all this started. This doesn't make me proud. I just want him home.' She was scornful, before changing tack, as if remembering where she was and who she was and, more importantly, who *he* was. 'Thank you, Mr Pargetter.'

He was saved by the ladies. All of them appearing at once through a set of French doors. Alec was gallant; he would take them all home, he said. 'I had one of my boys make ready the pony and trap.'

Magsy sat up front on one side of him, and Dottie the other. Magsy talked of Morgan and their dear dead boy, and Dottie talked of throwing up her guts every morning in Mrs E's lavvy.

On an uncomfortable plank seat in the back, Jane kept her handkerchief to her nose; Alec didn't hear how she snuffled, nor see how Kitty kept her arm about her, nor how Jane declared herself 'utterly mortified', and blamed her sleeping draught.

'Sometimes I forget I've taken it and I take another spoonful and it does make me dreadfully woozy and those children, they were at it again last night, Kitty, *sniggering* in quite a nasty way, although the poor dear things are dead, so I suppose one can't expect too much in the way of manners.'

Kitty hugged her tighter, and listened.

The hedgerow and the trees and the fields fell away and delivered them to the tighter landscape of cottages and brick and stucco. In the village nature was still abundant, but it was more polite, expressing itself demurely in gardens instead of shouting in fields.

One by one, the women were decanted from the cart, Dottie and Mrs Endicott insisting on having Caroline for a couple of hours, and Alec was left with – well, who could have foreseen it? – he was left with Kitty. The pony, a pretty grey, ambled out of Ambridge, and her passengers enjoyed the aimlessness.

Turning down a narrow lane overhung with trees, Alec put an arm around Kitty. With a glance to the left and the right.

'The letter writer can't see us here,' said Alec.

'And you know that how?' Kitty leaned in. 'I've been to

purgatory this afternoon, Alec. Pamela's so *kind* to me. If only she'd punch me in the gob.'

'Not her style.'

Does he think this is funny? Kitty's feet hurt in the Sunday shoes she'd worn to meet Pamela. Together, the Pargetters were formidable, a pair of thoroughbreds in harness. There was a rightness to their coupling; their marriage obeyed all the unwritten rules of British society.

But Kitty felt she had an advantage; Pamela didn't know about her, had no idea they were locked in a fight to the death. *I don't want to fight, but I must play the hand life's dealt me.* And fight she would.

She snatched the reins and the pony stopped, bending her head to the sweet young grasses. Kitty jumped down and pulled on Alec's arm until he had no option but to follow suit. She hooked his waist. 'I want you now, here,' she said.

'Good God, woman.' Alec pulled away, stepping back until his handmade shoes were safe on the dirt track. 'Stop it, Kitty.' He beat her off like a virginal maidservant in a melodrama.

With one of those hairpin mood changes that scared him (and gave his downstairs a certain lift, it had to be admitted), Kitty snapped, 'Why'd you have to be married to somebody like Pamela? She's so good and so proper. And her clothes. She always says the right thing. I want her to *like* me, Alec! And I think she does. Pamela likes me. Which eats me up.'

'Kitty ...' Alec glanced up the road, down the road. A

Horrobin could pop out of the undergrowth. A stout village woman could turn the bend. 'Not here.'

'That's my Irishness, of course.' Kitty paced and turned. 'Us colonial servants, we're doomed to need our overlords' approval.'

'Look here.' Alec took Kitty by the shoulders. 'You might not eulogize Pamela so much if you had to live with her.'

'No!' Kitty put up a forefinger. 'You're not to do that. Don't badmouth her to me.'

'What a strange little thing you are.' Alec looked down at her. The moment was a metronome poised to swing.

'That's why you love me.' The moment stretched. 'Oh, say it, Alec, you big fool!' Kitty pushed him, deftly, against a tree. 'It's obvious. You love me. You do. You love me. You should be telling me but here I am telling you!' She pushed her hand all over his face, as if squashing a sandcastle.

Alec's nose bent sideways and his lips flattened against his teeth. He laughed and laughed and a bird beat its way out of the hazel bushes.

She put her hand somewhere else. 'And that's why you can leave her, Alec. Because you love me and that *matters*.'

The roving little hand sobered Alec. He took it in his own and held it up, as if arresting her. Love as something more than a word to be used was novel to him.

Pulling her hand away and nursing her wrist, Kitty stepped back. 'Pamela's so sophisticated, and I'm just a peasant.'

'Please,' said Alec. He was appalled by this push-me-pull-you. Yet he wasn't bored, when so much bored him.

Alec had been bored all through school. Dammit, he'd been bored *at war*. But not with this girl. 'Look, darling, Pamela's only sophisticated to the likes of Doris Archer. In London she's a nobody. It suits her to be the glossiest fish in Ambridge's pond.'

Another about-turn. 'Be nice about her. I mean it.' And then another about-turn, of a different nature. Kitty flattened herself against a tree, her arms reaching backwards around it, as if cuffed. 'Let's do it. Come on. I want to feel the bark against my bum.'

Alec plunged into her like a man with no responsibilities, like a man who wasn't concerned that a neighbour might turn the corner and see his bare behind. 'You'll be the death of me, Kitty,' he snarled into her curls.

'I'll be the making of you, you eejit.'

When she came Kitty yowled and a fox answered from two fields over.

MAY

The warm, filthy smell of May shocked young Eugene.

Doris stifled her amusement. Did the young genius expect muck-spreading to smell of roses? He was insulted by farm life, and she imagined callouses forming on his soul just as they did on his soft hands. He was only a boy; he was feeling his way, like the rest of the nation. Being at war was, the politicians said, inevitable, but it felt unnatural to a woman brought up among pasture and ponds and the gentle sounds of cows talking to each other.

Jane Gilpin's unstoppable tears at the pageant committee had unsettled everyone else, but they'd calmed Doris. Weren't sobs the only sane response to war? If they weren't going to cry as they waved off cheerful young fella-me-lads to be shot, when *were* they to cry?

Doris saw Jane as courageous; *I could never break down in front of others like that*. But she wanted to. She wanted to heave the war off her back and lie in the dirt and press her face into the ground and cry.

But for now, there was work to be done. The men – her men – trooped in from washing up at the pump outside, big chapped hands in cruelly cold water.

Jez sat first. Mother Cat decamped. He glared at his plate. 'Do you really expect us to work all day on bread and dripping sandwiches, missus?'

'Blame the government, not me,' said Doris. 'I can't stretch the rations any further. You have a go, Jez, as you know better, and we'll see how you manage.'

The speed and ferocity of the answer took the men aback; they weren't to know of the morning Doris had had, of how long the day seemed to her. Eugene said, 'He doesn't mean anything by it, Mrs Archer.'

Doris put a hand on his shoulder as she passed. Felt how spare he was. Eugene was not designed to toil. She poured him tea, lots of it, in the biggest cup.

Love might not be everything to Doris, but it was everywhere. She loved the kitchen. She loved that it beat like a big healthy heart at the centre of the farm, of Ambridge, and therefore, surely, the world.

But lately the walls played tricks on her. They moved imperceptibly inwards overnight. The kitchen, once so expansive, had become a vice.

All those blessed pamphlets with their mock goose and their mock cream; they needed to eat real food, and lots of it. They had a war to win.

A cough from the parlour. Doris's ears pricked the way Glen's did when he heard a badger. 'You all right in there, Mum?'

'What, love? Yes. Just something in my throat.'

The parlour, hallowed and unused, home to the proper furniture and the one piece of silver and the family photographs in heavy frames, had been opened up and aired. Lisa held court there. A lonely court, but a safe one.

Family visits were promised, but Doris took her brothers' promises with a pinch of salt; caring for Mum was a family game of musical chairs and it stood to reason that the sole daughter would be left standing when the music stopped.

'Remember, Mrs Archer,' said Eugene, through a mouthful of bread Doris had baked that morning, 'I'm off to see the doc later. My asthma.'

'But you're the only one that can milk!' Doris flared up, as if another Doris, a Latina version, had been dormant inside her all these years. 'I can't do that on my own as well! I only have one pair of hands.' Doris bit down on the anger that stood primed and ready to fly. She didn't much care for this Latin Doris.

'Whoa there!' Jez pretended to be frightened of her. 'Why not rope in your sainted old man to help? He knows everything about everything. Although, I hear he's the ARP warden now, as well as doing his War Ag rounds.' Jez wiped the plate with a crust and sighed sympathetically. 'Sounds like he'd do anything not to be at home.'

'It's called doing your bit,' said Doris. She took away Jez's plate while he was still wiping. 'I'll have to show you how to milk, Jez.' She'd avoided it up to now. Didn't want him near her girls. The cows could be trouble if they weren't treated with respect.

She knew how they felt.

A pinprick of indulgence in the dour cloth of austerity, The Bull was full of men. Labouring men. Besuited men. Drunk men and men who could stop at just the one pint.

Dan was one of the latter, but this was his second pint. The landlord, Bob, had unsettled him.

'As a War Ag official,' Bob had said, 'you should be clamping down on these letters, Dan. People are unhappy. Things are bad enough with this blinkin' war without having a fifth columnist of our own.'

The War Ag wasn't the Secret Service, Dan had told him mildly. 'I'm a small cog in a large machine, Bob.' That suited Dan. He liked slotting into place, turning diligently, and feeling the great machine whirr around him. There had to be boundaries; he couldn't be responsible for farming, blackouts *and* petty crime. Now he said, 'You have to hand it to this letter writer, he's a cunning sod. Seems to be everywhere at once.'

'You make him sound like a will o' the wisp.' Bob wiped down the counter; it was a thankless task, it would soon be awash with slops again. Maybe that's why Bob used a dirty cloth, to underline the hopeless nature of his chore. The Bull was a haven of filth for the customers, lacking what they called a woman's touch, and a place where you could spill ash and sneeze without apology. A veritable wonderland of male behaviours. 'You mark my words, the letter writer's not a "he", Dan. This is a woman's doing. They have eyes everywhere, them ladies. My late wife, God rest her soul, knew what I was doing even if I was down in the cellar and she was over in Felpersham.'

'I'll try and step things up,' said Dan, with no notion of what stepping things up might entail. He was more tired than he'd ever been. His *hair* was tired.

Alec stooped at the low door.

'Hail Caesar!' shouted Dan. The second pint was having its effect. 'Did you call Ronald?' Alec brought with him news of the war and an excuse for a third beer.

'Yes. Just a half, please, Bob, and whatever Dan here wants.' Alec's friend, Ronald Furneaux, sister to Magsy and Morgan's brother-in-law, was member of parliament for Bristol West. Hard to get hold of, but a fount of back-channel information whenever Alec pinned him down. These titbits were hoarded; not everyone could be exposed to the unexpurgated facts of war. The ladies, for example, would be plunged into gloom. 'We've been caught on the hop,' said Alec, that 'we' meaning the Allies. 'We're rushing troops to west Belgium.'

'But the Nazis were supposed to invade via central Belgium.' Dan was sure of this for some reason.

'We got that wrong, I'm afraid.'

Dan put down his pipe and took up his glass. 'I'm not sure what I make of Churchill as PM. He's rash.'

'I like the man. Ronald was telling me there's been a slew of German officers bailing out over Devon. An *Unteroffizier* and an *Oberleutnant* were paraded through London. One can't shoot them once they land, they're prisoners of war, but there was talk of shooting them as they parachuted down. Churchill put his foot down. No, he said, it's like drowning a sailor. One has to have some rules, even now. If we lose our sense of honour, where will we end up? No, I trust Winston.' Alec would have liked to loosen his tie. But, well, *standards*. 'Where's your Jack these days?'

'Chatham, still. Bored stiff, poor lad.'

'You know they're saving him for the big push?' It would be hard, when it came, on the likes of Jack Archer.

'Doris keeps saying how she's glad he'll be protected by his tank.'

Alec opened his mouth but didn't speak. Why bother saying it out loud when both men knew that Jack would be driving a bomb across the battlefield. 'He's a good lad,' he said eventually. Pathetic, yes, but he had nothing more.

The street door flew open with a thud. Jimmy rushed in. His speed made him clumsy, even in this room he knew so well, and he ricocheted off the coat stand, knocking into Denholm's shoulder. No apology. Jimmy stormed up the stairs.

'There's no excuse,' said Denholm, mopping ale from a tie that was already patterned with stains, 'for rudeness, even if the boy *is* blind.'

Bob agreed, apologized on Jimmy's behalf, said he'd

have a word, and added a muttered, 'You mardy old get,' as Denholm lumbered to a stool.

Jez smelled of cigarettes, sweat and something else besides, something warm and sharp, like vinegar. He was slightly too close to Doris as she cajoled a wide, slow, red and white cow along the concrete aisle of the cow shed. She put up with his closeness; to point out his presumption would open up a conversation she didn't feel able to have.

She needed Jez and Eugene. No land girl had materialized. It was just her and her two miscast men against the world.

'See, here, how we get her up onto the raised part, and just gently slip the chain round her neck.' Dan had relaid the floor over the winter. It was pleasingly hygienic. He'd also made the wooden partitions that bookended the shed. They were raw. Doris had become adept at persuading out splinters with an open safety pin. 'She's new to this, so go gentle with her. There you are, my lovely,' she said to the cow, who had found the hay set out for her. 'You have a nibble and don't mind us.' The animal chewed unhurriedly. Her dark eyes were beautiful, Doris thought. Why weren't there any poems about cows' eyes?

'Sit yourself on that little stool and dampen that cloth,' she said, 'and give her udder a good wipe.' She took care to sound conversational; Jez resented any form of instruction. Doris could feel his breath. It wasn't sweet and summery like the cow's. It was coarse and hot, like him. 'If we wipe her, then no bits of dust get in the milk.' The milk was ordinary and precious. Like the eggs. Like the wheat. Like Glen who sat in the barn doorway watching them with the air of a headmaster. Firm but fair.

Jez wiped the cow's teats with warm water, and Doris sensed rather than heard his micro-chuckle. That, she realized, was why she didn't want to milk with him.

It was easy, if you had a dirty mind, to be lewd about milking. And Jez had a dirty mind. Life on a farm brought you up hard against the basics. Birth. Sex. Death. If you were given to sniggering at anatomy or fluids you'd be ho-ho-ho-ing all day. None of it was funny to Doris. It was necessary, could be hard work, and it was relentless. Not funny, though. Not when it was your life.

'That's right, take a teat and don't pull, just tease out the milk.' Doris put her hands over his and soldiered on with the double entendres. She made sure not to look at his face. She couldn't have borne the smirk. 'Like this. Squeeze the base with your thumb and index finger, like I'm doing, then kind of squeeze right along the teat with the rest of your fingers until, see, the milk squirts out.'

Doris stood back. 'You're doing well, make sure it goes into the bucket. *Into* the bucket.' She was glad of an opportunity to snap at him. 'Hey, go easy! The cow's new to this as well!'

When the small galvanized bucket was full, Doris lugged it to the bigger bucket and dumped the creamy milk. The smell of it was powerful, like paint coating the walls. It was warm, cloying, perilously near to unpleasant.

Doris chained up another cow, her favourite, one with

strawberry roan markings that made her think of fruit fool. Squatting on her little three-legged stool, she heard regular squirting from Jez's cubicle. She heard nothing but unruffled snorts from his charge. He was good at it, she had to admit. 'You're a natural,' she said.

'She loves it,' said Jez. 'Don't you, girl? She loves me getting my hands on her.'

Doris leaned into the cow's warm flank and wet it with tears.

'Bananas?' asked Magsy, with drooping, hopeless intonation.

She knew Frank Brown wouldn't have bananas in stock. He never did. They were rare now; she missed their yellow silliness.

'Sorry.' Frank was balding, but he lovingly curated the stripe of grey hair left to him. Empathetic eyes looked out from a weather-beaten face; he was slight, knocked back. A take-no-notice-of-me man, the ideal shopkeeper. 'But I do have any amount of beetroot, and Morgan loves a bit of that.'

'Not as much,' said Magsy sorrowfully, 'as he loves a banana. Still, as they say, I'd rather take pot luck with Churchill than eat humble pie with Hitler.'

Waiting his turn, trying to be philosophical about the long list in Magsy's hand, Alec said, 'You spoil Morgan.'

'No, no, Alec, I *look after* him.'

Frank was chipper. 'That'll soon be my Nance's job. I'll pass that on to her, that Morgan favours a banana.'

Mrs Endicott had to chip in. 'Do *not* ask my digestion to cope with beetroot. A beetroot could end me once and for all.' She clicked her fingers. 'Like that!'

Magsy decided to take a couple of large beetroots and bake them. Like most of her thoughts, she shared it. 'When I bring Morgan's dinner over to Homeleigh I might whisk round the rooms with a broom. The house is in a sorry state. Bachelors, you know. They don't *see* dust.'

Hearing her cue, Mrs Endicott said, 'It was immaculate when you lived there, my dear. One could eat one's dinner off the floor.'

Why, wondered Alec, *would you want to do that?*

Magsy tried to look modest. 'Men need looking after,' she said, as she left with her jewel-red spoils in a string bag.

'Being looked after by Magsy,' said Alec, 'could kill a man.'

Even Mrs Endicott, who was known to disapprove of what she called clever-clever comments, laughed at the truth of that. 'But we shouldn't tease. She did bring those two boys up, and then to lose poor Anthony so early in the war ...'

A moment of reverence, no, a moment of *pain*, was bestowed on Anthony. He was just a memory now; he would do nothing new. He was neat and ironed, and dead.

'A young fellow from Hollerton, navy chap, drowned up at Scapa Flow,' said Alec. 'Bad business.'

'Scapa Flow,' said Mrs Endicott wonderingly. 'Every day one hears of places one never heard of before.' She shuddered. 'A gypsy once told me I would die in the arms of the sea. That's why I could never join the navy.'

That, and the fact that the Royal Navy isn't crying out for old ladies, thought Alec. 'You a navy man, Frank?'

But the shopkeeper was gone. Sourcing something 'out the back' for Mrs Endicott.

Caroline barged in. She had the gait of a drunkard, careering along as if about to fall over, only to miraculously right herself just before her tipping point. 'Bacon!' she shouted.

'It's more usual to say hello,' laughed Kitty, bringing up the rear. She was slightly out of breath. She was in green, like a shoot, and she rippled with life.

'Here's my best girlie.' Mrs Endicott and Caroline had an intense friendship. 'Who's a pretty little thing?'

'I am,' said Caroline with great confidence. She was pudgy and grabbable, and Mrs Endicott bent creakily down to do just that.

Frank, back again, told Kitty he'd be with her soon. Alec offered his place in the queue. Mrs Endicott said she loved to see a proper gentleman.

'I've been saving coupons.' Kitty brandished them. 'I'm frying up bacon and eggs today for a special treat.'

'Ooh, lucky you,' said Mrs Endicott to Caroline.

They're for me, thought Alec. A bubble filled the inside of him. There was no room for anything else. He was made of happiness for a good, solid minute and a half.

With the ladies gone, Alec ran through his mundane needs and Frank brought him tobacco and shoe polish and a box of pencils.

There was a stock phrase to be used about each Ambridge

resident. Kitty's was, 'What a misfortune, a lovely young woman like that being widowed', and Frank used a variant of it now. When Alec nodded, he went further. 'She'll be snapped up soon enough, lovely-looking lass like that. Mind you, the kiddie . . .' He sucked his teeth.

'What about her?'

'Well,' said Frank, slightly uncomfortable, as if tackling a truth nobody liked to acknowledge, 'taking on another man's child, that's bound to make any bloke think twice. It'd be easy to trap a chap, make him feel responsible for a lovely little tot like that. Two and six, please, Mr Pargetter.' He repeated the amount. Mr Pargetter was staring at the floor.

When Sunday came, a reliable and pious full stop to the week, the vicar pontificated from the pulpit on the infamous poison-pen letters. They were, he said, adulterating the well.

Whether he noticed that Walter Gabriel was fast asleep, or that Gerald Pargetter was carving his initials in a pew, is not known. The vicar was keen to restore the status quo, a dubiously foreign phrase that meant nothing to many of his flock.

'Weeks have passed since the second morbid little message. An end to worry! Why should we care about slander that some cowardly soul won't even put their name to? Do we really believe the esteemed Alec Pargetter is unfaithful to his wife? We do not! Do we really believe that our dear sister Blanche Gilpin and our esteemed postman Whitey White commit the foul sin of adultery again and again and again? We do not!'

If looks could kill, Pamela's expression would have raised Henry above the altar and detonated him, cassock and all, above the heads of the congregation.

Beside her, her husband tilted his inherited nose even higher, all the better *not* to catch the eye of Frances Bissett. Sympathy from the vicar's beige little wife could not be endured. In his peripheral vision, Frances seemed to shimmer and blink; she wore a silvery blouse. Alec recognized the fabric, last seen in a bolt under Connie Horrobin's arm. It seemed the rectory was not above a touch of black marketeering.

At the back of the church Agnes, most un-crow-like in red, noticed the discomfort and smiled into her hymnal.

Outside, in the mellow sunshine that Ambridge was daring to get used to, all talk was of the misjudged sermon. Until a Pargetter or a Jane drew near, and then the topic changed.

'This war spoils all our fun,' said Mrs Endicott, her arm through Dottie's. It wasn't clear who was leaning on whom, the eternally terminal old lady or the skittle-shaped pregnant woman. 'Now I hear this year's farm show has been cancelled.'

'You lot, you villagers, your idea of fun,' said Dottie, 'is to look at, like, cows n' that. I don't get it. You can see a cow any old time. There's one now.' She pointed at a horse on a distant slope. 'I'll never understand country people. I mean, in the shop yesterday everybody was talking about drenching sheep.'

'Ah, but that means—' began Dan, who had caught up with them among the headstones.

'I do *not* care what it means,' said Dottie.

'Her ankles are at her,' said Mrs Endicott. 'Poor girl. I was advised never to bear children, you know. It would have—'

'Killed you, yes, Mrs E, can we get a move on? I want me lunch.' Dottie propelled her towards the gate.

The rat-a-tat-tat of make-believe gunfire rang out. Billy, in the kind of mismatched, some too long and some too short clothes that marked him as a Horrobin, staggered backwards, groaning and exclaiming, *'Mein Gott!'*

'You got him, John,' said Nance approvingly, her hand in Morgan's. Now that they were 'official' such displays were possible, and it was clear that Nance delighted in her changed status. In her muted way.

'One more German gunned down by our brave boys,' laughed Morgan, as they sidestepped the histrionic casualty of play war. The doctor had put on weight. He was perky. Even if his other arm was held, trophy-style, by Magsy. He was the filling in a peculiar sandwich: Magsy wasn't giving up her rights without a genteel fight.

Slowly, like a new bride, Doris exited the church with her mother. Lisa, so rarely seen in the wild, was lionized. An hour earlier, Lisa had been packing her suitcase and sobbing that she was going home to her parents.

For now, the old lady was calm. If she didn't recognize the faces milling around her she didn't say so, and kept to platitudes that didn't give her away. She might have been colluding with her daughter; she might have been maintaining the courtesy that ran so strongly through her it outlasted her wits.

'Not much wrong with those legs, Lisa, my old beauty!' Walter Gabriel had woken up; the final blast of the organ for the recessional hymn always did the trick, propelling him out of the pew like a whippet. 'I'll race you round the gravestones!' His father's mound, proud of the grass still, had as yet no stone. Just a cross with Jonjo's name and his vital dates. Walter brought a posy every Sunday, and now he veered off to lay it carefully down before heading for The Bull, his other place of worship.

Dan's oh-so-casual comment that he might pop in to see Bob and have a quick pint irked Doris as she wrangled Lisa along the gravel path. There was so much to do, so many disparate strands of the farm to take up. She rattled off a hissed précis for him, ending with the chore allocated to her by the pageant committee. They needed an opulent cloak for Walter Raleigh to throw over a puddle for Good Queen Bess; Doris would sew it, of course.

'You can knock that up sitting by the fire tonight, love. Don't you panic. I'll give you a hand with the dinner when I get back.'

'A hand?' Doris was talking to Dan's back. She couldn't envisage how Dan would help with a roast chicken and roast potatoes and gravy and carrots. If roasting a chicken stood between Dan and starvation, her husband would be discovered dead beside the stove.

'Doris, and who's this? Dear Lisa, too! We're honoured.' The vicar, fresh from his triumph in the pulpit, was in high spirits as he stood by the lychgate, glad-handing and holding up his parishioners from getting on with their day.

Doris managed a smile. Held on a little tighter to Lisa's arm, as if she could contain her mother that way.

'Good to see you.' Henry bent and spoke slowly and clearly, his horsey teeth bared as he enunciated each word distinctly.

When in her right mind, Lisa loathed being patronized. She was wont to say 'I'm old, not foolish'. Now, she simpered.

The vicar was gratified. He was proud of his ability to communicate with all, whether high-born or low-bred. He was proud of the many skills he didn't possess. 'You're looking well. Our good Borsetshire air clearly agrees with you.'

Lisa lifted her skirt. High, right up to the thigh. She stuck out her leg, in its droopy lisle stocking. 'Like what you see, sailor?'

'I, um, oh.' The vicar straightened up. 'Doris?'

'We should be getting back.' Doris hurried her mother away as if she was arresting her.

For the men of Ambridge that Sunday, all roads led not to Rome, but to The Bull. Dan and Alec met each other and walked in companionable silence until Dan said, 'Funny how Kitty Dibden-Rawles is never at church.'

Alec twitched. *Why's he mentioning it to me?*

'Ah, yes.' Dan answered his own question. 'She's Irish, of course, she'll be a calithumpian.'

*

'They seem happy enough, don't they?'

Doris had press-ganged the children into helping her check on one of the calves. Its dung was loose. It might be something or nothing, but farming had taught Doris to keep a close check on even simple matters. She'd lost a calf earlier in the week and it rankled. An animal's death was costly and melancholy and a judgement on her care of it. The calf had fitted, his skinny legs kicking out and his eyes bewildered.

'He's lying a bit funny.' Christine tugged her mother over to the corner of the barn. The weather was warm enough for the calves to sleep out, but prevention being nine-tenths of cure, the patient was inside.

'You're right.' Doris knelt. The straw crackled beneath her. Sweet-smelling but liable to turn; no farmyard is ever truly sweet. 'I can't really see in this light . . .'

'Come on, he's fine.' Philip kvetched from the door.

'Here comes somebody,' said Christine.

Across the yard a lantern swayed at head height.

Not you, thought Doris. *Stay away.* Help from Jez came at such a cost it wasn't worth it.

'Eugene!' Christine clapped. 'How'd you know we needed you?'

'Just call me the farm fairy,' said Eugene. He stood with the lantern over their heads while Doris checked over the patient and declared him sound. 'I was on my way back from The Bull.'

He smelled strongly of ale.

Doris thanked Eugene and let him limp away, all the while

feeling the awkwardness that so disabled her. She felt like she was asking the college boy for a favour if she gave him an order, and she was unequal to asking about his drinking. The relationship was off-kilter with these new men; she knew the rules with genuine labourers, but these press-ganged recruits flummoxed her. She recalled Dan's face earlier when she snapped at him for telling her, all glee, that there was now a farm labour deferment in place. 'And how is that good news, Dan Archer?' she'd said. 'Bit late for me, isn't it?' And all this while he was 'helping' with the roast.

All day, her husband had had that look on his face, the one that told her he wanted a serious chat. Doris would rather have stayed in the warm barn with the murmuring music of the cows' breathing, but a velvet cloak lay expectantly on the mantel, alongside a pile of stupid glass jewels.

'Come on, kids.' They trooped across the yard.

'Mum, I hate the new stuff Dad's putting on the crops.' Christine was indignant as only a precocious eight-year-old can be. 'It's not natural. It shouldn't be allowed. The king should say something.'

Doris agreed. The war pushed them onwards into a bright technological future, but it suppressed beauty along the way. Normal, insignificant beauty that Doris took for granted. Columbine. Kingcup. The daisies that Glen wore when Christine wove him a chain.

Mother Cat stood sentry at the door. Yowled when she saw them. When Christine scooped her up, both girl and cat jumped at her father's voice.

'Bed!'

'But it's only—'

'But me no buts. You too, Philip. Chop chop.' Dan watched them stomp sullenly up to their chilly rooms. He turned to Doris. 'Love . . . your mum. It's time we had a talk.'

Doris wanted to run back out to the barn. Instead she put the kettle on. Felt Dan's eyes on her as she battled the arthritic tap. 'That needs looking at,' she said. 'Getting stiffer and stiffer.'

The closest of couples have their deceits. Doris and Dan had refused to name what was happening in their home. Now, Doris sensed there was no fending off the inevitable. Their own phony war was over.

'Lisa's senile, Doris. Sorry, but she is. There's no other way to describe it. And she's getting worse.' The farmhouse walls were thick, but Dan whispered. 'You have to face it, love.'

Doris faced ten things before breakfast. She was good at facing things; she had put in years of practice. 'I know.' She bit back the impulse to flare up. None of this was Dan's fault. He was unafraid to do the right thing; she had always treasured him for that. 'Yes,' she said, in a whisper. Giving in.

Putting out the cups and saucers helped. Pouring the tea, bemoaning the empty sugar bowl, fetching the milk. But then they began to talk.

'Her confusion lasts longer now, when it comes,' said Dan. 'She'll know where she is, who she is, but suddenly . . .' He pulled apart his hands, let out a little huff of air. 'Suddenly she doesn't. We used to rely on a few hours a day when she was just good old Lisa, but now . . .'

'Her memory's slippy. Mum knows she knows us but she can't put her finger on our names.'

'I just thank God she's happy-go-lucky most of the time.'

Doris was in no mood to thank God. He wasn't keeping his end of the bargain. She was holding him to account, for once, as opposed to the other way round. Blasphemy gets easier, she was finding.

Dan said, 'It happens, love. Old people, they get simple. Nobody knows why. Maybe they wear out, like cars. My old gran lived with us when I was a boy and she was, well, *frightened* the whole time. It was terrible to witness.'

'Mum never runs away, nothing like that.' It was something, Doris supposed. Still no thanking God, though. Not for such a crumb. 'I don't mind looking after her, Dan, you know I don't. I'd do anything for Mum, it's only fair, it's just that she's *not* Mum anymore.' Doris gave herself permission to cry. There was no torrent. Just a couple of stinging tears that cost forty years of self-respect. She rubbed hard at her eyes, as if they'd let her down. 'It's not fair.' She balled her fists. 'It's not *fair!*'

'Easy, easy.' Dan used that voice with the livestock. 'All that frowning, you'll give yourself wrinkles, girl.' When he leaned over to smooth his wife's forehead she batted his hand away. 'Fairness doesn't come into it, Doris. It's the way of things.'

'Easy for you to say, Dan Archer. She's not your mum.' Doris would have taken her hasty words back if she could. Dan had been only a boy when he lost his mother. In many ways he still was a bereaved boy, beneath the War Ag overcoat. *Maybe*, thought Doris, *I've only been a nice person up to now because I had nothing to break me*. The war showed her true colours. She was a woman who would maul her husband when he was trying to help.

The soft *sluff-sluff* of Lisa's slippers announced her. 'Ooh, I've had a lovely nap,' she said.

They watched her carefully as she made for her rocking chair. They glanced gratefully at each other. This was one of the good hours. Lisa was herself.

Mother Cat leapt onto the old lady's lap and was petted, not tormented. Lisa asked after the calves, and was appropriately scandalized by Eugene's drinking. 'He'll have to watch himself, that boy,' she said. She rocked gently, and fell back into a doze.

'If our friends knew, they could help,' said Dan.

'Help? Gossip, you mean.' Doris saw Dan's expression flicker. *He's disgusted with me*. 'Nobody can help us. She's our responsibility.' *And our shame*. Doris was ashamed of the shame she felt; she would have felt only compassion for any other family in their position, and yet she didn't feel able to accept that balm. She turned it on its head, and made it unwelcome. 'We're in this on our own.' Doris put her finger to Dan's lips. Lisa was waking up.

'You there!' she called to Dan. 'You're a cheeky one, aren't you, Simon!'

Later, after they had inveigled her up the stairs, Dan asked, 'Who's this Simon I remind her of?'

Doris was unbuttoning her dress. It had an awful lot of

buttons; it took time. 'An old neighbour of ours when I was Chrissie's age.'

'I hope he was handsome.'

'Not really. Dad used to say he had a face like a slapped arse.'

That was it. That set them off. Fits of laughter. Until Doris began to sob, and said against the haven of Dan's chest, 'Oh, Dan, my mum, my lovely mum.'

AMBRIDGE MIDSUMMER PAGEANT
COMMITTEE MEETING MINUTES

Date: 22 May 1940
At: Noon Cottage
Chairwoman: Pamela Pargetter
Present: Frances Bissett, Margaret
Furneaux, Emmaline Endicott, Doris Archer,
Dorothy Cook, Kathleen Dibden-Rawles,
Jane Gilpin

1. Kitty thanked everyone for coming to her house for the meeting and was glad that the committee had agreed to her suggestion that we take turns to host as 'it is more democratic'.

2. Mrs Endicott asked if the window might possibly be closed as she was in a

draught and that was as sure a way as any
of dropkicking her into the grave.

3. Dottie suggested we sell kisses at
the pageant. As Vicar's wife I objected to
the impropriety of such a thing and I did
not appreciate Dottie's implication that
I can't care much for our brave boys if
I won't even part with one measly kiss on
their behalf. (Note to self: ask Henry to
have a word with Dottie.)

4. Doris said 'No the cloak is not
finished yet'. Pamela reminded Doris
that the pageant is less than two weeks
away. Doris assured Pamela that she was
perfectly aware of this thank you. Pamela
said she hoped Doris wouldn't let us down.
Doris got up suddenly and knocked over
poor dear Jane's teacup and went to use
the facilities.

5. Mrs Endicott asked if the window
could be opened as she was feeling stifled
and her chest is at her.

6. Dottie went to fetch Doris who
had spent rather a long time in the
facilities.

7. Kitty dropped her handkerchief on
the rug and we all had a good giggle
because it looked for all the world as

```
if she threw it! Pamela asked us to
concentrate and Mrs Endicott apologized
for being giddy.
   8. Jane suggested we start an Ambridge
Pig Club. Doris said her husband is kept
busy tracking down illegal pigs and Kitty
asked how can a pig be illegal and Doris
said pigs have to be licensed by the
SPKC and Pamela said there is a blessed
organization for every silly little thing
since the war began and this committee
is not about pigs thank you so could
we get on.
   9. Kitty asked did we know that
midsummer is a witches' sabbath called
Litha. (Note to self: check sp.) She said
'Crazy things happen at Litha'.
   10. Mrs Endicott came over queer.
```

The meeting didn't end, it just dribbled to a standstill.

Doris was off like a goat, and Dottie followed with Mrs Endicott. Jane was still sitting, still bellyaching about Agnes's failings, and Pamela was arranging her witty little hat in the mirror over Kitty's fireplace.

It had been a mistake to host. The sight of Alec's cufflink winking up from the rug had made Kitty want to throw up. The gilded 'P' glinting from its oval of indigo enamel had reared up, enormous, right by Pamela's foot.

She felt she had made a good fist of pretending to drop her hanky. The cufflink sat fat like a smuggled gun in her pocket. *That was close*, she thought, still sweating.

The room looked shabby to Kitty. Why hadn't she noticed that everything was too small. Too worn. Pamela's svelte silhouette emphasized the sagging upholstery and the faded chintzes that argued with each other from every chair. Kitty couldn't supply the little sundries that Pamela showered them with. No cake. No cordial. Her larder was barren. The bill at Frank Brown's shop made her reluctant to go in and face his gentle, persistent query about when might she settle up.

'Who are these lovely people in this photograph? Are they mother and father?' Pamela spoke with a hatpin in her teeth, the hat cocked.

'Yes.' The Hennesseys, framed on the mantelpiece, were small and round and sheepish; they were unused to being photographed and it showed. It had never occurred to Kitty before, the tawdriness of the portrait's black and white background. The limp curtains. The wallpaper marbled with damp.

'They must worry about you, on your own with a little one, and the country at war.' Pamela smiled at Kitty in the mirror.

'They do.' Kitty had never thought to be ashamed of her parents until this minute. Pamela would be baffled by the Hennessey home, a Georgian mansion of strict symmetry in the centre of Dublin. Abandoned by its colonial owners, it now housed fourteen families, each clan sharing a single room to eat and wash and sleep. Her own mother had long since burned the shutters, with their ornate carving, for firewood.

'No doubt Noel's people are good to you.' Not a question. Pamela assumed the British did their duty.

'Well, yes.' The Dibden-Rawleses paid Kitty a tiny allowance to stay away from them. They imagined themselves generous, no doubt, as people removed from poverty often do. They didn't know, as Kitty must, the price to the nearest farthing of children's shoes.

A foreigner, and a low caste one at that, Kitty heard the *whoosh* of air in her ears as she fell through the cracks of English life. She felt misunderstood on a fundamental level – the way she walked, the way she spoke, what made her laugh and what caused her to retreat.

She only felt known when she was with Alec.

As Pamela took up her handbag and gloves, the former patent leather, the latter hand-stitched kid the colour of setting plaster, Kitty re-examined that thought. Surely, she and Alec were too early in their love affair for such depth. *Does he know me yet?* Were they still acting with one another?

The women were so slow, so careful with their goodbyes and their gratitude. *Oh, just go!* she thought, feeling second-rate. She had none of their bovine self-confidence; *I am all need.* She needed protection. Security, both financial and emotional. A father for Caroline.

'We must be vigilant at the pageant,' Pamela said, as, last of all, she took her leave. 'Mustn't let those naughty witches of yours use their sabbath to ruin our carefully laid plans.'

'They wouldn't dare!' *Why did I mention Litha?* Everything Kitty said and thought and did seemed idiotic when Pamela turned her gaze upon it. Pamela and Alec were two of a kind. They needed nothing; they had everything already. *And here's me, scrabbling at the windowpane of their life.*

If Kitty was going to win Alec she would have to fight for him. And Pamela looked like a woman who had never lost an argument in her life.

May, true to the adage, had come in like a lamb and was going out like a lion.

Clouds had been bullied away, and a determined, jolly sun shone on the clearing where Kitty sat on a torn and patched picnic rug sprung from her attic.

She was awaiting her . . . *what?* There was no title for Alec. Not one she could countenance, anyway. 'Lover' sounded thrilling only if you were European. 'Fancy man' made her imagine him in lace and velvet. 'Husband': this was one title he could claim.

He's a husband, just not my *husband.*

Lying back, propped up on her elbows, she tapped her shoeless feet together, enjoying the pagan feel of it. She scanned the trees. It was secret, this patch. But not silent. Summer hummed in the grass. She fancied she heard a giggle, and chided herself for listening to Jane Gilpin's ghost stories.

Which excuse, she wondered, would Alec offer his wife for today's absence? She hoped he could get away; their trysts were by nature provisional. She had put on her best suspender belt. Washed her hair, with vinegar in the final rinse for the shine he always commented on.

Lower Loxley was the epicentre of pageant activity; the house would be a-buzz. Possibly he could slip out under cover of the melee; Pamela would be absorbed in banners and bunting, and besides, a wife who doesn't suspect is less liable to ask questions.

The sordidness of duping Pamela, who trusted him and, if it came to that, trusted Kitty too, tended to suck the colour out of the day, so Kitty pushed, hard, with the small hands that could sew and soothe and arouse, until there was distance between herself and the beastliness.

Edicts had been issued from the big house over the past few days. Tasks and chores allotted, favours called in. Kitty had sewn bunting from old bandages. She had ferried cornflowers, sweet peas and blowsy peonies for Elizabeth I's headdress from Mrs Endicott's garden to Brookfield. She had let out the smocking on Caroline's best dress, or perhaps it was Caroline's least bad dress; all the child's clothes had lived a life before they reached Noon Cottage. There was nothing new for Caroline, nothing shiny.

A cracked twig made her sit up. Nothing. Nobody.

Kitty had spent much of the morning daydreaming about sex with Alec. It was different to sex with Noel, the only other sex she had to compare it to. For one thing, she was a willing partner with Alec, not cornered, not begged, not hectored. Alec didn't sweat onto her face, and he didn't cry afterwards. He didn't tell her that she was the reason he was the way he was.

Noel had been drinking since he could get up on tip-toes and reach the family decanters. Kitty knew his thirst wasn't her fault. *It wasn't*, she repeated again. It took a great deal of repeating because Noel had worked hard to make his accusations credible. *Where are you, Alec?* His kisses would drown out the grim march-past of images that was Noel's legacy.

He might pass her a few bob, too. The first time he'd done it she'd hesitated. Should she be insulted? What was he suggesting? The second time she saw it for what it was; he was attempting to look after her in the way a man like Alec looked after those around him.

She had taken the three shillings here, the odd pound there. It kept her the right side of the red line that meant no supper, no soap. And it helped her send money home to her parents. She didn't tell Alec that. He wouldn't understand why she had to do so; he had grown up in comfort, with money trickling one way only, down to the next generation.

'Ow!'

'Darling!' Kitty leapt up. She was all energy. She vibrated. She laughed at him as he struggled through the hedging that ran, as if planted to protect Sleeping Beauty, all around the clearing.

'Damn and blast it!' Alec laughed with her as he faltered, hostage to the brambles. He freed himself and raced to her, almost knocking her flat, but instead sweeping her up and swinging her round in their magic circle where such behaviour was possible.

She was breathless. She tried to kiss him but he didn't want to kiss. He wanted to hold her. His arms were tight, and he rocked, his head dug into her shoulder.

This urgency was familiar from Caroline, when the child woke in the night, or encountered some fearsome bug on the floor. Kitty let herself be held, and she held him back. She stroked his hair and felt him sink into her.

She wondered if anybody had ever stroked his hair before, and felt powerfully sorry for him. He had ebullient dark hair which he coerced into a glossy swimming hat. *I would have you grow it*, she thought. He would be a wild thing, with a head of black curls that moved in the wind.

They sat awkwardly, still entwined. They lay. She found a way of nestling into him that meant they were closer than close and could both watch the unrelenting blue of the sky.

Alec talked and talked and talked. Dunkirk. Retreat. 'It looks bad. We're on the run, Kitkat.'

'Never,' said Kitty. 'You Brits, you win, that's what you do. It'll work out.'

'They've asked for civilian boats. We're on our bloody knees.'

'Boats? What, to go over and, like, rescue the soldiers?' That did sound bad. Making-do taken to extremes. Could wars be won with little boats?

'I've offered my boat, of course.'

'You have a boat?'

Yes, there was a family boat, of course. A 'pleasure launch',

moored at their 'summer place in Cornwall'. Kitty was alien-
ated by the vast hinterland of experiences and *things* Alec
shared with Pamela. 'Lookit,' she said, leaning over him on
one forearm. 'We're on our own-io here. We have this wonderful spot in this wonderful wood. No eyes on us. Nobody
scribbling notes to pin up in the middle of the village.' Kitty
undid his watch and laid it on the blanket. 'Let's steal one
hour. I'll time us. One hour when this hedge is a moat and
nothing can get at us. We deserve it, Alec. Love deserves it.'

'*You* deserve it, darling. Oh, you really do, Kitkat.'

'No, *we* do.' Kitty threw a leg over him. She leaned down
and kissed him. His mouth was so familiar. She loved the
way he leaned up, straining to kiss her harder. She sat back,
as if he was a horse and she was not a transplanted townie
and could actually ride.

He said, 'I've sent one of the estate boys down to Porthleven.
He may be able to—'

Kitty reminded him they were on their hour.

When the hour was up, and Kitty had put her torn nylons
into her pocket, and Alec was rubbing at the grass stains on
his trousers, he told her that Pamela had requested an emergency pageant committee meeting at the village hall. She
was in a week-long terrible mood; the pageant always got her
that way. She'd engineered a terrific row about, of all things,
the cufflinks she'd bought him as an anniversary present.
He couldn't place them, and she'd been vitriolic, when it was
most probably just some issue with the new housemaid.

Picking up his watch, Alec said, 'And you're late, darling.'

He kissed the top of her head. 'Obviously, we should get back separately.'

This tacit admission of the wrongness of what they were doing, of what they *were,* meant they didn't catch each other's eye as Kitty said, 'We should come back here, it's so private,' and Alec agreed.

When they left, the clearing was returned to its natural inhabitants, the shrews and the mice and the midges, until Billy and John stole out from HQ beneath the camouflage of dry old branches and fresh greenery.

They stared at each other. John's mouth hung open.

'Grown-ups,' said Billy, with a gurn of distaste, 'are crazy.'

The maypole rose higher and higher above The Green. Painted a bright white, with a golden ball shining at the top, it wobbled as the beefiest male villagers heaved it up. Mrs Endicott oversaw matters. She was less use than Mavis the Pekinese, who gambolled leadenly through their feet.

'Heel!' Mavis ignored Pamela, who was striding across The Green to greet her husband. 'Alec, at last. How do I look?'

Alec seemed confused by the question.

'The dress, Alec, it's new, and as that's quite a rarity these days I thought, well, that you might . . .' Pamela shrugged.

It was, thought Alec, a shrug both hostile and expectant. 'It's nice,' he said. 'Yes, very nice.'

She stared at him for a long moment. 'I can't believe I'm begging you for praise,' she said. She was angry with him; her face, always tight, shrank even flatter against her bones.

'It's only a dress, after all, just a damn dress.' She turned and clapped her hands. Without preamble she declared the pageant cancelled.

Doris, the cloak in her hands and the bags beneath her eyes testament to how late she had stayed up trying to make the stupid thing's collar lie flat, let out a much louder and much ruder exclamation than Ambridge was accustomed to from an Archer. 'Hang on a blessed minute, Pamela, that's not up to you! No, I mean, just ... no!'

'Cancelled is perhaps the wrong word.' Pamela pivoted, so all the worker ants could hear. 'The pageant is *postponed*. Ask yourselves, can we truly enjoy ourselves while so many British servicemen are standing on a French beach in mortal danger?'

'But,' said Kitty, just turning up, her passion tripping her words and mangling her meaning. 'Pamela, hold on, I mean, aren't servicemen in danger every single day? And everyone's worked so hard and the children are looking forward to it and—'

'I don't think any of us has worked as hard as the brave men and women of the British armed forces, Kitty.'

Afterwards Kitty would scold herself for her bad mind; Pamela had *not* stressed the word 'British'. Almost certainly she hadn't.

Mrs Endicott was mumbling. 'I suppose ... with the awful news ... perhaps it would be wrong to ... *frolic*.'

'I was looking forward,' said Dottie, slumped behind her bump, 'to a bit of frolickin'.' She dropped the Union Jack she'd been mending to the grass where it lay in a heap.

Nobody else questioned Pamela. She raised her arms, rallying her serfs. Mavis did a terrible shit right by her shoe. 'We'll have our pageant on Guy Fawkes, make up for the fact that fireworks are banned this year. It'll be marvellous. Same theme. Indoors if raining!'

And that was that. All that was left to do was for Pamela to click her fingers at the men to take down the semi-erect maypole.

Alec considered the metaphor rather heavy-handed.

31 May 1940

Dear All,

My fiancée and I have taken the decision *not* to postpone our wedding. As our brave boys make their perilous journey home across the Channel, let's show Herr Hitler that Ambridge won't be beaten!

Yours very truly,

Dr Morgan Seed

JUNE

The radio was on in the back room of The Bull.

As wedding guests filed through the front door, Stan, in his habitual Dickensian grime, sat huddled over the wireless. He had barely left his post since news came through that Cliff's division was caught up at Dunkirk.

'Keep it down!' he bellowed, as villagers expressed noisy glee at being handed a glass of warm white wine the moment they stepped in off The Green.

'Oi!' Bob's rebuke was gentle. He was tolerating Stan, despite the extra work the wedding made for him. 'Don't make me chuck you out, Stan.'

'He's all right, he's all right.' Morgan's face was pink with bonhomie. 'Now, Stan, I'm sure Cliff will—'

'You're not sure of nothing.' Stan stood up. He was taller than the doctor. Taller than everybody, really, and more accustomed to fighting.

Jimmy was there, suddenly. 'Stan, Stan, come on now,' he

said. He laid careful hands on him, his eyes looking blankly at the floor. 'Sit, friend, and I'll sit with you.'

Stan fell into the chair, and Morgan backed out towards the front bar, where Mrs Endicott ambushed him to say lovely things about his lovely bride, which Morgan could only agree with. 'I don't deserve her,' he said, and he felt the truth of it very keenly. There was something he should have told Nance before the knot was tied. Each time he'd approached the telling of it, he had suddenly felt it didn't need to be said. Then, alone in his bed, he'd reproached himself, and braced himself to tell her the next day.

Tonight, for the first night in decades, he wouldn't be alone in bed. But Nance still didn't know.

Kitty crossed The Green in emerald chiffon that was a relic of one of Noel's spending sprees and allowed herself to feel light, to feel young for once. *Because I am young.* Ahead of her Caroline was already a parody of a well-looked-after child, with berry stains on the smock that was just too short despite the hem being let down as far as it would go. But Caroline had flowers in her hair and she was giggling fit to bust; *she's grand.*

Good humour is infectious. Dottie had caught it from Dan and she passed it on to Jane as they met outside The Bull, each unfamiliar in pressed pastels, each buoyed up by the ceremony they'd taken part in, each anticipating more lavish food than they'd eaten since last summer. Jane had made her peace with tripe, but she would never learn to love it.

'Hello, gorgeous, don't you look a picture!' hollered Dottie as Kitty drew near.

'And you, I do like your hair like that.'

'I done it special. But look at this bleedin' tent I have to wear.' Dottie held out the voluminous material. 'I ain't seen me ankles in a month.'

Kitty took up the rear, following them from the bright outside to the dim interior of the pub. She faltered slightly when she realized Gerald Pargetter had fallen into step beside her. As he pushed past her, he said 'War!' hotly, slyly, into her ear.

Peculiar, thought Kitty, and put out a hand to stop Caroline disappearing into the forest of legs.

Everyone who was anyone was there, as the saying goes, but everyone who was no one was also there. Squashed, hemmed in, Kitty had little choice where she went. The tide of people swept her up and set her down beside Nance Seed, Brown as was. Not a Brown anymore.

They weren't close, but they had the camaraderie of young women to call upon. Kitty knew Nance was shy, that her role as the village's dolly in her lace and her veil didn't come naturally. 'Soon be just you and Morgan,' she said.

'Yes, yes.' Nance's eyes didn't meet Kitty's. 'We have a hotel.' She seemed both mortified and thrilled. 'Just one night.'

Kitty leaned in. 'Relax, Nance, he'll know what to do.' She read much in Nance's expression.

'But . . .' Nance pulled a face.

'No buts today!' Kitty squeezed the bride's hand. Felt how it shook. Remembered that poor Nance had no ma. Mind you, given the advice Kitty's mother had given her on her wedding night – *Sure, lookit, it'll be over soon enough and it won't kill you* – perhaps that didn't matter. 'The big secret, Nance, the thing they don't tell you, is that it's *fun!*'

'Horses doovry?' Agnes thrust a platter of eggy some-things between them. She had stepped in for Connie Horrobin at the last minute, and was now a hybrid guest/waitress. Connie lay in bed at home, silent and braced for the bad news she felt sure was her due. 'Dunno what Dan Archer'll make of the catering, Nance. All them eggs is illegal.'

'True,' said Nance. 'But Doris supplied them, so . . .'

'Lovely brooch,' said Kitty, pointing with an egg (she was *starving*) at a sparkly diamante swirl on Agnes's lapel.

'Isn't it just,' said Agnes. 'A present from me admirer.' She pirouetted away on knitting needle legs.

The food heightened the mood every bit as much as the alcohol. If asked, most of those present would have admitted they didn't think much about food before the war; now it was a preoccupation. The spread was no feast, but it was consid-ered and *special*. Mrs Endicott took her life in her hands with three vol-au-vents, one after the other.

Arranged along a wooden bench, Blanche sat against cush-ions borrowed from Lower Loxley, a satin quilt covering her knees. She was perfumed, curled and a little grotesque, her eyes sparkling with consumptive vitality. As she called out to people they came to her, and bent or knelt. She was greedy for company, scooping it up, holding onto hands, and throwing back her head to laugh.

Kitty felt bold enough to smuggle some closeness with

Alec under the cover of chit chat. 'Say hello to Mr Pargetter, Caroline.'

'No!' Caroline guffawed at her own wit.

'Pick her up,' said Kitty. 'She loves it when you throw her in the air.'

'Everyone can see.'

'But even Walter Gabriel picks her up. It doesn't mean anything.' She leaned in, spoke lower. 'I love it when you and Caroline play together.'

'It's not *seemly*.' Alec felt her recoil. She sometimes shrank when his vocabulary became what she called 'too Brit'. Bob's comment about Kitty trapping a man by making him a father figure had lodged in his mind.

'Right y'are,' said Kitty, her smile taking on a rigid quality. 'Gerald called me a whore,' she said, just realizing it. The boy hadn't known to pronounce the H. That was what he'd meant by 'war'. 'Alec, oh Jesus, Gerald *knows*.' She took in his fastidiously even expression. 'And you know that he knows!'

'Kitty, not here, please.'

She smiled still. Her eyes sparkled; pain and happiness can have the same effect on beauty. 'Holy Mother of God, Alec, could you not trust me with that?'

'Not. Here.'

'This matters, Alec.'

But he had moved away.

The thick old walls, white-plastered once but now drab with smoke, absorbed talk as they had done for decades. From the back room came the drone of the Home Service, serving up not music but facts and figures that had oppressed the village for days.

Or, those villagers who took note. Death was far away, muffled by the acres of tilled land that swelled and sank between Ambridge and Dunkirk. Jane heard the phrase 'Over sixty-eight thousand men are expected to be evacuated today alone' and reached for another sherry.

Beside her Frank Brown took up a fiddle, and played. It was the first time he'd ever done so in public, and his face was pink with pleasure. The shopkeeper had hidden depths, as does everyone. Ambridge's hidden depths had been exca- vated and reported on with salacious joy; the triumphalism of a wedding, its two fingers to the war, helped them forget the enemy in their midst. They had a day off from being spied on.

The air Frank played was quick and flighty, and Walter Gabriel took up the tune after a fashion.

The radio couldn't compete.

Jane sought out Denholm, stage-managing it so she walked backwards into him. She regretted refusing his proposal. She regretted it more than anything else she had ever done, but then, she had done so little. Denholm was the road not taken, the prize left unclaimed.

She decided – it was a firm decision, made with the same conviction as a captain turning a liner – that she loved him. It felt so good to love. It suited Jane, and woke up all the kindest parts of her. For years, Jane had felt herself wither and des- iccate, as mean thoughts multiplied. Loving Denholm made her soft, and sweet.

'Denholm!' She feigned surprise and begged his pardon, and arranged herself so that he could notice how well her blue two-piece suited her. 'A day like today,' she said, her lips delicate around the words she had prepared, 'leads one to dwell on what might have been, does it not?'

'Does it?' There was salad cream in Denholm's eyebrow. 'Keeping well, I hope? Good.'

She hadn't answered. Jane was *not* keeping well. 'You seem altered,' she said. She spoke quietly; a Victorian ploy to make sweethearts lean in.

He didn't lean in. 'Do I?' Denholm had put on weight. His hair needed a cut. He smelled, slightly, of mould. 'Are you going to finish that sandwich?'

'Um, no, do have it, I insist.' Jane watched her triangle of bread and fish paste disappear. 'You are welcome to unburden yourself to one who understands, one who is, oh, how can I put this, in the same exquisite pain.'

Denholm looked suspicious. He stopped chewing.

'You seem depressed, dear Denholm,' said Jane. 'Are you? Are you awfully sad?'

'No,' said Denholm slowly. His expression suggested he was trying very hard to understand what Jane was talking about.

'Oh,' said Jane. Then, clearing the disappointment on her face, she said, 'Good, good, I'm glad. Yes, that's right, you toddle off to the buffet and we'll speak again later,' she said to Denholm's vast back.

The groom, on a processional with his new bride, asked

Jane if she was enjoying herself, if she had everything she needed.

'Now there's a question,' said Jane. She found herself tearful when Nance kissed her cheek. As if a goddess had leaned down from Olympus. The white dress transformed the shopkeeper's daughter; Jane would never experience such a metamorphosis. 'Don't mind me,' she said, as she hunted in her handbag for a handkerchief. 'I'm just an old fool.'

'You have a tender heart, Jane,' said Morgan, in the same voice he used when he cajoled her out of her fear of ghosts. 'This is a day of high emotion.' He put an arm out and caught his sister-in-law as she passed. 'Isn't it, Magsy?'

She was in heavy crepe, the colour of spinach. 'I do love it,' she said, attempting girlishness, 'when Morgan calls me that!'

Morgan could indulge his sister-in-law – *ex*-sister-in-law? – today. He had woken up fretful that a poison pen would spoil his wedding. But the service had gone off beautifully, and the sight of Nance in white, along with the emotional wallop to the chops of being a married man once more, all intoxicated him.

The fiddles set toes tapping. The courtiers around Blanche changed shift; the older, the infirm, the averse to dancing, settled down with her.

The reels set Lisa fidgeting. She was spick and span, blameless, characterless, with her grey bob and her plain suit and her flat shoes.

'S'all right, Mum,' murmured Doris. She had searched for and found a safe spot. Lisa was propped against a dark wood pillar in such a way that, to the casual onlooker, she was merely lounging as opposed to being supported. Doris knew that in a small community like Ambridge there's no such thing as a casual onlooker. She was on high alert. Ears pricked. One eye on her mother, the other on the crush, over the rim of her glass.

Doris had never been one for drink. Now, though, she envied Stan his befuddlement as he slouched in the back room. She could do with some oblivion. She took a large gulp and almost choked on the sherry's nutty fumes. No, sobriety it would have to be.

'Chrissie!' she called, and yanked her daughter to her, straightening her hairband and smoothing the shoulder of her blue dress. Doris had been intensely proud of Christine's solemnity as she followed Nance up St Stephen's aisle. She should tell the child so. Instead she found herself saying, 'Don't you spill nothing on that dress after all those hours I spent on it.'

'Christine!' The girl was enveloped in a hug. The bride, still on her rounds, seemed relieved to have reached the Archer corner. 'You look a picture,' she said into Chrissie's ear. And to Doris, she said, 'I'm getting so many compliments for my dress, Doris. I never thought I'd wear something so beautiful and it fits like a glove.' The dress was plain, like Nance, and lovely, like Nance. 'When I was stood on your kitchen table and you were hovering around me with pins in your mouth, it was like I was a daughter again for a little while.'

'Oh, love,' said Doris.

The crowd spirited Nance away.

'We should begin our farewells,' said Pamela, as she pushed away from the long table. It was covered with a medley of tablecloths and splattered with the fall-out from cheese and potato pie and a roast chicken or two and a strange dessert which involved powdered egg and mock cream. The finale of strawberries, red and sexy and bursting with summer, had incited a cheer. 'Before the serious drinking begins.'

'Bit late for some.' Alec was monitoring the back room, where Stan's shape had turned devilish as the day wore on. More hunched, more malevolent, more pissed. 'Won't it be rude, darling, if we're the first to go? People notice what we do, you know.'

Pamela looked at him. Levelly. For quite a while. 'You are so transparent,' she said eventually. She sat back down. 'Another half an hour. Then we go.' She lowered her voice. 'I offered Lower Loxley to Morgan for the celebration, but instead he chose *this*.'

'It's the bride's family who organizes the "do", Pamela. Frank Brown loves The Bull.'

'And it's *cheap*,' said Pamela. 'I do wonder at Morgan. Allying himself to trade, after marrying a Furneaux.'

He could have said it. But he didn't. Alec could have reminded his wife that her family were 'trade', that her father's money couldn't rewrite history. Instead he said, 'Pity Ronald couldn't make it today. He's very fond of Morgan. Considers him more a brother than a brother-in-law.' Alec was privately relieved that Ronald Furneaux was absent; Pamela was wont to make a fool of herself, showing off 'my dear friend, the member of parliament'.

'Of course he's not here!' Pamela scoffed at his naivety. 'Ronald can't possibly approve of this marriage.'

'Ronald takes people as they are.' Alec swallowed hard as he saw his wife reach out and catch Kitty.

'Will you dance, Kitty?' asked Pamela, her smile a slash of vermilion. 'I suspect a jig will break out any second.'

'I don't know.' Kitty was alarmed. Like Bella the cat when she sensed Hero on the path. 'I might. If anyone asks me.'

'You must have a queue of suitors.'

'Not really.'

'I can see you with a settled, older gentleman, Kitty.' Pamela was this side of arch; she knew her husband well enough to know he hadn't told Kitty she was rumbled. 'Somebody like Morgan, but sadly he's taken. Nance has done well, has she not?'

Before Kitty could answer, Alec stood and said, 'Ask any fellow here and they'll tell you Morgan got the best of the deal. Nance is quite the best-looking, most sweet-tempered girl for miles.' It was neat, he thought later, how he managed to offend both his wife and his mistress with that remark. He strode to the bar.

'I should find Caroline,' said Kitty. Serene in her belief in Pamela's ignorance, she followed Alec. He sped up. He avoided her. She stopped, irresolute, lonely in the midst of the babble.

Magsy took Alec's vacated seat, and sat herself down next to Pamela. At last, they both had a conspirator. Magsy gently maligned Nance's dress, her veil, her accent. None of it explicitly bitchy, all of it drenched in envy.

Only when the vicar joined them did their talk turn vanilla once more.

'Don't, Kitty dear,' said Mrs Endicott as she passed her, 'even *consider* dancing after such a meal. You could drop down dead of the head staggers.'

'I'll remember that,' said Kitty gravely. She took another glass of whatever Agnes was handing out, and asked her, 'Are you getting a chance to enjoy yourself, Agnes?'

'You bet your life I am,' said Agnes, shouldering past. She was, Kitty realized, plastered.

Mrs Endicott wasn't done. 'If we'd started a pig club when dear Jane suggested it, we'd have roast pork today. But oh no, nobody listened. Brampton Green's pigs are *beauties*, I hear.' With a sly glance at Kitty, she beckoned to a tall man trapped by the vicar's wife in intense, mundane intercourse. 'George! Frances, dear, might I borrow young George?' Without moving her lips she whispered to Kitty, 'Handsome, isn't he? And a bachelor.'

Introductions were made. Mrs Endicott's shorthand was comprehensive; Kitty discovered that George Seed, Morgan's remaining son, was a 'boffin', engaged in something so very clever and secret that he couldn't even tell them where he did it. George, in turn, was furnished with the information that Kitty was a widow, a mother, 'an Irish colleen', and gentle and nice and kind and all those uber-feminine attributes Mrs Endicott so admired despite working her way through Ambridge society like a steamroller.

'The old puss is matchmaking,' said George, as Mrs Endicott discreetly backed away to hector Bob about The Bull's hygiene.

'Is she?' Kitty laughed. She felt unmatchable, as if she was covered in scales beneath her pretty dress. Only Alec would do. Only Alec could understand her strange ins and outs.

'How d'you do?' George stuck out his hand. He was tall and man-shaped, blondly forgettable. Urgent eyes, maybe, with a vulpine glint, but essentially just another chap. 'Mrs Endicott got it a little wrong. I *can* tell you that I'm based at RAF Bawdsey in Suffolk. People say my work's very important, but how do they know? Perhaps I'm just a coward who doesn't want to fight. Much as I'd like to, I can't tell you what I'm working on.'

Kitty, who had no interest in what George did, feigned disappointment. 'How mysterious.' Her eyes tracked Alec.

George downed his drink. 'God, I hate weddings.'

'What have weddings ever done to you?'

George looked at Kitty as if just noticing her. 'Aha, a feisty one!'

'Not really.' Kitty edged an inch away. George edged an inch nearer. 'I suppose you're glad to see your father happy?' She gestured at Morgan, his arm around Nance's waist, both of them enduring the vicar.

'Happy?' George let out a little *hmm*. 'We're none of us happy. Not since Anthony.'

'I'm sorry.' Kitty felt her peep-toe court shoes turn to heavy boots. 'I didn't think.'

'You don't have to think. You're far too pretty to think.'

'Surely, we all have to think.' Kitty – feisty, far-too-pretty Kitty – didn't like being described to herself by this man, bereaved or not.

'Come on, relax.' As George put an arm clumsily around her, Alec looked their way.

'I am relaxed.' Something stopped Kitty shoving George. Something that had been piped into female veins since time immemorial. She didn't want to cause a scene. 'Hands to yourself, please!' She kept it light.

'Kitty, Kitty, Kitty.' George sighed her name on a sliding scale, as if she'd been giving him the runaround for years.

Magsy inserted herself. 'George, dear, it might be time to switch to lemonade.' She didn't seem able to translate the look he gave her. She carried on, turning to Kitty. 'I do have to babysit this boy-o! I'm more than a mother to him, especially since I lost dear Anthony, and—'

'*I* lost him,' growled George. His pink-pale face flared red. 'You didn't. You can say you're our mother 'til hell freezes over but that doesn't make it true, *Auntie*.'

Kitty put a hand on Magsy's arm.

'Georgie,' began Magsy.

'Don't call me that.' George turned away, as if dismissing a valet.

'Let's get some air, Magsy,' whispered Kitty.

'No, I'll, it's quite all right.' Magsy blundered away, almost treading on Caroline.

'There you are.' Kitty gathered up her daughter. Inhaled her myriad smells of clean hair and dirty hands. Thanked God for her. Felt sorry for her. And danced on the spot with her until Caroline laughed.

A voice in her ear. 'Why the hell are you encouraging that Seed boy?'

Kitty turned. It was far more suspicious for Alec to talk into her hair than it was for her to face him. She kept her expression neutral as she snapped, 'I was being friendly.'

'Well, don't. Give him the cold shoulder, Kitty. The fool's half-cut at his own father's wedding.'

'Do you have the right to tell me what to do, Alec?' Such words were risky; they would be pure gold in the hands of the poison-pen writer. 'If either of us is permitted to be jealous surely it's me?' *Ignored, sidelined, shameful little me.*

Oblivious to mood, Jane approached them. She was bright. Too bright, like a candle guttering. 'I was thinking, Kitty,' she said, 'about what you said. About Litha.'

'Litha?' Alec frowned.

'I looked it up. The witches' big midsummer party.' Jane pulled her shoulders up to her ears. 'Awfully spooky. *Anything* can happen during Litha. Mischief, death.' She grinned, as if mischief and death were just the ticket. 'Although we poor victims *can* ward off the evil eye.' She raised her eyebrows and spoke confidentially. 'But it's rather *risqué*. One must jump naked through the flames of a fire!' She tittered, delighted with her bad self. She recovered. 'Not very Ambridge, of course,' she said, and moved on.

As did Kitty. Nudging her way through the press of people, she felt Alec watch her. Her feet were not following orders, they had a life of their own. So careful to preserve her ties to him, she was testing these ties, and it made her dizzy.

By Lisa she stopped. Kitty didn't know this lady, and it struck her that Lisa stood awkwardly against the timber strut. Doll-like. 'Mrs Archer,' she said discreetly. 'I'm afraid you have a little stain on your dress. Would you like me to help you with it?'

Doris had heard. Her head swivelled like a bird of prey. 'Where? Where?'

She was horrified, too horrified, thought Kitty, at the grassy smudge. It was not 'little', it was a broad stripe, hence Kitty's decision to mention it.

'Oh, Mum, how did you ... ? Kitty, what must you think of us?'

'I think, well, I don't think anything,' smiled Kitty. 'Sure, we all have little mishaps now and then.' She went to take Lisa's other arm; Doris was manoeuvring her away and it didn't look easy.

'Thank you, *no*.' Doris's face fell at her own sharpness. 'Please, sorry, there's no need.'

Comically lopsided, Doris and her mother lurched through the party.

'Had one too many, Lisa, old girl?' hollered Walter Gabriel, his face glowing red like Mars.

Doris's laugh sounded horrible. She paused in her struggle to let Jimmy go by. A glass dropped from the tray he held. A hoot went up from drinkers, and Doris couldn't bear it. She was inside out, finely tuned to the suffering that was suddenly everywhere.

It took her back to the months after her babies came. The exhausting empathy. 'Come on, Mum,' she muttered. 'Let's get you cleaned up.'

'You'll never guess,' Dan said to the neighbours clustered around him. Like him, they were the other side of a lot of beer. It was late. Nance had taken off her veil. Nobody wanted to leave. And yet, in what Pamela saw as an unforgivable breach of etiquette, the speeches had yet to be made. She was, in effect, a hostage to this interminable reception. 'You'll never guess,' Dan repeated, 'these so called labourers, this, um, Jez and Eugene, they've only gone and given *barley* to the horses and *oats* to the cattle!'

The men bent double. Dottie screwed up her nose: farm humour. She never got the jokes. She was bored. She was enormous. Her legs ached but sitting down didn't help, so she roamed the bar, feeling out of place and teary. That internal spring that kept her going had failed; she was homesick. She missed her mum, which was unexpected as her mum was a trout of the highest order.

The only hint of khaki in the place belonged to Jack. He was back, on a special pass, and he was dancing to Frank Brown's haphazard fiddle with a girl who worked in a dairy the other side of Lakey Hill. She smelled of cheese and, crucially, she wasn't Peggy Perkins. There might be a kiss later, and a bit of a feel, if the cheesy mademoiselle was willing. When Jack asked after Peggy his mother had rolled her eyes and wondered why he was so interested in that stuck-up madam.

'Because, Ma,' he'd said, 'she *is* a stuck-up madam.'

Shouts from the back room – now levitating in a marsh gas of cigarette smoke – drowned out the music. Stan Horrobin, on his feet and swaying like a reed, bawled at Jimmy, who stood, head down, taking it.

'Why're you here, useless and blind, when my clever son's probably lying dead at the bottom of the sea?'

From nowhere, Alec appeared. The voice of reason. The *posh* voice of reason. 'Now, now, Stan. It's not Jimmy's fault. Let me buy you a drink.'

'That's what it takes for you to drink with the likes of me, is it?' Stan was never so eloquent as when he was drunk. 'My boy dying?'

'Stan, the flotilla will collect Cliff. They'll look after him.'

Stan tugged an imaginary forelock. 'Thanking you kindly for your interest, lord of the manor, but do you think I'm an imbecile? The likes of Cliff don't matter.' His fist on the table made the pewter dance. 'Nice to see the Archer boy home *again*.' He nodded at Jack, who stood behind Alec, shoulder to shoulder with his father, a male phalanx against what might be about to happen. 'Having a tough war, aren't you, Jack?'

It was Doris who stepped forward. 'You ought to be at home, looking after Connie. Off you go, Stan.'

He swayed some more, until he seemed about to topple. Jimmy darted over, and slung Stan's arm about his own shoulders.

'Come on, let's sit you down outside for a bit.' Jimmy steered Stan out to the yard. The fiddles struck up again. Jack cold-shouldered the dairymaid. Doris went back to Lisa. Mrs Endicott was helped to a seat. Glen the sheepdog lapped up spilled ale.

Caroline rammed her hot little head into Kitty's knee. 'Mama,' she said, perturbed.

'S'all right, chicken, the men are playing nicely again.' As Kitty took the girl's hand, George Seed took Kitty's other elbow.

'I need some air,' he said.

She was moving, she was walking. Caroline also needed some air, so Kitty let herself be steered by George. It was only when they stepped out into the dim, balmy night that she saw how flushed and hectic he looked.

'Here. Over here.' He herded Kitty and her daughter as if he was a border collie, and they recalcitrant lambs. They stood to the side of the pub, beneath an overhanging gutter. The blackout curtains made the pub a blank box, out of which music leaked.

'Jaysus, that Stan's a beast of a man,' she said.

Caroline recovered. She twisted her hand out of Kitty's and teetered off to peer at God knows what on the ground.

'Kitty.' George stared at her. 'Kitty.'

'George.' She mimicked his accent and his deep voice.

He didn't laugh.

'You know, I really should get back.' Kitty cocked her head towards the door. Only feet away, it seemed distant.

'I want to tell you what I do. For the war effort.'

'Oh. Right y'are.' One eye on her meandering daughter, who seemed to be speaking to a weed she'd found, Kitty assumed a listening face.

'You've heard of Watson-Watt.'

'No.'

'Yes you have. Man's a genius. He heads up my team. We're developing a way of detecting aircraft using radio.'

'Goodness,' said Kitty, as she was clearly expected to.

'Where's *my* medal, though?'

'Ha ha! Where's mine, come to that!'

He still didn't laugh. Perhaps he couldn't hear her. *Perhaps,* thought Kitty, *I'm just an enormous, anonymous ear.* She nodded along to George's story. She kept a little distance. His drunken self-pity reminded her of Noel.

'Anthony's a hero, even though he walked into his own side's bullets. No church service for *me*, Kitty. No sombre toast at Sunday lunch. I just drink alone and muse on God's sarcasm. I mean, why would my father's favourite son fall so early and the also-ran carry on living?'

'I'm sure Morgan doesn't—'

'Oh, Morgan *does*.' George put his face close to hers, so she could smell the whisky on his breath. 'But it doesn't matter now, does it? All the family dosh will go to the new lady of the house anyway.'

This maudlin man needed to be shaken and refolded, but Kitty didn't suggest he pull himself together. Life with an alcoholic had taught her not to waste her breath. 'Caroline!' she cooed. 'Here, chicken, we'll go in.'

'Please.' George reached out and circled Kitty's thin wrist with his fingers. When he said 'stay', it was with desperation.

'No, I really should go in.' She was calm. *Nice*. She saw Caroline wander a few feet further away.

'Everybody leaves me.' George was angry.

'My wrist, George,' said Kitty. 'Please.'

As she pulled away, he moved his hands to her shoulders and pulled her hard towards him.

She made a tiny mew, but capped it. 'Listen,' she said, sweet and persuasive, suddenly so close to this stranger. 'The speeches are starting. They're always gas. Let's go in, you and me.' She smiled. She encouraged. She could see George wanted to cry.

His mouth crashed down on hers. His teeth caught her lip. His arms, as if motorized, snaked around her and jammed her body against his. He bent her painfully backwards until he found the hem of her dress and yanked it upwards.

She saw, over the bulk of his shoulder, her little girl crouch to draw shapes in the earth with a stick. She struggled without taking her eyes off Caroline. Willing the little one not to turn around. She made no noise; she mustn't scare Caroline.

They tussled. It was unequal. He dug his fingers into the flesh of her behind. An insistent shape dug into her front. Her face was wet with his saliva.

The door of The Bull opened. Noise and light and Jack Archer spilled out. He didn't see them as he crashed back against the wall and pulled out a packet of cigarettes. He didn't see Kitty grab the split second he bought her. She wrenched away from George and picked up Caroline, barging past Jack and having to steady herself as she landed back in the bosom of the wedding.

People. Noise. She checked her dress was decent. She wiped her face. She hushed her startled daughter. She didn't cry. She didn't draw attention to herself.

Dan stood on a chair, holding a sheaf of telegrams and letters. He was laboriously reading a pun-heavy message from some Seed cousin. Kitty scanned the faces – so good-humoured, so unaware of the primal scuffle that had taken place just feet away – and found Alec's.

She started forward. She stopped. He might blame her. He might punch George. Kitty pretended to listen to the telegrams, aping the reactions of the others as she stood, stunned, hot and cold and numb.

'And this one's from Mr Ronald Furneaux esquire, MP.' Dan waited for the theatrical 'Ooh!'s to die down. 'To Morgan and Nance felicitations on this day stop I hope to see you both as soon as duties allow stop I wish you a long and happy life together stop.'

Alec threw Pamela a look that told her so. She ignored him. She checked her watch.

'Now we have a *letter*.' Dan shook out a sheet of paper. Perhaps if he hadn't lifted that last half pint he'd have recognized the handwriting and gone no further. But he was surfing on the good spirits in the room. 'Dear Friends, as you enjoy this wedding feast and toast Morgan Seed and Nance Brown, here's a puzzle for you.' He broke off to say, 'I love a puzzle!' The crowd was expectant. Somebody yelled, 'You *are* a puzzle, Dan Archer!'

'Question: when is a Brown not a Brown?' All looked at Frank. Frank, alone of everyone, was not gay. 'Answer,' read Dan. 'When it's a Braun.'

'Eh?' shouted Dottie.

Nobody got it.

Dan carried on reading out the letter. Until he didn't. '*Achtung!* The father of the bride was born among the swastikas in Berlin. What fun to have Germans living in Ambridge . . .' Dan dropped the letter as if it was hot. Those who passed it around later were able to read the rest of it.

WHAT FUN TO HAVE GERMANS LIVING
IN AMBRIDGE WHILE OUR BOYS ARE
BUTCHERED ABROAD.
    SIGNED
    YOUR NEIGHBOUR

There was puzzlement and laughter, before silence worked like a virus through the guests. One after the other, they fell silent, and looked at Frank, and then at Nance, and then at each other.

Frank was the colour of his daughter's dress. 'It's not true,' he said. 'How could we be German? It's a lie.'

Morgan blinked. Nance's hands went to her face.

'No!' Blanche sat up and shouted. 'No, this is all wrong!'

'The first two weren't true!' said Frank, with desperate spirit. 'And this one's not true either.'

Billy goose-stepped across the floorboards. '*Heil* Frank!' he shouted.

A clip on the ear from Walter Gabriel put a stop to that. And to the wedding party.

Kitty, Caroline cradled in her arms, pushed roughly out, and was the first to hit the night air.

Like a mahogany Stonehenge, the big old wardrobe and dressing table loomed in the dark of the Archers' bedroom. Cosy, hiccupping beneath the quilt, Dan watched his wife move about in her slip.

He liked doing this.

Doris was going about her solemn, stately end-of-day routine. A drawer opened and closed. A small glass bottle was set down on a surface. She rubbed something into her neck.

A loud creak.

'Was that Mother?' Doris turned her head.

'No. Get into bed, woman, will you?' Doris would warm up the cold sheets. The wonderful furnace of the marital bed. He wasn't imaginative; Dan didn't envisage the Seed marital bed, and so didn't wonder if Nance had stopped crying and if Morgan had rediscovered his wits.

Some of the women had whispered superstitious twaddle about witches and a sabbath. He'd been quite sharp with that

Agnes, from Woodbine Cottage. It wasn't black magic, it was some nasty human being, someone they all knew. 'Doris,' he said, gently.

She sat regarding herself in the oval mirror. The bedroom set had been their first purchase when they married. Doris remembered standing, awestruck, in the furniture shop, stroking the polished wood. She had been half afraid the debt would land them in the poorhouse.

Lovely arms, my Doris, thought Dan. He liked the soft lushness of them. The gentle arabesque – not a Dan word, not exactly what he thought – as she lifted her hair from the nape of her neck and took up the heavy hairbrush.

We haven't had you know what for an age. There had been a drought. He'd learned to weather them; in fact, the lean periods were often of his own making. Was it the beer, or the peril, or the sight of Doris's arms that moved him to woo? 'Fancy a spot of rumpy pumpy, love?'

'Go to sleep, Dan,' said Doris.

It's noisier than you think on the forest floor in the small hours.

Wee things wake up and go about their business. Foraging is efficiently carried out, sex is had, murder is done.

The moment shimmers.

Up the road in Ambridge, flames flicker in the dry garden of Noon Cottage. Kitty feeds a small bonfire with twigs. Her tears are violent and loud as she tears off her dress and flings it into the fire. His dirty hands were on the lovely chiffon, on the flesh beneath it. She is not safe here. She is prey, and vultures circle. She pulls down her silk camiknickers and they follow the dress.

Up a tree, one of the hornbeams that march in formation through Lower Loxley's grounds, Gerald sits and regards the sleeping valley. He can't work out if he wants to fight or cry. He lets out a loud howl which bounces off the hills.

Communing with her reflection in the cheval mirror, Doris brushes her hair, taking out the curl. A hank leaves her scalp and sits in the brush. She stifles a sob and checks to see if Dan has heard. He's fast asleep.

The hotel bed is so correctly made that Morgan isn't sure he can insert either himself or his new wife between its starchy covers. She is still crying. The tears seem to be in inexhaustible supply. He takes her hand. 'Let's try and get some sleep, Mrs Seed.'

Alec will notice as he passes her door that it is open. A mere inch or so, but he will recognize the cue. Pamela arranges herself against the pillow. She hears his tread along the hallway. Hears him pause. She tenses. He gently closes her door and his footsteps continue to his own room. Pamela takes up an eye mask, pleasantly weighted and embroidered with lily of the valley, and puts it on.

The rooms above the shop feel empty without Nance. Frank pulls up the floorboards beneath his bed, cursing how well he nailed them down in the first place. He is light-headed with anxiety. He reaches into the small suitcase stashed among the cobwebs and he weeps. The feel of it, the memories it carries, the loss it implies. Frank takes out the small cloth book, a children's tale with beautiful illustrations, typical of its time. He remembers the story. Aloud, he croaks the title. '*Aschenputtel, Scholz Künstler-Bilderbücher.*' He whispers, 'Cinderella'.

By the side of The Bull, two figures merge into one. Agnes giggles. 'Get off, we shouldn't!' she says, but pulls her partner deeper into the dark.

Naked, Kitty balls her fists and leaps through the fire.

The sun was out.

The village green was a perfect island of grass. Birds sang and children played. Dunkirk was done with. The boys had come home; they were not boys anymore. If anyone privately felt that the nation had been humiliated, that the war had been almost lost as soon as it began, they kept quiet about it; Britain had lived to fight another day.

Frank Brown rinsed out a rag in a bucket of scalding water. Magsy stood by and watched as he wiped manure off the store's window. The 'B' of Brown was indeed brown.

'This is a disgrace!' Magsy told the empty lane; she knew curtains were twitching. 'To treat a valued member of our community in such a way. Animals!'

'It'll blow over, Miss Furneaux,' said Frank. He breathed through his mouth; the cloth stank. It was the second time that day he'd had to come out and clean the window. 'The fiend will move on to his next victim.' He rubbed at the raised letters of his name. 'Some other innocent will suffer.'

Dottie bowled up on a bicycle.

'Should you be exerting yourself like that in your condition?' Magsy looked askance at the juxtaposition of bike and belly.

"Course!' Dottie swung her leg, with some effort, over the saddle and propped the bike against the shop. 'Fancy anyone mistaking Frankie boy for a Nazi!' She chucked Frank's cheek, then recoiled from the smell. 'According to that blinkin' letter writer Ambridge is a den of whatsit.'

'Iniquity?' offered Magsy.

'That's the thing.' Dottie reeled off a list of Ambridge's iniquity on her fingers. 'First, posh old Pargetter's having it off with some trollop or other. We don't know 'oo. Probably not you, Magsy, eh? Then it's Blanche's turn for some ooh la la with the *postman*, of all people.' Dottie loved that detail. 'And now, apparently, the Browns are German! I've never met anyone as English as Frank. Whatever next? Am I from the moon? Are you a spy, Magsy?'

Affronted, Magsy said, 'Why would you say such a thing? Me a spy! My family have only ever served this nation.'

'That's the point, duck, this letter writer says whatever comes into his head.' Dottie turned to Frank and pointed a finger. 'Now, don't you dare tell me you don't have no tea, or me and Mrs E will riot on The Green, I swear we will.'

It was a hot and dusty slog to the Horrobins' place.

Doris was suspicious of sunshine; like so many Brits she'd

been fooled by it before. Given in, bared her shoulders, only for it to retreat and leave her shivering. She tended to hang on to her comforting armour of foundation garment, thick hose, dress, pinny, cardigan and coat. Today she regretted the coat.

Her steps slowed. There would be no welcome for her at Connie's. She had no official business today, but a suspicion had nagged at her, and pushed her out of Brookfield and away from her own concerns.

What if Connie doesn't know Dunkirk is done with?

The Horrobin homestead stood apart, insulated not only by Heydon Wood, but by Stan's belligerence and Connie's distrust. It wouldn't surprise Doris if Stan had smashed the radio, and surely nobody in that shack took a newspaper.

Crossing the yard, she heard Billy and John whooping somewhere. They should be at school, but Doris would leave that for now; tackling Connie was like moving a wardrobe – best to heave one side at a time. 'Hello there!' she called, with a brightness she didn't feel.

The house looked burgled, as ever. Connie was in shadow, peeling turnips into a pail.

'Connie, dear, have you heard the good news?' No use expecting the elaborate Ambridge geisha rituals of tea and home-cooked this and that at Broom Corner today. 'The boats are all home. The whole sorry business is over.'

'Why should I care?' Connie was peeling a turnip to nothing. 'We had a letter. Official.'

Doris felt as if Connie had slapped her. 'No,' she said, pointlessly. 'No, Connie.'

'Cliff's dead.'

The roof had fallen in on this family; Doris stood in the rubble. 'I'll fetch Henry.'

Connie grunted. 'The vicar? Yeah, fetch *him*. When I lost my babby he told me not to be sad, I had other children. He doesn't think Horrobins are human, so no vicar, Doris. I'm busy. I've got to get the dinner on.' She dropped the sliver of turnip into the bucket, and picked up another one.

'Come to the table, Connie, please. I'll make us a pot of tea.'

Connie didn't move. 'I been thinking all morning of funny things.' Peel, peel, peel. 'When Stan took the boys out poaching . . .' She stopped, aware she'd incriminated her man, then carried on; the worst had already happened and besides, Doris knew Stan poached. 'The boys have to beat the field, see, so the rabbits panic and run towards Stan and his cosh. And same thing'd happen every night. I'd see Cliff come home on his own, down the back way. Stan'd send him back 'cos my Cliff wouldn't join in with killing, not any living thing, not even a rabbit, and there's hundreds of rabbits. And now look, Doris. Look at what they done to him.'

The letter lay on the table beside a sieve and an apple core and a salt cellar. Doris hated it. It was, in its way, another poison pen. 'Did he finish *David Copperfield*?' She remembered his voice, sonorous in the shadows. 'It's one of my favourites,' she said, and she had an urge to keep talking, to keep at bay her urge to weep. Because this sadness was not hers to own, it was Connie's.

But we all lost him, thought Doris. The piercing cruelty of it, the plucking, the turning to ash. It wasn't fair; Doris, who had never questioned the natural order of life and death, now railed against it daily. It was the imbalance, the way death rudely turned up everywhere.

Yes, she should keep talking, she should pull Connie through these first hot moments. 'Have you eaten, Connie? Got to keep your strength up. Cliff wouldn't like you neglecting yourself.' She paused. The envelope was unopened. 'Have you read this, Connie?' Doris picked it up.

'No need. They all say the same thing, them letters.'

Greedily, Doris tore open the envelope. *Connie can't read!* It was so obvious. No need to say it out loud in front of the woman. She imagined Connie realizing the envelope was 'official' and flinging it away from her as if it might burn her fingers. Doris unfolded the letter. Her fingers shook and so did the thin paper. 'Connie, he's alive.'

There was nothing from Connie. Then, 'You're lying to me, you wicked woman.'

Doris read out the stiff legalese. Cliff was injured but stable, and being cared for at Netley Military Hospital near Southampton.

'You promise? You promise?' Connie reeled out of the dim back of the kitchen. Her face in the light was a map of bruises.

'I swear it, love. Your boy's alive and well.' Doris would have liked to fold up the beleaguered little thing. She would have liked to sway there all day, Connie in her arms; it would be sweet to *help*. But Connie was what Lisa called – or used to call – a Touch-Me-Not. 'If there's anything I can do, anything at all—'

'Like what?' Connie returned to form; repelling all boarders. 'S'all right for you! There's your son loafing about, doing sod all. Jack Archer'll come to no harm learning how to march, will he?'

'I know you're upset, Connie, but . . .' Doris went no further. Her saintly robes chafed, but she couldn't fly at Connie. They were the same, really. It was the men who fought, but it was the women who waited and worried. It was a slow death she and Connie were enduring, of a thousand cuts. 'I'll be off,' she said, curtly; the Ambridge equivalent of a slap in the mush.

Nance agreed with Morgan that yes, it was lovely, really very kind, of Magsy to have Homeleigh ready for them when they came back from honeymoon.

Every surface had been polished to a high shine, every painting straightened.

'And my favourite dinner on the table.' Morgan was all appreciation, all gratitude.

'Yes, thank you, Magsy.' Nance had always called her Miss Furneaux when she'd served her at the shop, and the childish Christian name was bulky in her mouth.

It was a relief to see Morgan cheerful. The letter had hung like an awning over their short, utilitarian honeymoon, blocking out the sun that tried in vain to bless them.

Nancy had hoped that the shyness that bound her up, stilled her tongue, inhibited her hands, would dissipate when she said 'I do'. It had only deepened. She was restrained by shame, and borrowed shame at that. The disgrace belonged to the liar who had disfigured her wedding day. *What a wild and despicable thing to say about my poor father.* The depth of her hatred for this neighbour, and her desire to see them punished, was uncharacteristic. Her new husband had declared himself unsettled by it. 'And look, fresh flowers on the table, too,' she said. Nance really did try very hard to do the right thing. Even when, as now, she was dismayed.

Homeleigh intimidated her. Its fine detail. Its spare rooms, all of them painted and papered. It was too good for her, Nance thought. She might well be the lady of Homeleigh, but the role was bad casting, especially when compared to Magsy's easy ownership of its kitchen and its many, many cupboards.

'You sit, the pair of you, and tell me all your news.' Magsy fiddled and fossicked. She shook out Nance's napkin and set it on her lap. She scolded Morgan for suggesting wine: 'And you a doctor!' When the door knocker clapped, she said testily, 'Now who can *that* be on your first evening home? Surely folk know you want to be alone.'

It was Frank. He refused tea, he apologized for interrupting their dinner. He stood, hat in hand, like a penitent, until Morgan said to his new father-in-law, 'What is it, Frank? You seem troubled.'

'Please listen to what I'm about to tell you,' said Frank, 'and don't make me say any of it again.'

His parents came to London in 1887, he explained. 'I was less than a year old,' said Frank. He didn't take off his coat. He mangled his hat with his fingers. 'I grew up bilingual.

English and German.' He ignored his daughter's 'No, Dad!' and said, 'My family flourished here.'

Nance slumped as she listened. She changed as her father spoke; she was a different person by the time he finished and she didn't recognize herself.

'My father,' said Frank, 'was a violinist.' Manfred Braun joined a small orchestra and played the halls. Frank's mother sold haberdashery notions from their front room. They had enough, if not quite plenty. The house was quiet, industrious. Good neighbours on both sides.

'We never, not once, visited Germany after we left.'

His parents, Frank said, and repeated, were patriotic about the new country that gave them such opportunity. In fact, the family joke was how very British Frank and his brothers were.

'When the Great War broke out, we became enemy aliens overnight. All of us were sent to Mooragh on the Isle of Man. At least we were together.'

'You were interned?' Morgan sounded shocked.

'Only for six months.' Frank tried to describe the disgrace of not being allowed to fight. 'They re-interned my father when he broke our curfew. Enemy aliens had to be indoors by ten o'clock, you see, but Dad went out to fetch a doctor for my mother. She was, well, she suffered with her nerves.' Frank listed the restrictions. They needed permission to travel, their car was impounded, certain newspapers were forbidden.

'But, Dad.' Nance started forward. Her meal congealed

in front of her. 'I was alive then. None of this happened. I'd remember.'

'We made out it was a holiday on the Isle of Man, love. We kept things from you. It wasn't difficult. You were only five when the war ended. And your mum was so careful.' No need to revisit the horror and revulsion Marian Brown had felt for her in-laws' nationality. The spat insults, her new catchphrase of 'Why did I marry you when I had my pick of proper English fellas?' Frank said, 'We changed our names the minute the war ended.'

The Browns were scrubbed clean. When Marian insisted that this rehabilitation must include keeping little Nance away from her grandparents, and their accents and their bowls of *Eintopf*, Frank had complied. Reluctantly, but that was what his new country, his 'real' country, demanded.

The tale petered out.

Magsy left.

Nance pushed away her plate and laid her head on the tablecloth.

Morgan managed a few words. 'It'll all die down, Frank, you'll see. As you say, you're as British as the rest of us.'

'I should have told you. Before the wedding.'

'It would have made no difference.'

Nance would turn that moment over and over in her head. She would analyse it until it fell to bits. She would wonder if Morgan could have been more fervent.

* * *

All civilized persons know it's rude to shut the door in a dog's face, but Hero meant Alec, and Kitty couldn't face him.

Hero scratched at the familiar red-painted wood, and his master rapped and called Kitty's name.

She hid. Curled over herself by the coat stand.

'Kitty, Kitkat!' One blue eye was visible through the letterbox. 'It's somebody's birthday. Every little girl deserves a birthday present.'

'Burpday!' Caroline rounded the corner of the hall at speed. 'My burpday!' She screamed when a plump plastic hand poked through the brass slit of the letterbox. 'Mine!' she shrieked.

So in they all came. Alec, Hero and a massive doll in a tartan dress whose painted eyes were as flat and unresponsive as Kitty's.

'You can name her if you like,' said Alec stiffly. Even when he tried his best he tended to address the little girl as if she was a board meeting. The days when he had held her and laughed with her seemed distant. 'Oops, oh, mind out, Hero doesn't like her.'

When he had managed to extricate the doll's platinum blonde head from the dog's mouth, he stood on the doormat as Caroline ran, tripped, rolled with her massive new friend. 'Is it,' he asked Kitty, 'too big?'

He may have meant literally. She chose to answer as if he meant figuratively. 'I'll have some explaining to do. How a widow of limited means gives her daughter such a pricey toy.'

'Just say, um, just say . . .' Alec was marooned on the mat.

'Look here, Kitty, can't I come in? Can't we talk? I don't know what's gone on between us since the wedding.'

She was bored, suddenly. Her heart had begun to pump when he knocked at the door but now she drooped, all apathy. The sameness of it. Nothing as she would have it. And now this gift that overshadowed the second-hand tin tea set she'd gone without to buy. 'Come in, then, if you're coming. I've no tea.'

'I'm not here for tea.' Alec followed her into the parlour and found himself halted by her outstretched hand, palm out.

'Listen,' she said, and he powered right down; despite her dejection, Kitty felt a start at the authority she had over the tall, debonair foreigner. His hawk face was set, worried, *waiting*. 'Sometimes your stupid English reticence comes in handy. If you don't ask me why I've been avoiding you since the wedding I won't tell you. Is that a deal?'

'Um ...' Alec never felt so dense as when dealing with women.

'Just agree, Alec, and we can sit and, well, we can go right back to where we were. That's what you want, isn't it?'

Alec sat. He beamed. He looked too young to have a moustache when he smiled like that, all teeth, and Kitty, despite herself, was charmed.

Perhaps his presence would help. Dull the din in her head. Kitty had jumped through fire but was still not clean. She had come across men like George before, one of them a trusted relative. She had shoved and sweet-talked her way out of worse.

The letter that arrived three days after the wedding had twisted the knife. She hadn't known it was from George until she was two sentences deep in soggy apologies and self-justification. He had asked to make it up to her. He had asked her to let him know she forgave him. She had felt aggrieved that he was still asking things of her, and had washed her hands like Lady Macbeth until her fingers were wrinkled. Reading between the lines she sensed an ignoble offer being made. Of rescue. At a price.

'Tell me two things,' she said now. Noise would help. Chatter. And the knowledge that she was important to somebody. Not important enough to marry, never that, but important enough to make him buy a doll. 'One nice thing and one grotty thing that's happened to you since I saw you.'

'Well, cripes, old girl, you and your orders.' Alec leaned back, at ease. He took up so much of the room. 'I know! I heard about my Dutch friend, you know, the chap I was worried about. The Nazis are going easy on the Netherlands, it seems. Comparatively speaking.'

Kitty mirrored his relief. Alec was an interesting man, and listening to him was one of her chief pleasures. She'd missed his stories, and this particular tale of how a chain of encounters brought news of this fella, she couldn't remember his name, was new, positive, different.

She watched his face, so animated, and knew he was already recovered. His latest Kitkat emergency was dealt with.

Her interior monologue was particularly loud today, and it ran beneath Alec's 'grotty thing': an injury to his thumb sustained when he fell down the stairs while helping his men move furniture. Phrases from George's letter sounded in her ears, more perfectly recalled than her catechism. 'If I overstepped the mark.' 'You're a good-looking girl and you know it.' 'This war is hard on us chaps.'

This war was hard on them all, from Bella the tortoise-shell cat right up to the smug Pargetters behind their leaded windows. Kitty understood that the men left at home had guilt to contend with. She could imagine the impotence they experienced, and she despaired as she watched the war bend people out of shape.

But why must the women pay?

Kitty had underwritten George's anger and grief; she had paid with her body, still defaced with his fingerprints.

Alec had stopped talking. Tentatively, he took her hand. 'Have I done something wrong?'

She laughed. They were, by definition, *wrong*. His being on her sofa was wrong. 'No,' she said.

Her lack of status, her place in the pecking order some-where above Hero but many leagues below Pamela, had meant Kitty could only stew in her stifling cottage. She hadn't been able to call on Alec to mount his white charger and protect her from George. It was two-fold, this problem – he would have been unable to step in because then everyone would guess about their affair, or he would have belted George, which would have been yet another wrong piled on top of all the others.

Although, thought Kitty, *George would deserve it.*

'Men.' She said it bitterly, without thinking.

'Look here, I can't help being a chap.' Alec stood up. He seemed to be miles away from her when in fact he only crossed to the mantelpiece. 'I shouldn't have come.'

She was sorry. Acutely so. Frightened suddenly that her miserable introspection might have ruined things. Because Alec was the most important thing in Kitty's life. Putting Caroline to one side – in many ways, Caroline *was* Kitty, that was her way of mothering – Alec was all that mattered. He was the way. He was the key. He was pain and joy and *sensation* in a life where Kitty was numb much of the time. 'Don't say that!'

'You know I can't take these excesses of emotion.' Alec stared at the other parlour, the one through the looking glass. He didn't meet his own eyes.

'Yes you can!' Kitty leapt up. She sparkled; she could turn that on, an old trick. 'Because you love me, ya gombeen.'

Alec said nothing, but he turned to her and he smiled and she had schooled herself to feast on such crumbs.

They sat. He said, 'We have *hours* together, Kitkat. I let it be known I was off to my lawyer in Felpersham.'

'You're sure Gerald hasn't, you know, pretended to be a spy and followed you?'

He looked at her sideways. 'The boy's back at school.'

The delivery was just repressive enough to warn Kitty that Gerald, and his knowledge of their affair, was off limits.

'It's grand that we have hours, but we can't do exactly what we want, now, can we?' She raised an eyebrow so he would catch her drift. She leaned towards him, let her breasts melt into his arm for emphasis. 'Caroline's had her nap, so she'll be up for hours.'

Alec sighed. There was a growl in it. A thwarted yet happy noise. As if his duty pleased him. He clapped his hands. Caroline looked over. 'In that case, I think it's time we all played with dolly.'

They got to know each other a little better, the milk pudding of a little girl and the tall man who visited often and smelled of tobacco.

'Jesus, don't look at her fringe,' begged Kitty. She'd cut it herself, with the kitchen scissors.

'Nothing can mar Caroline's beauty.' She was a dear little thing, very quaint, he said. He no longer seemed afeared of touching her; indeed, he tickled her because it made her laugh until Kitty had to warn him to stop.

'She's an expert vomiter, that one,' she said. 'Unless you *want* to explain diced carrot all over your Turnbull and Asser shirt.'

'Why'd you marry Noel?' asked Alec over Caroline's head. She had crawled into his lap as if she owned it, and now sat there contemplating her doll with the contented languor of a despot surveying his gold.

'Why does anybody marry? I was nuts about him.'

'Noel? Really?'

'He was gas when he wanted to be. In the early days he was full of life.' When he was working hard to win her. When his Englishness was glamorous, and before she'd heard his

225

stories ten times. 'Remember his parties?' They both remembered the game of Sardines, their false start. 'And he was handsome, until . . .' Until he wasn't. Until he looked twenty years older than he was, and his sorrows crowded his face. 'You must've been crazy about Pamela at some point.' Kitty saw then that Alec never had been. 'You did love her, though, Alec? For an afternoon or so?' When he didn't answer, she said, 'Sorry. *Sorry.* Jesus, poor you. Poor Pamela.'

'Would you love me if I was poor?'

'I wish you were. Then we could run away together. The poor are free.' Kitty was troubled by her answer. She knew things Alec didn't know; that gulf between them frightened her. She knew that love struggles in poverty, that it can be dragged down and drowned by it. She took Bella up from the rug and stroked her the way the cat liked to be stroked, one long sweep from her nose to her tail. 'Perhaps only animals love us for who we are. The rest of us are, you know, *in context* to one another.'

'We are.' Alec said it wonderingly. He stroked Caroline's hair in the same fond, unthinking way he handled Hero.

'Speaking of animals, that Mavis hates me.'

'Pamela's dog? Nonsense. Mavis has no opinion on anything, she's a collection of tumours held together by fur and stupidity.'

'You're wrong, she hates me. Whereas Hero,' said Kitty, 'approves of me.'

Hero's tail whacked the floorboards at the mention of his name.

'His approval is worth more,' said Alec, who had never met a dog he didn't trust. 'I'm not poor, darling,' he said, as if sorry for some misdemeanour. 'I can't just run away with you.'

'Not now, I know that.' Kitty dropped the cat, who landed softly and padded away. 'But one day. Nothing can live without hope, Alec. If you don't water a garden, it dies.' She had the sense of going too far. Her head thudded. She had always been terrible at poker.

'You must have, you should have, hope,' said Alec. There was a web between them, a tightening of the air. 'I do want to, Kitty, I do, I just . . .' His face struggled. He was helpless; he didn't look like himself. 'It's so hard, darling, all this.'

Caroline pushed in between them. 'Play!' she ordered. 'Alkie play with Caroline.'

Summer

1940

Unhappy summer you,
Who do not see
What your yester-summer saw!

THOMAS HARDY
This Summer and Last

July

'Go on up to her room, she's holding bloomin' court.' Agnes straightened her apron and pointed Doris upstairs. 'As per usual.'

At the turn of the stair Doris met Win Gabriel. The elderly widow, portly and slow, took one step at a time. She was half turned, calling over her shoulder. 'You'll keep it to yourself, won't you, Blanche, about my poor Jonjo? Not a dicky bird.'

'Win,' said Doris, in greeting. And to let her know she was there, and had heard.

'Ooh, Doris!' Win blushed, her fleshy face purple against the white of her hair. 'Didn't see you, love.'

An awkward *pas de deux* got them past each other.

Whitey White sprawled across Blanche's bed. Shoes off, he lay full length, head supported on his hand, perfectly at home. When Doris looked askance she saw him wriggle with pleasure.

'Yes, it's me!' he said. 'Bad penny and all that.'

Doris had never liked him, not since that business of the

missing postal order in Christine's birthday card. 'Blanche,' she said. 'I'm returning this.' She held up the dinky blue handbag Blanche had lent Christine for the wedding.

'Leave it on the side somewhere.' Blanche was careless with possessions; if Doris had owned a satin handbag she would have tended it like a jewel. 'And don't look so disapproving, Doris!'

'Didn't think I was.'

'You've caught us out. It's time to confess all. Whitey and I are in love and we're planning to elope to Gretna Green.'

Whitey laughed more than the joke deserved. He had a big mouth and Doris had to look away; later she'd tell Dan it was like peeking over Cheddar Gorge. 'You're a one, Blanche,' she said.

'I'm no fool, I know what you're all saying to each other out *there*.' Blanche jerked her head at the window. She straightened her apricot silk bed jacket. 'You're all thinking, hmm, what if there's some truth in the letters after all. What if Alec *is* a lady's man and Frank Brown *is* a German and that poor old cripple *is* madly in love with Whitey White?'

There was more in this vein. Whitey said little but faithfully guffawed throughout, but Doris soon tired of being their audience.

'I haven't seen Nance since the wedding.' Blanche changed tack. 'No Sunday drives these days, I'm sad to say.' Blanche became coy. 'Tell me, Doris, are you boycotting the shop? My crow sends one of the village children in with a list.'

'Boycott Frank Brown?' Doris found it equal parts

ridiculous and mean-spirited. 'I'd soon starve if I tried. There's no other shop for miles. The man's a patriot.'

Whitey found his voice. 'Can't trust a Nazi.'

'He's not a Nazi,' sighed Doris. 'He's just Frank.' She saw a letter lying beside the postman. 'I'm going that way. Want me to deliver it?'

'If you like.'

After clearing her throat, Doris read the letter to Connie at a kitchen table that was home to a lump of meat Doris couldn't identify, a pipe, a rusting cheese grater and Wizbang. 'He likes it there,' was Connie's only comment when Doris saw the mongrel luxuriating.

'Dear Mum,' read Doris. 'Here I am laid up like an old feller and thinking of you there at home. I bet you are busy what with the war and everything else. They wheel us out into the sunshine and I think of Ambridge and all the colours in summer. The gardeners here work hard but it's nothing compared to Miss Gilpin's hollyhocks. Don't you worry about me, Mum, although I know I am wasting my breath. I'm not as pretty as I was but that doesn't matter. As the doc joked this morning it's a good thing I'm not a model. I have a face only a mother could love as they say but I am alive and there are many as aren't. I do miss my pals from labour division. They were good sorts. A right laugh. There was one chap from Glasgow and I couldn't understand a bleeding word but he could hold a tune and he was one of the first to go and so I think about him a lot. I keep cheerful and the nurses are nice. They have some right characters on their hands I can tell you but I am always respectful. Is Stacey keeping well? Clip her nails now and then. Tell Dad he'll have me to answer to if there's any funny business while I'm gone. At night I imagine I am at home with you and the little ones. Take care and don't worry. Your loving Cliff.'

Folding the letter carefully back into its creases, Doris gave Connie time to fold herself back into her own creases. 'He sounds chipper.'

'How bad is his face?' Connie asked as if Doris might have an answer. 'D'you think he's ruined? If he was dying, would he say?' Her fingers worried their way up and down Wizbang's knobbly backbone. 'It's not decent. It's not right.'

Doris silently agreed. There, in that cave of a kitchen, she felt at ease; Connie's hopeless reaction to the war was sensible, logical. Connie was flattened by it. Doris envied her ability to give in. The cardigan Connie wore was shiny with dirt. 'Sounds to me like he's getting better, Connie. He's got the best care and—'

'I want to see him.' Connie's fingers tightened on Wizbang, and the dog jumped down from the table with an aggrieved whimper. 'I just want to lay eyes on him. But Stan . . .' Connie let out a little sigh. She looked proud as she said, 'He can't do without me, see.'

'I'll go and see Cliff for you,' said Doris. The decision made itself. Before Doris could reconsider, it had pulled on its boots and put up its hand. Close behind the decision came the hundred reasons why Doris should have stayed schtum. Wartime travel was arduous, she was needed at home, the Horrobins were barren people to have dealings with.

'What? Why?' Connie's amazement didn't last, melting immediately to a gruff gratitude. 'Well, if you want to, I can't stop you, I suppose.' She was weeping and not bothering to wipe her face. As if tears were just weather. 'Stacey'll be chuffed, won't you, Stace?'

Cliff's dog didn't even turn at the sound of her name. She sat watching the wall.

'Stan *would* go,' said Connie. 'He loves his boy. Yes, he'd go, I know he would. But he's kept so busy.' As if her visitor had disputed that, she said sharply, 'He's a good man, Doris. And clever. We're going to be rolling in money soon. He's come up with this plan, you see. Stan's got it all up there.' She tapped her head and some microscopic winged thing flew out of her hair. 'He'll show you all.'

Noise in the yard announced the evacuees. John skidded to a halt in front of Doris.

'Hello, lady,' said the older brother. He had the brutal hair-cut of all the Horrobin males.

Giving them a fleet, discreet once-over – cleanish clothes, no bruises, no weight loss – Doris was struck by how very small John was. Too small, she felt, to be away from home. 'Do you miss your mum, John?' she asked.

'He don't,' said Billy. He stood a little in front of John, one puny protective shoulder stuck out.

John said, 'We haven't been to our secret place in the woods, honest.'

Doris smiled.

Vic Horrobin, hyena-sleek, came in with a brace of furry somethings behind his back. 'You be careful, boys. All the dead folk come out of their graves at night and dance in them woods.'

'None of that, thank you,' said Doris. She wanted to take Billy and John home. She wanted to take everyone home. She wanted to feed Stacey and liberate Connie and get Vic to stand up straight.

She just didn't have the time.

It was, apparently, the Battle of Britain.

Not *for* Britain; Pamela wondered at the grammar.

He was quixotic, that Hitler. Changing tack, never pressing his advantage. Pamela had, disloyally, worried that Britain was done for after Dunkirk, but there had been no decisive swoop, no cuff of England's ear. Now the danger had lifted from the sea and the soil, and taken to the air.

The aerial dogfights didn't take place in Pamela's patch of sky. Lower Loxley was as tranquil as ever.

In fact, it was sedated. The heat locked everything in place. Pamela herself was shackled to her desk. As usual. Behind her she heard the rustle of *The Times* as Alec read. She could feel him *thinking*, those male cogs whirring, rather slowly.

She was riled. He had belittled her – a talent of his, these days – by being stingy with details after a telephone call from Ronald Furneaux. She'd asked for titbits about the war; he'd refused to share.

'You can tell me, Alec,' she'd said, narrowing her already narrow eyes. 'I'm not some village woman.'

No dice. He'd taken refuge in *The Times*. She knew he knew she was gunning for a row. The heat pressed down on Ambridge like a lid. They waited, all of them, for news of the sky battle, and for the next poison-pen letter. Pamela wasn't sure which felt more real; life was about the tiny details, after all. She didn't personally know any RAF fliers, but she knew everyone in the letters' firing line.

She signed a cheque with an energetic flourish.

Alec was grateful he had his back to her. They were bookends, she at the desk in the window, he in his favoured armchair. He risked a touch of levity. 'This'll amuse you. Ronald told me about London Zoo. Would you believe they've put down the poisonous snakes in case the Luftwaffe scores a direct hit and the king cobras slither off into Regent's Park.'

Another piece of crisp paper extracted from a leather box. 'Plenty of snakes right here at home.'

'Hmm. Well. Yes.'

'Any day now another message in that deplorable hand-writing will land. They're laughing at us all, whoever they are.'

'We're on their tail,' said Alec. 'Dan's a terrier.'

'Good God, Alec, you and Dan Archer have *no idea* who it is. You're not Sherlock Holmes and Watson.'

Alec continued mild; Pamela was a tyre fire in this mood. He must resist the urge to throw gasoline. 'We have plans. All top secret, of course.'

'Be sure to write up your escapades for the *Boy's Own Paper*. At least we Pargetters have had our turn. The next one can't hurt us.'

'Whatever hurts the village hurts Lower Loxley.'

'Thank you for the sanctimony, Alec. It always helps.' There was a pause filled only by Mavis's breakneck panting from her post at Pamela's feet. 'Gerald will be home this weekend. Could you try and make some time for him?'

'The boy wants nothing to do with me. Let him be.' Alec shook the paper out and folded it. Pamela would make pawns of him and Gerald if he let her, moving them about the chessboard as her fancy dictated. And occasionally, the gormless Mavis would reach out and swipe the board with her paw.

Pamela said, 'And the other matter? Is there any progress?'

'Things are in hand.'

'One can't wait for ever. There are limits.'

'Yes. You're being very patient.'

'Oh, I am *not*.'

He heard a tapping. He recognized it. Pamela's thin gold pen drumming on the blotter.

She said, 'I gave up London for you.'

'Pamela . . .'

'I had offers. Better offers.'

Alec closed his eyes. If she reeled off the list of names now he would ... well, clearly he wouldn't do a single thing. He chanted in his head. *Reggie Wilson. Stephen Carlile. Dickie Carroll.* Pamela's Ghosts of Romance Past.

'I waited for you then, Alec. I'm rather tired of waiting.'

His stomach burned. A fire had taken hold of him. He'd felt like this in France in the last big stupid war. He swallowed. It was time. She was pushing him around the chequered board. 'Look, Pamela, if you really want to know, I—'

'You've never been much of a husband, and now you're not much of a father.'

It was a slap. Alec felt its sting. He sensed she had turned in her seat. She sounded chastened – by her standards – when she said, in a softer voice, 'Alec, I didn't mean ...'

He stood up. Turned to face her. His grasp on *The Times* was clammy. Mavis stopped panting, her hinged jaw snapping shut as she watched. 'I know what you meant, Pamela. I have to agree.' His mouth worked. The words would come, surely. He hadn't planned for this to happen today but he felt himself scream *go, go, go!* Make a break for it. Tell her the truth, all of it. The door was only feet away. In the style of the *Boy's Own*, with one bound he could be free, and in Noon Cottage.

Pamela stood too. Smartly. Sharply. 'I can see you're about to be foolish, and I won't stand for it.' She held up a forefinger as he went to speak. 'No! Thank heavens one of us has backbone. Even if you aren't doing your bit for your country I intend to make sure you do your bit for your family.'

She left the room. Mavis waddled after her.

'Like Piccadilly Circus in 'ere!'

Dottie fanned her armpits in Doris's kitchen. 'That's in London,' she told Chrissie. She explained no, it wasn't a real circus. 'Although there's plenty of clowns.'

'Dottie, sit down if you're staying.' Doris hovered with a huge pot of boiling hot stock. She couldn't get by.

'Sorry. I'm a nuisance, in't I?' Dottie took a chair and stuck her legs out in front of her.

''Scuse me, 'scuse me.' Doris cleared a path to the scullery, through Jez and Eugene and Christine and Phil and Glen and Mother Cat. They were iron filings, and Doris a magnet. 'Lunch in five minutes, boys,' she said. 'Shoo!' she told Mother Cat, who looked insulted but didn't move. 'Glen, out,' she said, and the dog was gone before she finished the word. 'Phil, nip out and fetch Grandma. Christine, make Dottie a nice cup of tea.'

'Just so you know, Dottie,' said Christine, 'I'm very bad at tea.'

'S'all right, duckie. I have low standards.'

Jez swung his leg over a chair and sat facing Dottie. 'Then you and me should get along fine.'

'Get away,' screeched Dottie. 'I'm eight months gone. Don't you flirt with me, you rascal.'

Jez dodged the flick of her scarf. 'Still pretty, even though you're up the duff.'

'Jez!' Doris was outraged. She was burning up with annoyance that had suddenly welled up from the rubber boots she'd forgotten to take off. 'Some respect, please.'

'Oops.' Jez winked at Dottie.

'How'd you put up with this one?' Dottie winked back. Pulled in what should have been her chin with pleasure.

'Dottie, it's lovely to see you but I'm in a bit of a rush, what with the men's lunch and all, so . . .' Doris stood, knife in one hand, a cheese and potato pie in the other. It was the fifth cheese and potato pie in a row; she expected ructions.

'Don't mind me, you won't even know I'm here.'

The labourers took their places. Phil could be seen going back and forth outside the window. Lisa could be heard saying the only thing she was saying today.

'No! No! No!'

The pie was cut. Milk was poured.

Eugene said to Dottie, who sat like a swollen bud in the midst of them, 'My sister had a baby last year.' He didn't usually talk to visitors, preferring to maintain a scholarly silence in the face of their humdrum preoccupations.

'What was it?' asked Dottie. 'Girl or boy?'

'Boy. Very difficult birth. Wrecked her uterus.'

'Her what?' Dottie recoiled. 'No, don't tell me.' She flashed a look at Doris.

'Not at the table, Eugene.' Doris didn't want reproductive organs discussed over her pie. She watched panic flood

Dottie's face; she remembered being that way when she was pregnant with Jack. The pretence that childbirth is nothing more than a room you will pass through. The refusal to imagine it. She sat, starving, and reached for the last slice of watery pie. Her hand stilled in mid-air, and she said, 'Dottie, love, you hungry?'

'No, not me, I'm fine, well ...' Dottie reconsidered. 'I *am* eating for two so if there's anything going, but don't go to any trouble.'

Doris gave her the last of the pie.

Phil stood behind his mother's chair. 'Grandma won't—' he began.

'That's fine, love. Sit. Sit.' Doris glanced out of the window. She could see Lisa pacing outside. The men were accustomed to the odd behaviours but Dottie wasn't, and Dottie was a connoisseur of gossip.

It occurred to Doris she had never seen Dottie's handwriting.

'Uterus,' said Eugene, 'is not a rude word.' He was huffy. He was hung over.

'Shut your trap,' said Jez. 'Ladies present.'

Dottie said, 'I'm sick of potatoes, no offence, Doris.' She reached behind her and took Raleigh's cloak off the dresser. 'Thought this was finished?'

'I'm adding to it. Pamela was, what was the word she used? She was *underwhelmed.*'

'Well, I'm whelmed. I reckon you've done a top-notch job. Ow!' She jumped and flung the cape away from her. A cedilla of blood showed on her finger. 'Bleedin' pins!'

Doris bent to pick up the cape. A paste jewel glittered. Outside Lisa chattered away. She called to Phil, to her dead husband, to Janet. She called most often, and most tenderly, to Janet. Doris passed a hand over her forehead. 'Dottie, I can spare Eugene to walk you home if you like.' She ignored his groan. She couldn't spare him but if it meant evicting Dottie it was worth the sacrifice.

'I'll be fine on me own. I come over to ask you something, Doris.' Dottie hesitated. 'You can say no, I won't take it bad.'

'Go on.' Doris began to clear the table. Jez helped. He had never helped before.

'Mrs E said she'll muck in when I go into labour, but, I dunno, I need someone a bit more ... Doris, will you be with me when Baby comes?' Dottie laid her hands across her stomach.

'Dottie, I ...' Doris raised a hopeless hand. There was a dirty plate in the hand; there generally was. Her mother began to sing in the yard. Jez threw cutlery into the sink with a clatter.

'Don't matter, s'all right,' said Dottie. She was hasty, making to go. 'Honest, I shouldn't have asked.'

'I'd be honoured, Dottie.'

The table juddered as Eugene pushed himself up. 'Everything here is so *small*,' he said. 'So drearily domestic.' He put his hands to his head. 'Doesn't it drive you people mad living in this toytown? The smallness of it? I mean, where are the *ideas*? I'm accustomed to thinking about the big things.'

'Who bit *his* bum?' asked Dottie.

'He's a brainbox.' Jez shrugged. 'They're different.'

'*I* ain't small,' laughed Dottie. 'I'm a bloody helephant!'

Doris agreed with Eugene; everything *was* small. She was a small woman in a small life and she was surrounded by small things. If they all rose up together they might suffocate her.

AUGUST

The harvest had a personality.

It was the yearly visitor who monopolized everyone. All shoulders bent towards the great work of cutting and collecting and binding into sheaves. Conversation never strayed for long from how dry the harvest was, or how meagre, or how bountiful. Cabbages were hoed and corn was stooked. A workers' camp had set up over Felpersham way, bell tents full of city folk drafted in for a 'holiday' bending and cutting.

Everyone fell into bed exhausted.

Of course, not *everyone*. Doris and Dan might crawl upstairs like zombies at nine each night, but Pamela sat up until eleven playing solitaire. Alec looked in on the Lower Loxley chaps and leaned on a stile to chat about yields. Jane was quite worn out with finishing a needlepoint kneeler for St Stephen's, and didn't know what stooking meant.

'Yes, love. Yes, love.' Dan was nodding and smiling, smiling and nodding, as his wife leaned out of the pull-down window in the train door. 'This isn't my first harvest, I've lived on a farm all my life, remember. You're not to worry about a thing, and you'll be back before you know it.'

'Do *listen*, Dan!' Doris competed with the banging of doors and the guard's whistle. 'Bring Mum her cordial, the black-currant not the raspberry, at noon sharp or she gets all funny. And keep Jez out of my kitchen. Make sure Christine clears out her chickens.' Doris lowered her voice. 'Mum's started taking her clothes off, so, well, keep an eye.'

The train began to move. Sluggish, playing with them.

She regretted it now, the commitment she'd made to visit Cliff Horrobin. What had she been thinking of? It was like a general deserting his troops on the brow of a hill before the final surge. She should be in her rightful place, in the kitchen, the signpost sending everyone right, left, up, down. The harvest didn't care about the Horrobins.

'Will you miss me, Dan?' Doris felt silly saying it out loud.

'You bet I will!' Dan waved his hat as the train picked up speed. Before it reached the bend he had turned to walk away, hands in pockets.

He's probably whistling, thought Doris. It had been the devil's own job persuading him to take a day away from his precious War Ag. Looking after the farm wouldn't be the doddle Dan seemed to expect. Things had changed.

The borrowed copy of *Stitchcraft* was soon set aside.

She saw a headline on a discarded newspaper, and imagined the RAF slugging it out somewhere overhead. She thought of the rat she'd ended with a shovel just that morning.

She thought of Jack, who had broken his finger on an assault course. She thought of the all-seeing eye of the letter writer and whether it had landed on Lisa yet.

Surely it's the Archers' turn next?

All the while the train burrowed south through a land floating in the heat.

The village shop was full.

Nobody was buying much; there was little to buy. The commodity being passed from hand to hand was news. There was no rationing *that*.

'I, for one,' said Mrs Endicott, 'never pause to read the church notices anymore, just in case the next letter is pinned there.' She dabbed her brow with an already soggy handkerchief. 'This weather doesn't suit my blood. The English aren't bred for the heat.'

The boycott of Frank's shop, feeble as it was, hadn't lasted. It couldn't; the nearest alternative was in Penny Hassett, and thanks to petrol rationing a wartime mile was longer than a peacetime one. There were whispers, the odd joke, but Ambridge had, apparently, healed over the wound.

'It's definitely a man writing these horrid notes, and an educated man at that,' said Jane. She was rarely so assertive. Beside her, Agnes asked how so. 'Because the spelling is perfect.'

'We're not in the Middle Ages,' said Agnes, remembering to add 'Miss Jane' for propriety's sake. 'Most folk can spell nowadays.' She gave Frank a hard stare before taking the

Wrapped sliver of bacon from him. 'And an egg, if you have one.' Agnes had a long memory; she would go to her grave believing Frank Brown to be a Nazi mole.

'One egg, love!' called Frank over his shoulder.

When Nance came out bearing just one perfect sand-coloured egg on a striped cloth, Mrs Endicott put her head on one side.

'And how is married life treating you, my dear?'

For an answer Nance smiled and frowned at the same time.

Agnes giggled. She studiously ignored the pointed look from her employer; the crow had already been warned about her 'suggestive' laugh.

'Think of the child, Agnes,' hissed Jane, gesturing to Caroline who was being contained by Kitty at the end of the queue.

'She's too interested in her dolly to listen to us,' said Agnes.

'Very true,' said Kitty, as Caroline, conscious she was being discussed, pressed herself against her mother.

The egg was examined. Sniffed at. Agnes looked dubious but eventually a buff-coloured ration book was handed over. It was a waste; there had been four eggs in the house when she went to bed last night, and this morning she had risen to find them splattered on the kitchen floor. Jane had blamed 'the ghostly tots'.

An outbreak of 'hello's as the bell above the door tinkled. Alec and Pamela entered, all smiles, all largesse.

'Kitty, Mrs Endicott, Jane.' Pamela nodded at each in turn. Agnes neither expected nor received a nod.

'Alkie!' squeaked Caroline, running the length of the sawdust-strewn floor. She leapt at him. 'Alkie! Alkie!'

There was much laughter. Much admiration of the sweet little thing's friendliness, and much wry eye-rolling at Alec's typically male ineptitude with her.

'Yes, hello there, um, Caroline,' said Alec, patting the girl's head clumsily. He ignored the little arms stretched up to him.

'C'mere, hen.' Kitty doused Caroline as well as she could.

'Bless her,' said Pamela. She was all in white. Spotless. Her hair like a shining helmet. Her nails like knives.

'I should get her home,' said Kitty, backing out and pulling Caroline away from Alec like a bodyguard protecting a movie star.

'See you at the pageant meeting, dear,' called Pamela.

'Mind out!' Dottie, outside on the hard-packed summer earth, jumped out of her way, then took Kitty's arm. 'Where you off to in such an 'urry?'

'It was so hot in there.' Kitty pushed a sweaty strand of hair out of her eyes. She had been awake all night with her daughter. Some existential toddler fear had seen them singing nursery rhymes until the sun came up. 'Lord, Dottie, look at you. You're about to pop!'

'Tell me about it,' said Dottie. She chivvied Kitty's hair with her hand. 'Tell you what. I'll nip over tonight and set your hair for you, yeah?'

'Really?' Kitty was touched. 'It's a long way to nip, Dottie, in your condition.'

'I'll take it slow, I like to walk, I get fusty sitting indoors all evening. Now, look 'ere, girl, just 'cos you're a widow, no need to get like them older ladies, Doris and Jane and whatnot, all flat shoes and baggy coats. You'll always be a beauty. You don't give that up, girl.'

Traipsing home without the twist of sugar she'd come out for, Kitty yearned to graduate into flat shoes, tightly knotted headscarves, wrap-over aprons. *I'm a show dog, prized for my looks.* The eternal other woman, doomed to preen herself unto death.

Facts must be faced; Kitty had a short shelf life.

Alec knocked at the front door of Noon Cottage, but had no time to smooth down his hair or press on the ends of his moustache before Kitty opened the door and leapt into his arms.

He staggered backwards, and laughed, trying to contain her bounce.

She gasped, 'It's you! It's you!'

'Who were you expecting, old girl? Winston himself?'

'I wouldn't give that auld goat houseroom.' Kitty pulled him inside and slammed the door and kissed him hard against it.

Alec rubbed his lips. Amused. Shocked. Happily scared. 'I see. Like that, is it?'

'It's always like that,' growled Kitty. 'Caroline's with Dottie and Mrs Endicott. Get in there. *Go!*'

He allowed himself to be shoved to the sofa. He was blown

away, again, by Hurricane Kitty. They did it quickly, with the ease of old lovers and the ardour of new ones.

He sat up. His hair hung over his eyes. He was still panting when she began to talk.

Wriggling back into her zigzag-patterned dress, Kitty said, 'God, wasn't it *awful* at the shop earlier, when you came in with Pamela? I almost died.' She pulled all the pins out of her hair and it fizzed around her narrow face. 'She makes me feel so *bad*, even though she doesn't know.'

Alec would later wonder just what had happened on his face. He'd thought he had it under his control. But Kitty paused, a clip between her teeth and her hands sunk in her hair.

'Holy Mary Mother of God. Pamela *does* know.' Kitty bollocksed her hair up any old how. 'When did she find out?'

'She's always known.' Best to be honest, he thought. A little late. Alec tidied his hair and his clothes. A button on his fly was loose. 'Please, darling, calm down.'

'Calm down?'

Only then did Alec recall that each time he'd told a woman to calm down they'd simply echoed the instruction back at him, louder.

'Why are you always done up so tight?' Kitty, so languorous a moment ago, sizzled with voodoo energy. 'Even with me. *Me!*' She beat her breastbone so hard Alec smothered her hand.

'Kitkat, you'll hurt yourself,' he said.

She snatched her hand away. He felt a nail graze his palm.

'We share, Alec. Or we should. We're in love, that's how it works. We *talk*. Otherwise what's the point? I could be anyone!' Kitty found her knickers and balled them up and threw them at him. 'I've been feeling wretched about Pamela and now I'll go back over each time we met, knowing she *knew* what we get up to, and I'll feel ten times worse.'

'That's the Catholic in you.'

'Why can't it just be the human in me?' Kitty let out a rasping, irritated sigh. 'Guilt isn't exclusive to Catholics, surely? I know you're ashamed, at least I hope you are.'

'Of course I'm bloody ashamed!' Suddenly Alec matched her vehemence. He had never been angry with Kitty before. He saw her jump at his shout. 'There's no right way to go about this. We make decisions on the hoof. The thing is, the thing *is*,' he said, struggling after his strong start, 'that it's all bad and all devious no matter what we do. The very first step we took condemned us to lie. I've tried not to lie to you—'

'Thanks very much I'm sure.'

'But I've been protecting you and scared you might end it and just, well, confused.'

He looked it. Kitty didn't let herself feel sorry for him. They were galloping towards something and she wanted to see the view from there. 'It's simple, though. Shut up, shush, Alec, it *is*.' She felt certain he and Pamela never had stand-up fights like this. She imagined a touch of sarcasm over their 7 p.m. martini, or a suppressed sigh at breakfast. Well, Kitty came from a family that threw rocks. 'Do you not understand

what's happening here? We're not playing, this isn't sordid.'
Shouting her worst fears didn't, it turned out, help with them.
'Or is it?'

'Of course it isn't,' Alec snarled at her. Even though he was
reassuring her. 'But your constant insistence on discussing it,
well, it wears me out, Kitty. Because we're both trapped, not
just you. Do you ever think of me?'

'The *selfishness* of you!' She screamed now, not caring if
anyone was passing the open windows. 'The towering, epic,
bloody self-regard of you, Alec. It's me who'll be ruined by
this. Me who'll pay. The woman pays, Alec, or have you not
been paying attention?'

'Do not lecture me, Kitty.' Alec did up his tie, and the
knotting of it seemed like a murder. 'My hands are tied.' He
hesitated, but he said it. 'You can't pretend you didn't know
from the start how it would be.'

'Oh, there we are, there's the nub of it. I know the rules so
I can't expect anything. Well I do bloody expect something
because there are new rules now. Do you love me, Alec?'

It was a simple question. The daring of it knocked the
breath out of her. And made Alec quiver.

'This is hardly the time—' he said.

'Jesus Christ!' bawled Kitty. Her hands, nailed to her hips,
dropped. There was a weapon she hadn't used because she
wanted all to be natural and organic between them. Because
she wanted love to drive them. But he was an idiot and
needs must and so she looked levelly at him and said, 'That's
it, Alec.'

'No, that's not it.' Alec was spluttering. 'Be careful, don't say things you can't take back.'

'I can't lecture you, but you can lecture me?'

'Kitty, come on!'

She folded her arms. She thought again. She decided. She pushed the button. 'It had to come to this, and now here we are. Alec, it's her or me.'

Alec stood up. 'No, no, don't, Kitty.' He held his hands out in front of him as if she advanced on him with a blade. 'Think, darling, don't do this.'

'Did you think we'd never reach this moment?' Kitty neighed like a horse at his lunacy. 'Have you never read a book or watched a film? Choose, for the love of God. Be a man.'

She flew at him and he let her. She hit him on his broad chest with the flat of her hands as if he was a door she was trying to get through. 'Choose! Her or me! Who? Who do you choose? Pamela or me?'

Kitty gave him one last insolent shove. She turned away, and leaned on the sideboard, panting.

And Alec? He left.

His feet took him directly to The Bull. Alec had no say in the matter.

As sweet a sanctuary as Notre Dame cathedral, as male an environment as tobacco and spit could make it. Apparently, the other men of Ambridge felt the same; there was a lock-in under way.

'Don't tell the War Ag!' Bob winked and held up another tankard for Dan. 'Jimmy, lad, feel your way over to the window corner with a chaser for Walter, and clear his table.' Bob watched his son negotiate the maze of low tables and tipsily leaning stools. 'Getting good at it,' he said, and there were nods all round.

'Bloody shower, they are,' Dan was saying as Alec arrived. He leaned back, loquacious, in the snug. 'Don't know how my Doris puts up with them. Labourers? Don't make me laugh. One day of dealing with 'em has me spitting nails. Don't know one end of a scythe from the other. Dangerous, they are. Downright dangerous.'

Alec turned his squat glass of whisky round and round in his hands. Crouching over it, he stared at but didn't see its marmalade depths. 'Dangerous,' he repeated encouragingly, not listening. He didn't know who or what was dangerous and he couldn't muster up the oomph to care.

The door swung open. It hit Denholm, who was nodding off behind it, arms crossed, head back and mouth agape like a walrus.

'Blackout!' yelled Dan, then, 'Son? What are you doing home?'

The war meant that people popped up and disappeared at odd hours and in the wrong place, like toys thrown about by children. Jack was out of breath, his pug-nosed face bright pink. Words spewed out of him.

'I got him! The letters! The bloke! I got him!'

Men stood and wiped their mouths with the backs of their hands.

Dan slammed down his drink. 'The poison pen?'

'He got away from me at St Stephen's, he was too fast, Dad.' Jack was flattened as drinkers pushed past him, out to The Green.

Jack ran with the posse towards the church, panting out his story as he went. 'He was sticking something up on the church door. He wriggled away from me in the dark but I recognized his coat. That old regimental overcoat. It was Stan Horrobin.'

'No note 'ere,' growled Walter when they reached the church's dim porch. 'Maybe it got blown away.'

'You look for it, Walter.' Dan had sobered up. 'Alec, search inside St Stephen's, and you others come with me and we'll see if Stan's hiding among the graves.'

Once the door banged shut behind Alec, he could have been the only man alive in Ambridge.

St Stephen's at night was a different beast to the church on Sunday. The stained glass was dead. Arches faded to shadow. There, in the centre of the aisle, Alec saw a grotesque man, bent and gaunt.

The heavy crucifix was shocking in its size and its realism. Retrieved from an ante room where it had spent the last fifty years, the sculpted body had been taken down and propped up against a pew while the vicar decided on its fate. He didn't fit in at St Stephen's, this dying Jesus with his eyes cast down, his skin grey, and paint peeling on his skeletal knees.

Alec approached him. The cheekbones were sharp enough to cut. He laid a hand over one of the Lord's. Palm to palm.

Pushed at the nail that went through the plaster flesh. It was real and jagged.

Alec squeezed.

He sagged against the cross, and pressed harder. He closed his eyes. Blood dripped on the tessellated floor.

'Alec?' Dan ran up the aisle, oblivious. 'We can't find him. We should get over to Broom Corner before he burns that bloody coat.'

'Yes, yes.' Alec straightened up.

Dan pointed at the Rorschach blot of blood. He hesitated. 'Is that yours?'

'Dan, have you always been faithful to Doris?'

Dan's face was a perfect illustration of bemusement. He looked from the blood to Alec's face. 'Of course.' He laughed, a quick snort, the kind he made reading the funnies in the *Echo*. 'What a question. Where'd we be if we carried on like continentals? There's nobody like Doris and I know what side my bread's buttered, thank you very much.'

Not laughing, not matching Dan's tone, Alec was fierce. 'But what if your bread isn't buttered? What if you're unhappy? Does that matter? Or are we all just tiny tiles in a huge mosaic, condemned to stay in place so we don't spoil the damn pattern?'

'Alec, I'm at sea here.' Dan was still trying to laugh but his face wouldn't co-operate. 'Do you need something for your hand?'

Time to make light of it. To pretend it was tomfoolery. 'Your expression, old boy!' Years of training by nannies and public school and the army and his wife meant Alec could snap back into shape double-quick.

'I thought you'd gone doolally tap. This war, it makes us all a bit . . .' Dan circled a finger at his temple. 'This air battle. The RAF boys. It's getting to us.' He punched Alec gently on the arm.

Alec sensed Dan was trying to communicate, to understand, while keeping it all carefully manful. 'It does,' he said, and then, all movement, 'Let's go get Stan Horrobin.'

This heat, thought Doris. It was too hot. It wasn't right nor proper.

It had been too late to visit Connie when she got back to Ambridge the night before. Much had happened since then, ugly scenes at the Horrobin place. But visit she must, despite all that.

Ahead on the road, she saw Stan. His Vic was beside him, like a smaller version designed as a spare. Their faces were black with bad humour. Doris didn't offer a hello. She stood and waited for them to reach her.

'We've had enough of the Archers round here,' said the father. The son sliced the air with a switch. 'You're sweatin', missus,' he jeered as she hurried on. She put a neurotic hand to the back of her head, where the hair was growing scanty, and hoped they couldn't see.

The house was empty. Doris found Connie in the wash house, kneeling at a tin bath full of sopping clothes. She came slowly out into the sun, her legs no more than threads hanging from the hem of her skirt. 'What do you want? We told that husband of yours last night. My Stan never done it. Silly kiddies' games, writing foolish letters, why would he? Stan lost that coat last winter. Some bugger nicked it. It's not *always* the Horrobins when something bad happens, no matter what those stuck-up Pargetters and the cuckoo Gilpin sisters think.' She lowered her chin and pointed, all malevolence. 'It's one of you good upright churchy folk what's writing the letters.'

Doris held up a hand to stem the flow. 'That's not why I'm here.' She'd heard all about it from Dan. How Connie had flown at him, nails out. How the language from her would take the rust off a bucket. He'd bathed his bloodied face, and said, 'She's a demon, love.' He'd been disappointed, rebuked. Without the coat, they'd had to leave Broom Corner with the mystery still intact.

No letter had been found. There was a stay of execution for the next victim. It lay somewhere underfoot. Maybe too mangled to read. And maybe not.

Doris smiled, aware it was probably only a ghastly attempt. 'Connie, I'm not here about all that business. I went to see Cliff yesterday, like I promised.'

Connie changed utterly, from Medusa to mouse, her mouth a hen's bum. 'Best come inside.'

Indoors, amid the clutter and a new smell, warm and redolent of the insides of living things, Doris performed her piece. Edited, concise, washed clean of strong emotion. 'You should see the hospital, Connie, it's a palace.'

The turrets and towers had been a surprise. Cliff was a pet of all the nurses, Doris said. 'Lovely girls, so brave, and all sweet on him. It wears him out to write, so he was very particular that I tell you you're not to fret if you don't hear from him, the poor lamb.'

Avid, greedy, Connie asked many questions but not the ones Doris feared. Was he eating, she asked. Did he have books, was he missing home? Nothing about his injuries, a peculiar oversight Doris was grateful for. She didn't know how to describe walking through the rows of iron beds in the aggressively clean, high-ceilinged ward to find Cliff at the very end.

His hands on the coverlet were raw from grenade burns. Inside out, they seemed. A nurse in a bell-shaped apron was obscenely healthy beside him. Cliff's dull eyes stared out from bandages, and, beneath them, Doris saw an evident lack of face where face should be. No jaw should look like that. Cliff's face didn't hang together behind the dressings, which had begun to spoil and turn a marbled grey and pink. The boy was wonky, and seemed different, *lesser*, because of it.

He had left his face in France.

Leaning over him, Doris had mopped up his tears. She held onto her own; plenty of time for that later and Cliff didn't need her pity. He needed company and news, and that's what she had given him.

Hard to know with the unknowable Connie whether she was leaving out certain questions because she didn't want the answers. Her 'Thank you, Doris' was clumsy; gratitude was rarely called for in that house. 'All I want now is to have him home.'

'It might be a while yet. And, Connie, well, he might be a bit different.'

'He'll be fine when he's home.' Regal in her rags, Connie dismissed Doris. 'Won't he, Stacey?'

The dog didn't offer an opinion.

When Doris saw the trio gathered outside The Bull, she made a diversion, hurrying towards them like a worker bee ferrying nectar to the hive. She would shake off the miasma of Connie and her sorrow with application of some mundane and healing chatter.

'You back again, Peggy?' she said.

'Me mum made me come.' Peggy seemed to have aged a decade in the months since her last visit. She was groomed, sure of herself, a grown-up in grown-up's clothing. 'She doesn't understand how tricky it is hoofing out to the sticks with the trains the way they are.'

'We're hardly the sticks, Miss Perkins.' Jane was mildly insulted on behalf of her cosmopolitan Ambridge brethren.

'Oh, we are.' Dottie nudged Jane hard enough to send her flying. 'Love your hat, Peg.'

A twirl was executed, to show off said hat. It was swanky, bought with Peggy's first week's wages at the shoe shop. She told them how her mother suffered bad dreams about Billy and John. How she feared lice and rickets and beatings. 'I only come here to stop her going on about it.'

'You're a good girl,' said Doris, meaning it but glad all the same that Jack was otherwise engaged back at Brookfield. There was something of the minx about Peggy; she could ruin a boy's life. Especially if that boy didn't have the sense he was born with.

'You ain't going down no lane in those shoes.' Dottie was in awe of the strappy cream sandals. 'Hang on. I'll nip into the pub and get you a lift.'

'Bad business last night,' said Jane, her waxy, barely there face criss-crossed with worry lines. 'No news of the letter, Doris? Nobody's handed it in? We don't know, erm, who it might be about?'

'No, no news.' Doris saw Dottie emerge with Jez, who spat energetically into the tub of begonias that was Bob's pride and joy.

'I've dragged this one away from his pint!' said Dottie.

Doris was quick. 'Are you in the truck, Jez? How come?'

Jez was unruffled. 'Ask your husband. He sent me for a lend of a subsoiler.' He turned to Peggy. 'You the damsel in distress?'

'I'm never that.' Peggy looked him up and down, clearly and rudely dubious about what she saw.

So, it's not just me, thought Doris. She admired Peggy's acumen; Doris would have accepted a lift from Beelzebub at her age.

'Scuse me, I need a wee!' Dottie, not noticing Jane's fluttered eyelids at such candour, bent double and scooted back into The Bull, almost colliding with Jack, who was tugging on his jacket as he barrelled out.

'I'll take her, you're busy, Jez mate.' Jack smiled at Peggy who didn't smile back. 'I don't have wheels but I can walk you there. If it gets muddy just hop on my back.'

'Sir Galahad.' Peggy pursed her lips. Made him wait. 'Go on, then,' she said.

'You *are* good, Jack,' said Jane, as Doris tried and failed to catch her son's eye.

Bob was out of his pub; this was a rare sighting of him out in the open. He was agitated. Bouncing on his toes. 'Ladies! Your little friend! She's creating in the lavatory!'

Shrieks filled the pub. Female cries that had the clientele a-twitter.

'Can't be the baby,' muttered Doris, hurrying through The Bull and out to the yard, to listen at the raw wooden toilet door. 'She's not due.'

Jane held back, tentative in this male stronghold. 'Is it the baby?' she asked across the cobbles, mouthing the words as if swearing.

'It's the baby!' screamed Dottie as she burst out of the lavatory.

Men scattered. Doris, whose only thought was *I do not have time for this*, took charge. She flung orders as she held up Dottie and steered her into the snug. 'Bob, I'll want all your towels. Fellas, out, the lot of you! Jane, I need you.'

'But Doris, I'm of no use.' Jane was quaking. She had never seen another woman's parts; she'd never really studied her own.

'Will I do?' Peggy appeared. She cleared a table with

a swipe of her forearm. Tankards, glasses, ashtray all hit the floor. 'Up you hop, Dottie, and stop screaming, for gawd's sake.'

Dottie was panting with fear. 'Is it now? Really? I don't want to do it.' She clung on to Doris, who had to prise off her fingers. 'Please, Doris, I can't.'

'Be brave, now, love. We'll look after you.'

'I can't look,' called Jane from the door.

'Get yourself home, dear,' said Doris. 'Now,' she said when Jane lingered. 'And you, you horror!' She flapped a hand at a whiskered old man peering through the window like a theatre goer in the cheap seats. 'Forgive me, Dottie,' she said, and felt inside the woman's underwear.

She's near. Doris had presided over the delivery of countless lambs and calves. This couldn't be that different; *we're never more animal than we are giving birth.*

Interrogation revealed that Dottie's waters had broken hours before.

Events took them over. The baby, like the war, didn't give a fig for Doris's timetable. Time stopped, in fact. They could have been labouring for hours, or maybe it was all done in minutes. Sealed up tight, the three women were in it together. Dottie and Doris and Peggy, all doused with gore and sweating like boxers.

In another way, Dottie was on her own.

'Good girl, good girl, you're doing well.' Doris mopped and held and encouraged.

'Crikey, men have it easy,' said Peggy, running in with

264

a cold spoon to lay on Dottie's forehead. She had left Bob cowering by the sink. 'I'm never having a baby, Mrs Archer.'

'I can't do it,' said Dottie. She was crying again. The words were just gasps. 'Help me. Stop it.'

The doctor had, as they say, been sent for, but Nance, whey-faced, had dashed in to explain he was over Edgeley way, standing in for their GP. A boy had been sent but . . .

'No, Dottie, don't push. I know you want to, love, but don't.' Doris tethered Dottie to the table with instructions and commentary. The woman was writhing and full up, yet seemed liable to float away, such was her longing to be free of the pain.

It rushed at Dottie, this pain, then shrank away. She was its toy.

'The head!' yelped Peggy. Her hand went to her mouth.

'Turn her over.' Like other things Doris just knew – if an egg was fresh, how many teaspoons of cornflour to add to icing, when not to bother Dan – she knew that Dottie needed to be on all fours.

'What, like a dog?' said Peggy. She disapproved.

'Like a woman giving birth.' Doris had brought her own children into the world like this.

'Oh, God. Oh, God, help me.' Dottie was enormous, a planet. She pulsed with pain. The blood had stopped mattering.

'*Now* you push, girlie! Now! Do it for me!'

Dottie strained. The room grew and shrank. A baby came out of her and landed in Doris's waiting arms.

Doris sobbed and Peggy brought a boiled, cooled towel and Dottie toppled onto her side.

'Is it done?' called Jimmy from where he sat sentry on the other side of the door.

Nobody could tell him. They were catching their breath. They were welcoming Dottie's son.

'Can you take me all the way back to London like this?' Peggy was surprisingly comfy on Jack's back, her legs stuck out either side, her forearm throttling him as they lurched back from Broom Corner. Her cavalier had kept his word.

'If you like.' Jack felt, all things considered, he'd rather be at war; *she's a lot heavier than she looks.* 'Move your arm, girl, I can't breathe,' he squeaked, then, 'I haven't taken out a single girl since I met you, Peggy Perkins.'

'Why would that interest me? It's up to you who you court.'

'No reason. Just ...' Jack hoiked her upwards and she whooped. He tottered on. He almost fell a couple of times, but he got her to the bus stop in good time.

'I'll wait with you,' he said.

'Up to you,' said Peggy.

Like everyone else, they talked about the Battle of Britain. He pretended he was chums with an RAF ace. He even named him, and saw Peggy bite her lip at the mention of 'Reggie, erm, Farquharson'. Nothing worked with this one. He asked her about London.

'Sandbags everywhere. And uniforms. Plenty of soldier boys. Dancing most nights. There's so many new ones to learn. Do you dance?'

"Course.' Jack sneaked a look at her. She'd kept her hat on throughout everything; it was wonky. It didn't spoil her looks; nothing could. He found her spectacular. Like a firework that kept going off. He had watched her, with a sense of ownership that was not his right, as she grilled her brothers in the Horrobin kitchen.

She was an empress visiting the poor. The way Peggy crossed her legs made Jack want to sing. And Jack *couldn't* sing. She had scolded Vic Horrobin for filling the boys' heads with foolish ghost stories. She'd pulled a face when Billy said his best friend was a ferret. And she'd seemed deeply sorry for Stacey, the dog who pined for her master.

'You told your brothers off good and proper,' he said, taking out his cigarettes. He offered her one and she shook her head. He thought for a moment, then put the packet back in his pocket. 'But I saw you slip them a shilling when you left.'

The only time Peggy's composure had faltered was when John had asked after their dad. She had brushed him off.

'It's you, isn't it,' said Jack, 'who has bad dreams about the boys, not your mum.'

The bus came.

Jack leaned in for a kiss.

Peggy dodged him. Hit him. Laughed at him.

She was gone.

And Jack was bereft.

* * *

The grass thrived in the graveyard.

All those dead bones below, supporting all that green life above. Caroline had to pick her feet right up as she tailed her mother, the doll tight in her arms against her chest. The doll was Emily; Kitty had christened her. She looked like an Emily.

Skirting The Green, Kitty felt sweat gather under her arms. The blue seersucker was one of her favourite dresses; she looked ornamental in it, but she couldn't feel that way while the heat made a Borneo of Borsetshire. Her freckles had almost joined up; it was the nearest her Celtic skin got to a suntan.

Outside the shop was a blackboard. Frank chalked up the score each time there was news about the Battle of Britain. Today, apparently, the combat up in the clouds – no, hang on, there were no clouds – had gone England's way.

But Frank could be lying. She recognized his mission to prove his loyalty. Englishness wasn't a club she had ever belonged to, but unlike Frank she had no wish to do so.

Only an hour ago, Alec had talked of the aerial dogfights while they lay together in bed. Not her preferred pillow talk, but that was what you got for falling in love with a Brit. While he'd gassed on about Hawker Hurricanes versus Messerschmitts, she'd put up her blackout boards and pulled the curtains tight.

They never got to have a night together. How sweet it would be to lie beside Alec right through, until the next day got going. She wanted them to have a dusk and then a dawn, all joined up. She wanted continuity. She wanted to get bored of him. What odd ambitions she had these days. To eat a dull dinner opposite Alec, to argue about a bill for something frivolous she'd bought. To not have sex. To not have momentous discussions. To not watch him greedily as he left because it might be the last time she saw him.

Fake bars of chocolate stood smart in the window. It was time Frank removed them. Seeing what you can't have depresses a person; this Kitty knew. 'No, sweetie, not today,' she said for the umpteenth time when Caroline pointed and cooed.

After her outburst, she and Alec had simply picked up where they left off. No milestone choice had been made, no plumping for Kitty or Pamela. This, it seemed, was their pattern.

I explode.

He retreats.

He returns.

We are naked.

Inequality was nothing new. Kitty was accustomed to it. She had run towards it earlier that day, in their *faux* night, in her all-or-nothing way.

Her whisper had been hot in his ear. 'You can do anything you like to me.' She was nothing. They had proved that now. She existed at Caesar's whim. The sweat on Kitty's skin from their lovemaking hadn't yet dried when she hurled her fireball of the erotic and the emotional. 'Hurt me if you want to.'

'I don't want to do anything to you! Do *not* talk like that.'

His disgust was an unflattering coat that nonetheless

keeps out the cold. She'd wondered then, and she still wondered now, staring into the shop, if she was fooling herself that Alec, a totem pole of privilege, would ever be able to listen to and know her.

He's a well I've dropped a stone into. It might take the rest of her life for Kitty to hear the *plop.*

'Come on, in we go.' Kitty squared her shoulders. She would have to beg another week's grace from Frank, and hope he would allow her to add to the bill. She had collected nettles in the churchyard; they would make good broth but Kitty thought of the bones forming inside Caroline's stout little legs and knew man cannot live by homemade soup alone.

Once inside the shop, Kitty picked up on the festival atmosphere. 'What's going on?'

'Cherries!' Agnes's lips looked bloody. 'Mrs E's cherry harvest is in.'

'You should ration them, Frank,' said Jane.

'Finders keepers, I say!' Agnes grabbed another handful.

Looking on with pride, Mrs Endicott bemoaned her inability to enjoy her own produce. 'They're full of acid, or is it gelatin, and just one could put me in bed for a week.'

'Dig in, little one.' Frank tilted the basket towards Caroline, who didn't need to be asked twice. 'What's that stuck to dolly?' he said, nodding at a muddy scrap on Emily's dress.

Kitty picked the torn rectangle of paper from the tartan, and crumpled it in her palm.

Outside once more, she turned towards Brookfield. She would have liked to go straight to Alec, but of course she could not.

While the cherries were cheering up the shop, Dan was following Doris into the scullery, out again, to the range and then to the table. 'Love, you can't avoid me for ever. I'm making a good point, and you know it. It's time we told the truth about your mum.'

Dejection reigned in the farmhouse. It had been a watershed moment, fitting a lock to the outside of Lisa's bedroom. It felt so cruel. 'Confused' was the term they tacitly agreed on for her condition.

It was a diplomatic word, and manageable, in a way Lisa's behaviour was not.

'The children ignore her,' said Doris, as if Dan hadn't spoken. She slammed down a fork, a fork, a knife, a spoon, a ladle into the drawer. Her mother was fading from view, becoming a non-person.

'No they don't.' Dan flinched at his wife's furious glance. His customary downsizing of problems didn't fly with this topic. 'Doris, have some faith. God is good.'

'Is he?' snapped Doris. 'Is he, Dan?'

A timid tap at the door and they both turned to see Kitty. She had Caroline in her arms and held out a piece of paper. 'Letter number four,' she said.

* * *

In the circle of thorns, sequestered by the woods, Billy and John sat in their sumptuously appointed HQ.

A cushion had been added. It was too fancy to be Connie's, and fitted the description of one Jane Gilpin had left in her porch to air. There was a bottle of lemonade, and Wizbang.

They talked, as gentlemen do, of society.

'What's so great about a baby?' Billy screwed up his face. Dottie's kid was boring, yet it was all the village women seemed to talk about. 'So what if he opens his eyes? If *I* burp I get told off.'

'Not by Connie,' said John, approvingly. 'Only by Mum.' He missed getting told off, now that he thought of it. 'How did they get the baby out of Dottie's bum?'

'Dunno. With a stick?'

AMBRIDGE WINTER PAGEANT
COMMITTEE MEETING MINUTES

Date: 21 August 1940
At: Woodbine Cottage
Chairwoman: Pamela Pargetter
Present: Frances Bissett, Margaret
Furneaux, Emmaline Endicott, Doris Archer,
Kathleen Dibden-Rawles, Jane Gilpin
Absent: Dorothy Cook

1. Jane welcomed us all to her home and apologized for the smell and said 'Agnes is distempering the outhouse'.

2. Pamela asked if there was any joy with finding a pony to borrow to pull Elizabeth I's cart.

3. Magsy said how could anybody concentrate on the pageant when an actual miracle has occurred in Ambridge. Pamela said the restoration of Jimmy Little's sight is not a miracle. (Note to self: ask Henry to have a word with Pamela re: miracles, God etc.) Kitty said she would make a card for us all to sign before Jimmy leaves to join the army. Doris made a noise that startled us all but she assured us it was only a frog in her throat.

4. Jane said it was a shame there would be no ploughing match this year because most of the local young lads have joined up and when will this dreadful war ever end. Pamela asked what had that to do with the pageant exactly. Jane did not know.

5. Jane suggested a change of theme from Elizabeth I. Doris suggested quite loudly it was a bit late for that after all the

work put into the costumes. Pamela said
the theme will stay the same.

6. Caroline fell over and began to cry.
Pamela took her on her lap.

7. Magsy asked if we thought poor dear
Dottie had noticed about the baby and what
will the poor girl do? She said we must do
all we can to help. She asked if somebody
should gently point out what was amiss
with the baby. Doris said 'Don't be daft of
course Dottie knows'.

8. Pamela said could we please get on
with the meeting.

9. Jane said she couldn't sleep for
wondering what had happened to the
anonymous letter Stan Horrobin had nailed
to the church door. Kitty said it hadn't
been Stan but Jane said there's no smoke
without fire. Magsy said it could be any of
us, even Jane, and Jane said she had never
been so insulted in her entire life.

10. Pamela said everybody should calm
down and said 'Sit down Jane' and could we
please get on with the meeting.

11. Doris said this might sound silly
and asked if everybody was feeling
all right and Pamela asked how did she
mean and Doris said doesn't the war and

the hate and the aggression seep into
them and Pamela said if there was no
other business then we might as well
call it a day.

SEPTEMBER

The farmhouse lay soaked in sleep.

Snoring – whimsical from Philip and intermittent bronchial thunder from Dan – lulled Doris to sleep.

Another noise, alien, woke her. Not because it was loud but because it was out of place. Diligent Doris, sentinel of Brookfield, shoved her feet into slippers and was out on the landing in her dressing gown before she was properly aware of what she was doing.

Jez.

Always her first thought when a detail was out of place. What if he was prowling, touching things?

There it was again. A soft voice – not Jez's – and the gentle drag of a chair across a rug. Doris pulled the bedroom door closed behind her when Dan stirred. The harvest left them so few hours to sleep; no point in them both being up.

Down the stairs, feather-footed, Doris looked forward to catching Christine in the act. No scolding, just a hug and a 'Back to bed, young lady!' It wasn't the first time Doris had had to break up a midnight feast with Christine's teddies. The teddies had survived the eight-year-old's recent purge of 'babyish' toys and Doris was glad, but she sped up at the thought of a bear sticking his embroidered snout into her carefully hoarded sugar.

Flat and silver in the moonlight, the kitchen was not itself.

Doris put her hand to her throat and watched, possessed by what she saw.

In her nakedness, Lisa was a pale flame as she stood at the table, her back to Doris. Slight, blueish, she was cutting a slice of bread from a loaf. She cut it beautifully thin.

As Doris watched she buttered the bread. Carefully, going right to the edges. 'I'm making soldiers for you, love,' she said, over her shoulder. Not to Doris. She spoke to the empty rocking chair, spotlit by the moon on the flagstones. 'You do love soldiers with your dippy egg, don't you, Janet?'

The chair rocked just once, up and back.

Doris walked past her mother and out of the back door.

A mac thrown over his pyjamas, Dan made for the top field at speed.

'Love,' he said, stopping a little short of Doris. He pulled his belt tight. It had trailed in the mud.

Her slippers filthy, Doris stared up at the moon. Huge, low, it was a true bomber's moon. 'Don't worry, Dan. I'm not mad. I'm not my mother. It's just that it's beautiful out here.'

'It's always beautiful out here, Doris. You don't need to stand in the cold to appreciate it.' Dan took a careful step forward, holding up his pyjama bottoms with one hand. He was at a loss. He needed someone to show him how to deal with this peculiar circumstance. His wife was always where he expected her to be. He relied on her to be utterly Doris-like around the clock. And now this. He racked his brains. 'Is it your mum? What if I helped more? If you won't let anyone else give you a hand, at least let me muck in, love.'

He meant the offer, yet he didn't want her to say yes. He didn't have any energy to spare. When she shook her head he was shifty about his relief.

'Come on, love, let's get you back into bed.'

She let him take her hand, but her own was dead against his fingers. She let him lead her home. As they reached the gate of the yard, Doris kicked off her slippers, and her feet bled on the paving.

The summer was still doing its damnedest but there was the sense of an ending in the early September day.

Daisies were everywhere, modest and exquisite. They carpeted the slope where Hollerton Junction's platform gave way to nature, their chalky white and yellow outfits slightly stained. They were on the turn.

Only one person stood waiting for the train. Slight, slim, Jimmy Little was in khaki. His boots were too big. As was his hat. His eyes were fixed on the daisies. As if memorizing them.

They were supernatural, Jimmy's eyes. His happy ending was a heaven-sent dollop of pure good news in the midst of casualty figures and a ranting Adolf stomping all over the map. It was a miracle. The vicar encouraged use of the word, asking what else could they call proof of God's benevolence.

God had been particularly busy the last couple of days. Alongside tinkering with Jimmy's eyes, he'd found time to punish the Luftwaffe for their arrogance. Believing the RAF to be beaten, the German planes had turned their attention to London. And then, literally out of the blue, the RAF had found their second wind, picked up the Battle of Britain where they left off, and inflicted record losses on the Luftwaffe. The tide had turned. Or, as Dottie put it, 'Take *that*, Adolf!'

Bob Little had wanted to see his son off, but Jimmy had been firm. 'No fuss, got it, Dad?' The photograph of Hilda was in pieces, swept into the dustpan back at The Bull. The miracle hadn't impressed his sweetheart; she'd found another. A navy chap. Sub lieutenant.

Alec, approaching Jimmy on the platform, didn't know what the boy was thinking, had never heard of Hilda. 'I know, I know,' he said, when Jimmy turned. 'Your dad told me you don't want goodbyes. My apologies.'

Jimmy nodded. Shy.

'I just wanted to tell you that I was frightened too, when I went off to France in '17. Nothing wrong with being frightened. Quite the opposite, if you ask me. It shows common sense.'

A cigarette was handed over. Alec's gold lighter sparked. His blue enamel cufflinks showed for a moment. 'Six weeks basic, is it? Then the infantry?'

They smoked in silence for a while. Jimmy looked down the track.

'It'll be hell, Jimmy. I promise you that. Either boring or hellish, sometimes both. But know this. Ambridge is rooting for you. We're proud of you. We won't change. We'll be waiting for you to come home in one piece.'

Jimmy didn't look at him. Wouldn't use the miraculous eyes on Alec. He must have heard, though, the rustle as Alec took a piece of paper out of his breast pocket. He must have heard the click and hiss of the lighter, and smelled letter number four burning on the platform.

DEAR FRIENDS,
   CAN YOU SEE WHAT I SEE?
   I SEE JIMMY LITTLE. I SEE THAT
HE CAN SEE. I SEE THAT HE DODGED
THE CALL-UP BY DIGGING UP HIS OLD
GRANNY'S WHITE STICK.
   SIGNED
   YOUR NEIGHBOUR

'We should have burned this when Dan and I came to see you. Rest assured that nobody knows, and it'll stay that way. Not even your father will ever hear about it from us, Jimmy.' Alec tapped Jimmy's elbow, and when the boy turned, he held out his hand.

Jimmy ignored the hand and leaned into Alec's chest. It took a second, but then Alec's arms folded over the younger man. He held him tight. Then let him go.

The daisies shut their eyes, one by one.

* * *

The moment shimmers, and above the ordinary roofs of the ordinary people, the sky pulls out all the stops and presents them with a dawn of deep cherry reds and juicy peach and a spectrum of blues that would exhaust Thomas Hardy's pen.

Frank doesn't look upwards. He's intent on rubbing out the swastika on his door. The whitewash is still wet; it's coming off. Frank scrubs harder. He didn't hear a thing, no footfall, no giggling. Like the letters, the swastika landed from thin air and could be the work of any neighbour, any friend. As if he has such a thing anymore. Frank doesn't know where the shame stops and the fear starts.

The sky is invisible to Kitty. She has no idea of the time in her dark bedroom. It's very late, or maybe very early. She's not sure when the crossover happens from late night to early morning, but since she had Caroline she's been in that territory often. She lies with the little one in a tumbled bed. She tolerates the small dirty foot laid across her face. She thinks not of words but of numbers. Is zero a number? Noel's life insurance has run out. Like Noel, it has gone. Like Noel, it didn't do much for her even when she had it. She wishes she missed him; it might add meaning to losing him.

Mornings, evenings, what do they matter? Dottie has torn up her diary. Little Chaz is in charge now, and like all tyrants, the baby doesn't consider his servant's needs. She kisses his knee. She presses her cheek against his. She likes to regard him in the mirror, his face close to hers. Her pale skin, his dark brown face. Her thin hair, his tight black curls. He is, and Dottie knows this and doesn't need any input thank you very much, the most beautiful little baby God ever put together.

The tube station is carpeted with people. Peggy doesn't like the early hours; introspection visits, and she hates its insinuations. She's doing the right thing not telling the boys that Dad's missing. They're too young, too far away, they'd be upset. Before they were evacuated, Peggy thought of her brothers – when she thought of them at all – as nothing more than a portable block of monkey business that got under her feet. Now that Mum has lost the plot, Peggy is in charge of Billy and John's wellbeing. And that's fine, she's up to the job, she really is, and anyway she can have a secret little cry while the old bat along the platform hacks up last night's rations.

The sink has been scoured. Glen has been let out and then let in again. The jars in the scullery are lined up, their labels in perfect order. Capital letters spelling out 'RHUBARB CONSERVE' and 'GOOSEBERRY JELLY' and 'POTTED BEEF'. Doris wipes the kitchen table again. She keeps away from the back door. It's a lure, a shining exit. She wants to nip out of it, and run and run until she is a dot on the horizon, like a hare fleeing the hounds. But the hounds always catch up.

The dark stained glass comes alive in St Stephen's. Red and gold stripes flay Jane's back as she kneels. 'Forgive me, Father,' she says, staring up at the refurbished Christ. 'Forgive me for my many sins. Forgive me, *forgive me*, for resenting poor Blanche, for praying the ship she came home on would sink. Forgive me for the things it makes me do.'

AUTUMN

1940

'O I am tired of waiting,' she said,
'Night, morn, noon, afternoon;
So cold it is in my lonely bed,
And I thought you would join me soon!'

THOMAS HARDY
Something Tapped

OCTOBER

The purr grew louder. As if a gigantic cat stalked the twilit back roads.

The purr became a growl, a throaty 'R' endlessly rolled. The avenue of bare trees, silver in the dying light, stood to attention as the motorbike sprinted past.

No headlights, not in wartime. Just apocalyptic noise.

The riders bent into the corner. A skid, then the bike corrected itself. The shriek gave the game away; the passenger riding pillion was a woman.

It was Kitty.

The motorbike stopped. Kitty had been bounced and jiggled for a couple of miles, and she was sore. The heavy goggles bit into the bridge of her nose.

'What's the verdict?' Alec twisted on the seat. 'D'you like her?'

Kitty was breathless. She gave him a senseless smile, one that didn't happen often. She had been lifted out of Ambridge by the hand of God and swung like a child. 'Again, please!'

She wondered how she looked with the goggles pushed back and dirt drying on her face.

'Christ, you're something else, old girl.' It was awkward for Alec to kiss her from his position, but kiss her he did. 'I'll let her have her head this time.'

The BSA M20, a skinny dun-coloured thing, lived in a lean-to distant from the main house. Pamela knew nothing about it; Alec took care to change back into wool and tweed after visiting this new paramour. He wiped his face of oil with a handkerchief and pegged down his smile. Pamela would lecture about misuse of petrol, about safety, about the folly of trying to recapture his youth. But Kitty had simply cocked her leg over it, wrapped her arms around his waist and urged him onwards.

He let the bike go. Together, Alec and Kitty covered ground. But only in circles.

The deception about the motorbike was an extra layer of skin grown over their affair. They lived in a negative image of love, comprised of what they could get away with. While it grew bigger, it also grew smaller, yet they kept building.

Recently Kitty had stopped holding her breath. It happened behind her own back, this relaxation of her fears. When Alec had ignored her ultimatum it had felt like an ending, but now, if she squinted, she could pretend her passiveness had been a clever tactic.

Because Alec was putting the hours in. When she woke up alone she knew he still wanted her; that he was wanting her from a distance, and that he would want her tomorrow.

Each day was progress. They crept nearer the date, as unknown to her as the date of her death, but surely as inevitable, when they would pull the negative image inside out and *voilà*! She and Alec would be the couple, the sanctified pairing, and Pamela ... *We'll take care of her.* Kitty made this vow to her rival.

'Faster!' Kitty thumped Alec on the back.

'Yahoo!' Alec screamed.

'Stop!' Another thump from Kitty. 'Alec, stop. What's that up ahead?'

The bike skidded, stopped. Kitty fell, turning it into an awkward jump.

Quick, fairy-like, the wraith hopped off the road and into the trees. The dark ate it up.

He'd seen it, too. 'Was it a trick of the light?' Alec walked to the trees, swinging at the sparse late grasses with a leather gauntlet. 'There!' He pointed, then sprang back. It was quiet now the bike was still. A wispy somebody blundered on dry twigs.

'Come back, I don't like it,' said Kitty. October was a death mask of a month. She wanted to be roaring along on the bike again, thumbing her nose at the night.

'Could be a German flier.' Alec winced at how unlikely that was; he'd heard stories but saying it out loud smacked of children's tales.

Half a mile away, Billy and John were enjoying Connie's benign neglect.

Their mother's neurotic parenting would never have seen

them plunging about a graveyard after dark. Their fear of the place was minutely calibrated to the fascination it held for them.

Less keen than Billy, John nonetheless kept up with his big brother. It was unthinkable to be left behind among the tombstones.

'Listen!' Billy stood stock still. His Aran, far too big, glowed in the gloom.

'What's making that noise?' John was filled with woe, as if a tap had been turned on.

Something groaned. Then came a hectic scream, like souls being torn out of chests.

They crouched behind an Endicott tomb.

They were very unhappy. John closed his eyes but couldn't bear that. Opening them was as bad. He heard the demon make a circuit of the churchyard on heavy feet or paws or *claws*.

'Let's make a run for it,' hissed Billy.

John couldn't. He shook his head.

Over at Brookfield a truck pulled out, slitted covers over its headlights. Doris was at the wheel and she drove as if pursued by the thing in the graveyard.

A bicycle followed, then took the opposite direction along the back lanes too narrow for the truck. Dan dinged the bell as he disappeared.

He'd call the police from Lower Loxley, but realistically, thought Doris, what could the police do? The village would help. Dan would mobilize all the able-bodied men and women. *They'll find Mum.*

They had to. It was freezing tonight. And Lisa was getting so thin. Her mother's bone-white arms, skinny and poor, flashed into Doris's mind.

No prayer would form in Doris's mouth. It was a forgotten dialect, put away, and dead. Instead she was prey to imaginings. Her mother as just another mammal in the vicious night. A shrew. A mole. She'd seen them all, curled up in death. Why would one life matter to a warrior god who snuffed out so many each day?

Up that way. Down the lane. Across the crossroads. Doris drove recklessly. Neighbours appeared at gates. She saw Bob poke the bushes opposite The Bull. The blacked-out streets were alive with volunteers.

Everybody knows about poor Mum's sickness now.

Nobody checked out St Stephen's, where Billy and John were face to face with a monster. It had proved amiable, and when Billy reached out to rub its snout it tolerated him.

They had never been so close to a pig. It was dense. And not as pink as storybooks had led them to believe. More of a dull beige. Its ears were raggedy.

'Is it a ghost of a pig?' asked John, who didn't rub its snout, and wouldn't have done so for a hundred pounds.

'Nah! He's just a pig and he's ours.' Billy took a piece of twine out of his pocket. He'd known when he filched it from Stan's pocket that it would come in handy. 'Finders keepers, innit?'

As they persuaded the pig out of the back gate of the churchyard, half a mile away Alec was stepping out in front of the truck.

Braking like a racing driver, and feeling the big old vehicle revolt at such treatment, Doris slumped with relief. Her mother stood with Alec, his arm around her and his jacket over her shoulders.

AMBRIDGE WINTER PAGEANT
COMMITTEE MEETING MINUTES

Date: 19 October 1940
At: Woodbine Cottage
Chairwoman: Pamela Pargetter
Present: Frances Bissett, Margaret
Furneaux, Emmaline Endicott, Doris Archer,
Dorothy Cook, Kathleen Dibden-Rawles,
Jane Gilpin

1. Pamela said she was grateful to
Jane for hosting once more at Woodbine
Cottage, and she was grateful to Doris
for attending at a time when she had so
much to attend to at home with Doris's
mother being senile. Pamela said there was
nothing like that in her family. Jane said
that having an invalid in the family traps
one. Dottie said that Lisa was a poor old
girl but it was always a laugh when her
own nan said something silly and we all

need a laugh nowadays. Magsy said Doris
didn't need to hear all this, she only has
to know we are there to help. Everybody
said they would help. (Note to self: ask
Henry to have a word with Doris.)

2. Pamela said could we get on please.
Jane said could Pamela kindly ask Magsy if
she had finished the dried flower wreath for
Elizabeth I's head. Pamela said 'Why can't
you ask her yourself when she is sitting
right there'. Jane said that Magsy knew
why. Magsy said that Jane has got it into
her head that Magsy is the letter writer.
Jane said the handwriting looks like
Magsy's and Magsy has never liked Blanche.
Kitty said 'Oh for God's sake'. I, myself,
Frances requested that she not take the
Lord's name in vain even though we are
all aware Roman Catholics like to do so.
Pamela said 'Ladies you are behaving
like a bag of cats'. Dottie laughed until
baby Charles woke up in his basket and
began to cry.

3. Pamela said could we get on please.
She had to step outside because of an
altercation happening outside the window.
Walter Gabriel shouted at Stan Horrobin
'You was supposed to take care of it but

```
you let the silly so and so get out, and
we have lost a lot of money'. Pamela told
them to be off.
    4. Pamela said really could we please
get on. Blanche called from upstairs that
she needed a foot massage and an extra hot
water bottle. Jane began to cry which set
baby Charles off again.
    5. Pamela declared the meeting over.
```

Macintosh viciously belted, Doris was off to do her duty.

It was no Dunkirk, but the stakes were high all the same; every available individual had been whistled up to help with the last big push before the pageant.

Halloween approached, and the hedgerows were shutting up shop for what promised to be a hard, wet winter. Cattle were back in barns, potatoes were out of the ground, wrens were hunkering down in the bushes.

Like the other committee members, Doris supported the pretence that everything was fine, that holding the pageant in October instead of high summer was just the ticket. But the days slithered to darkness early, and The Green was a bog and nobody was in the mood for outdoor fun and games.

The Battle of Britain dribbled on, seemingly endless despite the RAF's heroic resurgence. Every day there were tallies of planes lost, and planes safely home. Doris worried about whether the pilots were eating properly; how could they defeat the Hun on watery pie? Chucked up into the sky like pigeons, the pilots were boys, and they were her sons. Jack himself was still in training, still blithe, still untested. The open skin on Doris's soul made even ordinary days a challenge; today, putting together a makeshift Elizabethan tableau, she was running on fumes.

Squaring her shoulders, Doris made her way into the oil heater fug of the village hall. Umbrellas lolled in puddles of their own making. Somebody was singing; somebody who really shouldn't. Mavis the Pekinese was underfoot, dragging her behind across the lino. Doris put a finger to her nose; Mavis had a powerful signature scent.

'Dress rehearsal, everyone!' shouted Kitty. She clapped her hands and then laughed at herself. 'Sorry, I'm not very good at being bossy.'

As a Lady of the Court, Doris wore a ruff made out of curtain tape. She put it on. It drooped.

Like everything else.

Dan popped his head in at lunchtime, regretted it, and scarpered. Doris had listened to his list of all he had to do that day. She could top it, she could always top it, but she had remained silent as he huffed and puffed. 'To cap it all,' he'd said, pulling on his coat, 'I have to placate Brampton Green's pig club. They're demanding compensation for one of their pigs, the one that got stolen. I reckon it got out and somebody nabbed it. Honestly, Doris, people think the government's made of money.'

Money. Doris never thought about it. On the treadmill of the farm, they planted, they fed, they slaughtered, they sold, and the house was kept warm and the roof was made sound and the children were shod. Money, surely, had become less relevant in the war. The only things that mattered were things you could *use*, solid things. Machinery. Bread.

'You look like you stepped out of a history book,' said Kitty, picking up a fold of Doris's skirt and holding it out like a bridesmaid.

'Do I? It's only Christine's old nursery curtains.' Doris had put them up when she was pregnant. A hundred years ago and quite a different Doris.

'Pamela found me some old velvet.' Kitty ran her palm over the nap of her amber costume. 'I couldn't do it justice, though. I can't really sew. Is the hem all lumpy?'

A triptych of pock-marked mirrors stood in a corner. Kitty turned to frown at the back view of the dress in the glass.

Three Kittys stared back, alongside three Dorises. Then three Pamelas joined them, pulling at the fur-trimmed neckline of her costume.

I'm so stout! It shouldn't have been a surprise. Doris looked down at her solid body every day. The comparison was stark. Beside the heft of Doris, Pamela was a few brushstrokes and Kitty was both voluptuous and petite, quite the trick to pull off.

Sucking in her belly, Doris stared at herself. She had her father's soft eyes, and his unreasonable hair. She stroked the slalom of her hip the way she stroked the sateen quilt on the bed at home. Doris was all of a piece with her habitat; she imagined a rangy, chic cow in a Brookfield barn and had to smile.

I'll do.

Frances leaned over her shoulder. A shortage of men, or of men willing to step into hose, meant the vicar's wife was William Shakespeare. Her moustache was, Dottie had whispered, not a prop. 'I assume, Doris, it's looking after poor dear Lisa that keeps you from church on Sundays?'

Doris fussed with her ruff.

The vicar's wife hesitated, then said, 'And Philip? You said he had a cold, and of course he couldn't come to Sunday School with a runny nose, but I bumped into him yesterday and he seems ... better.'

More fussing – a tad brusquely – with the ruff.

'You know I'm happy to babysit your mother if it means you can attend service.'

Babysit! Doris had left Lisa in her younger son's care. Yes, it was too much responsibility for a twelve-year-old but you grew up fast on a farm. Phil hadn't complained; still reeling from Doris agreeing with him that, yes, Sunday School *was* a waste of time. He hated looking after Lisa, particularly on a bad day. That morning, he'd looked on, wide-eyed and clueless as his grandmother cried for Janet. Ransacking the rooms. Begging Doris to call the police and report Janet missing. 'That's quite all right, Frances. We're managing just fine.'

And I don't want to come to church!

The road to hell was paved with thoughts such as those. But Doris had them anyway.

'This ched tastes lovely. What's that, dear? I said the ched is lovely.' *Oh, fiddlesticks, what's the boy's name?* 'The ched, dear. I'm talking about this, my piece of ched and butter.' *Why can't he understand me, I'm being perfectly clear.* 'Bread, yes, why, what did I say? Ched? I never.' *He's a joker, this one, oh, look at him, he loves a laugh!*

How am I suddenly in bed? Where did that little bit of time go? Where do all the little bits go? I keep losing time and I don't like it, you shouldn't lose time, it should just unroll nice and neat. 'Who's that? Who's there? Show yourselves!' *Sounds like kiddies. These aren't my hands! Good heavens, the wrinkles.* 'Who are you?' *What if they're burglars? Is Janet all right? She's such a light sleeper, that girl.*

This is peculiar. I didn't walk here. I did not walk to this window. 'You, boy, how did I ...' *Oh, he's Philip! My grandson. Doris's middle one.* 'Did you sit me down here, pet? Well, aren't you good to your old granny.' *The rain, all cool against the window, just lovely dripping off the branches.*

I'll go and see what my Bill's up to. My husband can't find his head without his hands unless I'm there to help.

'Get your hands off me, you little twerp! How dare you!' *Is that me screaming? Where's my family? Where's my mum? Why hasn't somebody come to fetch me and take me home? I want to go home.*

The amiable woman who ran the laundry in Loxley Norton sat to have her hair teased up into what Dottie imagined was a Tudor 'do'. 'Dead spit of Mary Queen of Scots, I am,' the woman said, picking her teeth. She lowered her voice to speak treason. 'Silly, ain't it, having a full dress rehearsal? That Pamela Pargetter might have nothing better to do but the rest of us have lives to lead.'

Jane, pitching in and holding hairclips because Agnes had refused to – 'I don't do nothing I don't get paid for,' she'd said – was pained. 'Mrs Pargetter is a wonderful leader,' she said. 'And please don't let her hear you.'

Industry was the order of the day. The village hall hummed with women intent on their work. Talk of the letters was inevitable. The merest of glances passed between Kitty and Doris; alone of everyone there, they had read letter number four, and were braced for number five. Jimmy's letter was sealed up inside them. They would never tell.

'Happen you're next for a poison pen, duckie,' said Win Gabriel to some gentlewoman of generic appearance who featured in no gossip, no speculation. If she'd gone missing, the village would have been hard-pressed to give police her distinguishing characteristics. 'Or you, Doris. Or you, Miss Gilpin. Could be any of us.' Win Gabriel used her own spittle to position a beauty spot on a Woman of the Bedchamber. 'Mark my words, one of they letters will cock up our pageant if your Dan doesn't hurry up and put a stop to it.'

'Him and Mr P,' said Mary Queen of Scots. 'They fancy themselves a pair of detectives.'

'Defectives, more like!' said Dottie.

'They're doing their best.' Doris was mild.

Pamela didn't react. Her head was bent over a casket of Spanish treasure which stubbornly refused to hide its provenance as a child's vanity case. She was all thumbs, hopeless at detailed work. She preferred broad strokes, delegation. She never cared to peer too closely.

Her rabid desire for war news ran counter to her nature. Every fact, every figure, each analysis was leapt upon. Even when they robbed her of sleep. She had dreamed of the Luftwaffe hovering like vultures on the other side of the Channel, ready to swoop down and pick England's bones clean.

The stakes, too high, too hard to confront head on, brought back memories of Mayfair nights, when, too young to be up, Pamela watched her father bet her mother's engagement ring on a spin of the roulette wheel.

'Those Nazis take the biscuit,' said Mrs Endicott, who would live to the age of one hundred and two and never forgive the bombing of Buckingham Palace. 'Why doesn't the letter writer pick on *them*?'

Such questions can't be answered.

In the middle of the room, Nance coached fourteen-year-old Isabella Mackenzie in queenly deportment. Holding an orb, with a book on her head, Ambridge's only juvenile redhead processed in a circle.

'I don't feel like a queen.' She was whining. Close to tears. She was not a volunteer, Pamela had conscripted her.

'Chin up,' said Nance.

'You're doing so well,' said Kitty

On The Green, Eugene and Jez had arrived. They stood around, waiting to be activated by some woman's word. They had also been conscripted. They would hoist the maypole.

Again. 'Or is it an Octoberpole?' Eugene had asked, proud of his wit.

Her raincoat thrown over her olde worlde finery, Doris told them where to find the pole and the rope.

Eugene cursed, Jez did most of the work. Perhaps it was the audience that made him flex his muscles and exert himself in a way he never did at Brookfield.

'Innee strong?' Dottie moved Chaz from one arm to the other. Her son was fractious. A handful.

'You know maypoles are just pagan phallic symbols?' Eugene's educated voice carried.

'Ooh, not in front of the vicar!' Dottie nudged Henry Bissett, who laughed as if copying a laugh he'd once heard from an adjoining room.

'We're all pagan at heart, aren't we, Rev?' Eugene waited for a response as he leaned back, pulling on the rope connected to the very top of the striped pole. Its damp ribbons were bound along its length.

No response came apart from vanilla-flavoured mumblings that signified neither agreement nor disagreement. 'What, no opinions?' Eugene was all scorn. 'Why don't you people debate? Don't you ever talk about feelings and life and death? The big things?'

'Oi!' called Jez. 'Less chat and more pulling your weight, posh boy.'

Doris backed him up; she and Jez were seldom in yoke together. 'He's right. Get that maypole up and then I'll debate you a nice hot cup of tea.'

Eugene made a disgusted noise in his throat as he strained and the pole rose. 'It's not religion that's the opium of the masses in Ambridge,' he said. 'It's tea.'

There was applause when the pole took root. Jane, admiring its girth and height, said, 'Such a marvellous symbol of Great Britain. No wonder God is on our side in this dreadful war.'

'That's exactly what the Germans think,' said Doris. She saw the vicar hesitate, then carry on trudging back to the village hall. Henry wasn't about to debate with her, either. 'We can't rely on God to see us through, Jane.'

'No, *no*, Doris.' Jane was keen to put her right. 'Whatever else Jesus is, he's always been a gentleman.'

'Our Peggy's getting even fatter,' said Billy.

It was a heartfelt compliment; he loved to cuddle Peggy, and the fatter she got, the more comforting the cuddle.

'That's what pigs do,' said John. 'That's their job. They get fat.' He had wanted to name the animal Mrs Pink, but Billy had been so adamant he'd given in, and the pig was Peggy.

Something between pet and tsarina, Peggy took up all their time. HQ had been refurbished to reflect her needs. Fresh straw beneath her trotters every morning. A small pencil portrait of her best side tacked to the planked wall. Fallen apples and contraband scraps in her stolen china bowl throughout the day.

God, they loved her. Her bristly skin. Her smell, her noises, her merry eyes.

'Look at her lashes!' John exclaimed at least once a day.

'Stan was flippin' angry with Connie this morning.' Never having read Freud on displacement, Billy didn't know that Stan was transferring his impotent rage from its proper subject to another lesser target. So Billy simply hated him more with each thump of Stan's knuckles on Connie's poor body.

'He was going like this.' Billy stood up. His Stan impressions always went down well with his brother. Especially on days like this when they had fled one of Stan's rages, when Billy had cried, and he knew John knew. 'All my plans come to nothing, woman! That animal was gonna make us a fortune!'

They managed to laugh at despicable Stan. They had no idea which animal he referred to. *If only*, thought John, *I could get between him and Connie and knock him out flat!*

Four days to go.

Life was a series of countdowns Jane must manage. The pageant. The next letter. The end of the war. At least she knew exactly when the pageant would be. And how it would feel; the war could end one of two ways, and if Britain didn't prevail against those unspeakable Nazis would Ambridge be burned down? Would her greenhouse topple beneath a tank?

Feet on the stairs were a welcome diversion. Lately, she

and Blanche had talked less. She still kept a vigil at the side of the high bed, still handed Blanche her pots of hand cream and combed out her sister's flossy fair hair. But distrust had burrowed in between them.

'Dottie, dear!' Jane jumped up, vacated the highest-status chair. 'How lovely to see you and, um, little Chaz.' Jane couldn't look directly at the baby. The child's blackness wrong-footed her. Was it rude to mention it? Was it rude not to mention it? He was a dear squeaky little thing. Never having been 'blessed' – her mother's phrase – Jane found babies disconcerting. The jerky movements. The bodily fluids that exited their bodies without warning. The innocent eyes which nonetheless conveyed judgement of the adults around them. But she liked Chaz.

'How's your nerves?' asked Dottie as she took a seat, settling her boy on her lap.

'My nerves? They're ...' Jane wasn't sure how one described nerves. She was aware nobody believed in her spectral visitors, but the dead children had pit-pattered past her door again last night. 'I'm well, dear.'

'Good, good. Ladies, I'm here to say goodbye.' Dottie waved Chaz's mittened hand. 'Bye-bye, ladies,' she said in the high, fluting voice she gave her son when ventriloquizing. 'I'll miss oo.'

Jane felt her throat constrict. Another loss. She didn't approve of Dottie, nor even particularly like her, but Dottie had woven herself into the fabric of the village, and therefore Jane's mindscape. Change must be resisted in the lanes of Ambridge. She felt panic nibble at the edges of the static bedroom.

Blanche, from her bulwark of pillows, evidently felt the same. 'Must you go back to London? It's safer here for, um, Chaz.'

Dottie didn't speak French or Italian but she was fluent in Spinster English and she knew just what the 'um' before her son's name meant. He was most definitely the first mixed-race visitor to Woodbine Cottage and possibly the last. 'Yeah, it's time. Me mum hasn't even met this little hero yet.'

Hanging around, Agnes stood most un-maid-like, arms crossed, lounging against the doorjamb. 'How's your old man feel about Chaz?' She knew Dottie would understand the question. The boyfriend was a Viking; there was no Venn diagram in which he and the baby connected.

'You tell me.' Dottie shrugged. 'I've written and told him, before someone else gets there first and does the job for me.' She rubbed her nose against Chaz's. 'He can hardly complain, I mean, he's married, so . . .' As faces fell she howled with laughter. 'What am I like?' she asked, and nobody could tell her.

Tears. Embraces. A pain in Jane's chest and a pounding in her ears.

Dottie left. Off to London and a different, harsher war. 'You'll remember me, ladies, wontcha? I'll never forget you all,' she said as she took up her bags. She was already spare again; she had ricocheted back into shape. She was indomitable. She was Dottie.

Jane apologized profusely to Blanche, and even to Agnes. 'Sorry, *sorry*, I don't know what's wrong with me.' She cried until teatime.

Stripped to the waist, Dan splashed himself clean at the deep old sink.

A folding screen, once dark green, shielded him from view of his family. And from the cat, and from the men. Brookfield's kitchen was chugging and hot, filled to capacity, throbbing even.

Unravelling an old school jumper of Jack's to make socks, Doris kept an eye on Lisa, who was cuddling Mother Cat and murmuring into the cat's teepee ears. She kept an eye on Jez, who couldn't be trusted around food. She kept an eye on Philip, whose cough troubled her. She could have done with more eyes.

Mother Cat yowled and darted down from Lisa's lap. 'Christine, love, get Grandma to help you winding this yarn, there's a pet.' The gentle repetition of such chores helped Lisa stay calm. Today there had been only one 'high spot', as Doris called them. If she could steer her mother through the evening and off to bed without misadventure, Doris would consider the day a success.

Winding, winding, Christine said, 'How many hours in two days? That's how many it is to the pageant. If Isabella Mackenzie gets sick, can I be Queen Elizabeth?'

'She's not going to get sick,' said Doris. 'And don't remind me how little time I've got left to tick off everything on

Pamela Pargetter's blessed list.' Just as Doris wondered what on Earth she'd found to worry about before the war, she wondered what she'd done with her time before the pageant committee.

'Dan'll wash himself to nothing behind there,' said Lisa.

'That he will,' said Doris. Her mother was one of them tonight. She spoke of concrete things, not the fluff that lined her head.

Dan whistled.

Christine said, 'Dad! We can't hear the wireless.'

'Doris,' said Lisa. 'That child's too near the fire.'

'Scooch up, Chrissie.' Again, Mum was right. Mum was normal.

Jez carried his plate to the sink, said ''Scuse me, guv,' to Dan, and laid it on the draining board.

When he and Eugene left it was just the family, all together while October came to a freezing end outside the back door.

Even Jack was still safely bored somewhere they spoke English and ate proper food, and nobody was shooting at him.

Lisa said, 'Doris, have a look in on Janet, dear.'

Christine's head turned so quickly her ponytail caught her in her eye. 'Mum?' she said. As children do, she had long since raised her antennae at the current that ran through her mother at mention of Janet.

'Not now,' said Doris.

'Not *ever*.' Christine was sulky. She would stay sulky until offered hot milk, or allowed a biscuit.

Only when the jumper had been reduced to a ball of grey yarn did Doris summon Dan to the parlour. Her breath formed shapes in the air. The parlour was too costly to heat in winter, and Lisa no longer sat in there. It had reverted to its chilly self.

Doris walked up and down the rug that was too expensive for daily use, and sat finally on a good chair.

'What's all this, then?' Dan was dressed again, in a jumper she had made for him. It itched, but he was a man of duty.

'Janet's my sister.'

'You don't have a sister, old girl.' Dan sat too, on another of the high-backed, unfriendly chairs. He and Doris shared everything. Every triumph, and every little sin. She was the only other human being who knew about his caution for cycling drunk that May Day. He'd know if she had a sister.

'I do. I did. She died when she was five. I was eight.' Christine's age; they both thought it.

'But, why have you never ... What did she die of?' Dan sounded fearful, which in turn made Doris fidget.

'Diphtheria. I was kept away, in case I caught it. She had a fever, she could barely speak.' She described as best she could Janet Forrest's long, slow, hard death. 'It took just a few weeks, to end her.' Her suffering in a short, narrow bed under the eaves had consumed the house.

'Mum nursed her. You should have seen her, Dan. She was worn to a thread.' Strenuous, magical, there had been an unspoken hope that Lisa's love could keep Janet aloft, alive.

306

'She looked like Mum. You know how I take after my dad? Well, Janet was all Mum.'

'A little sister,' said Dan.

'When she died,' said Doris, 'we were kind of bunged up. Me, my brother, Dad, Mum. We were *composed*.'

'That'll be shock, love.'

'I know that now. Back then I thought I'd been frozen.' Talking about Janet didn't feel the way Doris had assumed it would. Her mouth worked just fine. The words to describe her sister formed easily. She didn't choke. 'We just got on with life. We didn't mourn. We didn't talk. The habit took hold. She – Janet, I mean – disappeared. Not as if she'd died, more like she'd never lived at all.' Doris so rarely had tears in her eyes. They glimmered as she looked at Dan and said, 'Janet. Janet, Janet, Janet!'

'Janet!' said Dan, in his nice woolly voice. He held her. She was good to hold, like a warm loaf.

Still there, against him, Doris kept talking. 'Dad used to fly off the handle if anybody mentioned her name. I had to do my little cries in private. It made him furious that I missed her. But I did miss her, Dan. She was so funny.'

In Doris's memory, Janet stomped about, alive, in her Start-Rite T-bars.

'She had this cute hair. All curls. But oh, she was a minx. Spiteful, too, when the mood was on her. Used to pinch me under the covers, and her face angelic all the while.'

'She'd be what age now?'

Doris knew to the nearest month. 'I've said happy birthday

to her every fourth of June. She'd be married now, Dan. Her kids'd be big. Or maybe, listen, this is silly, but I have a fantasy she became an actress and went to Hollywood and made films with Fred Astaire.'

'Not very likely, love.'

They sat, her hand in his, at the gleaming table used at Christmas and when somebody died. 'Don't you tell this to a soul, Dan Archer, but when Mum had to come and live with us, I didn't want her. When you're a child you accept everything, don't you? Like Christine looks up to us, I looked up to Mum and Dad, and did what they told me to do. I'm an adult now and, well, Dan, they were plain *wrong*.'

God's authority had been challenged and his famed compassion found wanting; it was a hop, skip and a jump to examine her parents' omnipotence.

'Now it's too late to talk about her. Our Tom only came along after Janet died. Imagine that, Dan. My own brother doesn't know he had another sister. It was cruel of Mum and Dad to silence me. *Cruel*.'

Dan demurred. He was a demurrer of long standing. 'They were doing their best, though, eh?'

'Yes, I know that, but all the same. Janet has no memorial, no marker. It's like she never existed and she did. I remember her, Dan! And now Mum's reliving the nice moments, the boiled eggs and the bread and butter soldiers; and I'm glad, I really am, I'm glad for her.' Doris stumbled here. Squeezed Dan's calloused fingers. 'But it brings it all back.' Lisa kicked away the delicate scaffolding Doris had constructed around the forbidden subject. She didn't go further. Didn't tell Dan that it wasn't fair that Lisa, who insisted on the silence, got to break it.

I'm angry with the mother I'm losing.

A row with Lisa, one adult to another, might clear the air. But how to argue with a child-woman? How to berate someone who depended on her so completely?

'Doris,' said Dan. Then he said it again, but differently. Sadly. 'Oh, Doris.'

Their muscular unspoken love stretched between them but Doris felt his helplessness. She also felt his need to help. Which helped. Words weren't Dan's strong suit. She didn't expect a rousing speech.

There was more. She felt her pulse pound in her ears. It was time to make confession. Because Dan must *know* her.

'Dan,' she said, and the dreadful majesty of what she was admitting made her quail. 'There is no gentle Jesus, he's not on our side in this rotten war. How would my Sunday School God let this happen?' Earth, Doris now knew, was a football lobbed about the stars. Jesus did not have his eye on the sparrow. Hitler stood between Doris and the Almighty; she shivered in the eclipse of her personal sun.

'I don't believe that, silly billy, and neither do you.'

'I'm going to hell, Dan,' she whispered. A hell she didn't believe in.

'Nobody in Ambridge is going to hell, Doris.' Dan seemed sure of this. He stood up, and bent to kiss the top of her head. 'But I'll tell you where I'm going. I'm off to stand watch over the maypole. Only two nights to go, and Alec's convinced we'll catch the bugger.'

Doris settled Dan's scarf, handed him a thermos, told him not to do anything daft. She watched him go and took a comb from her pocket. She always kept one stowed on her person these days, so she could tease her hair over the ever-growing barren patch of skin.

He doesn't understand, she thought.

NOVEMBER

There it was again.

That hesitation, that moment of distance when Kitty held Caroline out for a goodbye. Alec resisted the child; as if she was infectious, as if he might catch love from her.

Kitty brought him his coat. 'It's freezing out there tonight. You and Dan Archer'll catch your deaths.' She settled him into the coat, enjoying the proprietorial feeling, smoothing out the collar. 'Will you swing by on your way home? Jump in with me, fella, and I'll warm you up.'

'Don't tempt me.' Alec's hand was on the latch. He said, all earnest, 'You know, even when I'm not with you, Kitkat, I *am* with you.'

Excitement fomented in her stomach. The night outside was without colour, but hope blossomed and unfurled in Kitty's head, where she lived the life that mattered. He was trying his best: this love stuff was new to him. 'Be safe,' she whispered. 'I love you.'

They both jumped at the sound of a high voice from the gate.

'Got any scraps, miss?'

'Is that Billy? And little John?' Kitty laughed at the wan faces.

Alec didn't laugh. 'What the blazes are you two doing out at this hour? Home with you, now.' He turned his hawk's face, disgruntled, to Kitty. 'Connie doesn't look out for those little chaps.' He paused. 'They won't squeal on us, will they?'

'That you were here? Why would it even occur to kids to talk about that?' Kitty laughed and pushed him down the path. Pushed him and the reminder that their love was illegitimate out of the gate and turned her back on them both.

The enemy was defeated.

Well, not defeated; *seen off*. The Luftwaffe had had their nose bloodied, if you were being polite, or handed their balls in a bag, if you were Walter Gabriel. The RAF had, with their stiff upper lips and their Spitfires, filled the sky with bullets and won the day.

Alec, feeling like a buffoon in a brocade jacket, told Frank Brown, who wore a feathered hat, 'Funnily enough, according to Ronald, a Polish squadron took most scalps. One hundred and twenty-six! Damn good chaps to have in your corner, the Poles.'

'Do come *on*.' Pamela marched ahead, staunch shoes squelching in the muck beneath her billowing gown. The dress swayed on a hoop made from sweet pea supports. She was tense, telling everybody, even Mavis, to come on, come on now, do come on.

They all obediently came on, with their doublets and their corsets and their headdresses. Some costumes were laughable and last-minute, others, like Kitty's amber velvet, a sensation. Doris had altered it, and taken great care over the fit; Kitty's freshness did the rest.

'Chop chop!' shouted Pamela, moving among the villagers as if she, and not Isabella Mackenzie, were queen for the day. Her nose red from the cold, she accepted congratulations for the Battle of Britain ending just in time for the pageant as if she had personally sealed Germany's retreat when she plucked the date out of the air.

Only the weather dared disobey her. The day was cold and damp and drear, the bunting hanging limp like washing. But apples were bobbed and country dancers slithered stoically in the mud. Frank's feather soon gave up the ghost as he oversaw the tombola out in the sleet. Nobody complained, not out loud, although there was a certain amount of naysaying over by Bob's beer stall.

And then the sun came out. It carved a space in the clouds and threw a rug of dim gold across the village green. A breeze titillated the bunting. Spirits rose. Frank's feather dried out. Billy and John chased Wizbang through the crowd, and Nance tutored those who were interested in an Elizabethan court dance. The enormous Union Jack at the top of the maypole woke up.

Kitty curtseyed to Dan. Beside her, Caroline clumsily

did the same. 'Good morrow, Sir Archer of Ambridge,' she said. 'Prithee, erm, whither thou, something, that's all I can come up with.'

'Verily,' said Dan. 'Forsooth!' He ruffled Caroline's hair and she scurried behind her mother; she didn't like men she didn't know. 'Tell me, Kitty, does Doris seem all right to you today?'

'Yes, why?' Kitty drew nearer. Doris was the rock of Gibraltar; so long as she was in good working order no real harm could come to the village.

'Oh, nothing, just, well, I've just lost her and, oh, there she is.' Dan rocked onto his tiptoes, checking out his wife. 'I'm being an old woman, but she's not been tiptop.'

Kitty was jealous. Suddenly and absolutely. She wanted a man who would worry about her wellbeing. Who would scan a mob and find her face and evaluate its expression. 'You're a good husband, Dan.'

'That's easy, love.' Dan winked. 'Getting yourself a good wife, now *that's* the bit most chaps get wrong.'

'Will tonight be your last night keeping watch on the maypole?'

'Yes. I've given up hope of catching our poison pen, to be honest. Everyone knows what we're up to and this character's too bright to show up. But you know Alec . . .'

She certainly did. But she couldn't talk to him in public beyond a hackneyed greeting. Alec had returned the night before for that warm hour she'd mooted. Kitty's thighs ached, hollow. He had taken her, and she had given, and then she had laid down the law.

This was their pattern; the steps every bit as formulaic as the one, two, feet together Nance was demonstrating. Kitty looked forward to tonight's mandatory reconciliation. The knock on the door, and then their secret sport, the sublime indoor game. There was glue in their lovemaking, she trusted it now.

And Pamela? *We'll take care of her. She'll want for nothing.*

Behind the village hall, screened from the hoi polloi, the queen's float was finally ready. Just a cart that lugged milk from the Gabriels' to market, it was festooned with gold boughs and bronzed leaves. None of summer's slutty colours made it into the design, but the deeper, knocked-back earthy metallics made for a pleasing whole. If it was a poem it would be one of Hardy's melancholy ones, written after his wife's death. If it was a song, it would be the laments Kitty crooned after a whisky.

'Looks smashing,' was Walter Gabriel's opinion. 'Well done, Mrs P.'

And Doris and Jane and Magsy and Kitty, thought Doris and Jane and Magsy and Kitty.

Now that Kitty had pledged to look after Pamela, she could see her more clearly. Freed from guilt, Kitty allowed herself to dislike Pamela's snobbery and hauteur. Arctic winds swirled around Pamela; Kitty shivered. Soon, soon, she and Alec would live ... where?

That was a happy game. The war was over, Alec was hers, Caroline had two parents, and they house-hunted in Ireland.

Or America! Or maybe just down the road; there was Gerald to consider.

They had come a long way, she and her man, since that game of Sardines.

'One hour,' said Pamela. 'And then we start the procession.'

Another countdown.

A sudden brouhaha by the apple bobbing. The committee ladies toiled over in their upholstery fabric finery.

'Denholm!' Jane's shriek was perhaps the first time that lady had raised her voice outside of Woodbine Cottage.

He lay full length, letting out terrible noises. One leg lay awkwardly, *weirdly*, beneath him. His jowls were white.

'He went down like a tree,' offered Win Gabriel. She scolded Billy for laughing, and Billy, stung, said, 'But he's 'orrible, missus.'

The huddle cleared for Morgan, who diagnosed a broken leg, and marvelled at how Denholm had accomplished it. This prompted colourful bystander re-enactments of the man's fall, its speed, its spectacular nature, the role mud had played. Morgan ignored these, and organized a stretcher of sorts.

'There, there, Denholm.' Pamela's solace had a perfunctory ring. 'Can we move him before the procession, *please*, Morgan?'

'I'll come with you to the hospital, Denholm.' Jane knelt at his side, ruining the needlework panel she'd made for her costume. 'Take my hand, dearest.'

'Ow,' said Denholm. Over and over. And 'sod it!' and 'God damn it to hell!'

'I won't hear of you missing the pageant, Jane.' Morgan was avuncular.

'But he shouldn't be alone.' For once life was matching Jane's feverish daydreams. She envisaged a heartfelt rapprochement in an ambulance. 'He needs me, Doctor!'

'He'll be fine. You've worked so hard, why let a little accident spoil your day?'

Now covered in mud *and* disappointment, Jane slapped away the crow's offer to help her up.

The sun did its bit. Kept going, even if it sputtered, while the wind tried a little too hard. The maypole was the epicentre of gaiety, its ribbons knotting as bad boys danced in the wrong direction. Jez was one of them; he and the girl from the dairy seemed to have an understanding. They were absent for a short while; he sank a restorative pint afterwards.

Eugene kept himself apart from the revels. He drank steadily and his face darkened with each pint, like a battery storing up energy.

'Ladies of the Court!' Pamela marshalled her committee. 'Chop chop!'

'That's what Henry the Eighth said!' Dan toasted Pamela's retinue as they passed him.

'Make that your last ale of the day, Dan Archer,' said Doris over her shoulder. She would need him later; Lisa was making slow circuits of the pageant with Christine and Phil. Her mother was a UXB who could detonate at any moment. Always in her eyeline. Always constricting her heart and its chambers.

Behind the hall, all was quiet industry as the worker bees buzzed about the float and their queen. The floral arch chose this moment to collapse. Doris heaved it upright, and glanced over at Isabella Mackenzie in her finery.

Whenever Doris saw a little girl doing intensely little girly things – dressing up, playing with dolls, picking apart a fairy cake with her fingers – she had a stab of feeling that had a specific colour, a specific taste, a specific burst of sensation. They all added up to Janet, a mingling of all the imagined Janets in Doris's heart. She had only known the girl, but a woman had been cocooned inside her. And buried.

'Come on, queenie!' called a voice from The Green. 'Let's be havin' you!'

'You ready, Isabella?' Kitty put her hands on the girl's shoulders. 'Orb up, chicken, like we practised.'

'I can't.' Isabella's eyes pleaded with Kitty. 'I can't. I just can't.'

'Yes, you can.' Stepping in, blocking Kitty, her face close to Isabella's, Pamela was brisk. 'Hop up on the float, there's a good girl, and don't keep the village waiting.'

'I can't.' Isabella's face was plague-pale beneath the papier mâché crown. 'Sorry. I. It's. Sorry.'

'She can't do it, Pamela,' said Kitty. She took the crown off the girl's head. Reverently as if the Koh-i-Noor made from a painted pebble was a real diamond. 'It's all right, Isabella.'

The girl fled, face in hands.

'Oh, goodness gracious,' said Magsy, looking to the others.

'We need a new queen,' said Doris. 'Jane, go and look after Isabella. *Jane!*'

The woman was off with the fairies. Pretty miserable fairies, by the look of her. She came to, and scuttled after the abdicating teenager.

'Might I suggest little Gaye? Gaye Wallis.' Magsy's goddaughter was bow-legged but gung-ho.

'Gaye hasn't rehearsed.' Pamela snatched the crown from Kitty and let it dangle from one long finger.

'There's not much to it,' said Doris. 'Just waving, really. And smiling.'

'Kitty, *you* rehearsed the Mackenzie girl.' Pamela held out the crown. 'You do it.'

Kitty's shoulders flew up to her ears. 'Jesus, no, I don't think so, Pamela. It should be a proper villager.'

'Nonsense.' Pamela lifted her chin. She narrowed her clever eyes. 'Obviously, *I* am not suitable. I'm too old. You're the only one young enough and pretty enough for the job, Kitkat.'

Kitkat.

Pamela knew what lay inside Kitty under lock and key. And Pamela was not one tiny bit scared of it. She used it. She was, as ever, on top, ahead, *queen*.

Magsy bustled forward. 'Here's your cape, my dear.'

'And your orb.' Doris pressed the tarted-up tennis ball into Kitty's hand.

'And here, Queen Kitty, is your crown.' Pamela let it settle on Kitty's curls, then rammed it down.

The crown cut into Kitty's forehead.

'Allow me.' Pamela held out her hand, and supported

Kitty up the step into the cart. It lurched. The pony was impatient.

'Can I have a moment?' said Kitty. 'Alone? Just to gather myself.'

'We'll wait on The Green.' Doris shooed away the women. Pamela went first, upright, not hurrying but covering ground. Doris said, 'I'll send the lad round to hold the pony for you.' She looked a little closer at Kitty, and reached up to rub her arm. 'Oh, Kitty, love, no need to look so woebegone! All you have to do is smile and let us cheer you as you go by.' She gave the arm a squeeze.

Alone, Kitty gave herself a talking-to. Lined up her thoughts. It wasn't as if Pamela's knowledge of the affair was anything new. Yes, the use of her pet name was masterly. *Brava, Pamela.* But what did it mean, really? It didn't change a thing.

She needed Alec, though. Just the shape and solidity of him, to rubber-stamp her confidence. He hadn't so much as looked her way all day.

When he turned the corner, his brocade jacket over his arm, she laughed. 'I conjured you up,' she said. She bent, not easy with the dress and the crown. 'Quick! Give us a kiss before the pony boy appears.'

Looking up at her, Alec didn't smile. That should have warned her. But no, she remained stupid, or naïve, or both.

'Hop up,' she whispered. Kitty didn't like looking down on him from her regal cart. She didn't want to condescend. She smiled at his hands gripping the side of the cart. She saw his blue cufflinks. She had always assumed the P stood for Pargetter. Might it stand for Pamela? He looked eerie, ironed, his face empty and heavy.

Her father had looked like that when he told Kitty her brother was dead.

'What? *What*, Alec?'

'I can't do this.'

She looked away from him. She looked ahead of her. Threw the orb in the air and caught it. Her foot tapped maniacally against the wooden boards. 'Where *is* that boy?'

'Kitkat, it's wrong. We always knew that. I never said we'd ...'

She looked at him. She had to because this was real. This was an ending. She needed a tray to put this sorrow on; it was so very heavy. She needed to leave it behind because no way could she carry it.

He said, 'Pamela and I, it's not something I can just leave behind. It's unconscionable to untangle a marriage. My son, he's unhappy, too. Really, I'm thinking of you, darling. It's for the best. Weren't we always on borrowed time? It hit me last night, sitting out in the dark with Dan. We argue and argue. We know it's not right, and it can't ... *hold*. Call me a coward if you like.'

She didn't like. Kitty took her seat on the wicker throne. She grew more and more stiff. She would be a fossil by the time he finished, if he ever did. And she waited for the one word that would make it better. Or maybe worse.

'Truly, Kitty, this is the best option for you. You deserve

a man who can take care of you. You'll find somebody who puts you first. I can't bear the thought of that, of course, but I don't matter. I'm doing this for you, I promise.'

'Ey up.' The boy was tiny. He was farm-strong, and didn't waste words on Kitty. It was all about the pony. 'Come on, girl. Easy now.'

The cart jolted. Kitty shot forward, then steadied herself. She braced her feet against the slats.

'I'm sorry. Forgive me.' Alec didn't follow her. 'I'm sorry,' he called after her, as loud as he dared.

A roar went up as the trap jerked around the corner. Berserk happiness, far greater than the moment deserved, broke out. Dried flower petals rained on Kitty. She waved with one hand, held up the orb with the other.

The smile on her face revved up the cheers from her subjects. It amazed her, from the other side of her beautiful face, how her features swung into action so readily. She felt her lips pull back, she felt the slight pressure of her front teeth against them, she knew her eyes had creased into slits, she knew her nose had flattened. She felt her freckles sing.

It would ruin it all if she vomited, so she swallowed the foul taste in her mouth. She picked out Caroline, in Doris's arms. Saw Caroline's face open like a pansy with amazement at the sight of her mammy in such splendour. Saw Doris press down the cowlick that fell in Caroline's eyes and hold her up higher to witness Elizabeth I's triumphant progress around the duck pond.

Lurching, smiling, Kitty was transformed and so was the

village. The pageant would sustain them for another year, despite the needle-branches of the trees and the washed-out sky. They were happy, they were in it together, they were transformed from disparate, desperate people into a patriotic clump.

Good Queen Bess's loyal, beloved Raleigh waited by the pump in the shape of the vicar. He lacked the legs to carry off hose, but his bejewelled cape was so vivid nobody noticed.

Dan stepped out from the crowd to hand Kitty down from her carriage. He beamed into her face. And Kitty? She beamed back.

The big moment was upon them. Kitty stood, pole star of Ambridge, with everybody watching.

Everybody except Mr and Mrs Pargetter. Pamela was listening to something her husband was saying into her ear, her head bowed and to one side, her Elizabethan get-up adding to the grace of how her neck curved.

'It's done,' he said.

Pamela straightened and watched the vicar throw down his cape. Clumsy, not as rehearsed. She applauded with the crowd. She clapped very hard.

At her feet, Mavis did a minuscule shit on Alec's shoe.

It was midnight or later. The moon was put out. Ambridge was dark.

Hunched, his nose to his knees, Dan suspected that Alec was asleep beside him. This bush opposite The Green was no feather bed, but Alec had come straight from The Bull, and then taken a nip from his flask every two minutes. Dan had refused the Scotch; they were on maypole duty, and you wouldn't find Dan Archer asleep at his post, no sir.

Hang on! What the blazes? Why was Walter Gabriel in bed with Dan and his Doris? Muggy, he began to protest but other details bothered him. There was no bedroom wallpaper, just the cold slap of outdoors. And that wasn't Doris beside him!

Dan hastily un-spooned himself from Alec and creaked to his feet. 'Say that again, Walter? I wasn't asleep, just—'

'I got him! The letter bastard! I got the blackguard!'

Wrapped in Walter's thick arms, the figure struggled but only in a token way. Limp, head bent, frame buried in a military greatcoat.

Dan plucked off the beret, roughly unwound the scarf. 'Good God.' He drew back, as if the letter writer was indeed poisonous. 'It can't be,' he said.

'Good evening, Dan,' said Blanche.

They spoke in whispers.

They were not in church, they were in the parlour at Woodbine Cottage. Blanche was upstairs in her bed, and Morgan was attending to her.

In rag curlers, Jane was diminished, a doll. Furniture had frozen in the room, all wore coats. Except Agnes. The crow was busy, buzzing from kitchen to parlour and up the stairs, keeping up a supply of watery Ovaltine and salty one-liners. She wore her brooch every day now, despite Jane's disapproval of such 'showy' jewellery on duty. It glowed in the lamplight as she nipped about the cottage.

Alec was there, blank-eyed, and Walter, glorying in his role as saviour of Ambridge. Dan couldn't sit still. 'Blanche,' he kept repeating. 'Blanche?'

'But how?' Jane added little except questions. She was drowning. A current far beneath that had always tugged at her toes now had her legs. 'I blame myself.'

'Pish.' Agnes sounded more angry than consoling.

Dan stepped in. 'Now, Jane, you're not to do that. Your sister . . .' He hesitated; nobody knew better than Dan Archer how thick and muddy blood ties could be. 'Blanche fooled us all, not just you.'

'A spot of something stronger, gents?' Agnes winked. 'In your Ovaltine?'

Nobody refused.

A call from upstairs. Morgan used the voice he reserved for homes of the dying. 'Miss Gilpin is ready to see you now.'

Slotted in like knick-knacks at a second-hand emporium, the men lined the walls of Blanche's bedroom. All was peachy, tranquil, low-lit. All was sour, and baffled.

By the head of the bed, Morgan said, 'I've examined Miss Gilpin.' There was distance now from their friend and neighbour; she was a 'Miss'. 'I have found nothing wrong with the patient's legs. She has complete mobility. She is well enough to answer your questions.'

'This,' said Blanche, 'is a kangaroo court and I don't recognize it.'

Jane covered her face with her hands. She sat forward, and her wrap gaped to show her chicken chest.

'Would you rather,' asked Morgan, 'that we fetch the police?'

There had been a hurried consultation between the men. Wasting police resources in wartime was, they agreed, wrong. None of them needed to say aloud that they didn't want this getting out beyond the village.

It was, essentially, a family matter.

'I'd rather,' said Blanche, 'you let me get some sleep.'

Glances were exchanged. Evidently nobody had shown Blanche the script; where was her humility? Her mortification? Leaning against a bookcase of romance novels, Alec was elsewhere, somewhere unpleasant by the look on his face, and Dan's questioning frown didn't bring him back to them.

Their natural leader having abdicated, Morgan stepped up. 'Miss Gilpin, it's clear that you're responsible for the spate of malicious notes that have blighted the village. What do you have to say for yourself?'

Blanche looked at the beamed ceiling. Then, as if bored, at her hands.

Suddenly, vehemently, Jane said, 'Why's she in bed? She can sit.' Her face contorted and she growled, 'Put her in a chair.'

The men were irresolute. 'Well,' said Morgan, but went no further.

'It's all the same, surely,' said Dan.

'It is *not*.' Jane seemed to notice her dressing gown was

scandalously open and pulled it around her. She wished Denholm were here, to take charge, to protect her from the she-witch masquerading as her sister. 'Get her up!' Jane didn't look directly at Blanche. As if that might burn her retina. 'Get her out of that bed.'

'Will you agree to sit on this chair?' Morgan set down a pretty, spindly boudoir seat.

'No.'

More glances. More disquiet.

'I believe we can get through our business without moving Bl— Miss Gilpin,' said Morgan. His tie sat sideways and he had brushed only the front of his greying hair when pulled from his bed.

'Get on with it.' Walter's beery fragrance argued with the tuberose of the bedroom. His meaty arms were crossed, his fingers tapping impatiently. 'We know she done it, she knows she done it, don't matter if she's lying in the bed or dancing on the bloody roof.'

'True,' said Morgan, 'but we must proceed with some semblance of order.'

'You did it, Blanche.' Jane looked at her at last, all venom, a wasp in curlers. 'Just admit it. You've dragged dear friends through the mud. When I think of Nance and Pamela and heaven only knows who tonight's victim was.'

Dan perked up. 'That's a point! Walter, did you find a letter when you tackled Blanche?'

'Nah.' Walter shrugged.

'We must search.' Dan was always grateful for something

practical to do. 'Can't have some poor soul happening on slander about themselves.'

Blanche spoke. She was bored. 'It's not slander, though, is it? It's all true. Nobody can say I smeared their good name. I simply shone a light on their true selves.'

'And who made you God Almighty?' Walter's head wobbled. 'Eh? Who gave you the right to pick out all the little things what folk have done and show 'em off to the world?' He pushed something deeper into his pocket. If Blanche wasn't so compelling a figure, if Alec had been taking note, it might have been noticed.

'Don't pretend you're righting wrongs,' spat Jane. 'You make up horrible lies, you're not a public service! You just want to do damage. Morgan here knows full well what a liar you are. How can you look him in the face when you claimed his father-in-law is German? And Alec? The things you said about him are unforgivable.'

Morgan flicked a look at Alec, but Alec was elsewhere entirely. He took another run at it. 'Miss Gilpin, it may go better for you if you refrain from justification and simply explain yourself.'

In the silence that followed, Agnes spoke. Nobody had noticed her, neatly hidden between the bookcase and the door. 'Hold on, something's fishy here. The second letter was about Blanche, weren't it? She'd hardly bad-mouth herself!'

Jane said, 'You're forgetting how clever my sister is, Agnes. Letter number two put her above suspicion.'

'Ooh yes, I get it.' Agnes seemed impressed by Blanche's

guile, and asked her, "'Ere, are you really having it off with Whitey White?'

'If I were to have it off, as you put it, I'd set my sights considerably higher than Whitey, I assure you.' Blanche was simmering. Like a rocket preparing to blast off.

A personality like hers could never be contained in a frilly single bed. She punched her pillow, all eyes upon her, and settled herself comfortably. 'If you're waiting for a boohoo apology you'll be waiting all night. The best I can tell you is that it gave me something to do.' She held out her hands. '*There*,' she said.

'Shocking,' whispered Jane. Humiliation crept over her like moss.

Morgan said, 'I see it now. This bed is the fulcrum of village gossip. All you had to do was turn it into something salacious.'

'It's all catalogued up here.' Blanche tapped the side of her head. 'I know *everything*.' She savoured the word. 'People are indiscreet around me, thinking it'll go no further, they're only telling a poor cripple.'

'And of course you're adept at opening people up,' said Morgan.

'She's like a squirrel,' laughed Agnes. 'Only she goes for scandal, not nuts.'

'But it's not merely listening to what people say.' Jane was agitated. They were fudging an important point. 'She makes up these insinuations.'

Nobody backed her up. The men were quiet. Agnes folded

her arms, as if relishing her front-row seat at the discomfort in the room.

Dan, who missed his bed and missed his wife and missed the very recent good old days when the letter writer was some faceless git, said impatiently, moving matters along, 'First off, how come she doesn't have polio?'

'Hmm.' Morgan blew out his cheeks. 'I've never, well, one doesn't, I didn't question the diagnosis. I took over Blanche's care when she was . . .' He hesitated; gallantry forbade him name too precise a year. 'She was in early middle age, and had been crippled since girlhood so I assumed . . .'

'I did have polio,' said Blanche. 'It was horrible and I was far from home with stupid Aunt Maud over in the United States. It was mild. A temperature. A fever. But Auntie died before she could cable home the good news that I made a good recovery.'

'So, as far as the family were concerned,' said Jane, creeping along the story, 'you were terribly ill and getting worse, when in fact you were *better.*'

'I was wheeled onboard for the voyage home. Just a precaution, because I'd been bed-bound. I was tired and exhausted, bereaved, and quite alone. People were kind. I was a celebrity.'

Dan understood. 'You liked being the centre of attention, so you stayed in your wheelchair when you got home.'

'It was a game, at first. Then Mother and Father were so solicitous. They'd rearranged the whole house for my comfort.'

'Not to mention my life,' said Jane. Her naked anger

discomfited the men, who were accustomed to hearing her simper, and to tuning out that simpering. 'My entire life's been built around your comfort, Blanche. You've made me a handmaiden to *nothing*.'

'Nobody forced you into a thing.' Blanche rolled her eyes; the discussion might have been over a quart of spilled cream, and not a life. 'Jane, dear, you suit martyrdom. What else would you have done? You're hardly marriage material.'

'Blanche!' said Dan.

'You old bitch,' muttered Walter.

Jane thought of Denholm now, the man she had given up for Blanche. She thought of him the way she thought of her parents' house; a crumbling place she had once loved and was now torn down. She wanted to scream, but that was not allowed.

'I kept expecting to be found out.' Blanche sounded amused. 'Back then, our dear old family doc didn't even correspond with the American medics. All I had to do was say over and over that I'd had enough of treatments and hospitals, and nobody mentioned cures or therapy again. It's not your fault, Morgan. My history was set in stone by the time you arrived.'

'I've been your accomplice,' said Morgan. Perhaps he was remembering all those drives, how he carried his patient downstairs, and used up precious petrol. 'Alec, there are ramifications to this. Can we really keep it to ourselves, or should we fetch a police officer?'

'No police,' said Alec, unfolding his arms, coming to.

'Let's wind this up. Everybody's exhausted, and Jane needs her rest.'

'I'm perfectly all right.' Jane bridled at the suggestion. 'I say we thrash it out. Confess, Blanche, do the decent thing at last. Tell us how you did it.'

Alec pushed his hand over his face.

'Ugh,' said Blanche, her mouth turned expressively down. 'What do you need to know?' She yawned. She was ruined-looking in the early light. 'Here goes, for what it's worth. I wrote the notes with my left hand. Mind you, it *still* looked like my handwriting. You people, you don't see what's right in front of you. For years now I've been getting out of bed in the middle of the night to stretch my legs. Yes, Jane, make *that* face again. I've been capering around the house while you sleep. *I* am your ghostly children, waking you up with creaks and giggles and smashing your eggs on the kitchen tiles. The freedom of it! And then I began to venture out, and ooh la la, the things I saw. People in places they shouldn't be, with people they shouldn't be with.'

Alec kept looking at the floor, at the cutesy design on the rug.

'The *best* fun was leaving the letters.' Blanche unfurled a finger for each note's location. 'The gate outside the church, that was *yours*, Alec. Letter number two, I tiptoed into Frank's yard and hid it in the box of Walter's rhubarb. That was the one about my torrid romance with the postman. Then, let me think, ah yes, then it was back to the church where Jack Archer grabbed me by the collar and almost put an end to my career. That letter went missing.' Blanche lowered her chin, looked Dan dead in the eye. 'I wonder if we'll ever know what it exposed.'

'We have no wish to hear,' said Morgan.

'Speak for yourself,' said Agnes.

'Where was I? That brings us up to date. Tonight I visited the maypole. I knew you two swashbucklers would be lying in wait, but I also know you're too old for night-long vigils. I didn't foresee Walter, though. Well done, Walter.'

'Don't you well done me.' Walter, too, was counting on his fingers. 'You missed out the letter about the Browns, the one as was read out at his wedding.' He looked at Morgan, who'd clearly rather he didn't. 'The one about your new missus, Doc, and her old dad being a Nazi and that.'

'Hardly a *Nazi*,' said Morgan.

'That,' said Blanche, 'wasn't me.' She shook her head, stubborn, absolute. 'I hold my hand up to all the rest but that wasn't me. I had no idea Frank's a Kraut.'

'He's *not* a . . .' Jane faltered at the ugly word. 'Tell her, Morgan. Tell her to stop pretending she's a soothsayer.'

Morgan's mouth worked but he said nothing.

'I did *not* write the letter about the Browns. Believe me or don't, but there it is,' said Blanche. 'You have another bogey-man in your midst.'

'Your word,' said Morgan, 'is worth little at this juncture.'

'My dear doctor,' murmured Blanche, 'your bedside manner has deteriorated somewhat.'

'Why don't we reconvene in daylight?' Alec sprang up, his

333

motor jumping suddenly to life. 'We can't achieve much more at this hour and we're all exhausted.' He was halfway to the door before the others could agree or disagree.

'There's a lot of questions left hanging,' said Dan. He thought of bed. 'But it *is* late, so ... Alec, I'll walk with you.' He gathered his hat, hoping Doris would let him hop under the covers for a couple of hours' kip when he got home.

'Sorry, man, no. I have to dash.' Alec must have levitated down the stairs; they heard the front door slam only seconds later.

'Too bad the last letter is lost.' Blanche reached for her sleep mask and pulled the covers up to her chin. 'I've been saving it up.' She lifted the mask and one eye peeked out at them. 'It's the one about murder.'

Nothing mattered except Kitty.

Alec had made a mistake. A towering mistake, fantastically wrong. What had made him preach at her and offer that stilted, insulting 'goodbye and thank you for all your hard work' speech? It couldn't have been Alec, because Alec loved Kitty. He needed her and he loved her and he had to reverse matters. He ran all the way to Noon Cottage.

It was still dark, even though it was already tomorrow. On the doorstep of the house before Kitty's place, he saw a tiny shape crouched. Bella the cat was being disloyal, too, as she lapped milk from a bowl.

Somehow, he would square matters with Pamela, end it all. The language would arrive when he needed it. *That doesn't matter now.* Just as Blanche's imbecilic spree didn't matter, and the war didn't matter.

The universe had narrowed to Kitty's outline.

Her gate. Her path. Her door. Alec knocked, then hammered. His teeth framed in the letterbox. 'Let me in! Please!' Did it matter if anyone heard him? Not anymore.

Pounding round to the back of the house, Alec battled the dogwood and stood in the skeleton of a rose bush to peer in at the sofa and the shelves and the rug.

They were still, as rooms are at night.

The back door was unlocked. Once in, Alec swarmed over the house like smoke. It was empty.

Not just of people. Of *things*. Kitty had erased herself and Caroline in a matter of hours. The only evidence they had ever been there was Emily reclining stiffly on a footstool.

Alec held the doll to his face. It smelled of Caroline. He made noises into it. Animal sounds. Then he rubbed his eyes with his knuckles like a baby in a picture book.

Kitty's nearest neighbour opened his door with an aggrieved look, both for the hour and possibly for Mr Pargetter's wild expression and the doll he held to his chest.

'There's a telegram,' said Alec. He was gabbling. He didn't care whether he was convincing; if he could have shaken the man for the information he would have. 'It came to Lower Loxley by mistake. Where's Mrs Dibden-Rawles?'

'She gave Bella to me to look after, asked me to be kind.' Each word was reluctant, the still-sleepy man standing well back from the whirlwind on his step. 'Said she was leaving. She seemed upset.'

'Leaving? Leaving, you mean *leaving*? When?'

'A few hours ago. Look, all I know is Kitty went off about nine o'clock in George Seed's car.'

At dawn, Alec finally left Noon Cottage.

He looked back through the front window at the denuded house, at the doll prim in her tartan on an arm-chair. He wanted to take it with him, but Pamela would ask questions. He had made Emily comfortable, posing her stiff limbs.

Birds, who didn't know about the war and hadn't heard that Alec had ruined his life, sang crazily around him.

Too late. Too late. Alec's wisdom arrived too late. Now, in the ruins of their love affair, he saw Kitty's vulnerability. Too late. She had been reduced to accepting an offer – *of what?* – from the likes of that Seed man.

He entered his solemn house and hated it.

From mouth to ear, over teacups and pints, the news covered ground rapidly.

The identity of the poison-pen writer knocked Hitler off Ambridge's front page. Agnes did her best with the dis-semination, and Walter was no slouch. Nobody was above discussing it. The vicar found time for it even while formu-lating what he would say when he visited the Gilpins, for visit them he must.

'Blanche has a nasty mind,' the vicar's wife said to Frank and Nance over the pitiful loaf they allowed her. 'She listened to everything we all said, and put two and two together to make five.'

'She's brought unhappiness to many homes,' said Frank. He was measured when he talked about Blanche. Careful.

Not so Pamela. 'She should be run out of town,' she said confidently to Ronald Furneaux, when she picked up the phone and hung onto him instead of passing the handset to Alec. 'Not the anaemic little sister, just Blanche.' She listened, then laughed, prettily, not the way she laughed around Alec. 'Ronald, you're so right! The cabinet could make good use of her espionage skills! Here's Alec, and do be gentle with him, he's moping around like a lovelorn housemaid.'

The baddie herself was seeing her sitting room and kitchen in daylight, and she found them lacking.

So shabby. Jane shouldn't be trusted with décor. Sludgy colours with no light and shade to the whole. Blanche needed sensuality, something to stroke. Downstairs was all worsted and hemp and Jane's walking shoes lying dejected on the mat.

She took up a magazine and put it down again.

I am in quarantine. Like an imported pet with flecks of foam on its snout. No visitors, and Jane kept to her room. Her faithful crow, a raised eyebrow in human form, tended her with rude succinctness. They were all eaten up with curiosity. How she'd done it, how she knew such arcana.

Because deep down they all know the letters speak the truth.

They may deny her to each other, and add slander to her

crimes, but they knew she had put two and two together and made exactly four.

While they slept she'd been haunting Ambridge, breaking flowerpots and scaring cats. One midnight had delivered her a wonderful gift: Alec Pargetter taking his leave of Noon Cottage, and Kitty's dressing gown suggesting her nakedness beneath it. Blanche had been obliged to shrink into the camouflage so handily available at that time of night, and had just missed bumping into the boy, Gerald, as he tailed his father back along the lane.

It was child's play to deduce who had given Alec his shiner. Then, the divine moment of inspiration. She still mewed when she remembered it. Why not devise a game that entangled the entire village? Like they were dolls. Like she was Nero. Like she was God.

Hippity hop to the gate of the church where Blanche pinned up her first note. Safe from suspicion, with her withered legs and all. She wore the coat she'd pinched from Stan Horrobin one night as he slept off a skinful outside The Bull. She'd simply sauntered over and plucked it from where Bob Little had laid it over the sleeping man. It transformed her from genteel to dangerous; she liked its heft and its yeasty smell.

The commotion in the village was exhilarating. She would write one more. Just the one. About herself and Whitey White. It would absolve her for ever from any suspicion.

It was something else, too.

Blanche never confronted just how much she enjoyed

having Whitey lie across her bed. It was a simulacrum of the romps hinted at in the novels she read and reread. The closeness. The interlocking of male and female. Blanche wondered what sex was like, knowing she had relinquished it along with responsibility or expectation or duty when she disembarked in her wheelchair. Letter number two had the delicious stink of wish fulfilment.

The third letter, read out at the wedding, took the wind out of her sails. It didn't bother Blanche that she would go to her grave damned for it, but the mystery intrigued her. She hadn't written the letter exposing the Browns and she wondered who hated them enough to do it?

I've taken the fall for you, whoever you are.

Unwilling to have some stranger call time on her game, Blanche had rushed out a fourth poison pen. And found herself in the arms of a man for the first time when she'd been caught.

Jack Archer had been so hard, all knobs and gristle, and so unexpectedly strong. But Blanche had wriggled and kicked and scooted away. The loss of her precious, cleverly worded note had irked her for days but then, when she'd all but forgotten it, Jimmy's sight returned.

Funny, that.

She and Jimmy had both used the night to show their true selves. Sitting cross-legged at her window, eating toffees and throwing the wrappers over her shoulder, Blanche had glanced next door at The Bull and seen Jimmy creep, sure-footed, out into the yard. He had bent his head over the photograph of, was it Hilda, yes, that was her name. He spent *ages* mooning over his land girl Cleopatra. He wept. He kissed her image. The blind boy was, like herself, a malingerer.

She stood and prowled the room. Despite years of practice, Blanche was bad at waiting. The fifth – and alas final – note lay unread in someone's pocket. She put her money on sly old Walter Gabriel. It would surface; she had whetted everyone's appetite with her mention of murder.

People, thought Blanche, *are very simple, when it comes down to it.*

The 'how' of her crime was simple enough. But the 'why' of it? That was a secret even to Blanche. She didn't know why she enjoyed sowing misery and wasn't curious.

It's fun.

Fog made a Gothic apparition of Denholm's house.

Jane, scarf up around her nose, knitted hat limp on her fringe, stared up at the windows of Turnpike. The man of the house was absent, its windows black. A niece was looking after him as his leg healed, according to the crow; she had her ear to the ground even when the ground was November-hard.

What must Denholm think of me? Some of Blanche's infamy must surely rub off on the sister who shared their small quarters. Denholm's regard, proven by his proposal, was one of the struts that held up Jane's frayed tent.

It was hard to trust now. Not just people, but her thoughts. Old certainties had turned to dust. The spectral children were gone, replaced by something much worse. Jane's head was a derelict place.

The cold bit into her joints and made her feel ancient. She had never been young, it wasn't her thing. As the 'late arrival' in her parents' lives she had been earmarked to see them through their old age. With Blanche incapacitated, Jane had nursed their mother through a long illness, only for her father to succumb, with perfect timing, to his own malady. As one parent was waved off at St Stephen's graveyard, the other started a nasty cough.

I could never leave.

It pleased Jane to think she'd have been brave enough to do so.

Despite the fog, another circuit of Ambridge was preferable to going home. A queer, wintry stasis prevailed as the village waited for the last letter to be found, and she met nobody. It was an odd hour, just after dinner, when children were got to bed and pipes were smoked. She had nothing to return to, except anger.

Every sugar bowl had been smashed, but it had not satisfied her rage, which renewed itself overnight, every night. If her name was not held in high regard in Ambridge, well, then Jane was nobody.

Through the years she had begged God's forgiveness for the petty revenges she wreaked on Blanche. A lukewarm hot water bottle. A delay in ferrying the newspaper upstairs. Now all that was expunged, forgotten; she could have done worse and still not scratched the surface of what Blanche truly deserved.

She heard the truck before she saw it. The mist gave it up suddenly, like a pantomime genie. Its lights were blinkered.

'Brookfield?' said the man who wound down the window. 'Can't see a thing in this fog. Not that there are any signs if I *could* see.'

'That way, up there, take a right.' Jane pointed with her glove.

'Thank you, ma'am.'

'Ma'am' pushed Jane from old to Neolithic. Time to go home. She wouldn't speak to Blanche. She would keep the promise she made the night of the pageant, and never address her sister directly again. *Thank God for Agnes.* Not a statement Jane had ever thought she'd make, but Agnes was somebody to talk to, somebody who shared her distaste for Blanche.

Visitors would return. Blanche would be rehabilitated to some extent. Jane would never falter, though; she would keep the sooty flames of remembrance burning.

Doris heard, then saw the truck rumble through the goose-grey mist. It parked down by the five-bar gate. 'He's early,' she thought, but it wasn't Dan's mate come to collect rams for auction. It was, she realized, Mr Wyer.

Glen led the way to the gate, his tail a flag. A figure firmed up in the fog as they picked their way along the tyre ruts. 'Jez,' called Doris. 'Do me a favour and round up Eugene and Dan. There's a bigwig from War Ag checking up on us and no doubt he'll want to talk to you all.'

'Glad to, missus. All right if I pop to the house first? I left me glove.' He waggled a bare hand.

'You don't have to ask, Jez.'

He blew her a kiss.

Kids banished, Lisa napping, Doris went about her Sisyphean kitchen work as Dan and Robert Wyer talked at the table.

Between less affable men it could have been tense, but Mr Wyer managed to lean on Dan for results and Dan managed to defend himself without rancour. *A pity*, thought Doris, *that Winnie and Adolf can't take a leaf out of their books.*

'How's the census going?' Mr Wyer set everything down in small, cryptic writing.

'Great guns,' said Dan. 'It's all in this folder. Every labourer, every machine, every clapped-out little nag.'

'You included telephones, like I asked?'

'Not many to include,' laughed Dan.

'You know you'll be getting a telephone?'

Dan pulled in his chin. 'Cripes,' he said.

'Us?' Doris was astounded.

'Yes, Doris, you,' said Mr Wyer, smug with his largesse. 'Now, rabbits. They can't move for the little blighters over Lyttleton Cover.'

'Stan Horrobin's doing his level best. Goes against the grain, letting him poach, but needs must. You might have a word with the powers that be about coal, Mr Wyer. I couldn't get my hands on nearly enough for the steam traction engines this harvest.'

'Noted, Dan, noted.'

Butting in with scones – and luxuriating in their appre-ciation for such wonders – Doris added a gripe of her own. How, she asked, was she supposed to manage with untrained, unwilling labour?

'No point in giving farmers silly targets,' she said, hands on hips, using her I-made-the-scones power while it lasted. 'If you only give 'em incompetent men.'

'Fair dos, Doris.' Mr Wyer reached into a briefcase. Took out a folder that tore and showered the table with documents. 'Let's see if we can sort you out.'

Dan took out his pipe and, on a squinted signal from Doris, put it away again with a slight, almost interior sigh.

'Here we are.' Mr Wyer smoothed out a form. Neat cop-perplate writing trammeled by boxes. 'Yes, yes, oh, that's not right.' He looked up, took off his glasses. 'It's damn silly, one labourer's insufficient for a farm the size of Brookfield.'

'Two,' Doris corrected him, and then, hastily, 'That still isn't enough!'

'No, one.' Mr Wyer swivelled the paper to show her. 'A Eugene Haldane.'

Jez did not appear anywhere on the official paperwork. Dan remembered noticing that, and creating a supplementary form, assuming it was an oversight. 'I gave it to Jez to post,' he said, the sentence slowing as they recognized its implication.

As for Doris, she remembered waving Jez into the truck at Hollerton.

Hey, you! You for Brookfield?

The two-second delay. The nod. Her senses in revolt as she ignored her intuition.

And then Dan's bemusement about the lack of reply from War Ag. Then finding Jez's wages from the farm's pockets, knowing they'd be reimbursed.

Doris ran, with neither coat nor hat, to the men's digs. He was gone, of course, as were his meagre belongings. There was a dent in the bedclothes where he had sat to pack.

Back at the house, she shoved Dan out of the way and began to open drawers. Jez was a germ floating through the war, and she had ushered him into her kitchen. She checked her handbag. She checked her purse. She checked the scullery.

'Come on, love,' said Dan. 'He's hardly going to steal your pickled onions, now, is he?'

Peggy was back.

'You again?' Stan Horrobin slouched in the doorway. 'It's a long hike from London for a little piece like you.'

'Is your wife in? I prefer to deal with the organ grinder, not the monkey.' Peggy pushed past him. It *had* been a long hike. 'Down, Wizbang, I haven't come to see *you*.'

She petted the grubby dog all the same. And called to Stacey, who limped over to lick her hand. 'Still missing your master, eh?'

Connie, wiping her hands with a cloth, hurried in. 'We all miss our Cliff,' she said, and she seemed happy to see Peggy, who didn't know how unusual this was.

Later, as Peggy gathered her handbag and her coat, she said, 'Here you go, Connie,' and held out some rolled notes.

Connie's hand was a blur as she grabbed the money and secreted it into a hidden pocket.

'That's for the boys, got it? Not booze for *him*.' Peggy nodded at Stan, asleep in the one soft chair. 'You giving them some veggies? And a bit of pudding and custard now and then?'

'I look after them like they was my own.'

That was what Peggy was scared of. 'I'm still reeling about what you told me, the crippled lady and her poison pen.' Peggy went to the broken mirror and surveyed the Picasso face it threw back. 'Who says nothing ever happens in the countryside?'

'You *are* lucky,' said Connie, keeping a respectful distance from Peggy as she tucked her hair into her fluffy beret and applied a dab of lipstick to her cupid's bow. 'Going back to London.'

'Yeah. Well.' Peggy's mouth turned down. She was still pretty; it didn't matter what she did with her features. Peggy was used to her own beauty and it had stopped impressing her. The Blitz was beyond Connie's comprehension. Before the middle of September it had been beyond Peggy's; now she was a 'plucky Londoner' picking her way through fallen masonry to get to work. '*You're* lucky, Connie, that nobody's bombing the tripe out of you.' She wheeled around, arms outstretched; this cuddling business was new, but felt right. 'All right, kiddos, I'm off.'

The boys had been spirited today; the oinking whenever Connie said Peggy's name would have earned them a glare at home, but not here. She didn't care overmuch about manners or reading or behaviour. She had no ambition for her brothers beyond getting them through the war in one piece; Billy and John had become important to her. No longer short-trousered cyphers who got under her feet, it had taken distance, and danger, to render her little brothers fully three-dimensional. Her anxiety was a stiff wind that kept blowing her to Ambridge. 'John, love, I'll be back before you know it.'

He had to be peeled off his sister. Even Billy's oinks didn't help.

'Who's this?' said Connie as barking from the yard alerted them to a visitor and woke up Stan.

'Only me!' said Doris, evidently unsure of her welcome. 'Wondered if there was another letter from Cliff.'

Stan swore, or probably did; the gargled exclamation as he settled back down sounded ugly.

'Nah. Nothing. Here, you in the truck? Give this one a lift.' Connie pushed at Peggy, and John gave up and retired to a dark corner with Stacey, who was always available for collective melancholy. 'Heard from your Jack, have you? Having an easy war, you Archers.'

Doris took a moment. Ignored Connie. The effort was visible. 'Ready, Peggy?'

'My other boy, my Vic,' called Connie as she followed them out, 'he'll be eligible for conscription in two years. Something to look forward to!'

As Connie grew smaller in the rear-view mirror, Doris tried to evict the woman from her thoughts. Good house-keeping habits now extended to the inside of her head; sadness was the enemy, like dirt in her kitchen. Sadness slowed her down, and if Doris slowed down, well, where would it all end?

'My Jack'll be sorry to have missed you,' she said to Peggy. Doris had a brief, forbidden thought: *Our Janet would've been every bit as pretty as Peggy if she'd lived.* There was no way to prove this, nobody to corroborate her bias. 'Have you noticed he's sweet on you?'

'I'd notice from the moon. He's a nice boy, your Jack. He looked me up when his unit came up to Bushy Park to, oh, I don't know, do *something* in the mud; they keep the lads busy. He can't hold his drink, that's for sure. I didn't tell him about my regular fella. He's a big shot, Doris. Owns a factory.' Peggy paused. The truck threw them in the air and caught them again in its scuffed seats. 'D'you think Jack'd be jealous?'

'Do you want him to be?'

They laughed.

'I'll scribble down his service address.' Doris sensed a maturity in Peggy, a forced growing, like Walter's rhubarb squeaking in the dark. 'You could write to him.' Doris fished an envelope out of her bag as they idled behind a trailer full of quizzical sheep. 'If you like.'

'I'm too busy to write to some boy.'

They set off again, with a toot on the horn for the sheep's chauffeur, who Doris, naturally, knew. 'First the air battles, now the Blitz, there's always someone getting it, isn't there?' she said.

'It was so funny, the other night.' Every Londoner had their Blitz story, the one they trotted out, and this was the Perkins'. 'Mum and me, we were just coming up out of my nan's shelter and there was another explosion, a biggie, and I put out my arm like, you know, *get back*, and I got Mum in the nose. Blood everywhere. Mum creating. So Nan hands me a towel and I mop up Mum's poor face and it's only the towel we keep to wipe down the outside lavvy!'

'No!' Doris was grateful for the laughter. Jez might be gone, but he remained a surly, stubborn blot on the landscape. The Archers were out of pocket. They'd fed and housed him, and paid his wages in the expectation of being reimbursed. *It's my fault.* Thrifty Doris felt responsible for every penny. Each time she mislaid something – a key or a comb – she thought *Jez!* But then she'd find it. She knew, in her bones, that he had taken some trophy with him, and daily she searched for a void, a lack, but nothing was missing.

That was only true until she disproved it.

She said now, 'Awful about Balham tube station, though. Did you hear about it? A month ago now, it was. All those people asleep on the platform, sheltering from the bombs, and they weren't safe at all.' The picture had been on the front page: a double-decker bus face down in a crater. 'A water main burst as well. Those poor, poor folk.' Doris gasped. 'Oh, Peggy, I didn't think, it's not near you, Balham, is it?'

'No,' said Peggy. 'I'm the East End.'

'Bet it's lively!'

'It's lively all right.' Peggy had a new habit. The morning after a raid she would leave the house early and jog a tour of her friends' houses. She didn't knock on any doors, she just checked that the houses were still there.

Death, she knew, was coming for her. She couldn't keep eluding him, no matter how nimble she was on her feet. As Peggy picked her way over the smashed innards of fallen houses, over sideboards and sewing baskets and snatches of dress fabric, Peggy braced herself. One morning the tour must end in tears.

She'd fallen to her knees over a cat, its furry outline pressed into hot tarmac. She'd sobbed for that cat as if it was her nearest and dearest. It was just a cat. It was just another death.

Hollerton Junction. Peggy didn't get out. Doris waited, but when the train arrived she said, gently, 'Peggy? You'll miss it.'

'No. Yes.' Peggy hugged Glen, who had stuck his big hairy head between the front seats. She stepped out, straightened her coat, and slammed the door. 'Fresh air's not so bad once you get used to it.'

Halfway back to Brookfield, glad of solid old Glen and his undemanding camaraderie, Doris noticed the scrap of envelope with Jack's address on it was gone.

By the church she slowed down alongside Walter Gabriel. *Where's he off to in his Sunday jacket?* 'Need a lift?'

He shook his head. Walter was one huge scowl. He walked on. Or marched, rather, holding a piece of paper in his hand. All the way to Homeleigh.

Nance let him in. Accompanied him to her husband's surgery door. Got no response to her small talk. 'Walter for you, Frank,' she said, and closed the door on them both.

'You need to read this, I reckon, Dr Seed.' Walter didn't take the offered seat. He approached Morgan's leather-topped desk and tossed a piece of paper onto it. Folded and refolded, it was limp.

Morgan pushed his chair back. He put a hand to his mouth.

He knew it was the missing letter. He had anticipated this moment time and again in his mind, and now it was here. 'Walter,' he said. 'Your father was suffering horribly. He was struggling, and I—'

'I suspected but I didn't know for sure until I found that letter on Blanche when I nabbed her. You overdosed me dad, didn't you? You nudged him over the edge. Mum couldn't bear to watch him in his pain. I thank you with all my heart, I do, and you should count yourself an angel, Dr Seed.'

Morgan rose out of his chair and took the raw, red-fingered ham of a hand that Walter held out. He waited until the man had stopped sobbing. He saw him out.

He ripped the note into pieces.

DEAR FRIENDS
    IF YOU HAVE A COUGH, GO TO DR
SEED. OR A SNIFFLE OR A TUMMY
ACHE. BUT OH DEAR KEEP YOUR
EYES ON HIM AS HE DISPENSES YOUR

TABLETS. OUR MEDICINE MAN HAS a
HOBBY AND IT'S NOT GOLF.
  IT'S MURDER.
  JUST ASK JONJO GABRIEL. OH
I FORGOT, YOU CAN'T. HE'S DEAD
AND BURIED.
  SIGNED
  YOUR NEIGHBOUR

DECEMBER

Two weeks until Christmas.

Billy and John, who didn't yet know what Christmas with the Horrobins looked like, foresaw plum pudding and stockings, and a merriment that lasted the whole day from getting up early to going to bed late.

The wood had shrunk back since the summer. They didn't have to beat a way through. Their path to HQ was clear, an easy route through the trees. No mud today; that was a plus.

'Keep up, John,' said Billy.

John's wellingtons were slightly too big. When he sped up they made a funny, sucking noise. Whump, whump, whump. 'Stan's being nice,' he said, suspicious.

'Yeah! He's even not saying horrid stuff to Connie. Maybe it's his birthday.'

'No, it was his birthday before. He got really proper drunk, remember? He went to kick Stacey. Something's happened. Something good. Good for *him*.' Both boys knew that would entail a horrible downside for somebody else.

Billy said, 'He was going on about being in the money soon.' He stopped dead in his tracks. 'Peggy!' he said and began to run.

The clearing was different. The painting of Peggy was face down. All her little accoutrements scattered about, and HQ leaning drunkenly over, its door caved in.

'She's gone, John!'

They roamed all day and shouted her name. It was no good. Their pig was gone. John, of course, cried, but so did Billy.

'It's like Morgan,' said Agnes.

'I shouldn't laugh,' said Frank, 'not now he's my son-in-law, but yes, you're right.'

The poster above a box of foraged mushrooms imagined a cheery Father Christmas who exhorted Ambridge to 'Make it a War Savings Christmas!' He did bring Morgan to mind. The cheeks. The round glasses. The benign gaze above a hefty tum.

'Any chance of an orange?' Agnes knew the answer.

'Some nice dates there.' Frank pointed. His breath froze on the air.

'I 'ate dates.'

Nance handed the box of Christmas cards to Doris who rifled through them and said, 'All very flimsy. This wartime paper is just useless.'

'More like blotting paper,' said Pamela, who was carefully

selecting her allotted eggs. She wore a stovepipe hat, velvet, brown. She was rarely seen in the shop, and there was generally an air of performance to her visits. As if she was an actress who had researched domestic chores for a role.

'There's *some* good news for Christmas,' said Magsy. 'Bigger rations of tea and sugar.'

Agnes was dour. 'Whoopee, let's have a party.'

'I find I stretch my personal rations perfectly adequately.' Magsy was pious. 'Now that I don't cook for Morgan.'

Nance blinked at the comment. Doris noticed. She had heard various similar remarks from Magsy. No malice in them, but still …

'I heard from Denholm's niece,' said Pamela, rejecting an egg and examining another. 'Patient's doing well, apparently, and expected home by Christmas. A man like that really ought to remarry.' She shook her head as if Denholm was, say, a bicycle minus a saddle. 'Awfully thin-shelled, these eggs, Nance.'

'Sorry, Mrs Pargetter,' said Nance. The apology was reflexive. 'Hello, young men!' She greeted Billy and John. 'Such long faces!'

The two boys were unusually subdued. They each wore two handknits, and John had worsted stockings on under his flannel shorts.

Magsy leaned down. Her fleshy nose wobbled near their own dainty frozen ones and made John shrink. 'Aw, are you missing Peggy?'

Billy side-eyed John. *How does the old bag know?*

'Yes.' John's word came out wet, on a sob. 'She was took.'

'No, no, she's in London, dear,' said Magsy.

'Eh?' John stopped crying in shock. *'London?'*

'I heard,' said Nance, leaning comfortably over the counter to talk kindly down to them, 'Peggy has a job in a shoe shop.'

The boys forgot what Connie had sent them to buy and trailed out into the arctic street, keen to be alone and discuss this unexpected turn of events in the pig's life.

They were in Alec's way. He sidestepped them, glancing in at the shop.

Pamela raised her hand at him. Smiled. Alec didn't break step.

'Pamela, Pamela!' Magsy pointed to the egg cracked in Pamela's glove.

'As I said. Thin shells.'

Pamela removed her glove, placed it tidily in her hand-bag and left.

When Agnes, too, pulled up her collar and left, Magsy spoke to Nance in a conspiratorial whisper. 'Any more trouble, dear? You know, the slogans, the breaking of the window.'

Frank answered for his daughter: 'That's all died down, thank you, Magsy.'

Doris recognized the full stop; Magsy did not.

As Nance's cheeks ignited, Magsy said sorrowfully, 'If I could turn the clock back and snatch that letter out of Dan's hand I would. When I think of the trouble it's caused.'

'Yes, well.' Doris was vigorous, brandishing her chosen

Christmas cards at Nance. 'It's all done with. Blanche was caught, and stopped.'

'We must all thank God for small mercies, as the vicar said on Sunday.' Magsy seemed to remember something. 'Were you at Eucharist, Doris? I missed you.'

'No.' Doris had run out of credible excuses, and just left it at that. She felt exposed by the innocent question, as if Magsy had seen how she winced at her children's prayers. She patted her hair nervously; she'd taken to combing it over the bald patch, like a travelling salesman.

Doris had always fitted in. Always been a straightforward woman of her time and place; losing her faith made a guerilla of her. Her divorce from the genial God who kept Ambridge ticking over had left no mark that anybody could see, but still she feared them – *the others* – somehow smelling it on her.

She wanted a way back. She wanted to go home. She wanted to trust again.

It was like those puzzles in the newspaper: 'What's Wrong with this Picture?'

'Where's old Bob?' Dan leaned over the scratched counter. Bob was ever-present within The Bull's four walls. A little bald god always on hand to lay a beery salve on their wounds.

'Bob!' shouted Morgan.

'Do come along!' called Alec.

'Get your arse in 'ere, Little!' roared Stan.

Morgan tapped the counter. Schooled to notice such things in his patients, he had observed his own growing dependence on Bob's medicine. The tot of whisky in the evening was looked forward to with carnal anticipation. This midday beer with his sandwich was less a habit than a *sine qua non*.

Nance had noticed, too. She was a noticer, his girl, and he loved that about her. That didn't mean he answered her soft questions with any frankness.

Truth be told, they didn't know each other terribly well. Despite his age and his experience, Morgan saw now that he had naively expected marriage to solve that, to flesh them out, reveal her to him, and vice versa.

It was a slow process. A lick of the finger and a turn of another page. And what was there for Nance – graceful, swan-necked Nance – to read about her ageing husband? Morgan had been duped by two fakers; he'd danced attention on Blanche and propagated the lie of Jimmy's blindness. The best use of his skill was in dosing an old man to death. He should have told Nance. *She deserves to know what kind of man she married.* It's tough to come up against one's own coward-ice, and Morgan called 'Bob!' again, his eye on a bottle of his favourite ale.

'At last!' Stan slammed down his tankard when Bob, shiny head bent, took his rightful place behind the bar. 'Pint, and quick about it.'

With something approaching reverence, Bob lined up five squat glasses. He took down the bottle of Glenmorangie with both hands. Like a high priest he poured exactly the same measure into each glass.

The men were quiet. Church-quiet. When Bob raised his

glass, they raised theirs. They were waiting. They were, though none would admit it, trembling.

'To my boy,' said Bob.

'Your boy.'

They drained the glasses and put them down with a thump that felt appropriate.

Alec said, 'When, Bob?'

'Four days ago. Egypt.'

Morgan said, 'I'm so sorry.' He didn't look at Dan or Alec; he couldn't. *We made Jimmy join up*, he thought, and it burned more than the Scotch.

'He gets his sight back, and now . . .' Bob poured another for them all. 'Doesn't seem right.'

Stan took off his cap. 'I'm sorry for your loss, Bob.'

Bob took a deep breath. 'My only boy,' he said.

WINTER

1941

Woman much missed, how you call to me,
call to me

THOMAS HARDY
The Voice

The village was quiet.

Only if you were on foot, as you passed the houses, would you hear the clamour of everybody at table.

But why would you be on foot? Only the snow was on the streets on Christmas Day. Tradition resisted the war, and it ground on behind closed doors. Doors decorated with holly wreaths.

A steady granular crunch was the only noise on the snow-muffled air. It grew louder as the figure drew nearer. A military man, in bulky khaki, only his eyes visible in the letterbox slit between hat and scarf.

He passed Woodbine Cottage without a glance for the candle in its window.

Within, Blanche saw him go by. She knew he wouldn't knock; there had been no visitors all day. It surprised her. It led her to do something alien to her nature; she reappraised her situation.

It was new to her, this feeling of hurt. The timeline was awry; by now the neighbours should have begun to return. They were sulking, the fools. Blanche poked the fire, and felt her face smart from the heat. 'That bloody Agnes,' she shouted to the kitchen. 'Taking the whole day off! Probably snowed in somewhere with that *admirer* of hers, cooing over her cheap brooch. My crow's getting cocky, Jane, mark my words.'

Whether or not Jane marked Blanche's words she didn't respond to them.

Which didn't stop Blanche. 'I see Doris sent half a ham. She'll be back, you'll see. They're waiting for me to apologize. Ha! They'll have a long wait!'

From the kitchen came the ragtime noise of Jane's cooking. The ticking of the gas and then its *pah!* flowering as a match was put to it. A pan set down. The tap running.

'Oh, say something, Janey! It's Christmas. You can't keep this up for ever. Ah, here she comes, the cook!' Blanche bowed to Jane, who brought in a roast chicken on a platter that only escaped from the sideboard this one day of the year.

Carrots followed. Bread sauce was scraped into a jug.

'Bring the carving knife,' bellowed Blanche, as if the kitchen was at the other end of a castle and not four steps away. 'Although I could cut this scraggy bird with a butter knife.'

Jane wiped her hands and picked up the horn-handled carving knife. She turned it, studied it, and smiled. She untied her apron with one hand and let it drop to the floor.

Striding out of the back door, with its peeling apple-green paint, Jane flung the knife into the white square the garden had become. Her grey pumps turned darker with the icy dampness that soaked her stockinged toes.

She called a bright 'Merry Christmas!' at the soldier as she overtook him.

He didn't acknowledge Jane, just plodded on, zombie-like.

'I hear,' said Pamela, 'they're serving *murkey* at Brookfield.' She saw Gerald's expression. 'It means mock turkey, darling.'

'Ugh,' said Gerald.

'Quite,' said Pamela.

Their black market beef was magnificent. The carcass sat among trailing greenery and tall red candles; Pamela had seen the table setting in the *Lady* and had the housekeeper reproduce it. She loved the panelling by candlelight. The atmosphere. The air of plenty.

'It's so quiet,' said Pamela. The snow depressed her. Yes, yes, it was beautiful but it insulated Lower Loxley so well that they could be on the moon. Alec hadn't spoken since they sat down.

She reached over and swiped the paper hat from his head. 'You look ridiculous,' she said.

She had seen off the young pretender, but Pamela's was a pyrrhic victory. She had her husband still, but he was changed.

Right through his bones, along with the marrow, Alec was sad.

'What did you think of Henry's sermon at midnight Mass?' Pamela persevered because that was what Pamelas did. She supplied the conversation the same way she supplied the beef and the Christmas crackers and the *heir*, for heaven's sake. 'So thoughtful to mention Jimmy Little, but oh dear,

Henry can be banal, can't he? He might have been referring to a cat dying. Where *is* Sidi Barrani anyway? Too bad for Englishmen to die in all those hot little holes abroad.'

Gerald spoke. 'May I please get down?'

'Go,' said Alec before Pamela could say the opposite.

'Come back later, darling, for some plum pud!' Cook's gravy had begun to set on their plates. 'You might be nicer, Alec. It's Christmas Day.'

'I know what day it is.' Alec had given up Kitkat for this. For his seat at this table in this huge dead house. Kitty was everything; she was insubstantial but enormous. Some days he didn't remember her face, but it didn't matter because it would float back to him the next. He worried that he might stop mourning her; he needed the grief to feel alive.

'Are you happy?' asked Pamela.

Jesus Christ. 'Yes, I am. Aren't you? You got what you wanted, after all.'

'So I did,' said Pamela. 'Lucky me.'

'I dare you!'

John hated dares, and his big brother knew that. 'Don't dare me!' he yelled. 'That means I have to!'

'Go on, run through the graveyard!'

White snowy humps suggested the dead bodies far beneath.

Billy took his brother's sticky hand. 'I'll come too! And Stace. Come on, Stacey.'

The dog had roused itself for the first time in months. Black and white, refined, Stacey was aristocratic in the way mutts often are. Connie had suggested Stacey knew it was Christmas, and that's why she was finally cheering up.

'Like you two,' she'd said, handing a plate to each of the boys as the Horrobins – incredibly – all sat around the table to eat. 'I haven't seen smiles like that out of you in a while.'

They were drunk on pork. The smell of it, the crunch of the crackling, the insane moreishness of the Christmas banquet in a month of stew and parsnips. It eased the pain of losing their pig.

It would be years before either John or Billy made the connection; for now they were full of pork and looking forward to even more later on a nice bit of bread.

'I hate this place!' John stuck to Billy through the maze of graves. The sky over their heads was a sickly white, pregnant with another bellyful of snow.

Ahead of them Stacey lifted her nose and sniffed. Really sniffed, interested in something.

A figure was lurching through the drifts, head down. The man's pace was unhurried, consistent, as if he would keep walking whatever might stray into his path. As if he would walk to the ends of the Earth.

The dog bared her teeth. She let out a fluting growl. In her agitation she hopped stiffly backwards on all four paws.

The soldier kept coming.

Stacey turned and fled, barking and scattering the boys.

They fled with her and didn't look back, because they knew the dead soldier would be behind them.

*

Doris was flabbergasted. Where had Dan found the time to make a dolls' house, and in secret? Christine was absorbed by the tiny rooms and the tiny beds and the tiny family; it took four concerted stints of hollering up the stairs to bring her down for the murkey.

Paper chains criss-crossed the parlour ceiling. The room was thick with heat from the coals and the people in the room. It was transgressive, even at Christmas, to spoil its chilly perfection but oh, it was worth it.

Or so Doris thought, in the lull between clearing the table and embarking on the washing up. The port was out; Morgan's gift. She was on tea, and Magsy had asked for sherry. Luckily there had been one sticky serving left in a bottle under the sink.

Everyone wore a paper hat; it was mandatory. She had fed them all. *Over*-fed them all. Her own, even Jack, plus the Seeds, and Frank too of course, as well as Magsy, and Eugene, and at the head of the table, Lisa. Doris knew that look; Lisa was unsure but content. No fear. The fear was the worst, and it preceded 'acting up'. She didn't want her mother to act up in front of company, yet she couldn't bear to exclude her from family ritual. She would keep an eye.

'To absent friends,' said Dan, raising his port. He was soft-eyed; he'd be pawing her later. Doris felt tired as she anticipated finding the words to defuse him without hurting his feelings, all the while twisting away from his embrace.

She raised her glass. *To Janet*, she thought.

The day was Doris's creation. She had stayed home from

midnight Mass to wrap the modest pile of presents in brown paper. She had striven to emulate other Christmas Days, even though this one was different. And it had worked. The room vibrated with good cheer.

And me? Doris loathed the introspection of wartime. A loneliness of the soul that made her take her own temperature and compare her inner scenery to others'. Each of them around the table fought their own war. Paper hat or no paper hat.

'To my dear brother.' Magsy held up her glass.

'To Ronald,' echoed the others.

'Pity he's not here with us,' said Nance. She knew her generosity about Morgan's previous family went down well with her husband. It was nine-tenths genuine; the jealousy of the perfect dead wife only pricked her when she couldn't sleep. Or perhaps she couldn't sleep because of the jealousy.

'Bet Ronald's not eating murkey at the Houses of Parliament,' said Jack.

'Now, now,' said Dan. 'Your mother's murkey was excellent.'

'*My* murkey?' said Doris. 'I think you'll find it was Mr Hitler's.' She had stuffed a joint of mutton with breadcrumbs, then laid bacon over the top and added, to Jack's glee, parsnip legs. They had laughed at it, and sort of, kind of, enjoyed eating it. Because they had to.

'Ronald,' said Morgan, 'is *vegetarian*.'

As others expostulated at such wanton eccentricity, Magsy's attention wandered. She remembered how she had bugged and begged her brother to use his position to investigate the Browns' background. It had taken less than a day, even with the great motor of war running, for Ronald to call back with news.

'Margaret, my dear,' he had said, 'I do have something to report. I'm told the Browns are naturalized British citizens.' He had details, dates, documents. 'Now that I've told you, I need you to forget it. This family are now British. They deserve our discretion. Do you hear me, Margaret? I forbid you to share this information with any other individual. I shall need your promise.'

Breaking the promise she made to her brother had all been for nothing. Magsy wondered now what she had expected to happen when she wrote that letter. Yes, it had been read out at the wedding, and the truth broadcast, but Morgan and Nance were still together, and she was still the spinster aunt who nobody really wants but who is tolerated.

It was all for nothing! thought Magsy passionately. All for nothing the self-hatred she felt the moment her horrible words hit the air. All for nothing the peek into her dingy soul. Magsy's only gain? The revelation that her expectations of marriage to Morgan had been foolish and humiliating.

The Browns had done nothing to harm her, yet she had taken a sledgehammer to them. Penance was needed; Magsy would wear a hair shirt beneath her dowdy dresses if she could find one. All she could do was rail against the bigotry she had provoked.

And all the while she must stand witness to Morgan and

Nance's rapport, another circle she was excluded from. *I am lonely*, she admitted to herself (for it felt like a failing). But perhaps a woman capable of such spite deserved to be alone.

Lisa interrupted Magsy's self-flagellation. 'Are they married?' she asked loudly, pointing to Nance and Morgan. 'Or is he her father?'

Doris butted in. 'Mum, that's Nance and Morgan, you know them, they're married six months.'

'I like *her*,' said Lisa. 'But he looks a tricky bugger.'

Morgan quaked with laughter. 'You're quite right! I am.'

The moment teetered. Lisa's face blackened, then just as suddenly cleared. 'You're a funny onion!' she said, delighted.

They were all delighted. It became the *bon mot* of the day. Glen was a funny onion, and so was Christine. The murkey, they agreed, was the funniest onion of all.

Keen to join in – she was a child who grew an inch if the grown-ups laughed at her jokes – Christine said to Nance, 'If Morgan's a funny onion, that makes you Mrs Funny Onion!'

'Mrs F. O. Seed!' barked Dan.

'That's me,' said Nance. She felt Morgan glance at her. He was always so careful to reassure her that her ancestry didn't matter to him. *But it does*, thought Nance. In some small way it had to. She wondered what was the German for funny onion.

Across the table, her father cleared his throat. Noticing the cue, the others were quiet and looked to Frank. 'May I say something, please, friends? I feel the need to thank you.' He was quite red, poor Frank. The Browns did not relish the limelight. 'You've stood by me and Nance through ...' He evidently hadn't rehearsed how to describe their calamity. 'Through all that business. Especially you, Magsy.' He looked at her, and was tearful. 'You've stood up for me in public, and I want you to know how grateful I am. A friend like you doesn't come along very often in life.'

'He's right, Magsy, you've—' Dan stopped, silenced by Magsy's violent tears.

Chairs were scraped back as they all stood and gathered round her, the mad spinster aunt who cries at Christmas.

'Charades!' said Jack, when he felt the back rubbing and there-there-ing had gone on long enough. 'Mother, you write the clues.' He nudged Doris; he knew she hated acting out the charades.

She nudged him back, grateful for him, pushing away the sudden assaulting thoughts of where Jack would be this time next year. *If* Jack would be.

To the dresser, where, in the middle drawer, Doris would find the blue lacquered pen her father had used every day of his life. She used it rarely; she felt too much when it was in her hand. The lovely gloss. The clean nib. It was just right for a high day and a holiday.

It wasn't there. She pushed aside a receipt for a meal and a comb and a scrap of chintz.

Doris scrabbled, fingers anxious, turning everything over twice.

Somebody had stolen up behind her. Lisa touched Doris's arm.

She looked up at Doris, and laid her palm along her cheek.

It was dry and warm. 'I can tell,' she whispered, 'that you are a very special person.'

A bit pissed, but only a bit, Connie threw cabbage stalks onto the compost. Nearly had herself over. She tapped the bottom of the pail, then had to steady herself again as the little fellas and Stacey tore past her, well, *through* her more like, and almost knocked her down.

'Steady on!' she shouted. 'Seen a ghost?' She laughed and turned and saw the soldier.

He had stopped at the gate.

'Hey, you,' snapped Connie. Ready, as ever, to repel boarders. She looked again. 'Cliff,' she said.

She ran to him. 'Oh, my boy, my boy, my lovely boy.' She was crying. She was snotty. She threw her arms around his neck, had to reach up to do it, she'd forgotten how tall he was. Then she did something that she would never forgive herself for. She flinched.

The bottom left part of his face was not right, the flesh looked plastic and wet, and his lips were rolled meat, and his poor eyes were too bright to look out from such devastation.

Jane sped up when she saw the lights. It had started to snow again, fat, furry blotches. Denholm's windows, curtains drawn back, warmth spilling out, beckoned her on.

Feet soaking, hair a slick mess, Jane felt her transformation begin. She would leave her old sorry self out here in the snow. Why was romance not for her? Why had she believed that all her life? It ended here, now. She would say some magic words to Denholm and she would be mistress of Turnpike. It was a fairytale, all the better for its deferred happy ending. She looked through the window, into the room where she had refused him.

There was quite a gang in there, all of them standing and lively, with glasses raised for a toast. There were faces she didn't recognize, Denholm's family perhaps. But she recognized Denholm. And she recognized Agnes, who basked at the head of the table, holding up her left hand – that scrubbed and raw little claw – so the assembly could see her emerald and diamond ring.

Hero led the way.

His paws took him to Noon Cottage and Alec didn't quibble. He was drawn to the empty house with a pull perhaps stronger than when Kitty had waited there. Only in its emptiness could he find peace.

No, not quite that. Alec had given up on peace, the way he'd given up on being able to run the crest of Lakey Hill. A rightness, that was the best he could hope for now, and he felt more right inside the cottage than he did outside it.

'Nearly there, boy,' he said to the dog. Alec loved Hero. Alec hadn't known this until latterly. He had never classified the way he felt about his dog; now he cherished Hero's uncomplicated company. His loyalty. The way he looked at Alec as if all his options for happiness lay with his master.

Am I his master? Alec was, after all, following the dog. In order to, he might as well admit it, visit a doll. That silly doll, chosen without care, was now the only thing in Ambridge he sought out.

Emily the doll allowed him to be tender; he could hold it and imagine he held Caroline, and Caroline's mother. There was no outlet for tenderness at Lower Loxley. His wife was one big elbow – what else could she be, given his behaviour? – and his son was a desert island glimpsed now and then on the horizon.

He knew now the pleasure of being sweet to someone. Yet he couldn't be sweet to Pamela. He could only detest her, and know she didn't deserve it.

Hero disappeared through the open door of the cottage. Alec stopped, confused, then ran. 'Kitty!' he yelled, loud enough to surprise the rook who owned the yew in the back garden.

'Hello?' A little man stepped out of Kitty's parlour.

'Who the hell are you?' Alec's disappointment was sour in his mouth.

'There's no need to take that tone.' Glasses were taken off in consternation. 'Who are you, sir, for that matter?'

Introductions were made, and Alec apologized to the genial creature, dandruffy and blinking, who was interested only in the job he had come to do. One of a multitude of lawyers who answered to the Dibden-Rawles family, he was making an inventory of the cottage's contents.

'On New Year's Eve?' Good God, thought Alec, the man was keen. 'I doubt Mrs Dibden-Rawles stole anything.'

'Of course not. There's no implication of that nature, it's simply procedure.' The man had a clipboard.

Pamela had a clipboard. Alec suspected that people who owned clipboards would do just fine in the apocalypse.

'This little lady doesn't appear on my list!' The solicitor pointed to the doll.

'She's mine,' said Alec, snatching up Emily.

'I see.' A lifelong habit of not commenting on irregularities of personality came in handy for the stranger. He sighed, old-maid-like. 'I remember Noel being born. To think the Dibden-Rawles bloodline ended with him ... it's tragic.'

This was outrageous. Alec had to leave the room. Hero followed him, nails tapping on the stone floor of the kitchen. Alec picked up a jar, still half full of jam. Jam Kitty had made.

Noel's family was as short-sighted as his own, with their bloated pride in name and pedigree. *To paint Caroline out of the picture because they sneer at Kitty!*

The man followed him. Ticking. Peering. Scribbling. He talked to Alec as if talking to himself, in a murmur. 'Stove, good. Window dressing. Sink, slightly cracked. They were so relieved when Noel survived his brush with cancer, you'll know about that, when he was only a child.'

'He told me about it.' Alec kept his distance. Backed towards the big old cupboard where Kitty had kept her plates that never matched.

'Little did they know that the illness would have such an effect on the entire family.' When Alec frowned, the solicitor dropped his voice even further. 'Infertility,' he hissed.

Alec pushed his way out of the kitchen, past the silly man. Out to the hallway, where he bent double.

The child's hair. Caroline's hair would never lie flat. Alec straightened up and stared at himself in the pitted mirror.

Just like mine.

He looked up at the ceiling. Guessed that he was probably standing more or less beneath the old wardrobe. He remembered the smell of it, the glamorous softness of the old fur coat behind him and the warmth of Kitty against him. He closed his eyes and remembered how she smelled of Je Reviens.

And he remembered Morgan blundering in on his clodhopper feet.

'Room for a little 'un!' But he reconsidered. 'Dammit, too obvious, we'll be found,' he had muttered, and crept out.

As if a starting gun was fired, Alec and Kitty made fast, no-frills love. Silent, careful, hectic. The wardrobe rocked only a little. He remembered her face as she came, and he remembered how it had felt like standing on the edge of a cliff.

He had told her, as she told him, that it must never happen again. And it never had, until well after Noel's death.

Neither of them knew that night they'd made a baby.

A Caroline.

'I'll, just, um, if I may.' The man pointed upstairs with his pencil. He could have been a ghost for all the notice Alec took of him.

The family knew; hence the cold shoulder.

Dear God, Noel knew Caroline wasn't his.

Did he suspect Alec of being Caroline's father? It was an

ignoble thought, but it was Alec's first. Maybe Noel hadn't stood up in the boat to kiss the moon; he may have ended it all on purpose, knowing Kitty had been unfaithful.

He must walk this out. But he couldn't leave the cottage. He roamed it, avoiding the solicitor, who gladly gave him a wide berth.

In and out of the rooms, not saying goodbye when the man left.

He was angry with Kitty. *Why didn't you tell me?* he asked her dressing table, as if it might reply.

He should have guessed. He should have noticed the timing. He'd lived blind, staggering around, not even aware of his affliction.

Kitty could have used Caroline's paternity to force his hand. It would have worked; whatever happened to their love affair he'd have taken care of them both for ever. She wasn't chasing a meal ticket; she *had* a meal ticket.

Kitty had refused to play her ace.

She's stronger than me.

As if seeing another person, some cardboard villain in a Yank movie, Alec heard himself refusing to tell Kitty, 'I love you'. Avoiding it, as if the phrase was covered in germs. She had given him opening after opening, an opportunity every time they parted. She had told him, point blank, 'You love me'. Still he persisted with his dumb game.

Why?

Kitty, come back and I'll say it on the hour every hour.

Alec had left her love hanging on the empty air. All he

could do now was shout it to the chilly rooms. So he did just that, and Hero looked on.

It was quiet. The children were asleep, and so was Lisa. Her bedtimes ran to a toddler schedule, with much getting out and dashing away, and the constant threat of tears. Tonight, it had taken Doris half an hour to soothe her, to tenderly hoodwink her.

Doris picked up her knitting – another blithering sock – and eased off her shoes. The fire was past its best but still warming. The only thing missing was Dan, and that would soon be put right. They would observe midnight and the passing of the year with a drop of something. They wouldn't wake the children. Not this year. She didn't feel like celebrating.

Doris heard Dan's tread in the yard.

'Who was at The Bull, then?' She asked her customary question as he came in.

Without taking off his coat, or answering her, Dan pulled Doris out of the chair. She dropped her knitting and stumbled over a shoe.

'Hey now, Dan!'

He picked her up. Not without difficulty. With a grunt he swung her so he could carry her like a bride, across his arms.

'Dan Archer, you madman!' Doris put her arms around his neck, her cardigan rucked up, fearful of being dropped and her behind hitting the hard kitchen floor.

He carried her up the stairs. She exclaimed all the way. He

was red in the face, hoisting her awkwardly when his grasp failed. He threw her on the bed, which complained. Then he undid his trousers and kissed her, kicking the door shut with his foot.

Mother Cat, licking her paw on the chest of drawers, gaped at the activity.

'Well!' said Doris afterwards, now only in her slip and the wrong way up in the bed. She wanted to laugh or shout or something. Or sleep, that was it. She wanted to sleep with Dan's arms around her for forty-eight hours or so.

Dan wanted something quite different. He threw on his dressing gown. Held hers out for Doris. Old tartan things with frayed frogging, not appropriate for their new Hollywood roles as lovers. 'Come on, love, downstairs,' he said, and she obeyed him, because it was turning out to be more fun that way.

Midnight had trickled past, unnoticed, as they loved. St Stephen's bell was gagged. Behind their backs, Ambridge had sneaked into the future, and it was cold in the bottom field, the ground black beneath them.

'What's going on, Dan Archer?' Doris was still one big smile. She held her dressing gown tight about her throat, looking up at him.

'I do listen,' he said. 'You're so honest, but I haven't been straight with you, old girl. I'm bloody playacting, aren't I, with the War Ag? Letting you bear the brunt of the war, chasing your tail at the farm. I'm doing my bit, yes, maybe, but I should be *fighting*. I'm not an old fella yet.'

'You can't fight, Dan, you—'

He talked over her. 'Doris, love, this is my secret. I don't want to fight. I don't want to shoot some German farmer, some German *me*. I'm a coward, I'm a shirker. There. That's your husband, Doris Archer.'

They were weathervanes. When Dan sank, Doris rose.

'So you listen to me, do you, Dan? Well, listen now, fellow-me-lad. You're no coward. You're decent and you're strong.' Doris was on fire; she was necessary, she felt that, and she ran to meet the need. 'You do what's required, plus more besides. You're wearing yourself out! And do you mind telling me what's wrong with not wanting to fight? You tried to join up, you'd have gone if they'd had you. You're a human, Dan, and it's only human to be relieved.'

'You don't think less of me?'

'Why would I, love?' Doris believed in Dan. She said it now. 'I believe in you.' She took a step back. She laughed. Relief hit. She hadn't lost her belief. She'd refined it. She believed in her flawed, obliging husband. She believed in people. And the mighty and reliable cycle of nature. She said all this, but it came out wrong. Doris wasn't good with words.

She was better with her hands, so Doris bent and dug her fingers into the soil, coming up with a clot of dark earth that spilled on her slippers. 'That Eugene's a fool, for all his reading. Ambridge is stuffed full of the big things. These *are* the big things!' She closed her hand over the brown earth. It held life. She was grateful to it, and to Dan.

They were loons, laughing like the children laughed at Laurel and Hardy shorts.

Maybe there was a way back for Doris.

'We've gone right off the rails, haven't we?' said Dan. 'It's this war, love, but we're all right, aren't we?'

'All right? How dare you! We're more than that.' Doris kissed him, full on the lips, and forgot how cold she was.

'I love you, old girl.' Dan held her tightly, as if he'd just found her, and put away all thoughts of the conversation with Alec that had sent him dashing out of the pub and home to his wife.

'This'll be our last beer together of 1940,' Dan had said as the pub filled up around them. Walter was already unsteady in his patched boots. Elbows were bumped and pints were spilled.

Bob was busy. He was in five different spots at once, and that, said Dan, was 'good for him'. It would, he suggested, take his mind off Jimmy. 'Listen here, Alec, I'm doing all the talking. Cat got your tongue?'

Alec told him, then, about Kitty. The affair. The love; he used that word. He used it liberally. As Dan slowly put down his beer, and drew Alec to a high-sided settle – ears flapped all around them and Alec didn't seem inclined to lower his clipped, carrying voice – Alec told him about Caroline.

'She's mine, Dan.'

What to say? Dan was profoundly shocked. He looked at the table, at its knotty grain, its colour spectrum of brown and brownish and browner. Dan was moral, unimaginatively so. Children belonged in houses with their families; they did not drift above the chimney pots waiting to be claimed by this chap or that. 'But Noel . . .'

'He knew. Dear God, how he must have hated me.'

'He never showed it.' Dan could deal with problems of supply and delivery, or anthrax in sheep. He could also deal with matters of morality. There was right and there was wrong. 'Alec, I had no idea. You and Kitty.' He shook his head. He judged Alec. He judged him as his grandfather would have done. Without appeal, no room for nuance.

And it hurt Dan to do so.

'Kitty had grit, Dan. She didn't tell me about Caroline, but she should have, shouldn't she?'

Dan had no answers, and he wouldn't pretend to. The break in Alec's reliably upper-crust voice broke Dan, too. He heard the pain, and it pushed at centuries of conditioning. He saw a man, his friend, insofar as a farmer and a landowner can be friends, and he saw how hard that friend was trying not to cry. *Good God, don't blub, man.* Dealing with tears was Doris's department.

'It'll be all right.' That's all Dan had. He meant it, too, but then it's easy to say. He patted Alec's shoulder.

Alec pulled away, as if Dan had punched him. 'Who needs to listen to me whining on New Year's Eve, eh? You should be home with Doris and the children.'

'I should.' Dan's legs began to jiggle beneath the table. He wanted to run across the fields, leaping over hedges like he'd done as a boy. The road took too long. 'But . . .' He did it again. He scalded Alec with sympathy.

'Go, man. Get on. Go.' Alec laughed. Or the muscles in his face stretched his mouth over his teeth and a tinny *ha ha* escaped him. 'Happy New Year, Dan. Let's hope 1941 . . .' Alec had no hopes, he realized. He didn't care about 1941.

They parted company outside The Bull. Dan took off, overcoat flying behind him. Alec took the long way back to Lower Loxley.

He passed a cottage and the outbreak of hollers told him he had walked right through the year and out the other end.

As if taking in clouds massing on hills, Alec noticed details about himself for the first time. It had been a season of firsts since Kitty ran away. There was a hole revealed in Alec, one that had been stuffed with moss and twigs and family silver.

Now he had coughed all of that up. The ground rose beneath his feet, taking him away from the huddle of houses which was, when it came down to it, all that Ambridge was. The moon lit his way like a sarcastic sun. It was a changed man who trudged into the third year of war, one who didn't know he had never loved until he loved.

He'd given love a wide berth; the barren will do that. Give them a stick and they'll kill it.

Now love prised him open. Gave him words, all the damn words, and there was a sliver of Alec that wished himself back to ignorance. That, though, would mean no Kitty. So he accepted his pain and his loneliness as the price. Not of love, but of stupidity.

I could have her still if I wasn't such a fool.

And his little girl. He had never once looked at Caroline and thought yes, she was his. Never wondered about the shape of her eyes or the slope of her cheek. Her hair he remembered often, and he smiled every time, and patted his own cowlick.

Ahead of him, Lower Loxley grew with each step. It was inevitable he must return, no matter how circular the path. Alec must take up his shackles again, lock himself in with a woman he didn't understand. Had he ever tried to? That was a question for another night. There would be many nights, all of them long, and there was no hurry to index all the questions right now.

He wondered, for the hundredth time, how Kitty was coping. How she was living. If she'd risk travelling to Ireland, or if such a thing was even possible. What would she do for money; what black magic deal had been struck with George Seed? Kitty had surely signed in blood, believing herself as worthless as Alec made her feel.

She had compromised herself to get out of Ambridge. *And it's all my fault.*

And Caroline? How would the little girl know he loved her? Because he did. Alec was good at love, now that it was too late.

Nineteen forty-one is brand new. The moment shimmers.

Walter Gabriel is sound asleep. He reeled home for midnight and rattled the roof with a shout of 'And a happy new year to you all!' Just like last year. Just like every year.

But Walter is changed. His father is dead. Enemy planes have flown over his roof. His hangover clears its throat, awaiting its cue. For now, though, he sleeps.

Above the shop, Frank is awake. He turns over, pulling the covers with a grunt. He knows he'll dream of his father, and the old man will ask why he readily gave away his heritage for a country that will never truly accept him.

The murkey wasn't so bad. Eugene's tummy is full and his brain is a bit sloshed and his foot is aching in that familiar way. He was too tired to read when he turned in, or maybe too drunk. He wonders how his mother spent Christmas Day, and if she raised a glass to him. He assumes not. He lights a candle and scrabbles about beneath his bed until he lays his hand on a book. He finds his page. Books have never let him down.

It's hard to sleep in a tube station, with an unwashed bloke on one side, and your keening mum the other. Peggy closes her eyes and imagines herself a child again. Her dad will walk in, any minute now, and sort everything out.

Sitting in the faint light given by the embers in the grate, Jane reaches out her foot and sets the rocking chair going; a ghost would be company.

Shall I see another new year? thinks Mrs Endicott as she snaffles the last fugitive violet cream from a box she keeps under the bed. *My grasp on this life is so slender.* She belches and lies back on a dam of pillows.

Outside, not dressed for it, plunging through the night, Dan holds Doris's hand. A new word he heard on the Beeb has snagged on a nail in his brain. Blitzkrieg. What if the empire has had it? *What if we can't stop the Germans?* He speeds up, and Doris complains. 'Nearly there, old girl,' he says.

Pamela has left her bedroom door ajar. Alec is blundering about down in the drawing room. She abhors his new habit of sleeping on the big old Knole sofa, a bottle lolling on the rug. She doesn't blame Alec, she blames the girl. It's all the girl's fault. Standing in front of a cheval mirror in her best nightdress, that is, her briefest, she sees how meagre it makes her look. She tears it off and pulls a billowing cambric thing over her head, and closes her bedroom door with a bang.

There is the bubble made by the Anderson shelter's corrugated roof, and there is the bubble made inside it by Dottie and Chaz as they commune, nose to nose, in the chilly quiet. Her granddad twitches in his sleep like an old mutt, and her sister coughs on and off all night. Dottie murmurs to Chaz and he squeaks and sighs back and she is as happy, she thinks, as any human deserves to be.

That floor needs a sweep, but Bob ignores the dirt and pours himself a Glenmorangie. It is his nightly treat now. A treat without which he can't sleep. The silence after the singing and the carousing has his ears humming. He gets out the map again, rescued many times from the rubbish. He stares at Egypt. At Sidi Barrani. He drinks his whisky.

The trucks follow one another out of the barracks. Jack bounces on the plank seat and leans over his mate's shoulder to see the map. So that's where Egypt is, in bleedin' Africa. 'We're off!' shouts someone and Jack cheers, bashing shoulders with his friend, his teeth a white flash in the darkness. 'At last!' he laughs.

All very high-class, the hotel's reception desk cows the girl. She minds her P's and Q's, trying to look as if blokes squire her to such establishments every day. Jez smothers a laugh as he signs a cheque that he knows will bounce with a splendid blue-lacquered pen.

Out beyond the edges of Ambridge, a light burns at the Horrobins'. Connie has put the furniture back on its feet after Stan's latest tantrum. She has dried John's tears with the edge of her shawl and tucked him back in bed. From time to time she risks a look at where Cliff sits in the sketchily drawn shadows of the room. She can only look at him for a few beats. She is slowly piecing her son together. The jaw. The nose. The ear. The lips. She can only bear them one at a time, as if he is a broken jigsaw.

'It's awful long to leave the children, Dan.' Doris's feet are damp. It isn't an adventure anymore. She's freezing. She fantasizes about what Lisa might be getting up to, in the nuddy perhaps.

'They'll be fine. In here.'

'What? *Why?*' Doris lets herself be led through St Stephen's gate, and around the side of the church. She stubs her toe and could curse, she's *this* close to it, when Dan stops.

He strikes a match. She sees his silly, pleased-with-himself face in its flame.

'And you an ARP warden, Dan Archer,' she hisses. 'No lights!'

Then she sees it. A small plaque in the rough stone wall. It's new, the letters crisp and black on milky white marble.

In Memoriam

JANET FORREST

1903–1908

She was loved

Acknowledgements

The phrase 'dream job' is bandied about, but surely I have a right to use it. I've been invited to Ambridge to wander around and peek in its windows, to meddle in the history of a place so precious to so many.

I hope I've done it justice. Escaping to Borsetshire – and 1940s Borsetshire, at that – from our present day was the sort of holiday that Covid-19 made impossible. I found parallels between the first uncertain days of the Second World War and the UK's lockdown that enrich the story. It was a slender silver lining to a terrible time.

This book was born in a torrent of love and enthusiasm. Everyone who heard the idea got the 'tingle' that editors and booksellers live for. Many, many thank-yous are necessary, and here are some of them.

Thank you Charlotte Robertson, agent and chum, for dreaming up the entire enterprise and shouldering it through with equal parts charm and muscle.

Thank you Jeremy Howe, editor of *The Archers* and integral, beloved cog in the book's machine, and thank you to the other BBC folk who patiently answered my every question about horses and threshing machines and family trees. Charlotte Davey, Sarah Swadling, Mel Ward and Hannah Ratcliffe, your ideas are all over the story.

Of course, thank you to my editor, Clare Hey, for pushing and pulling and guiding us through a difficult period with all her usual *sang froid*.

Simon & Schuster I salute you all, but especially this lot – thank you Gill Richardson, Joe Roche, Amy Fulwood, Laurie McShea, Polly Osborn, Judith Long, Dom Brendon, Ian Chapman and Suzanne Baboneau. I will press wine on you when we can all be together in some ghastly pub once more.

Most of this book was written at one end of a long table while my daughter sat at the other end, taking part in her Zoom school lessons. So, the last thank you is to Niamh Strachan, who let her mother wander off to Ambridge at a time when all we had was each other.

Catherine Miller
London/Ambridge
July 2020

Catherine ⬛⬛⬛ by day and listens to *The Archers* by night. She lives in London but dreams of life in Ambr⬛ ⬛

Jeremy H⬛⬛ ⬛⬛⬛ ⬛⬛ *Ambridge* ⬛⬛⬛ ⬛⬛⬛ crucia⬛ ⬛⬛⬛ ⬛ insights into the nation's favourite radio drama.

Ambridge at War is fully authorised by BBC Radio 4.

Praise for *Ambridge at War*

'Intriguing, comforting and endearingly familiar'

Katie Fforde

'An inventive cosy crime prequel to the "everyday story of country folk", first aired 70 years ago ... tautly constructed and often laugh-aloud funny'

The Times

'You don't need to be a fan of *The Archers* to enjoy this ... It's a comfort blanket of a book with a rich vein of spicy intrigue'

Woman

'A novel that takes readers back to before the much-loved "everyday story of country folk" began ... Nostalgia for avid listeners with long memories'

Choice